THE
MURDER BIRD

Joanna Hines

SIMON &
SCHUSTER

London · New York · Sydney · Toronto

A VIACOM COMPANY

First published in Great Britain by Simon & Schuster UK Ltd, 2006
A Viacom Company

Copyright © Joanna Hines, 2006

The right of Joanna Hines to be identified as author of this work
has been asserted in accordance with sections 77 and 78 of the Copyright,
Designs and Patents Act, 1988.

1 3 5 7 9 10 8 6 4 2

Simon & Schuster UK Ltd
Africa House
64–78 Kingsway
London WC2B 6AH

www.simonsays.co.uk

Simon & Schuster Australia
Sydney

A CIP catalogue record for this book is available from the British Library.

Hardback ISBN 0-7432-4800-7
EAN 978074328006
Trade paperback ISBN 0-7432-4801-5
EAN 9780743248013

This book is a work of fiction. Names, characters, places and incidents are either
a product of the author's imagination or are used fictitiously. Any resemblance to
actual people living or dead, events or locales is entirely coincidental.

Typeset in Garamond by M Rules
Printed and bound in Great Britain by
Mackays of Chatham plc, Chatham, Kent

Also by Joanna Hines
from Simon & Schuster/Pocket Books

Improvising Carla

Surface Tension

Angels of the Flood

Acknowledgements

My thanks to all those who took the trouble to answer my many questions: Ayo Onatade, David Kirk and Amy for legal expertise, Nadja Corcas and Richard Stott for cellos, Ken McGregor for policing, Hugh Lander for ancient buildings, Mike Jecks for firearms and Mary Combe for wildlife. And thanks as well to Laura Longrigg and Melissa Weatherill for incisive and helpful editorial comments. But most of all, I'm grateful to Robyn Bolam, who wrote the beautiful stanzas for 'The Murder Bird' poem.

For John, Casey, Nicholas and Anna

CHAPTER 1

It was like it was happening in a dream.

Five weeks before Kirsten Waller's body was found in a clifftop cottage in Cornwall, Grace Hobden cleared away the lunch, checked to make sure her three children were playing on the climbing frame at the bottom of the garden, then went indoors to murder her husband. Paul Hobden, a large, blubbery whale of a man, was sleeping off the effects of a boozy lunch. In the corner of the room, a black and white film involving much swash and buckle was chattering quietly on the TV. While Douglas Fairbanks Jr swished his sword with laughing, lethal accuracy, Grace Hobden picked up a Sabatier filleting knife from the rack in her kitchen, went into the living room and, without hesitating for a moment, plunged the blade into the soft mound of her husband's chest.

He must have struggled to sit up at that point, though the first blow pierced the left ventricle of his heart and would have been fatal anyway: Grace was a qualified radiographer and knew her anatomy. The second blow struck his thorax at a forty-five degree angle, causing a large amount of blood to spill on to the check upholstery of the sofa, their new olive-grey carpet and, presumably, on to Grace herself. There was no need for a third blow.

When she had showered and changed, Grace gathered up her children – Angus, eight, Matthew, seven, and Susan who was only three – and told them they were going out for a treat. She drove them to the seaside, forty miles away, where they spent a pleasant afternoon playing beach cricket in the May sunshine, making sand castles and gorging on ice creams. Towards evening she phoned the police who were, in consequence, waiting for her when she got home.

'I couldn't take it any more,' she told them, as they contemplated the bloody remains of her husband. 'It was like it was happening in a dream.'

Raph Howes leafed through the stack of papers with mounting disbelief. His shirt was soaked with sweat, and not just because of the late summer heat. What in the name of all glory was his clerk thinking of? Like everyone else in chambers, Dermot was well aware that in the two months since Kirsten's midsummer death, Raph had avoided domestic briefs. And who would blame him? As he looked at the photographs of Paul Hobden's blood-streaked body, both gory and faintly ridiculous, it was Kirsten's corpse he kept seeing in his mind's eye. Always beautiful, even in death, with that cool, Scandinavian fairness, she was naked, one leg sprawled over the rim of the bath, head thrown back, not a trace of blood anywhere. But dead all the same. Horribly and irrevocably dead.

He stood up angrily and began pacing between the desks in his room. Even before his estranged wife's death, he'd always loathed this kind of brief. Domestic murders were too messy, too personal, too painful. Just imagine those three little innocents larking about in the garden while twenty yards away their mother dropped a bloodstained curtain on their childhood. If the poor little wretches had ever had a childhood.

Those kind of events don't strike your normal, everyday sort of family. No way.

Raph's throat was turning dry as the implications unfolded. Perspiration rolled down his cheeks. His nostrils detected a faint but unmistakable smell of burning; some witless bastard must have lit an early bonfire.

He leaned down, pushed the papers across his desk and shouted for Dermot to remove them. No one came.

A photograph slid loose from the pile. In her early thirties, Grace Hobden was pretty in an unremarkable kind of way; the woman who had lethally skewered her husband had a round face with stubby features. There was nothing in her appearance to indicate she was the kind of woman who should on no account be left alone with a sharp knife and a sleeping husband.

But then, as Raph knew, murderers seldom look the part.

She seemed lost and bewildered, as well she might. He glared at the photograph from a safe distance. How long had it taken, he wondered. Thirty seconds? Two minutes? How long does it take to commit the irreversible act that changes the lives of a whole family for ever?

He might have talked about it before. With Kirsten.

In the time when it was still okay for them to talk about murder.

'Dermot!' he yelled again, walking to the window. No air in here. That was the problem. Where was the man? Why didn't he just take the bloody stuff away?

Raph ran a stubby finger under his collar. Sweat spilled on to his knuckles. He couldn't deal with stress like he used to. Somewhere in the distance a dog was barking, that steady, unrelenting barking of a dog that is chained up, or trapped, or desperate . . . Barking as if its life depended on it.

The case would stand or fall depending on how Grace Hobden came across in court. For obvious reasons it was always difficult to prove self-defence or lack of premeditation when the victim was asleep at the time of the attack – difficult, but not impossible. The most promising line would be that she'd been driven to it over months and years of violence and abuse until suddenly, one breezy May morning, she snapped.

A phrase from her statement had stuck in his brain.

'*I just couldn't take it any more . . .*'

Take what? Paul Hobden's parents and sister claimed he was gentle as a lamb – but then they would say that, wouldn't they? Families never square up to the truth and state, 'He was a monster and deserved to die.' In her statement, Grace sketched a picture of a sadist and a bully. She had the bruises on her legs to prove it. Cigarette burns on her left hand. She said it was the psychological torture that was the hardest to bear.

Psychological torture.

Raph's heart was pounding and it was getting harder to breathe. These rooms in chambers were always impossibly hot in summer. He'd open the window but he didn't want to let in any more of that damned smoke. And where the hell was it coming from anyway?

'Dermot! For God's sake, man!'

Why didn't someone shut that bloody dog up?

Dermot Mercer pulled the chain and closed the lavatory door behind him just as Raph yelled for the third time. Dermot had very definite views about being shouted at by his barristers, all of them negative. His features, which even when he was in a good mood resembled those of an anxious hamster, grew more pinched and inward-looking. He moved fast, however. Raph's third shout generated urgency: the adrenaline kick of panic.

'What is it, Mr Howes? Is something wrong?'

A rhetorical question. He looked like everything was wrong. As a young man, Raph Howes had had the dark hair and swarthy good looks that might have suited a pirate in another century; since entering his fifth decade, he'd put on weight, his jaw was heavier under the blue shadow of stubble and his physical movements had slowed. Mentally, though, especially up against a worthy adversary in court, he was as agile and dangerous as ever.

Which made it all the more shocking for Dermot to see him like this.

'You're not well, Mr Howes.'

'Fine . . . perfectly fine . . . just take that damn brief away—'

But as Dermot reached down to remove the stack of papers, Raph banged his fist on the desk. Dermot's hand grazed the fine hairs on Raph's fingers; he drew back as though stung.

Raph's eyebrows collided in a frown. 'Who sent them?'

'Alan Caulder at Fergal and Smith. He was very insistent.'

'You know I said no murders. Not since . . .'

He didn't need to finish. Dermot knew what he meant. *Since Kirsten's death.* Even though no one else had been involved, that too had been a murder of a kind. Self-murder: the old-fashioned term for suicide. Dermot should have been more sensitive: two months on and the man was still hurting. 'Bob Holles made me promise you'd look at it. He's been convinced you've got the golden touch ever since you got that GBH client a suspended sentence. I'll take them away.'

'No. Wait.' Raph dropped down in his chair. He was breathing heavily.

Dermot went to open the window. It was airless in here; that was the trouble.

'Don't!' croaked Raph.

'But I thought—'

'That damn smoke is making my throat sore.'

'Smoke?' Dermot sniffed the air: traffic fumes, warm dust from pavements, maybe some pollen. But definitely no smoke.

'Some moron's lit a bonfire . . .' Raph's frown deepened as he registered his error.

Dermot said quietly, 'The Middle Temple's not exactly famous for its bonfires, Mr Howes', before adding, 'It was probably someone passing with a cigar.' He threw the window wide and smutty summer air gusted in.

'I must have imagined it,' said Raph. He rubbed his palm across his mouth, before muttering, 'And the dog . . .'

'Dog? What dog?'

Raph shifted, avoiding his eye. 'Just some damned dog.' He looked so bewildered that Dermot felt embarrassed, as though he'd caught him unexpectedly naked. Raph said, 'Look, now the instructions are here, you might as well leave them with me. I'll glance through them.'

'But I thought you said—?'

'I haven't made up my mind.'

'Let me give it to one of the girls. This would be right up Selina's street.'

'I said I'd look, didn't I? Just leave the stuff here.'

When Raph Howes spoke in that tone, no one argued with him. Dermot withdrew and returned to his office, but he was troubled. Dermot couldn't have the man cracking up on him: Raph brought in more money than most of the other barristers in his chambers put together. Dermot should have been more careful. From now on, no matter how persuasive solicitors were, he'd make sure Raph was fed a bland diet of armed robbery and corruption. With maybe a touch of arson for light relief.

If he'd known what his clerk was thinking, Raph would have been in full agreement. He needed Grace Hobden like he needed a hole in the head. Or in the heart.

Her story had all the ingredients he most loathed: the cosy domestic setting; vulnerable children who were going to lose out, no matter what; a messy dissection of family entrails – ugh, he'd be mad to take it on. Dermot was right: one of his female colleagues would jump at the chance to defend her.

The sensible course of action would be to tell Dermot he must be coming down with some kind of bug and take the

Basle fraud papers to work on at home. Home meant Lola, who'd talk to him about leg-waxing, or the love life of her friends, and he could lose himself for a few hours in his girl-friend's blissful inanities. Young, with a perfect body and a quite remarkably insignificant mind, Lola had drifted into his life at a time of crisis and had stayed because she offered an unlikely bastion against the torment that had almost destroyed him. Be prudent. Grace Hobden was not for him.

He watched, detached and mildly curious, as his hand reached out and pulled the Hobden brief towards him.

'*It was like it was happening in a dream.*'

Utter madness to take this case on. And it was a well-known fact that Raph Howes was a supremely rational man.

His throat was still sore. From the smoke. Only there wasn't any. Nor any dog.

He spread the papers in a fan on the desk.

It was the details that always got to you. The fact that Paul Hobden had boxed when he was in the navy and had been teaching his two sons to box the day before his death. The fact that Grace Hobden spent the afternoon before her arrest play-ing beach cricket and making sand castles, as though nothing at all was wrong. Asked about it later, she said she wanted the chil-dren to have some fun before 'things got a bit sticky'. The fact that her father had died ten days earlier. Maybe he could use that in her defence.

But, dear God, before *things got a bit sticky*? At moments of intense crisis, when you might expect the human spirit to come up with a tirade of Shakespearean grandeur, what did you get? Sheer banality. *It was like it was happening in a dream.* And it wasn't just the mute immortal Grace Hobdens of this world, either. What had been his own reaction when he heard about Kirsten's death? 'Oh no!' Just that. Oh no. An immediate and succinct denial of the tragedy. Oh no. The two most heart-breaking words in the English language.

(There were others, of course. *I'm sorry, Daddy. I didn't mean to . . . please don't.*)

A few years back, Raph had defended a young man who had taken it upon himself to murder a passing stranger with a bolt from a crossbow through the chest. When asked why, he replied calmly, 'I didn't like the way he looked at me.'

Yes, well . . . As people slip and slither through the thin crust of civilization into the depths of horror beneath, what paucity of language accompanies their fall.

Grace Hobden, he noticed, was described by a neighbour as a woman of few words. Who kept to herself, naturally.

He knew the type. Keep it private.

He'd have to find a way of using that in her defence, too.

What defence? What was he thinking of? The blood was pumping through his veins. Don't – *pump* – even – *pump* – go there – *pump pump*.

Too late. He'd gone already.

A strange silence was settling round him, the deep, numbing silence like snowfall, the silence that follows on after catastrophe.

It was the wrong murder, of course. He'd known that right away. It was always the wrong murder.

He reached for a pad of paper, took a fountain pen from his breast pocket, and began making notes in his elegant, small script. The law and all its certainties was a never-failing refuge;

the unbearable chaos of human grief reduced to a legal game. A game he happened to be good at winning. Raph Howes had come a long way.

And as he wrote he wondered, did the Hobden family have a dog?

A small boy runs through the grass. Long wet grass that soaks his bare knees. There's an unbearable ache in his chest. Fear and grief and he's out of breath from running so far. All the way from the road. In his arms a dead weight – and in his heart, terror.

Up ahead, the house. Where Daddy will be waiting.

I'm sorry, Daddy. I didn't mean to . . . Don't be angry, Daddy, please don't—'

CHAPTER 2

I had to do it.

On the back wall of Raph's house, halfway between the first and second floors, Sam almost quit.

The security light had come on and she felt exposed as a starfish on a rock. She'd gambled that the bathroom window above the kitchen would be ajar, but no luck. It was shut tight and locked from within. She daren't risk breaking glass until she was out of range of the security light, which meant going higher.

Twenty feet above the ground and serious vertigo kicked in. Her heart was hammering. This wasn't one of those useful, theatrical creepers that Romeos shin up, easy as a ladder; it was liable to give way at any moment. The paving stones below would make a hard landing. She imagined falling, her skull splitting on Raph's tasteful York stone patio.

Focus. Don't think.

Spreading her arms wide, she gripped a handful of creeper in each fist and leaned her cheek against the summer-warmed stone of the building. Vertigo gave her the illusion she could launch herself from the wall like a fledgling and fly. Don't do it. Breathe. Stay calm. Take your time.

No choice now, anyway, since going down is always harder. Besides, there was too much at stake to think of quitting.

On the far side of the house the traffic on Holland Park Avenue droned steadily. Even at two o'clock in the morning it never let up.

Grimly, slowly, testing each branch before trusting it with her weight, Sam edged higher. Her backpack bumped against her spine, skewing her balance. The hammer she'd stuck in her belt was digging into her ribs. Now her head and shoulders were clear of the security light. Now her body.

The next time she reached up, the knuckles of her right hand grazed the underside of a stone ledge. A windowsill. Pray God, let this window be open, just a crack.

She moved to the left, so she'd come at it from the side.

She was just reaching across, when the wall exploded in noise as a shriek of feathers skimmed past her cheek. She let go and floated free for a moment, muscles slacked with shock, and stared down into the pool of light below. She almost plunged, but at the last moment her fingers caught hold of the branch and clung on, while her heart pumped and the terrified black-bird screeched off into the night.

Damned bird . . . she was gasping . . . *it had almost killed her.*

A cold slick of fear covered her body as she gripped the creeper, sheer willpower holding her there till her thumping heart was steady enough for the final push.

The security light went out. Her eyes adjusted to the darkness.

In her nightmares, when she had to cross a missing space in the floor, it was always dark, darker even than this. Blind eyes looking into blackness.

Just climb.

Slowly, painfully, she eased herself up till her hips were level with the windowsill. Then, hardly daring to breathe, she adjusted her feet on the branch, grabbed a wisp of creeper with her left hand and reached across to test the window. Tight shut. Of course. Face it, Sam: they've gone away for the weekend. What did you expect? That they'd leave a welcome mat out for burglars?

Fumbling now, she tugged the hammer free of her belt. Before setting out, she'd wrapped its head in a cotton scarf and secured it with string. To deaden the noise. She hoped to God it worked.

A soft thud as the hammer hit the glass. No breakage. She tried again, putting more force into the blow. Still no good. The third time, a huge rage against all hammers and obstinate windows gripped her, and she swung her arm wide, forgetting the tug of the backpack on her shoulders, forgetting the frailty of the branch she was holding. As the hammer smashed through the glass her left hand still clutched at creeper that no longer held the wall and swung clear of the building; the backpack lurched away from her shoulders and all around her was black air, but at the last moment she gripped the window's edge, let the hammer drop down inside, glass slicing her palm as she held on, held on for her life, scrabbling for a toehold with the snub end of her sneakers, then gradually, painfully, each inch a mountain of effort, raised herself up until she found the catch on the inside of the window, released it, then hauled herself over the sill and fell, with a shiver of broken glass, into the deeper dark inside.

Safe.

She almost blacked out.

But no, not safe yet. Breaking in was just the start.

A steady beeping rose from the hall, growing louder all the time. Sam had less than four minutes to silence the alarm.

She picked up the hammer and was about to put it back in her belt when she noticed something warm and sticky oozing from her hand. Blood. Blood on her precious musician's hand. No time to think about that now. She pulled the scarf from the hammer and balled it into her right palm, staunching the blood flow as she raced down the stairs to the burglar alarm by the front door.

Maybe Raph had never changed the code. She punched in Kirsten's birthday: 4-5-52 followed by hash, but the beeping grew louder. From here on in it was guesswork. She tried Raph's dates, but the noise just increased. Any moment now and the alarm would trigger in the police station in Notting Hill. Desperately she punched in the first four digits of Raph's phone number.

Getting louder.

The second four numbers and then . . .

Silence.

Golden, ear-tingling silence.

The absence of noise was tangible, like a metallic taste against her tongue. She stood for a full minute without moving and listened to the quiet swish of traffic from the front. These houses were set back from the road behind thick evergreens, tall havens of quiet.

She held her watch up to the street glow coming through the fanlight. It was ten past two. She had over three hours before dawn, so she could take her time. Triumph surged through her and she felt capable of anything – and also, suddenly, extremely hungry. Well, at least the fridge in this house was always well stocked. She padded down to the basement kitchen, its acres of cool granite worktop gleaming smugly in the darkness, and pulled open the door of the huge fridge. As she'd expected, there were stocks for several feasts: cold duck and cheeses, olives and pâté, smoked salmon and quails' eggs. On the door were several kinds of fruit juice, Raph's ever-present bottles of champagne, a couple of bottles of Chablis and three kinds of mineral water.

Sam closed the fridge door firmly. She had her pride after all. It wasn't as though she was some kind of thief. She wouldn't touch anything of Raph's, not even the bottled water. She was only here to get what belonged to her.

Now all she had to do was find it.

Raph's Holland Park house had a raised ground floor, a huge reception room running from front to back down the left-hand side. To the right of the hall, a door led through into a large dining room. Raph's study lay behind this room, but could only be reached through the main reception room. Sam took the torch from her backpack and flicked it on as she turned left and went in. The pale beam of light picked out objects that had once formed a part of her everyday life.

She'd loved this room ever since her first sight of it when

she'd come to London seven years ago, a confused and rebellious fifteen-year-old. It wasn't just the scale and luxury of it that had impressed her, the two vast white sofas and the antique Persian rug as big as a tennis court, the urns that were always filled with lilies, the eighteenth-century porcelain and the stunning contemporary pictures. It was the sum total of all these things and something more besides: it was what the room said about Raph himself. This was a space that breathed self-assurance, a room created by a man who knew his own status in the world. Raph's house, especially this room, had given Sam confidence when she needed it most.

Instinctively, she moved to the grand piano near the tall windows overlooking the garden at the back. She raised the lid and touched the keys soundlessly, and in her mind's eye she saw Raph's fingers, short and purposeful like the man himself, picking out a simple tune while he roared encouragement.

With his usual mixture of arrogance, hard work and quick intelligence, Raph had learned the piano so he could accompany her cello practice. 'If I can play the bloody piece from scratch, the least you can do is get your part right!' he'd roared. And so she had, thanks to him. She'd probably never have got into the Royal College of Music without his encouragement and determination. So she owed the man, big time.

The bastard.

She let the piano lid drop with a soft thud and began her search. Apart from the bookcases, there weren't that many places in this room to hide things, but she'd look anyway.

Well, it wasn't here. She hadn't really expected to find it in the drawing room.

Raph's study was the most likely spot. High double doors joined the two rooms. After Kirsten's memorial service they had been flung open; now they were closed. Sam's right hand was still clutching the blood-soaked scarf, so she used her left to let herself in. A subtle alteration of the air marked the transition between the two rooms: beeswax and the heavy scent of lilies gave place to the smell of leather and an undertone of cigars. No longer a public room, but private and intensely masculine.

There was no shortage of hiding places here. Sam set down her torch and switched on the standard lamp, then hunted quickly through the leather-topped desk, but without success. Two whole walls were covered with bookcases and storage cabinets. It would be easy to slide a pale-blue leather-bound A4 notebook of the kind Kirsten always used into one of the bookcases. The casual observer would never notice it.

Sam would have to search every inch of bookcase methodically, starting from the top left. She dragged the library steps across the floor and began running her finger slowly along the spines of the books on the top shelf.

She'd reached the third shelf, second section, when she stopped suddenly. Frozen.

Every nerve in her body was humming with tension as she strained to interpret the new sounds. Not traffic. Voices.

Voices outside and coming closer. The front door opening and closing. Muffled laughter.

She shivered. Raph? But he'd said he was going to Basle to see a client. Had the trip been cancelled? Had he changed his mind and come back early?

A woman's voice, soft and husky. Sam cursed under her

breath. She would have recognized that voice anywhere: Lola. Oh God! Bloody useless Lola, trust her to turn up when she wasn't wanted. What was she doing here now? Sam thought she'd gone to Basle with Ralph.

There was a man with Lola. Maybe Sam had got the dates wrong and they weren't away for the weekend after all. Raph and his new girlfriend had gone out for the evening and now . . .

But that wasn't Raph. It was a man's voice, all right, but it was lighter, a tenor instead of Raph's rich baritone. A voice Sam didn't recognize.

What the hell was going on?

Just in time, Sam snapped off the light and hurried to close the doors leading into the drawing room. What was she supposed to do now? She looked around in despair. As if she had any choice. The windows in Raph's study, like all the others on the ground floor and in the basement, were impregnable with cast-iron grilles. The only escape was back the way she'd come.

A pencil of light appeared under the door.

'Ha! I can't believe Raph forgot to set the alarm!' Lola's voice was slurred but triumphant. 'And after all the times he's banged on about it to me. Just wait till I tell him! And you can be my witness. Mm . . .' There was a brief silence, and the next time Lola spoke her voice was softer, huskier. 'That was nice.'

Another silence. Then, 'I should go,' the man said.

'Hey, you just got here. I know, let's have a drink. I don't love being here on my own at night. It gives me the creeps, to be honest.'

'Well. I am Raph's pupil, you know. I don't want . . .'

'Just a glass or two. He always keeps something good in the fridge. You wait there. I'll get a bottle. Oops.'

'Steady. Are you sure you want another drink?'

'Uh huh. Sweetie, after what I've had, champagne'll sober me up. Oops again. These platforms'll be the death of me. There, that's better. I'm going to get the bubbles. Don't run away.' Lola's tuneless singing faded down the stairs. Sam gritted her teeth. Lola was a waste of space at the best of times; right now, she was a liability.

Why don't you follow her? Sam silently demanded of the stranger on the other side of the door. You'd like it in the kitchen. He was moving around, coming closer. Was he planning on coming in? Sam tiptoed towards Raph's massive desk, plenty big enough to hide behind. Her left sneaker squeaked in protest and suddenly the door into the drawing room was flung open and light poured in.

'What the fuck—?'

Her interlocutor looked every bit as shocked as she was.

It was easy enough to see why Lola was hitting on him. Even dishevelled and the worse for wear after a long party, the young man who'd mentioned he was Raph's pupil was attractive. Tousled brown hair and long brown eyes that were widening with surprise. And the jaw which had dropped open at the sight of her was lean and strong.

He blinked, drew in a breath and turned to call out.

'Stop!' Sam hissed. 'Lola mustn't know I'm here.'

'Lola? You know her?' He was facing her again.

''Course I do.'

'Then who the hell are you? What are you doing here?'

'I'm . . .' She hesitated. It went against the grain for Sam to divulge information to anyone these days, let alone a stranger, especially not a stranger who happened to be a friend of Lola's.

He said, 'How do I know you're not a burglar?'

'Don't be ridiculous.'

'Oh? So what are you doing in Raph's study? With the lights off? At two in the morning?'

'I'm . . . wait, I can explain.'

Shock had sobered him up. He was looking at her keenly. 'Go on, then.'

'I was looking for something.'

'In the dark?'

'Something that belongs to me.'

'Then why the secrecy?'

'There's a good reason.'

'Which is—?'

Sam could hear Lola calling up from the kitchen.

Sam said, 'It's personal.'

'I don't believe you. I'm calling the police.'

'Then you'll look like a prat.' Sam took a deep breath. 'And I don't think Raph would be very pleased either. I'm Kirsten's daughter.' His expression didn't change, so she added, 'You didn't know? Kirsten was his wife. She died.'

'Ah.' He retreated into the drawing room and pulled the door shut behind him just as Lola came back in. Sam held her breath. *Ah*? What did 'Ah' mean? That he believed her and would say nothing, or that he'd spill the beans?

'What were you doing in there?' Lola wanted to know.

'I thought I heard something. Thought it might be an intruder,' said the man.

'And?'

A brief pause, then Sam heard him say, 'I guess I imagined it.'

She breathed out a sigh of relief.

'There. What did I tell you?' Lola was triumphant again. 'This place is freaking you out an' all.'

CHAPTER 3

Even though he and Kirsten had been living apart for nine months by the time she died, the London home where they'd been happy together had been the obvious place for friends and family to gather to mourn her passing.

It had been raining the last time Sam was here. Only two weeks ago, but already the middle of August seemed to belong in a different era. Raph's huge drawing room had been packed with mourners who'd come back to the house after Kirsten's memorial service, the women in their black linen and grey silks, the men in dark suits. The double doors to Raph's study had been flung wide and people crowded in there, too. Beyond the windows green rain fell steadily on the summer garden.

And everyone was very kind to Sam.

Tactful, too. It was especially important that people were tactful. There hadn't been an inquest yet, so the 'suicide' word wasn't spoken out loud, but it trailed between the speakers like smoke, slipped into pockets of silence, flooded into the space left by an unfinished sentence. *Poor Sam. It must be so much worse for her, knowing how her mother died . . . It's especially bad when . . . One never thought Kirsten was the type to . . . do something like that. Poor Sam. Do you think she'll be okay?*

Poor Sam. Poor Sam wanted to hurl her glass at the tasteful walls and scream out that they didn't know what they were talking about.

Poor Sam wondered why the hell she was taking part in this farce; she ought to cut her losses and go, right now, but she stayed because there were people here who had genuinely cared about her mother, and even though they were deluded about the manner of Kirsten's death, in some way Sam felt supported by them, something of her mother's spirit lingering in the room as they talked about her.

People like Raph's sister, Miriam, and her husband, Johnny Johns. Sam had got on with Johnny right from the first. Everyone did. When she'd moved in with Raph and Kirsten he bounced into her life like a year-round Santa. Large and generous and honey-coloured, he had a voice like mulled wine and a laugh that lifted the spirits, no matter what. 'Darling Sam,' he said, enveloping her in a hug any self-respecting bear would have been proud of, 'you're so brave and wonderful. You must come down and stay with us at Wardley whenever you want. Isn't that right, Miri?'

Miriam clung to his arm and nodded. A paler, less angular version of her brother, Miriam seemed permanently exhausted by the effort of trailing along in the wake of her exuberant husband. Johnny was friends with everyone, and Miriam seemed to have no friends of her own – there was something aloof and

unbending in her manner which put people off – but the afternoon of Kirsten's memorial service, even she was being kind to
Sam. Distant and self-contained as always, but trying to be
kind.

Even Raph's mother, Diana, who was not famous for her
empathy, patted Sam on the arm and said, 'It's difficult, Sam.
Very difficult. But believe me, you'll come through.' She looked
away quickly, alarmed by what for her counted as gushing emotion. In Diana the strong nose and startled eyes of the Howes
clan created an almost parrot-like appearance.

Trevor Clay, Kirsten's London agent, was more direct. He had
loved Kirsten as a friend and championed her work from the
beginning. 'A double tragedy,' he said to Sam after he'd drunk
several glasses of Raph's wine. By that time, most of the mourners had left, only the hard core remaining. He sighed and said,
'Such a wonderful and unique woman – well, we all knew that.
But her work. She was just hitting the top of her form. This
next collection will be the best yet.'

'God, that's so terrible,' said Johnny, miserably. His forehead
was corrugated with wrinkles, like tide ripples in sand. 'When
you think what she might have achieved.' He shook his head.

They were sitting down now, an intimate little group,
exhausted by the emotions of the day. Raph loosened his tie and
refilled their glasses. His angular features were lean with strain.
Sam felt light-headed, more from a profound disbelief that this
was happening than from alcohol consumption, though that
was probably a part of it, too.

Trevor said to Sam, 'I can't believe she would have destroyed
her journal, though. That's just not like her. If only we knew

what was in her mind when . . . when . . .' Another sentence left hanging in midair. 'Before she died,' he finished wretchedly.

'Sam and I looked,' said Raph. 'When we went down. If there'd been a journal there we'd have spotted it. She didn't have that much stuff in the cottage.'

Sam said, 'Her journal wasn't the only thing we couldn't find.'

Trevor sighed. 'I just don't understand it.'

'Why?' asked Johnny. 'What else was missing?'

'A poem,' said Trevor. 'It was going to be the title poem for her next collection.'

'Did she destroy that, too?' asked Johnny.

'Must have done,' said Raph. 'It wasn't among her papers.'

'I'd seen some of it,' said Trevor. 'Work in progress. But she wouldn't let me keep it. She must have destroyed the only copy.'

'God, that's terrible,' said Johnny. Miriam slipped her hand into his arm and he patted it absently.

Sam said, 'Do you know what the poem was called?' And when no one answered, she said quietly, 'The Murder Bird.'

There was silence, broken after a few moments by Diana saying, 'What a strange name for a poem. "The Murder Bird". Quite morbid, really.'

Morbid? thought Sam. Or prophetic?

'"The Murder Bird",' said Johnny, rolling the title round on his tongue thoughtfully. 'I wonder what that was about.'

'So do I,' said Sam.

In the silence that followed, they all heard the front door open and close, light footsteps crossing the hall. A young woman who couldn't have been more than a couple of years older than Sam stood in the doorway. She looked as if she'd stepped off the pages of *Hello!* magazine, all streaky blonde hair, pouting glossed lips and impossibly long legs. 'Am I too early? I stayed away as long as I could.'

It was the first time Sam had met Lola. She knew Raph had a girlfriend, would have expected him to, in fact. He'd always hated being on his own and there'd been several since Kirsten's departure last October. But all the same, she was shocked at her appearance right now, when Kirsten was still such a presence in the room. She wasn't the only one. There was a ripple of unease.

Then Raph said, 'Lola. I didn't expect you back so soon.'

'Well, I'm here now. Aren't you going to offer me a drink?'

She came in and Raph introduced her. She looked bored, impatient for them all to be gone. The effect on Johnny and Trevor was electric. They both leaped to their feet, competing in their eagerness to pour her a drink, make space, introduce themselves. Lola possessed the kind of undiluted sexuality that could transform a bunch of grieving middle-aged men into a pack of tomcats. As he reached over to light her cigarette, Johnny threw Raph a 'Good work!' glance of approval. Kirsten, who had been in some way present in the room while they were talking about her, slipped away into the shadows.

Sam stood up. 'I have to go,' she said.

'Did you sort out about the keys?' Lola asked Raph. She hadn't yet acknowledged Sam in any way.

'Lola,' said Raph. 'I really don't think now's the time.'

'Keys?' asked Sam.

'That's right,' said Lola coolly, her eyes on Raph. 'Now that this isn't your home any more, it doesn't seem right for you to keep a set. No one else does.'

Sam hesitated, giving Raph time to intervene. He looked wretched and embarrassed, but he did not meet Sam's eye and he did not speak. .

She said, 'Raph?'

He said, 'You can give them back later, if you'd rather.'

Brilliant, thought Sam. No more pretending, then.

'I can do it now.' She reached down into her bag, pulled out her key ring and detached two keys. 'Keep the bloody things.' She dropped them on to a glass-topped table.

'Sam,' said Raph, 'there's no need to overreact.'

'Fuck you. This is restrained.'

'Well, really,' said Diana. She hated any kind of conflict and was always quick to smother it with a safe retreat to normality. She said, 'I don't know about anyone else, but I'm feeling distinctly peckish.'

'I'll whip us up some scrambled eggs,' said Raph. 'Sam, you'll stay for that, won't you? There's smoked salmon.'

'No thanks.' She was already at the door leading into the hall. She said, 'Since this isn't my home any more, I'm just going to get the last of my stuff.'

Raph caught up with her on the stairs. 'Sam, please. I don't want to fall out with you. You know you're welcome here any time. It's just a question of ringing first. I'm sorry about Lola, but – well, things are a bit delicate at the moment.'

'Delicate?' She almost laughed. 'Bad choice of words, Raph.'

'You know what I mean.'

'I don't care what you mean.'

She ran ahead, up to the second floor where her own bedroom had been, and pulled a box out from under the bed.

Photographs, mostly. Nothing else was important, but there was too much to carry all at once.

When she came back down, a quick glance through the door into the drawing room revealed Lola holding court, Trevor and Johnny jostling to be wittiest and most charming. Diana, glad only that harmony had been restored, smiled indulgently on the trio. Voices in the basement kitchen showed the whereabouts of Raph and his sister. Now that she had no keys, Sam had to tell him she'd come back for the rest of her stuff. She went down.

Halfway down, she overheard Miriam: 'You've got it, haven't you?'

Raph: 'Don't be ridiculous.'

But Miriam persisted, 'Does it say anything about – the family?'

'I told you. I don't – ah, Sam.' He flashed her a look – how much had she heard? 'Won't you change your mind and stay for a bite to eat?'

No, she was leaving right now. In that case, he insisted on calling her a cab. That way she could take all the boxes with her as well. He would have driven her himself but he'd had too much to drink. Ditto Trevor and Johnny. Sam didn't argue. She couldn't wait to get away from that house with its memories of good times and its present compromises and lies.

But – '*You've got it, haven't you?*' Miriam had said.

Raph had blustered. A sure sign that he was lying.

It was only a matter of time before Sam came back.

Which she had done, risking her neck to climb up the outside of the building, thanks to Lola's insistence about the keys and

Raph's weasel refusal to take Sam's side. Or maybe he'd been happy to let Lola do his dirty work for him. Maybe he had his own reasons for not wanting Sam to have free run in his home. Maybe he'd schooled Lola in advance.

Sam rubbed her eyes. Sometimes she wondered if she was making rational choices right now, or whether the horror of her mother's death had skewed her judgement. Whatever the reasons, she was now stuck in Raph's study, unable to make a proper search, while Lola partied with a handsome young man who was, it seemed, a pupil in Raph's chambers. It occurred to Sam that there was nothing to stop her from gatecrashing their jolly twosome and carrying on the search – nothing but her pride, which refused to involve anything which might even remotely resemble asking Lola for help.

She'd just have to wait.

Next door, the champagne cork popped and Lola squealed.

'Ooh, look. All down my dress!'

'Sorry.'

'You can lick it off it you like.'

'No thanks.'

'Suit yourself. I'm taking it off anyway.'

'Hey . . .'

'That's better. Mm. Let's get comfy.'

'Look, Lola. I really should go.'

'Stop wittering on. Anyone would think I was trying to seduce you. Don't flatter yourself, Micky boy. There, happy now?'

Sam's eyes had adjusted to the semi-darkness in Raph's study. She noticed with relief that her hand had stopped bleeding. She flexed her fingers – no harm done, thank God – and stashed the blood stained scarf in her bag. Silently, she unlaced her sneakers and pulled them off, then padded to the bookcase and ran her finger along the row of spines. Surely an A4 leather-backed notebook would be easy to find, even in this light.

Next door, the mood was changing.

'Mm, I feel woozy.'

'Go to sleep, then.'

'Yeah. But not here.'

'I'll help you upstairs.'

'Now you're talking.'

'And then I'm leaving.'

'Huh. Know something, Mick? You can be a real party pooper.'

Sam heard his soft laughter. 'Listen, Lola. You may be drop-dead gorgeous, but as far as I'm concerned, drop dead is what I might as well do if I start messing with you. I do happen to work for Raph, remember. And it's not going to look brilliant on my CV if I get thrown out of chambers for cuckolding my pupil-master.'

'Fuss, fuss, fuss.'

'Let's get you to bed.'

'Mm. All right then.'

More mumbling, shuffling and soft giggles. Noises vanishing up the stairs. The moment their voices had faded into silence, Sam flicked her torch back on and resumed her search. She was meticulous, feeling down behind the books, looking under the furniture and under the files in the two four-drawer cabinets.

She left Raph's desk till last. For the first time, as she fumbled through his old cheque books and a handful of letters, she felt a twinge of guilt at what she was doing. No time for scruples. A man's footsteps were coming down the stairs. Automatically, Sam switched off the torch, but the room was growing lighter. It was nearly time to go.

Just as she was about to shut the lowest drawer, her hand closed round something cool and metal right at the back, under a stack of padded envelopes. She pulled it out.

A gun.

It fitted neatly against her palm. Sam knew nothing about handguns, but this didn't exactly look like a toy.

There was just time to push it back where it came from when the door opened and Lola's date for the evening – Mick or Micky or whatever he was called – reappeared. His shirt was unbuttoned and he looked even more rumpled than he had done before. It suited him.

He grinned and started tucking his shirt into his jeans.

'She's out for the count,' he said. 'Did you find what you were looking for?'

'If I had, I'd have gone by now.'

'Tell me what it is and I can help.'

'Why would you want to do that?'

Mick was beginning to ask himself the same question. The intruder, who claimed to be Kirsten Waller's daughter and who had spent a ridiculous amount of time cooped up in Raph Howes's study, was about as friendly as a cactus. Put it down to curiosity. There had to be some explanation why this skinny girl with the cropped dark hair and bare feet was lurking in Raph's house while he was dealing with a fraud case in Basle.

He said, 'Suspicious, aren't you? Almost like someone with a guilty conscience. Maybe I was too quick to buy your story. I think I'll check it out with Raph after all. Do you always carry a hammer in your belt?'

'It's none of your business.'

'But I'm making it my business.'

'Oh, really? And when Raph gets back from Basle and finds you still here at seven in the morning and –' She jerked her head in the direction of the drawing room, where Lola's clothes were clearly visible on and around the huge white sofa. '– and all of this, you might have to do a bit of explaining of your own.'

'Shit.' Mick grinned. 'You'll vouch for me, won't you? All I did was see her home from a party. She wasn't in any state to manage on her own.'

'Yeah?' The cactus looked at her watch. 'And it took you an hour to help her up the stairs?'

'I guess I must have nodded off.'

'Raph might not see it that way.'

'Hmm. A bit of an impasse, really.' Mick was enjoying himself. The situation appealed to his sense of the absurd. 'What do you think we should do about it?'

'You can do what you want. I'm leaving.'

'I'll push off too.'

'Not with me you won't.'

Mick wasn't used to quite so much hostility. On the whole people tended to like him. 'Are you always this unfriendly?' he asked. 'Tell me what you're looking for and I'll have a look around.'

She hesitated, and seemed almost ready to accept his offer of help. It was getting light fast and, in that moment of hesitation,

Mick saw the uncertainty and raw pain that lay just under the surface of her hostility. For a moment, he really did want to help.

The moment passed.

She muttered, more to herself than to him, 'The bastard must have destroyed it.' She was pulling on her sneakers, slinging her backpack over her shoulder. In the garden, birds were singing.

'I won't say a word to Raph,' he said.

'Damn right you won't.'

And with that, she headed off towards the front door. He heard it bang shut behind her.

CHAPTER 4

The coroner's court was packed and airless in the August heat. Sam was sitting next to her father, Davy Boswin and a stout lady in a suit with lemon ruffles who Raph assumed was Davy's present wife, Linda. Raph had driven down that morning. He and Kirsten had still been married at the time of her death, even though they were living apart. No way would he have stayed away from the inquest. Sam was wearing a dark dress with a shirt over it loosely tied at the waist. With her cropped dark hair and her pinched, anxious features, she looked horribly young and vulnerable. He remembered her a year ago, radiant and full of energy. She'd been beautiful then. Raph wished Sam hadn't chosen to attend, but knowing how stubborn she was, never flinching from unpleasant necessity, he was hardly surprised. It was too bad that business with Lola and the keys had driven a wedge between them. But maybe such a wedge had been inevitable, eventually.

Several of Kirsten's Cornish friends were there, too, he noticed, including Judy Saunders who owned the cottage in which Kirsten had died and the farmers who had been her nearest neighbours. Dr Riley, the coroner, had an air of benign authority, like a strict but fair headmistress, as she introduced the case, then took the coroner's officer through the documentary evidence. There were statements from the policeman who'd been called to the scene when the body was found, from the doctor who'd pronounced 'life extinct' and from Andy Borlase, the local electrician who'd carried out work for Judy Saunders in the cottage; he had noted that the wiring was out of date and did not meet present-day standards but pointed out that it was not technically illegal either. There were photographs also. Most of them, the ones of Gull Cottage and the bathroom where Kirsten's body had been found, were circulated through the court. Those showing Kirsten's naked body slung over the side of the bath in which she had died so horribly were passed 'discreetly' between the coroner, her officer and those who had been first on the scene and therefore witnessed the real thing.

Raph, watching Sam's face, knew that she must be conjuring up those images in her head. He wished there was some way he could have protected her.

Raph had broken the news to her on the midsummer day Kirsten's body was found. He'd gone round to her flat and they'd driven straight down to Cornwall together. Mostly, they'd travelled in silence, but the bond between them had still been strong enough back then for words to be superfluous. She must have known how much he was grieving, too. He'd never quite let go of the hope that he and Kirsten might find a way to be reconciled.

They'd arrived at Gull Cottage early in the evening. Set back a few yards from the cliff edge, it had never been intended as anything but a temporary summer retreat. That first evening, the tranquillity of the scene made a cruel contrast to the tragedy that had just occurred. The sea was calm and blue; skylarks sang over the headland and gulls floated in the deep gulf between cliff and sea. Even Gull Cottage, so cramped and ramshackle, looked like the little house in a fairy story, evening light sparking gold on its windows.

'Are you sure you want to go in?' Raph had asked her when they got out of the car and walked, as people always did when they arrived at Gull Cottage, to the rabbit-cropped grass at the edge of the cliff. Kirsten's body had been removed by the undertakers, he knew, but otherwise everything was much as it had been when Davy found her body that morning.

'I've got to do it sooner or later. Best get it over with,' Sam had said. She'd hung back from the edge of the cliff. He remembered her vertigo.

'Brave girl,' said Raph. 'Okay then, let's do it.'

Sam nodded. She was still in shock, sleepwalking through the tasks that had to be accomplished.

Once inside the cottage, they found Kirsten's possessions scattered over every surface, just as she had left them: her walking boots by the door, her canvas jacket slung over the back of a chair, books and papers everywhere, her usual accumulation of practical and personal. A gypsy in her bones, Kirsten was able to make any place into an instant home, even hotel rooms were quickly stamped with her character. There was her favourite mug, wild flowers in a cheap vase on the table, photographs of

Sam, that photograph Raph himself had taken only the year before, mother and daughter together on the day Sam had graduated from the Royal College of Music. Sam looking as if the world was her oyster.

As they looked around, Sam was shaking, didn't seem able to stop.

Raph said, 'I'll make you some tea. Here, sit.'

She sat.

'I can help you go through her things, if you like.'

'Maybe . . . tomorrow.' Sam's hand was resting lightly on a thin stack of paper: *The Murder Bird and Other Poems* was written on the title page.

When he had made the tea and set it down in front of her, Raph glanced at the title and said, 'Trevor will want to see those. Let's hope they're ready for publication.'

'Yes,' said Sam.

With any luck, Raph thought, seeing her mother's last collection through to publication might be a help in the months ahead. She was going to need it.

'Oh, look,' he said, reaching across the table to a sheet of paper propped against the lamp. 'This looks like some kind of a note.'

Sam said, 'It's a poem.'

They read it together in silence. A single sheet of lined paper with the words 'The Farewell Bird' scrawled across the top. Not so much a poem, more notes towards a poem. If it hadn't been propped against the lamp that way, it would have been indistinguishable from the general mass of papers Kirsten was always surrounded by.

'Eradicate our love, eradicate the past', and 'Flying to grey-ness and beyond.' And ending up, 'I take my leave and go.'

'Oh God,' Raph said when they'd finished. Tears were sting-ing his eyes. 'So it wasn't an accident.'

Sam stared at him, not comprehending. 'What do you mean?'

'This note. It's proof – that Kirsten killed herself. I'm so sorry, Sam. I thought perhaps it was an accident. I *hoped* it was an accident. I'm so sorry.'

'She didn't kill herself,' said Sam, still not taking it in. 'Mum wouldn't do that.'

Raph turned away. He was looking out of the window, towards the sea and the far horizon. He had to get Sam to accept that Kirsten had taken her own life. He said, 'It wasn't an accident, Sam. I know it's hard to take it in, but there's no other explanation.'

'But . . . I was coming to visit. Next week. We'd talked on the phone. Made plans.'

'The note, Sam.'

'How about murder?' Sam asked him. 'Did you think of that?'

He sighed. 'It wasn't murder. I almost wish it was.'

She looked down, her tears spilling on to the title page: *The Murder Bird and Other Poems.* But she didn't argue with him after that.

There was silence in the courtroom as Davy Boswin was sworn in. In his early fifties, Sam's father was still a handsome man, medium height, with blue eyes and curly brown hair that was just starting to go grey. He was lean and muscular in the countryman's way – the kind of fitness that comes from a lifetime of physical work rather than hours in a gym. The only weights Davy had ever lifted were concrete blocks and boxes weighed down with fish.

But in the courtroom, he was out of his element. He was wearing a suit, for a start, and Sam's father had never been at ease in a suit. Nothing highlighted the difference between Kirsten Waller's two husbands so much as the suits they wore at her inquest. Raph's was pale grey light wool and had been made for him in Savile Row, as all his suits were; its expert cut made his ponderous figure look elegant and suave. Davy only possessed one suit; it had been bought off the peg and hung in a cupboard for years, to be dragged out for weddings and funerals – and now, for the coroner's court. The fabric was an odd shiny blue-black and it had never fitted. You could tell by the awkward way Davy Boswin held his shoulders, as though the hanger had been left inside the jacket, that he was itching to shove the wretched garment in his wardrobe and put his work clothes back on. He wore his tie, which was narrow and greenly spotted, like a garrotte.

It was Davy who had found the body.

'You were formerly married to the deceased, Mr Boswin?' asked the coroner.

'That's right.'

'But you were divorced several years ago?'

'Nearly twenty years ago, yes.' Davy was courteous, careful not to betray his distaste for the whole business.

Sam knew how much her father, the most private of men, would hate having to expose any of his private life in a court of law. And when he was unhappy he became quieter, and slower, than ever. That morning at breakfast he'd hardly spoken and, to Sam's frustration, they'd almost been late.

She'd travelled down to Cornwall by train the previous afternoon and stayed over at Menverren, the smallholding where she and her father had both grown up.

'We need to get there early, Dad,' she'd told him at breakfast, though without much hope that he'd pick up on her sense of urgency. 'There'll be press and everything there. We have to get to the court before they do.'

'You're sure you want to come, Sam?' he'd asked, anxious as ever to shield her from pain. 'The coroner said they wouldn't need to question you, you know.'

'Of course I'm going.'

'There's nothing new coming out, you realize that, don't you, Sam?' Davy knew her suspicions, but he seemed to have accepted the suicide lie, so she'd learned not to talk to him about it.

'I have to be there, Dad. Can't we be early, just for once?'

'Don't fret, Sam,' Davy had told her. 'The court's not going anywhere. The inquest will just be a formality, that's what they said.'

Linda, his wife, had taken no part in this discussion, but her pursed lips had said it all: Kirsten Waller had been nothing but trouble for Davy while she was alive, so it was hardly surprising if her death caused problems, too. Sam had hoped she wouldn't bother attending, but Linda was a loyal wife and wasn't about to miss seeing her husband give evidence.

They had arrived at the coroner's court five minutes before

Kirsten's case was called. As Sam had anticipated, the benches were packed with press as well as people who had known Kirsten while she lived in Cornwall and there had been a lot of shuffling and adjusting as the court's officer found space for them. 'Well, well.' Davy had been puzzled. 'Who'd have thought our Kirsten would have attracted such a crowd, eh?'

Sam hadn't bothered to respond. Davy had never really caught up with the fact that his first wife had become an internationally respected poet. To him, she would always remain the strange young American who had turned up with nothing, stayed for a few years then taken off as unexpectedly as she'd arrived, like one of those North American birds that are sometimes blown off course and fetch up in the far south-west of England, a lonely exotic, attracting brief attention before being forgotten entirely.

Except that Kirsten hadn't been forgotten; she'd become famous in the circles where poets are known. Hence it wasn't just the local press who were covering this inquest; journalists from the national papers were there as well, and a couple of TV crews. Unless new evidence came to light Sam realized that by the end of the day's proceedings the lie of her mother's death would be cast in media stone. Short of a miracle, and Sam had no reason to believe in miracles.

The coroner, deliberately informal, was sifting through the papers in front of her. 'At exactly what time, Mr Boswin, did you arrive at Gull Cottage?' she asked.

Davy weighed the question carefully before answering in his steady Cornish brogue. 'Well, it must have been about nine-thirty, because I'd dropped the boys at school and I was on my way to my sister Sheila's. I thought I'd just stop by at the cottage, seeing as how Kirsten had wanted to see me the day before and I hadn't been able to get there.'

'I see.' The coroner was making notes. 'You couldn't get there on the evening of the 20th of June because—?'

'There was a problem with the car, see. Wouldn't start.' Davy grinned awkwardly. 'Usually it's not that bad, but that evening, well, it needed some work doing.'

'There was a problem with your car?'

'Well, by the time I'd worked on it, it was getting late and she'd said not to bother. She was . . .' He hesitated, frowned, then repeated quietly, 'She'd said not to bother.'

A fist of shame closed over Sam's heart. The bare bones of her family's life were being exposed and picked over by strangers. Just for once, why hadn't he been able to get to the right place at the right time? Because if he had, Kirsten might be . . . No, don't even go there. She was angry enough without that. Davy had always prided himself on being able to pick up an old banger for a song and keep it on the road long after anyone else would have abandoned it. Her childhood years, before she went to live with Raph and Kirsten when she was fifteen, had been dominated by rattly old cars that smelled of oily rags, cars and vans that never started when they were really needed and got the character of cantankerous old relatives.

Sam glanced across at Raph, who would have driven down that morning in his dark green TVR – his long-distance car; there was a Citroën and an Audi as well. He was looking curiously at Davy, as though his choice of car was a mild eccentricity, rather than a habit born of years of making ends meet the best way he could.

'Ms Waller wanted to see you on the evening of the 20th of June?'

'Yes. She phoned me at lunchtime and said would I come round and I said I'd try.'

'When she phoned you from Gull Cottage, did she say why she wanted to see you?'

'Excuse me,' Davy corrected the coroner politely, 'but Kirsten never phoned from the cottage. There's no phone there, see. Never has been. It was one of the reasons she was always so happy there, because it was peaceful. If she wanted to use a phone, she either had to go to the Wearnes' place, that's the next-door farm—' He flicked a glance at the stoical figure of Ann Wearne, who was sitting near the back of the court, then went on, 'Or go into the village. Polwithick. There's a phone box next to the post office. I believe she called me from the post office because she mentioned something about posting a letter.' Mrs Wearne nodded her agreement at this remark.

'So she phoned you again when she told you not to bother?'

Davy's frown deepened. 'No, it was the same time. I said there might be a problem with the car, and she said in that case, not to worry. Come round another time.'

'I see. Thank you, Mr Boswin. And when you spoke to her on the 20th, did she sound anxious about anything? Depressed, even?'

Sam held her breath, waiting for her father's answer. As always, Davy gave the question full attention before saying carefully, 'No, I wouldn't say she sounded anxious. Or depressed, really. No.'

'So how would you describe her mood when she made that last phone call to you?'

'Well, now. That's hard to say, exactly. She sounded pretty much the way she always did, though you couldn't always tell what her mood was, by the way she spoke. And we didn't talk for long.'

'Can you try to remember precisely what was said?'

'That's a bit hard, but . . . it went along the lines of her asking if I could come by that evening and me saying I'd try. And she said not to worry if it got late because . . . Well, it wasn't that urgent, she said. And that was about it. See you later, then, that was the last thing I said to her before I put the phone down and . . .' Suddenly Davy's calm voice wavered. He paused, looked down at his hands which were spread out in front of him, then cleared his throat and said quietly, as if only addressing his hands, 'And Kirsten said, "Right you are, then. I'll see you some time, Davy." And that was . . . that was . . . it.'

He cleared his throat, then wiped his eye. He was still frowning with the effort of not giving in to emotion. A ripple of sympathy ran through the courtroom for the soft-spoken, still handsome man who was so obviously affected by the loss of someone who had left him over twenty years before. Davy Boswin had a quiet dignity that compelled respect.

Sam alone felt uncomfortable at Davy's choice of words. *Right you are, then* . . . Kirsten would never have used that phrase. They were Davy's words. Kirsten would have phrased it differently. Kirsten would have said . . . but Sam wasn't sure what Kirsten would have said. In the last few weeks she'd stopped being able to hear the echo of her mother's voice in her head and she panicked sometimes, wondering if in time she'd forget what she looked like, too. She just knew that Kirsten would never have said, 'Right you are.'

'Would you like a glass of water, Mr Boswin?'

Davy looked up, blinking. 'No. No, thank you. I'll do fine.'

'So Ms Waller didn't give you any particular reason why she wanted to see you that day?'

'No. Just said she wanted me to pop round. I thought she maybe needed help with a light fitting, or maybe moving something. Kirsten wasn't very handy 'bout the house, you know. I never imagined that she was . . . upset.'

'And when you arrived Gull Cottage at nine-thirty on the 21st—'

'It was *about* nine-thirty,' Davy interrupted her carefully. 'Might have been half an hour each way. Maybe nine. Or even ten. But most likely it was closer to nine-thirty.'

'I see. Can you tell us what happened when you arrived there?'

'Well, yes. I parked the car on the bit of ground to the left of the cottage and I went in through the side door.'

'Did you have a key?'

Davy looked startled by this question. 'I didn't need a key. The door was never locked at Gull Cottage. Kirsten didn't believe in keys and locks. It was one of those things she felt strongly about.'

'So anyone could have walked in?'

'Yes, I reckon so.'

'And when you went into the cottage, did you notice anything unusual?'

Here it came again. Sam clenched her fists. Each time she

heard this story was like the first time all over again and Sam felt the ground of her old life falling away, nothing but black panic swirling round her heart.

Davy had gone into the cottage and called out Kirsten's name. He hadn't noticed the note lying on the kitchen table because wherever Kirsten was there were bits of paper lying around with scribbled notes towards poems. It would have been more surprising, he said, if there hadn't been a note. He looked into the back room, then went out again into the garden and called her name a couple of times more. He thought she must have gone for a walk, but then something, he couldn't say what it was exactly, had made him feel that things weren't quite right, so he'd gone back into the cottage and called her name again – probably, he couldn't be exactly sure about this. Then he went up the stairs. Looked into the bedroom. Noticed the bathroom door ajar, the extension cord stretched across the landing. Glanced in.

The extension cord was looped over the side of the bath. The little radio drowned into silence, its lethal work done.

There were photographs – no need for them to be shown again, not even 'discreetly' – of what he'd seen there: Kirsten's body slumped half in and half out of the bath, naked and con-torted and dead . . . but Sam hadn't seen them and her brain refused to picture it. She hated it all the more, knowing how shy Kirsten had always been about nakedness. Years of bohemian life had not been sufficient to erase the strict code in which she'd been reared.

And now Davy's testimony had reached the puzzle of the switched-off plug.

'In your statement at the time, Mr Boswin, you said that the appliance that caused Kirsten Waller's death was switched off when you came into the cottage. Is that correct?' asked the coroner.

Davy hesitated. 'That's what I said, yes.'

'But subsequently, you told the coroner's officer that you may have switched it off yourself?'

'Well, yes.' He stopped. He was frowning as he went on, 'I don't remember exactly, but . . . what with the shock of seeing her like that . . . maybe I turned it off myself. Instinctively. Without even knowing that I was doing it.'

'Is that likely?' asked the coroner.

'Well, I reckon it might have happened like that. Yes.'

But Davy wasn't meeting the coroner's eye as he spoke and, almost imperceptibly, the sympathy that there'd been for him earlier was melting away. He wasn't being hesitant any more; he looked like he was being evasive.

Sam felt a kind of sick familiarity as she watched her father struggling. Give him a small boat that needed getting back to harbour in a force nine gale, or a stone wall that had to be rebuilt double quick, and there was no one in the world more competent than Davy Boswin. But put him up against any-one in authority – tax inspectors, schoolteachers, even doctors – and his self-assurance vanished. Often his manner was down-right shifty even when there was nothing at all to be shifty about. And now he was acting as though there'd been some-thing suspicious in his actions after finding his ex-wife's body.

There was silence in the little courtroom. A couple of people were fanning themselves with folded newspapers. Cars were audible through the open windows, but inside, all was hushed and waiting. The coroner had asked Davy something and he wasn't answering. If the power supply that had ended Kirsten's life had been switched off by the time the emergency services arrived, then obviously one of those first on the scene had done it. There was no need for him to look so guilty about it, as if he was being accused of having electrocuted her in the first place.

Davy started to speak, then coughed and cleared his throat. He glanced at Linda who had never taken her eyes off him for a moment. She was just two feet away from Sam, but it seemed like much further. Stout in her lemon-ruffled suit, she was sitting four-square on the bench, leaning forward slightly as though straining to hear what her husband was saying. Or as if she was getting ready to run away.

After a few moments, Davy nodded, almost imperceptibly, then turned his attention back to the coroner and said quietly, 'Yes. I reckon that's how it was.'

'You're sure of that?'

'Yes,' said Davy at length. 'I reckon I am.'

'Thank you, Mr Boswin. You may step down.'

And then it was over. The coroner had summarized the facts as she saw them in a cool, dispassionate voice, while taking care to stress the tragedy of the events and the sympathy the court extended to Kirsten Waller's family and friends, but her verdict was unequivocal. She had taken her own life. No one knew the reason, but the note left her in no doubt.

They drifted out and stood on the pavement in small groups.

Everyone was longing to escape but aware also that it would be unseemly to rush away. The coroner, who looked smaller, less headmistressy away from her position at the head of the court, was talking to Raph and Johnny. One or two people came over and commiserated with Sam. Judy was being interviewed by a local TV team: the 'best friend tells her story'. She was explaining, very earnestly, how much Gull Cottage and Cornwall had always meant to Kirsten, how she had often planned to update the cottage but friends who loved to stay there had always begged her to leave it just as it was. Linda was looking grim in spite of the lemon ruffles. She grabbed Davy's arm as though it was a package that she was taking possession of, but at the last minute he disentangled himself, murmured something briefly to her, before walking over to where Sam stood.

'All right, Sam?'

Sam smiled in spite of herself. *All right*, the Cornish phrase which covers a multitude of uses: How are you? I'm fine. I wish you well. Thank God it's over. On a visit to Gull Cottage a couple of years before, Kirsten had even written a poem called 'The All Right Bird', a bird with a single call for every occasion. Sam said, 'All right, Dad.'

'That was a grim old business, wasn't it, eh? Such a waste.'

'Yes.'

He hesitated, then, 'D'you want to come back home with us, Sam? You're welcome to stay another night, you know.'

'Thanks, but Raph's offered me a lift, and I'm working tomorrow.' She wasn't crazy about the prospect of travelling with him, but the TVR offered the fastest option, and she saw no reason to linger.

'Raph?' Davy's face darkened. He glanced across to where Raph was standing with Johnny and the coroner. Raph was looking increasingly stressed and eager to be away, so Johnny was doing most of the talking. 'What d'you want to go with him for?'

'It's easier than the train.'

'Ah.' He was still frowning. 'Seeing much of him then, are you?'

'Now and then,' she said. 'I think Mum's death has really got to him.'

'I thought he'd got fixed up with someone new.'

Sam could see Linda out of the corner of her eye. 'That does-n't mean he stopped caring about Mum though, does it?'

'Hm. Well . . . It's affected us all.' Davy slid his hand under Sam's elbow and drew her to one side, where he was sure they wouldn't be overheard. He said, 'Just between you and me, Sam. I'd keep your distance if I were you.'

'From Raph?'

Davy nodded.

'Why?'

'Come back with me and Linda and we can talk.'

'I can't. I've got to be in London for tomorrow.'

'Well. That's a shame, then.'

'What is it, Dad? What's the matter?'

Davy looked around him to make sure no one was within earshot, before saying in a low voice, 'Thing is, see, I don't trust him.'

Sam was about to dismiss it: Davy and Raph belonged in dif-ferent worlds so it was hardly surprising if . . . But then she stopped herself. Davy had always been generous in his praise of all that Raph had done for her. She said, 'Why not, Dad?'

'He knows more'n he lets on.'

'What?'

Instinctively, Sam looked across at Raph. He was shaking the coroner's hand, and doing a fair impersonation of the self-assured London barrister, but Sam knew him well enough, knew by the flex of his shoulders and the smile that was more like a grimace, that the strain of this day had got to him too. He started walking towards his car, then turned and seemed about to gesture towards her to tell her they were going, when Johnny must have said something to him, probably telling him not to be in such a hurry, because he rested a hand on his car door and began chatting with Johnny again.

'Someone was at Gull Cottage before me that morning,' said Davy, speaking so quietly that Sam could barely hear the words. 'I wasn't the first there. Don't ask me how I know, but it's the truth, I promise. A man, they said, medium height, dark hair, London clothes. And driving an expensive foreign car. Flashy. They think it was green or grey.'

Sam looked across at Raph's TVR. 'Raph? But Raph and I drove down together, later that day. He—' She broke off, quickly calculating the timing. It had been assumed that Kirsten had died some time during the evening before her body was found. Raph had been having dinner with friends at the time. And he'd broken the news of Kirsten's death to her just before noon. But in between midnight and noon? It was just about possible that if Raph had returned from dinner with his friends at eleven, he could have driven down to Cornwall and been at

Gull Cottage by four or five in the morning, then driven back to London for about 11 a.m. Then he could have contacted Sam, when he 'heard the news about Kirsten', and driven back down by late afternoon. It was a hell of a lot of driving, but it was possible. Just. 'Raph was at Gull Cottage just after Kirsten died? But why?'

'That's what I'd like to know.'

'Does anyone else know?'

'No point stirring things up.'

Why didn't you tell the police? Sam bit back the question. She knew the answer already. In a crisis, the Cornish close ranks. Bad enough that Kirsten was dead from suicide and an idyllic holiday cottage had been the location for a notorious tragedy: their strong sense of shame and an instinctive urge to grieve in private were more than enough to make them keep silent, Davy and whoever the mysterious someone was who had seen a man who looked like Raph at Gull Cottage just before Kirsten's body was found. No one understood this instinct better than Sam: after all, she'd learned to stay silent about her certainty that Kirsten had not taken her own life. Her reason was different. She'd tried telling the policeman dealing with her mother's death about her misgivings, but had been met by the blank wall of his disbelief. And worse, his pity. She couldn't bear to see people's pity, couldn't bear to see them thinking, *Poor girl, she can't accept the truth so she has to invent a murderer.* So she stayed just as silent as her father. She said, 'Are you sure, Dad?'

'I'm only repeating what I heard.'

Sam thought of the farming family who had been Kirsten's closest neighbours. 'Was it Ann or Bob Wearne?'

'Doesn't matter who it was,' said Davy. 'And best not to ask, either. Just keep your distance, all right?'

'No, not all right, Dad,' Sam drew in a deep breath. Maybe she would go back to Menverren with him after all. 'You don't think Mum killed herself either, do you?'

Davy looked away, to where Linda was waiting with undisguised impatience. 'We've had our verdict,' he said quietly. 'Doesn't matter much what anyone thinks, does it, not now. She's dead, anyway. Nothing's going to bring her back, Sam.'

'But that's not the point. If you think someone killed her—'

'I didn't say that, Sam.'

'Oh, for heaven's sake, what are you afraid of?'

'Don't go upsetting yourself, Sam. Life has to go on, now. We've all got our own lives to lead. You've got your music.'

Linda's patience had worn out and she walked over. 'Are you coming, Davy?'

'Yes, just saying goodbye to Sam here.' He lifted his arms to embrace her, but she moved away, too agitated for a farewell embrace. He nodded, accepting her decision, and said, 'You take care, now.'

'Bye, Dad.'

Sam went over to where Raph was waiting.

'Ready to go, Sam?' asked Raph.

She looked at him. Four hours alone in a car with Raph. She could use the time to ask him about what Davy had said. And have to endure his inevitable denials. What was the point?

She said coolly, 'I thought I might go back with Johnny.'

Johnny's face lit up. It was his happy spaniel face. 'Brilliant.

Fantastic. Couldn't be better. We've got to stop off at Wardley and pick Miriam up, but you don't mind about that, do you?'

'Of course not.'

'Suit yourself,' said Raph. 'Well, goodbye everyone.'

'Come along then, Sam.' Johnny was already heading to his car, pulling open the doors to let in some cooler air, chucking maps and wrappers on to the back seat. 'God, this has been a ghastly day. You were terrific. Can't imagine what it was like for you. God, Sam, sometimes life is absolutely bloody, isn't it?'

He couldn't hold back any more. He put his arms around her and wrapped her in a generous hug, while Raph got into his car and drove swiftly away.

Raph hardly noticed the large, blond-haired man, his oldest friend, who had given Sam the spontaneous comfort that seemed to be beyond the reach of both her father and her step-father. Right then, as he drove away from the courtroom and headed down to the roundabout, he was barely noticing anything. A pilot light of sanity was telling him he was in no fit state to be driving, not like this, but he knew he couldn't stop until he'd put some distance between himself and the horror of this day. As a criminal barrister, he was no stranger to the details of death; in fact, he usually relished the means by which unbearable events were tamed with legal tricks and phrases. But Kirsten's death was different. He could see her body, that body he'd known and loved like no other, naked and draped half in and half out of the bath. How long had death taken to claim her? Time plays tricks at the moment of crisis. Did it seem to be happening in slow motion? Had she tried to save herself, tried to escape? Had it been swift and painless, or had she suffered and screamed out in agony before the end?

He was gasping, cursing the traffic as it crawled up the hill out of Truro, desperate to get away before the horrors came back. But he couldn't drive fast enough.

Here it came, that other death, the first death, the one he could never escape from. The one that opened the door to the rest of his life. An unremarkable event, the kind of thing that happens so often that no one really notices any more. A small dog, white with a single black ear and a black splodge on its rump, a Jack Russell, yelps and sees him from across the road.

'*Chippy!*'

The small boy screams in anguish. He sees the car, a car speeding round the corner on the country lane where cars hardly ever come, where cars are not expected. He hears the dog's yelp of joy and then –

'*Chippy, don't!*' he yells again, but Chippy misinterprets the call, leaps into the road, straight into the path of the car. The driver never sees him, never even stops. The car roars off leaving emptiness behind, emptiness and silence and a small boy weeping in the wet grass at the side of the road.

'Chippy, wake up. Chippy, don't die. Chippy, oh Chippy . . .'

The twitches deceive him. He doesn't know they're spasms of death. He thinks there's hope. But when he picks the dog up to take him to safety, it's as if all his bones have been removed and there's only sawdust inside the skin. He tries to hold the head, keep back and legs together, still part of a living whole, but it's no good.

And as he heads towards home, the dog's lifeless body in his arms, a new terror takes hold of him.

His father's voice, echoing in his ears. 'Don't you dare take him out. He's not a pet. You know what happens to naughty boys, don't you?'

But Chippy had looked at him with those black eyes, just begging to go for a walk, just down to the stream where the horse chestnut grew and they could gather conkers together. So they sneaked out when Father went off for his Sunday drink. They'd be back before he knew.

And now . . .

He knew what to expect.

Once he was on the dual carriageway and the road stretched clear ahead towards London, Raph pulled the car into a lay-by. He was shaking, not fit to drive at all.

But this mood would pass. These moods always passed. He just needed time.

And then he could carry on. Again.

Just like he'd always done.

CHAPTER 5

Usually the last few miles of the journey to Wardley filled Johnny with a sense of contentment and goodwill towards life in general. It would begin as soon as he turned off the motorway and reduced his speed, concrete and bland artificial slopes giving way to ancient twisting roadways and hedgerows thick with green leaves and ripening berries. Anticipation mounted as that first sight of Wardley's ancient tower drew near.

But not today. While Sam slept in the passenger seat beside him, Johnny kept going over their conversation as they followed the A30 over Bodmin Moor.

'You visited Kirsten in March, didn't you?' she asked him. (Except when talking to her father, it was always 'Kirsten', never 'Mum', which was appropriate, he thought. They had been close, but not in the conventional way of mothers and daughters.)

'That's right.' No point denying it. She knew he'd made the trip out to Connecticut when he was in the States. He said, talking as though it had been a visit like any other, 'Miriam asked me to go – though I'd probably have gone anyway. Miri still thought there was a chance of patching things up between Kirsten and Raph.'

'Did you talk about Raph?'

'Oh, I expect we did. We talked about a lot of things.'

'She always liked you,' said Sam.

It was true, of course, but it still hurt to hear her say it. That sense, which he could never quite shake off, that he had let Kirsten down.

'It was mutual,' he said swiftly. 'And I admired her, too. She really was the most remarkable woman I've ever met.' Then, in case that had sounded too emphatic, he added lightly, 'Don't tell Miriam I said that, will you?'

Sam was quiet for a while, presumably mulling over this statement. Eventually she sighed and said, 'She wasn't depressed, at all.'

'She was unhappy about the split from Raph,' said Johnny. 'She told me she still loved him. That she'd always love him.'

'She told me that, too. I still don't understand why she left him.'

Johnny didn't answer. It hadn't been phrased as a question, so he didn't have to respond directly. On the topic of that final meeting with Kirsten, the less said the better, in his opinion. He said, 'Would you like to listen to some music?'

She shook her head. 'Do you think they would have got back together?'

'Impossible to say.'

'I suppose so.' Sam turned suddenly to look at him. He was aware of her gaze, though he didn't take his eyes off the road ahead even for a moment. She said slowly, 'I don't believe

Kirsten killed herself.' Pause. Still looking at him. 'Do you?'

He didn't hesitate. 'She must have done, Sam. What other explanation is there?'

'Did she show you that poem she was writing? The one that was missing from her final collection?'

'"The Murder Bird"?' In spite of the early evening warmth, a shiver ran down his spine as he spoke the name out loud. 'I suppose she may have done. I don't remember.'

Sam's eyes were on him still. Was she trying to evaluate whether he was telling the truth? She said, 'I think I know what the poem was about.'

'You do?' Johnny glanced quickly. Had Kirsten talked to her, too?

'It was a thrush. We saw it kill something.'

'A thrush? Yes, I see.' He was surprised at how relieved he felt.

The poor girl was just trying to figure out the truth and, naturally, he'd help her all he could. Sam had been 'family' for years and you can't switch off that kind of connection just like that. He reached across and patted her hand, frowning as he focused on the road ahead. Maybe that's why cars can be such good places to talk: there's a cast-iron reason for keeping eye contact to a minimum. He said, 'I know how hard it must be for you. Well, obviously I don't *know*, exactly, but I can imagine. Like the coroner said in her summing up, no one can ever be sure what was in Kirsten's mind that last day. What she did was so out of character. I know she got depressed sometimes – we all do – but she was always so positive and so full of life. God knows, it's hard for all of us to accept. But we have to. *You* have to. It must have been a temporary aberration. I don't know. *While the balance of her mind was disturbed* – whatever that means. Maybe it was just incredibly bad luck. We'll never have the answers. But you don't stand a hope of coming to terms with it unless you accept what the coroner decided. All the evidence points in the same direction.'

'Not *all* the evidence,' said Sam stubbornly. 'Just some of it.'

'Enough, anyway.'

She turned away to look out of the window, so he couldn't see her expression, but he could tell by the set of her jaw that he hadn't convinced her. It was going to take time, but sooner or later, Johnny was sure, Sam would have to fall into line with the conclusion the coroner and all those other professionals had come to, as well as Kirsten's friends and relatives. What other explanation was there, after all? Sam surely didn't think some psychotic stranger had wandered in from the coast path and murdered her mother while she took a bath? Gull Cottage was remote and the doors were never locked, but even so, the homicidal rambler was an unlikely scenario. There'd been no signs of violence. Nothing had been stolen.

All the same, their conversation had left a sour taste in his mouth, sour enough to spoil the pleasure of his return to Wardley. Here, round the next corner, he'd see the tower rising up across the fields before it was obscured again by the woodland on either side of the drive. He smiled – but only because he always smiled at this stage in his journey. For once it was an act of will, not spontaneous pleasure.

'Nearly there,' he said to Sam.

Silence. She'd fallen asleep just after Bristol, using that ethnic-looking shoulder bag of hers as a pillow. Asleep, she looked unbearably fragile and young. He remembered when she'd first left her father's home and come to live with Kirsten and Raph in Holland Park. She'd been a surly and in his opinion an unnaturally pale fifteen-year-old, dressed entirely in black, with rings in all the wrong places and hair that seemed to have been cut with garden shears. It had been hard to see how someone as vibrant as Kirsten could have produced such an unprepossessing daughter. Until, that was, he first saw her play the cello. From ugly duckling to glorious swan the moment she lifted the bow and drew it across the strings.

Over the next two or three years she'd changed completely. In some ways she seemed to get younger during those years with Raph and Kirsten, reclaiming her right to be a child, and innocent, while she grew in confidence and maturity and her music blossomed. That last summer before Kirsten's departure, Sam seemed to be riding the crest of a wave. One of the most talented students in her year at the Royal College of Music, she'd been beautiful in her success.

It grieved Johnny to see how, superficially at least, she'd regressed since Kirsten's death. Creeping back into her shell. He hoped it was only temporary, and that music would once again give her the way out. There was a major competition coming up, and if she did well in that, then her career would really take off. He'd help any way he could. Maybe because he and Miriam had not been blessed with children of their own, Johnny felt a fatherly concern for Sam. He wanted the best for her.

He changed down into second as he turned on to the Wardley driveway. Between the trees it was darker, but he didn't switch on his headlights. He knew this stretch of ground so well he could probably have driven it blindfold. Here the trees formed a tunnel and here, after this final turn, they thinned out, and that was the spot where Anthony had died. Always, the constriction of the heart as he passed the spot. He wanted to put some kind of memorial there, a stone with his brother's name on it, or a tree, but could never quite decide what was most appropriate. Now he was in the clear, house and tower rising up before him. Home.

At least Sam had agreed to stay at Wardley that night. He and Miriam were leaving for London first thing in the morning anyway, so she'd be there in plenty of time for her lesson. It was Johnny's profound belief, based on personal experience, that time spent at Wardley was always a healing experience.

He pulled to a halt in front of the house. An unremarkable but in its way quite perfect eighteenth-century house built on to a six-sided medieval tower. The tower itself was an almost unique survival from the days when even farmers needed to be safe behind high walls. Pevsner had waxed lyrical. For Johnny, this Englishman's home really was his castle. He let out a long breath of contentment and switched off the engine. Already he was feeling better. His earlier discomfort – guilt, even – at having been less than frank with Sam about the extent of his last conversation with Kirsten, that strange snowy March afternoon in Connecticut, was banished by the conviction that he'd acted for the best. If Sam knew what had really been on Kirsten's mind – obviously moving already to the place where its balance could be described as 'disturbed' – it would only make it harder for her to accept the coroner's verdict.

And he was convinced, in spite of everything, that the

coroner had been right. Looking at the facts objectively, suicide was the only explanation that made sense.

Diana was walking across the lawn with her dog Bobbo when she saw Johnny's car pass between the trees alongside the drive. At first she thought it might be Craig, coming to pick her up in her own Volkswagen Golf, but, of course, Craig wasn't expected until some time around ten. Even though her young driver was a relative – her brother Ronald's son, actually – it was always easier when contact between him and her present family was kept to a minimum. 'Not quite our sort of people,' she'd said once to Miriam and Johnny, at which Johnny had laughed that rather overloud laugh of his and said, 'Not anyone's sort, really, Diana. Must be why that lot spend so much time behind bars.'

It had been a lapse of taste, mentioning the unmentionable, and quite unlike Johnny who could normally be relied on to be discreet. Discretion was everything, in Diana's opinion. And Craig was a nice young man, on the whole, not at all like his father and his uncles. Thank heavens she herself had been a good girl and beautiful, so she'd been able to escape into an excellent marriage. She'd never really belonged in the family she was born into, had felt like a ladylike changeling in a house full of commoners. Luckily her children took after her. Everyone said, and it was only the truth, that Raph and Miriam were a credit to the way she'd brought them up, both so successful and – most important of all – so impeccably respectable.

Diana had been appalled when they informed her, after Anthony's death, that she would have to hand in her driving

licence. It wasn't entirely fair, because that whole business with
the accident had been the most terrible mistake. There wasn't
really anything wrong with her eyesight. But Raph had insisted
and, over the last couple of years, she'd grown quite to rely on
Craig. He kept himself to himself most of the time, but it was
nice to have someone she could depend on when there was lift-
ing or moving to be done. And Bobbo liked him, too. In lots of
ways it was a relief.

Diana believed in being positive about unavoidable circumstances. That's what gave her her enviable serenity.

Serenely, she entered the house by the garden door and made
her way to the hall where Johnny and Sam were saying hello to
Miriam. There was a certain amount of ritual cheek-kissing and
asking about the day. The inquest, apparently, had gone much
as Raph had said it would. He was always right about these
matters, thank goodness.

'That's excellent,' said Diana firmly. 'Now we can put the
whole unpleasantness behind us. Sam, you must tell me all
about your music. Will you play for us this evening?'

Sam stared at her as if she'd said something extraordinary,
then muttered vaguely about changing, or having a bath, and
vanished up the stairs with Miriam.

'Time for a drink, Diana?' asked Johnny.

'That would be very nice,' she told him.

'Sam's had a tough day,' he said, as they walked through into
the drawing room. 'You know, what with Kirsten's inquest and
everything.'

'And now it's over,' she said firmly. If she'd learned anything during her seventy years on this earth, it was that no

matter how difficult the circumstances – and heaven knows, her life had been far from plain sailing; only she knew the full extent of the obstacles she'd faced and overcome – a smiling face and a pleasant manner were always a woman's greatest assets.

'You're in the tower room,' said Miriam.

'I thought the tower wasn't lived in.'

'It's not actually in the tower. Just next to it. Mother's driver, Craig, will be sleeping in the second spare room tonight. If I'd known you were coming I'd have arranged it differently.'

'Don't worry. This is fine.'

It was more than fine. A smallish room right at the back of the house, separated from the other bedrooms by a long corridor, Sam's bedroom had a vaulted ceiling and a single thin window overlooking the garden.

'You've got your own bathroom.'

Sam put her bag on the bed and followed Miriam back into the corridor. A section of the wall, immediately before the bathroom door, was covered by a huge grey-green tarpaulin.

'What's that?' asked Sam.

'The way through to the tower. Or it will be, when the renovation work is done.'

'I might go in there by mistake in the night.'

'Oh, you mustn't do that.' Miriam's eyes widened with alarm; she grabbed her by the arm, as though Sam was about to hurtle lemming-like into the tower anyway. 'Part of the floor is missing. It's not safe.'

Sam removed her arm from Miriam's grip. She tended to

avoid physical contact with Miriam. The woman meant well, but she was so tense that a hug from her was like being wrapped in barbed wire.

'Don't worry. I won't.'

'We've got a man coming to look at it. To advise us.'

But Sam wasn't interested in the ongoing restoration of Johnny's family pile. Without any preamble, because this might be the only chance she got to talk to Miriam alone, she said, 'Why did you think Raph might have kept Kirsten's journal?'

Miriam stared at her. In Miriam, the hooded Howes eyes were wider, more bulbous, especially when she stared. 'What are you talking about?'

'Don't you remember, the day of Kirsten's memorial service? The subject of her journal came up and the fact that no one knew what had happened to the last one. I heard you asking Raph about it.'

'You must have misheard.'

'It sounded like you thought he had it.'

'No. We never spoke about it.' Miriam's stare was unblinking. She seemed to be thinking something through. Then she shook her head, as though shaking out an unwelcome thought, and said, 'Supper is at eight o'clock, but come down whenever you want. There are drinks in the drawing room. I'd better check on the food.'

She scurried off. Almost, one might think, in undue haste. Obviously the way to hold on to Miriam's company – if that was required – was not to bring up the topic of Kirsten's missing journal. Or maybe Sam was imagining it.

A small draught slipped out between the wall and the tarpaulin. Sam pulled it back and peered inside. Her eyes took a few moments to get used to the intense blackness of the disused tower. She looked upwards, where a few chinks of light were visible: obviously the roof was in need of repair. If there were any windows, they were all boarded up. At this level, there were joists and a few floorboards, with black space between them.

She drew back quickly. Vertigo again. Off and on, ever since her teens, she'd sometimes had a nightmare which involved having to step across an abyss, an empty space so deep there was no seeing where it ended. Like a well when you dropped a stone in and never heard it hit the bottom. She thought she could just manage to get across, but as she launched herself for the leap, the far side receded, shifting always further away, just out of reach, and she was going to fall . . . She always woke up at that point. Woke up shaking with fear and wondering, if the dream had continued, whether she'd have been able to make it to the other side.

So no, Miriam needn't have worried. There wasn't much chance of her wandering by mistake into the empty tower.

She went back to her room and looked out over the twilit garden. Since he and Miriam came to live here, she'd lost count of the times Johnny had encouraged her to come and visit them, and it felt strange that she'd finally got here on the day of Kirsten's inquest, this house which would be for ever associated in her mind with violence and sudden death.

Although she'd never seen the 'Murder Bird' poem, she had a shrewd idea that it must have been triggered by an incident she and Kirsten had witnessed when they'd visited Wardley together, the only other time Sam had been there. Two years ago, when Sam had still been a music student and Kirsten and Raph had been happy in their marriage and the sun had shone on their day in the country.

Remembering, she shivered, wished she'd gone straight back to London by train. Not returned to the house where the murder bird was born.

CHAPTER 6

This house means more to him than anything.

'Is this going to be an ordeal?' Kirsten had asked that summer morning two years ago, when they were getting ready to go to Wardley.

'An ordeal? What's that supposed to mean?' Raph was in the kitchen of his Holland Park house, packing a huge hamper: portions of smoked goose, wafer-thin slices of Parma ham, fresh rolls and several different salads and, of course, champagne. He pressed his thumb on a Brie to see if it was ripe, rejected it and took a Camembert from the fridge and sniffed it. 'That'll do,' he muttered, setting it in the basket next to a packet of oatcakes.

'You know,' said Kirsten, who was perched on the edge of the kitchen table, watching him. She was wearing pale blue cut-off trousers and a floaty linen shirt, her fair hair just brushing her shoulders. She had always been mistress of the casual look, whereas Raph only really looked comfortable in a suit. When he wore holiday clothes – this morning khaki jeans and a polo shirt – they hung awkwardly like fancy dress. Kirsten reached over and helped herself to a cheese straw. 'Is this going to be one of those Howes-special days, when everyone tiptoes round and pretends that everything is hunky-dory and no one says what's really on their mind?'

Raph glanced across at her with a grin. 'Not much chance of that with you around, is there?'

'Hm.' Kirsten wrinkled up her nose. 'That's what I was afraid of. I am getting kind of tired of my role as resident big-mouth American.'

Raph walked over and put his hands on her hips and drew her towards him. 'The only problem I have with your big American mouth,' he said, pressing his lips against hers, 'is that I just can't get enough of it.'

Kirsten draped her arms round his neck. 'That's okay, then,' she told him, rubbing her nose against his before kissing him back. Raph moved in closer. 'What time did you say we had to leave?' asked Kirsten.

'Not for hours,' said Raph.

Sam, who had been helping herself to a late breakfast after playing in a college concert the evening before, and who'd only got out of bed when she did because Raph had insisted they leave by eleven, groaned and took her coffee into the garden. She'd still been young enough, then, to be embarrassed by the overt sexuality between Raph and her mother. Davy and Linda had always been much more reserved, so much so that she'd never really understood what bound them together and had persisted in her efforts to make Davy get rid of his new wife long after they were married. Such tactics would have been unthinkable with Raph. Besides, Sam might be embarrassed, sometimes, but the happiness between him and her mother was infectious. She was learning that the best kind of love between two people creates more for everyone; it spills out and envelops those closest to them. Raph had never made her feel a stranger in his house, the way Linda had sometimes done, once she moved in.

She was glad the day was starting off so well, because this trip to Johnny's ancestral home had the potential for trouble. Kirsten and Raph's rows were rare and quickly over, but they were almost always triggered by something to do with his family.

She'd heard about Wardley, though she'd never been there before. She knew Johnny had grown up there and loved the place, but that when his father died it was his older brother Anthony who inherited. She knew also that Anthony now planned to sell; Johnny was, of course, bitterly opposed to the sale but lacked the resources to buy him out. No one knew whether this invitation for them all to go down to visit for the day was because Anthony had thought of a compromise solution to their problems, or whether it was to be a farewell visit, a last chance to see the place before it passed out of the family for ever.

'Did you remember to put arsenic in Anthony's sandwiches?' Kirsten asked later as they loaded the car.

Raph grinned his pirate grin. 'I admit nothing,' he said. 'But you might want to keep away from the pâté.'

On the journey down, it was easy to be optimistic. It was a summer's day out of a child's picture book: puffy white clouds in a blue sky, fields of golden corn rippling in the light breeze and contented cows standing in pools of shadow under the trees. Kirsten and Raph were in high spirits; Kirsten was never happier than when sitting next to Raph at the start of a journey. She said often that she'd never stayed in one place as long as she had with him and that she was having a hard time conquering her nomadic tendencies. She warned Raph not to let her stagnate lest she resort to desperate remedies.

'Not that an hour down the M4 and a picnic in a stately home really qualifies as life on the open road,' she commented cheerfully, 'but it'll have to do for now.'

But as they drew closer to Wardley, Raph's mood changed. 'Johnny's going to take it hard if Anthony's determined to sell,' he said. 'This house means more to him than anything.'

'Apart from Miriam,' said Kirsten.

Raph considered his sister's importance in her husband's life for a few moments before adding dutifully, 'Yes, of course. Apart from Miriam.'

'Maybe Anthony's thought of a scheme that will work for both of them.'

'Not very likely,' said Raph

'Why not?' Kirsten wanted to know. 'If Johnny and Miriam sell their London place, they could raise the rest of the money somehow.'

'Time is the problem.'

'So? If Anthony wants to keep it in the family—'

'But I don't think he does. That's the whole point. He doesn't want Wardley for himself and he doesn't want Johnny to have it either. He wants to offload the place for as much as he can get.

The trouble is, Johnny's so generous himself he hasn't cottoned on to the fact that big brother is a tight-fisted bastard who doesn't want to see him lording it in the family pile.'

'Jeez. Poor Johnny,' said Kirsten.

'Yup,' Raph agreed. 'Poor Johnny.'

They drove the rest of the way without speaking. Handel's Largo was playing on the sound system as they slowed to turn off down the farm lane leading to the house. Sam, who had been dozing in the back, woke up and looked about her with interest. You could see the tower first, above the trees, a fragment surviving from another age. She felt a tightening round her heart, that instant recognition she got when a building or a picture or a piece of music was something out of the ordinary, something created with skill and love and true originality. The feeling grew as they parked and she got out, her sandals crunching on warm gravel. Steeped in sunshine and silence, the house seemed to be sinking, gradually and gracefully, back into the ground which had formed it. Swags of roses gone wild billowed out from the old walls, ivy hung thick and mysterious in the shade, grass and weeds were everywhere, and little lizards scurried away as you walked.

To begin with it looked as though nothing was going to disturb the serenity of the place: its magic blurred the edges of tension. An outsider, observing as hampers were unpacked and rugs and cushions spread in the shade, would never have guessed that this was anything but a carefree day out in the country, family and friends gathered together to relax and have fun. Anthony had stayed there the night before – had camped there, really. The house hadn't been inhabited during the last years of old Mr Johns' life – he'd been in a nursing home in Bracknell – and Wardley had been closed up.

Anthony had invited a couple of London friends to join him: Yvette was in her late forties, something to do with the theatre and attractive in a rumpled sort of way with a thick tangle of hennaed hair, a full mouth which usually had a Gauloise in it and a richly husky voice, spoiled only by a hacking smoker's cough. Her much younger lover, Oscar, had the skinniest legs Sam had ever seen and giggled a lot, maybe from nervousness.

Johnny and Miriam had arrived before ten, much earlier than Anthony liked. In his eagerness to find a solution to the Wardley problem, Johnny had apparently woken at dawn full of energy and enthusiasm. As so often, Miriam was struggling to keep up with him, but she lacked his innate optimism and the strain was already beginning to show: behind her dark glasses her eyes were ringed with shadow, a sure sign with Miriam that she was falling into the grip of one of her punishing headaches. Her mouth was a taut line, battling the pain.

Sam had always thought Johnny and Miriam were an unlikely couple, Johnny so much like an overgrown puppy and Miriam so pale and edgy. Kirsten said it was a case of opposites attracting, that Johnny, with his endless exuberance and opti-mism, needed his wife's quiet attention to detail to keep his life in order. Today, as the champagne corks popped and glasses were filled and emptied with increasing speed, Sam saw Miriam was worried for Johnny, and no wonder.

'How's it going?' Raph had asked him soon after their arrival, when Anthony had gone inside to fetch more cushions.

'Not good. But I'm sure we'll get there.' Johnny was still

upbeat. 'He's determined to drive a hard bargain. We're just going to have to beat him down a bit.'

'And if you can't? Suppose he won't play ball because basically he's a mean bastard who doesn't want you to have Wardley?'

'But I'm his brother.'

Johnny spoke with such conviction that Raph stayed silent, watching with growing concern as they set out the picnic things and Anthony threw up one obstacle after another. Later, as Johnny was about to take a mouthful of game pie he burst out, 'But what's the rush, Ant? I don't understand. If we do it by stages, what's the problem?'

Anthony regarded him scornfully. His stringy, supercilious face did scorn very well. He said, 'Leave it, Johnny. You're being a bore. No need to spoil everyone's picnic, for God's sake.'

'But . . . There must be a solution, Ant.'

'Actually, I don't think there is. Not for you.'

'But what's the problem? Why are you being so difficult about this?'

'So terribly sorry, Johnny, but it can't be helped.' Anthony's phoney regret fooled no one. 'The sad truth is that people don't always get their own way. Not even you. That might be hard for you to take in, given that you've always had such an easy ride. I really hate to be the bearer of bad news, little brother, but it looks as if your luck has just run out. Oh dear.'

There was an arctic silence. No one had realized until then just how impossible the situation was. A lifetime of bitterness and jealousy was erupting in Anthony's cruelty. Johnny was dumbfounded, temporarily forgetting to breathe. It was like watching while a friendly spaniel got kicked. Johnny genuinely liked people and assumed they would like him back. And so they did. With the single exception, obviously, of his brother Anthony.

You could see the reason. When charm was being allocated in the Johns family, Johnny had got the whole lot. His older brother was a dry stick of a man, with a face that would frighten babies and a sneering manner. He was smirking as he turned to Kirsten and said, 'More champagne, dear one?'

'No thanks, Anthony,' she said coolly. And then, 'Maybe it's none of my business, but—'

Anthony smiled his chilling smile and interrupted her with, 'Absolutely right, darling. Best stay out of it, don't you think? It's time our golden boy learned to fight his own battles.'

'Maybe he didn't realize you were the enemy,' said Kirsten.

'Then more fool him,' said Anthony, holding up a thin hand. 'Ah look, the unlikely cavalry arrives.' He stood up. 'Your mother, I believe,' he said, glancing towards Raph. He began walking towards the front of the house. For someone with such long legs he had an oddly stilted way of walking.

Diana's Golf was negotiating the final turn. She'd driven up from her home near Exeter and, as she explained to everyone while a deckchair was placed in the dappled shade for her, there'd been a hideous pile-up outside Honiton and she'd been held up for nearly an hour.

For a little while there was an uneasy truce while Diana subjected them to the details of her disrupted journey and Bobbo, her little dog, snaffled food from half-empty plates. Anthony encouraged both of them. 'There, Bobbo, delicious pâté. Don't make yourself sick. Diana, which roundabout did you say the accident had occurred on? How many cars were involved? How long was the tailback?' Gradually everyone except Diana realized that he was spinning this out, partly as a diversion from the subject of Wardley, but also from a malicious desire to see how long she could continue with what he clearly regarded as a topic of no interest to anyone.

'Which villages did the diversion go through, Diana?' he asked. By now the atmosphere was thick with embarrassment. Only Yvette and Oscar were unaware of the growing tension. They had worked their way to the outer edge of the group, where they were feeding each other cherries and giggling like teenagers on a school outing.

Diana frowned, trying to remember.

'One of them began with P, I think.'

'For God's sake,' said Raph. 'Can't we talk about something else?'

'Anthony has asked me a question, Raph,' said Diana sternly. 'I'm trying to remember, Anthony. It may have been P, but I can't be absolutely sure.'

'A P? Really? I wonder what it was. I'll go and get my road map from the car so we can look it up.'

'Give it a break, Anthony,' said Kirsten.

'A break? May I ask what kind?'

'As if you didn't know.'

'Ah, riddles now.' He smiled. 'Party games time, is it?'

Johnny couldn't contain himself any longer. 'For fuck's sake, Ant. Why won't you compromise? Miri's plan would work fine, if you'd just give it a chance: you get all the money you want for Wardley, just not all upfront. Surely you can wait a few months while we organize the leaseback or whatever these things are called.'

Anthony leaned back on his arms and stared at his younger brother, so earnest and uncomprehending. 'Time's up, sonny boy,' he said. 'I've been meaning to tell you. Wardley's been on the market a month. Lots of interest already. A Scottish fellow has cash and is prepared to offer the asking price. It's too late for your footling little schemes. I'm not interested.'

'But . . .' Johnny was floundering.

'But . . . but . . .' Anthony mimicked. 'Oh deary me. Whatever can this be? Is it possible that for once in little Johnny's perfect life, he's not getting what he wants?'

Johnny stared, speechless. Yvette and Oscar stopped putting cherries in each other's mouths and watched awkwardly. Miriam put her hand to her forehead and bent over slightly, rubbing her temples. Raph was red-faced with anger.

'There's a map in my car,' Diana said. She alone remained oblivious to the conflict. 'We could check the name of the village. Pilkington, or something like that.'

Kirsten asked coolly, 'What's it like being the world's biggest shit, Anthony?'

Diana wiped the corners of her mouth with a napkin. 'Really, Kirsten. Here we all are having a nice picnic.'

Kirsten said quietly, 'Sometimes you have to say it how it is.'

Diana gave a little cough. 'We'll check the name later, then. Well, yes, Anthony, I don't mind if I do.' She held out her champagne glass for a refill.

'Diana, you're a woman after my own heart.' Anthony was gloating.

'That's very nice of you, Anthony. Families.' She gave a little laugh. 'We have our ups and downs, but never anything serious, thank heavens.'

'Of course not,' said Anthony.

'Oh, for Christ's sake,' said Kirsten.

'I don't think we want that kind of language here, do we?' said Diana. 'It's so pleasant to have a family day in the country.'

'Sorry, I forgot. God's in his heaven and all's right with the world. Is that it?'

'Something like that,' said Anthony. His own enjoyment seemed to have risen as everyone else's vanished. He was never happier than when those round him were at each other's throats.

Johnny said, 'You've put Wardley on the market, Ant?'

'Chink. Do I hear the sound of a penny dropping?'

'Why?'

'Because I want to sell it. I believe that is the usual reason. And I have a buyer. Cash.'

'But *I* can buy it from you. That's what I've been explaining to you all morning. Miriam's got this scheme—'

'Fuck your scheme – sorry about that, Diana. I want cash, Johnny. Stop living in a dream world. Wardley's gone. End of story.'

'Oh.' Johnny looked as though all the air had just been punched out of him. 'Oh,' he said again. Sam watched in horror as his face crumpled and turned red, like a boy's. Tears began rolling down his cheeks. 'I can't believe it.'

'Believe it,' said Anthony. Mission accomplished, he wasn't bothering to smile any more. He stood up and began clearing the plates and glasses.

'I'll help,' said Oscar. He looked confused, in need of an occupation more demanding than feeding cherries to Yvette.

'I can't believe it,' said Johnny again. 'You're winding me up.' Anthony just shrugged, dismissing him, before walking with jerky little strides towards the house, out of earshot. Oscar, his arms full of plates, hurried after him. Yvette watched him hungrily, then settled back on the rug and closed her eyes.

Johnny's choking sobs were magnified in the silence that followed. Sam glanced down and realized she'd been pulling the heads off daisies and shredding them. A little mound of white and green was heaped just beside her knee. Raph was looking embarrassed and angry. He reached in his pocket and pulled out a large, folded white handkerchief and handed it to his friend. 'Come on, Johns, let's walk this off. Is that old boat of yours still moored on the pond?'

Johnny shook his head, but he allowed Raph to pull him to his feet and lead him across the lawn, away from the house. Just before they reached the hedge that marked the end of the formal gardens, Johnny turned, as though he was going back to the house to talk with Anthony some more. Raph put his arm round his shoulders, keeping him to their course, and together they disappeared from sight.

'Well,' said Diana, picking a magazine out of her bag and settling back in her deckchair. 'That was a very pleasant picnic, I think. So enjoyable to eat outdoors.'

'Shit,' said Kirsten. 'What an almighty fuck-up.' She stood up, filled with surplus energy, but for once she didn't seem to know what to do with it.

Yvette stood up also and stretched. She ran a hand through

her thick tangle of hair. 'I'll go see if they need help with the clearing up,' she said, and set off towards the house.

'Right,' said Kirsten to no one in particular. She looked down at Miriam and Diana who were both leaning back in their chairs with their eyes closed, Diana's face settled into her habitual blank smile, Miriam's a study in tension. She turned to Sam. 'Do you want to explore?' she asked Sam. 'We can't just stay here.'

'Sure,' said Sam.

'That sounds nice,' said Diana, not opening her eyes.

Kirsten hesitated. 'Are you okay, Miriam?'

'Just my head,' said Miriam. Talking seemed to be an effort.

'Can I get you something?'

'I took a pill earlier. It should work soon. If I just close my eyes for a bit.'

'If you're sure.'

Miriam nodded. Even that slight movement made her wince.

'Such a nice afternoon,' said Diana serenely. 'I may just have forty winks.'

'Why don't you?' murmured Kirsten, adding in a soft voice that only Sam could hear, 'God knows, you've been sleeping all your life. Let's take this stuff inside and then head off some place.'

They gathered up the rest of the plates. As they were nearing the back door, there was a shriek from inside. 'Jesus,' Kirsten groaned. 'Now what?'

Yvette erupted into the garden, dragging Oscar behind her. 'That's it! We're leaving! Kirsten, you have to take us to the station.'

'What's up?'

Anthony sauntered out into the sunlight. He was smiling that thin, supercilious smile. 'Stop overreacting, Yvette, it was just a kiss, darling. You can't keep your pretty boy all to yourself.'

Oscar's red face as he shambled on to the lawn revealed who it was Yvette had surprised with their host. 'No, we're going,' she said. 'Right now. Kirsten, you have to drive us.'

'Sorry, honey. I've drunk too much champagne and anyway, I don't do gears.'

'Sam?'

'She doesn't drive.'

'I'll ask Miriam then.'

'She's getting a migraine.'

In the end, it was Diana who volunteered to drive Yvette and Oscar to the station. Anthony had offered his services, but Yvette refused absolutely to go anywhere near him; her most flattering description of him during the turmoil was 'a snake in the grass'. Raph and Johnny were still down by the pond, presumably. At the last moment Miriam insisted on accompanying her mother; Diana had already had a long drive that morning and it wasn't fair for her to go alone.

Sam and Kirsten stood beside Anthony on the edge of the lawn and watched as Diana's Golf trundled off down the drive. Diana was behind the wheel, peering ahead as though into fog, with Yvette beside her, still shouting abuse at Anthony through the window. Miriam and Oscar were silent and shadowy in the back.

When their car had disappeared from sight, Anthony turned to Kirsten and asked smoothly, 'Coffee, anyone?'

'I'll pass, thanks. You sure know how to make a fun day out for everyone, don't you?'

'Are you referring to our lovers' little tiff? Just think of the delightful reconciliation that awaits them.'

'Yvette and Oscar were just a sideshow,' said Kirsten. 'I'm talking about your brother.'

Anthony smiled with mock regret. 'Alas, Johnny has to learn to face facts. Sometimes it is necessary to be cruel to be kind.'

'Oh really? Why don't you just go pull the wings off some flies?'

'Darling, I did that before breakfast.'

Kirsten always looked magnificent when angry. Her eyes flashed fire. 'It must help when you get a kick out of being cruel,' she said. 'Where's Raph anyway? I'm ready to split.'

'Down by the pond, probably,' said Anthony. 'Playing Ratty and Mole. D'you want me to fetch them for you?'

'Don't bother,' said Kirsten. 'We'll wait till Miriam gets back.'

'Ah yes. Little Johnny mustn't be left alone with his wicked big brother. That would never do.'

'I never realized you hated him so much,' said Kirsten.

'There's a lot you don't realize, sweetheart.' His thin smile was chilling.

Kirsten turned her back on him. 'Okay, Sam, let's go some-place we can breathe clean air. I'm getting poisoned here.'

'Why's he being such a shit?' Sam asked, as she and her mother strode across the lawn together. 'If he doesn't want the house, why should he stop Johnny from getting it? It's not fair.' Sam was almost in tears. She'd always liked Johnny – as far as she knew, everyone did – and it made no sense that someone should deliberately set out to hurt him, especially his own brother.

'Honey, I've no idea. I could come out with all kinds of stuff about sibling rivalry and scapegoats and favouritism and all of that crap. But right now, my gut reaction is that Anthony's a sadistic bastard who gets pleasure from hurting people.'

'But Johnny's his brother!'

'So? Don't go underestimating how much hate there can be in families. Ugh, when I think back to the stuff my brothers and sister got up to – no wonder the whole idea of family life has me reaching for a suitcase and checking plane schedules.'

Sam had heard about her mother's family, and had even spent a few weeks with them during one of her American summers. It was always hard to reconcile those slow, hard-working relatives with the children her mother had described. Uncle Vernon, for instance, who passed the collection round in church, was supposed to have left Kirsten tied to a tree one spring evening as night fell. Sam was fond of her two younger half-brothers, even though they'd been a nuisance, mostly, when she lived with them, but she hadn't seen them much recently and couldn't imagine the violent emotions that were tearing Anthony and Johnny apart.

She and her mother were about to follow the path that Johnny and Raph had taken earlier when Kirsten turned aside and unlatched a low gate. She said, 'Best to leave Johnny for a bit. Raph'll help him if anyone can. And there's something I want to show you.'

'What is it?'

'My favourite bit of the garden. It's my Wardley bolt-hole.

You know how I never like visiting anywhere unless there's some place I can escape to.'

Kirsten led her into what to Sam looked like an overgrown vegetable garden. Out of sight of the house, with thick hedges all around, it was the kind of place Kirsten loved.

Raspberry canes were growing up through the long grass and weeds; a handful of currant bushes sprawled between metal posts where once there had been a fruit cage. 'And look,' said Kirsten, 'this is the best bit.'

At the far end of the plot of land an ancient bench leaned in the shade, some kind of fruit tree growing on the wall behind it. Kirsten sat down, testing the wooden seat with her hands first, then closed her eyes and inhaled deeply. 'Ah,' she said, ' "Peace, perfect peace—'

'"With loved ones far away".' Sam finished the quotation with her. The words Elizabeth von Arnim kept pinned above her desk had long been Kirsten's mantra and Sam recognized it at once.

'But not you, honey.' Kirsten put her arm around Sam's shoulders.

'Sometimes me,' said Sam.

'Sometimes everyone,' Kirsten agreed.

Sam had trouble explaining why she and her mother got along so well, in spite of the fact that Kirsten had left her with Davy and her grandmother when she was hardly more than a baby. *She'd been abandoned by her mother*, was how other people told the story. By rights she should have been bitter, messed up, resentful, and all the rest of it – but she wasn't. Kirsten's friend Judy Saunders, who was always telling anyone who'd listen that she'd put her children first, didn't get along with either of her offspring now. She thought it was highly unfair that Sam and Kirsten were so close; she said it must be because Sam had never known anything different. That was part of the truth, but there was more: Kirsten had never made excuses for herself, had never apologized or pretended the situation was different from how it was. The way she explained it to Sam, there hadn't really been any choice: Kirsten had known she couldn't stay with Davy, and she'd known also that, on balance, Sam would be better off with her father and grandmother in the home she'd always known than traipsing round a distant continent with a rootless mother. And that was true, at least until Linda arrived on the scene. Sam got all the love and security she could have wanted from her father and grandmother. From Kirsten, she'd got something no one else could give her, a glimpse of a world where there were more important things than home and family, a world where it was worth making sacrifices for the sake of the things you believed in. As her music came to take centre stage in her life, Sam was better able to understand the hard decisions her mother had had to make.

Which was not to say that Sam wasn't pleased when that impossible choice was no longer necessary: in the few years they'd shared in Raph's London home, Sam had grown close to her mother, just at the age when most of her friends were growing away from their parents.

She joined Kirsten on the bench. The air was hazy with the hum of insects and a deep stillness lay over everything. She hadn't realized how keyed up she'd been by the tension at lunchtime until she began to relax. After a while she said, 'Do you think Johnny will get this place?'

'He can't. Not if Anthony's determined to sell.'

'Will Johnny be okay?'

Kirsten was silent for a few moments, before saying quietly, 'That's up to him, I guess. Wardley's just a house, but houses get invested with such a lot of other crap.' Kirsten turned to her with a sudden smile as a possibility occurred to her. 'Maybe he'll get to discover the joys of travelling light.'

'But what if—?'

'Ssh,' Kirsten interrupted her. 'Look.'

Sam looked. There was a bird about five metres from their bench. At first Sam wondered why her mother was so interested in it, but then she saw that it wasn't alone. Head cocked on one side, black eye bright, the thrush was peering intently at a lizard, which faced it on the rough, dry ground. The lizard looked like a tiny dragon, head raised, tail raised, all four feet splayed in the dust, poised to attack.

But it was the bird that moved first. It bounced forward on its stiff legs in a friendly sort of way, then thrust its beak towards the lizard's head, a quick, darting movement like the flash of a rapier, before hopping back to where it had started. The lizard squirmed briefly, raised its head once again. The thrush tilted its head the other way and observed it for a few seconds, as though someone had just presented it with a new toy and it was curious to see how the lizard would respond. Then it attacked again.

Sam turned to her mother. 'Why are they fighting?' she asked in a whisper.

Kirsten shook her head. 'I don't know,' she mouthed. 'Maybe the bird is defending its nest.' It was more of a question than a statement.

Sam shifted. She wanted to intervene and stop the fighting, even though to begin with it looked like a fair contest, one both combatants had chosen. If anything, the advantage lay with the thrush, but then she figured that if the lizard was after the bird's eggs and she chased the bird away, she'd be guilty of helping the nest raider.

Gradually Sam understood the contest was far from equal: the lizard just wanted to survive. Again and again, as the thrush darted forward to attack, the lizard twisted and thrashed in the dust, but couldn't escape from the rapier sharp stabs of the bird's beak. 'Why doesn't it run away?' asked Sam in a whisper.

Kirsten shook her head. *I don't know.*

'We have to stop them,' said Sam.

'Too late,' said Kirsten. And Sam saw she was right. If they shooed the bird away now, they would be condemning the lizard to a lingering death. Each time the thrush attacked and the lizard attempted to raise its head, its movements were less agile, a desperate writhing, a hopeless spasm of life. It couldn't ward off the blows any longer.

And then suddenly, it was over. The lizard lost its footing, slipped sideways, and the thrush's beak became a spear, piercing the pink membrane of his belly. One last spasm, and the lizard's secret entrails spilled through its skin and on to the dust. Its legs twitched, it gave a final thrash of its tail and then lay still.

Too late, Sam leaped to her feet. 'Go away! Go away, you bloody bird!' She flapped her arms and the bird flew off. She felt sick. 'Ugh, how come we just watched and let it happen?'

'It's nature's way,' said Kirsten tersely, but Sam could tell that she was shaken too. 'It's happening all the time; the only difference is this time we saw it.'

'It was disgusting. We have to bury it.'

'Ted Hughes wrote a poem about thrushes,' said Kirsten. 'He called them killing machines – can't remember the exact words. I always thought he was a bit hard on them, but he was right. I'll check it out when we get home.'

'The lizard didn't stand a chance.' Sam was close to tears.

'No, poor Mr Lizard. But we didn't know how it would end. I thought maybe the lizard was the aggressor – wanted to raid the nest or something.'

'Me too.'

'So to begin with, our killer fooled us into seeing it as brave defender. It was only gradually we saw the real picture. And then the bird even started to look different. Did you notice?' She dropped her voice. 'By the end, it looked kind of evil, didn't it?'

'But it was just following its instinct,' said Sam.

'Yeah. But all the same. When it moved in for the kill, it looked like a murder bird.'

Sam shivered. 'It was just a bird,' she said.

'A murder bird,' Kirsten repeated. Her eyes had the soft, unfocused look they often got when the seed of a poem was taking root in her mind.

That was when they heard the siren. Faint and far away, but getting louder.

Sam smiled, glad of this reminder of the outside world. She said, 'Do you think they've heard about poor Mr Lizard?'

'Reptile paramedics? They'll be too late, I'm afraid.' Gradually her smile changed to a frown.

'Listen, Sam, sounds like it's coming down the drive.'

'Maybe it's the farm,' said Sam.

'No, it's coming to the house.' She sprang to her feet. 'Something's happened. Quick!' Sam followed and together they ran across the abandoned vegetable patch, through the little gate and across the lawn towards the house. Johnny, she thought, he's done something. Tried to drown himself. Fought with Anthony. A disaster just waiting to happen.

There were two cars between the trees on the near end of the driveway, just before it opened up into the forecourt. One was a police car, its warning light still flashing in the shadows between the trees. The other was Diana's Golf and you could see right away, from the angle at which it was slewed across the road, that something was wrong. Two uniformed police, a man and a woman, got out of their car. The man crouched near what looked like a shirt that someone had thrown down in the shade. Raph was helping his mother out of the driver's seat of the Golf. Johnny stood at a little distance, his arm round Miriam's shoulders. The policewoman moved over to talk to them, but they weren't looking at her.

'Oh my God!' gasped Kirsten, slowing up.

Sam stopped. Not a shirt, it was Anthony lying between the car and the tree. His body was barred with sunlight and shadow. One of the Golf's headlights was smashed.

'Is he—?'

The policeman stood up slowly. 'A doctor will have to confirm it,' he said. 'But it's not looking good.' He glanced at his watch. 'Four-fifteen,' he said.

'What happened?' asked Kirsten.

The policeman glanced towards Diana. She was standing, now, leaning against Raph. She looked suddenly much older as she put her hand up to her face, shielding her eyes from the sight of Anthony's mangled body: his legs were twisted and there was blood seeping through his pale shirt.

Raph still had his arm around his mother. He said, deliberately calm, 'Diana never saw him. That bright sun and shadow is blinding. She must have panicked when she hit him.'

'I think she was trying to reverse,' said Miriam. Her face was pale as death but she too was speaking quietly, deliberately. 'She must have been trying to move away from him, but he'd fallen down when she hit him the first time and she couldn't see. She reversed, but then suddenly she was going forward again. I shouted at her to stop, but she didn't seem to know what she was doing. The second time, she drove right over him.' She shuddered.

'Jesus,' said Kirsten.

Raph detached himself from Diana, leaving her standing on her own near the crushed headlight of her car. He came over to Kirsten and Sam. 'Don't look,' he said. 'Sam, keep back. I'm sorry. It's too late.'

But, of course, she did look, drawn by the same compulsion that made them stay and watch the death of the lizard. Sam had never seen a dead body before, but she knew at once, knew from the unnatural way the head was twisted on its neck and the frozen inertia of his fingers, clutching at nothing, that Anthony was dead.

'She didn't mean to hurt him,' said Miriam.

'Of course she didn't,' said Raph. His voice was mechanical.

Diana took a couple of steps away from the car. She swayed slightly, then said in a voice Sam had never heard her use before, 'I will not take responsibility for this. I absolutely refuse. It wasn't my fault.'

'No one's saying you did it deliberately,' said Raph, going over to her again. 'Of course, it was an accident. A terrible, terrible accident. Everyone knows that.'

Miriam let her hands drop to her sides. 'It was my fault,' she said. 'I blame myself.'

'Miri,' said Raph. 'Don't be insane.'

'But it's true!' Her voice was rising with emotion as she went on, 'I should never have let mother drive back from the station. For God's sake, she's been driving all day. She probably fell asleep or passed out or I don't know what – something!'

'Did you see what happened?' Raph asked her.

'Not right away. We weren't going very fast. Mother is always such a careful driver. I had my eyes closed – because of my head – and the first I knew was when I felt the car hit something and Mother started screaming and then I opened my eyes and saw Anthony. He must have fallen, but he was okay, I think, because she can't have hit him very hard, and he was trying to get up. You could see his head just coming up behind the bonnet and his mouth was open. I don't know what he was saying, maybe crying out. Then we were going forwards again. I tried to grab the wheel, pull on the handbrake, but it was too late and then the car kind of lurched forward and Anthony screamed and his face disappeared and – oh! Oh, it was so horrible!' She buried her face in Johnny's shoulder. He still hadn't spoken. Couldn't take his eyes off his brother's broken body.

'It wasn't me,' said Diana. She sounded suddenly petulant, as though it was somehow unfair for her to be blamed for what had just happened.

'No one is saying you did it deliberately, Mother,' said Raph. He looked at her with disgust, but he was still trying to make it easier for her. 'With the shadows and the light between the trees, it can be hard to see properly. It's like camouflage. The police will understand that.'

The policeman sighed. 'We'll have to take statements from everyone,' he said.

'Of course,' said Raph. 'You've got to do your job, obviously.' He was pulling himself together, asserting his authority and taking control of the situation. He put his hand under Diana's elbow and addressed the policeman in his most persuasive bar-risterial voice, 'But as you can see, officer, my mother has had the most appalling shock. We all have. I suggest we take this one step at a time. There's nothing to be gained by rushing things. Maybe when the doctor gets here he can give her something. My mother has always suffered with her nerves. You're not going to get much from her while she's in this state. Come along, Mother. I'll take you inside. It's all going to be all right. Trust me.'

'Are you sure, Raph?' She looked up at him, desperate for reassurance.

'Just trust me, Mother; you've nothing to be afraid of.'

'Well. If you're sure.'

'Quite sure, Mother. The doctor will be here soon.'

He led her away slowly. She was tottering on her slender heels in the gravel and leaning against him for support.

Kirsten said, 'Can we cover him up?' She took off her linen shirt, revealing her skinny white T-shirt, and moved forward.

The action galvanized Johnny into life. He sank down on to his knees beside Anthony's corpse and caught him by the shoulders.

'Don't move him, sir,' said the policewoman, gently.

But it was too late. Johnny, clinging to him, had begun to cry. This was a different kind of weeping from the rage and frustration that had siezed him earlier in the day.

'Oh, Ant, Ant, what's happened? Oh, Ant, don't die!'

Crying without hope.

They stood and watched, helpless.

Eventually the doctor arrived and pronounced Anthony dead. The undertakers came.

And yet, in spite of everything, when Sam remembered that afternoon, it was the memory of the lizard and the thrush that was most painful. It was the only time she'd seen something fighting for its life, all its essence pared down to a single imperative, the need to survive. And she'd been fascinated. Sickened and repulsed, yes, but fascinated, too. She and Kirsten could have stopped the slaughter, when it was still early enough for the lizard to escape, but they hadn't. Like spectators at a gladiatorial contest in some dusty Roman arena, they'd been totally absorbed in the life and death struggle.

Anthony's death had been a tragic accident. It was the murder she remembered most clearly.

Because she'd witnessed it. And because her silence had made her a part of the crime.

CHAPTER 7

'Breathe! Let the music breathe and sing!'

Grigory was shouting over the sound of the cello and the piano, rocking and waving his arms. 'Sing, Sam! Give it your heart!'

Sam was trying. God knows how she was trying; she'd never tried so hard with a piece of music in her life. If making music had been a question of willpower alone, she'd have been a second Jacqueline du Pré by now. Shirt damp with sweat, she hunched over the cello, its curves familiar against her body, going in close to capture every detail, hitting the note right in the middle, her trademark 'true' sound. Then she arched back, expanding her torso, as the bow swooped across the strings for the crescendo. Every trick she had ever learned, every nuance and shade – and all for nothing. The soul of the music, the alchemy that takes a sequence of notes and transforms it into a work of art, stayed tantalizingly out of reach.

She ended with a flourish, her bow suspended in mid air as the final note faded into silence, and waited. She did not even

look across at Nadira, seated at the piano, also waiting. Grigory
was a hard taskmaster; it was the reason she revered him and
had chosen him for her teacher in the first place. One of the
great cellists of his generation, he had left Hungary in 1956 but
never really reached his potential in the West. He was widely
respected by his fellow musicians, but unknown to the general
public. 'Just another music has-be,' he used to say bitterly, his
love of idiom as usual galloping ahead of the grammar. And that
was in the days when he could still play. Now that he was in his
late seventies, arthritis had ended his music-making, and turned
an irascible man into a tyrant. 'Leave now!' he had roared at her
halfway through their first lesson together. 'Hit a road and not
return without you study Schumann's heart!' and, more
recently, 'Do you fob me off with garbage? Am I kindergarten
teacher now? Is that the big idea?'

Head bowed, staring at the worn threads of the carpet, she
waited for his rage. She dreaded looking up to see the anger
and disappointment on his face. Most probably, he'd realized
by now that it wasn't worth keeping her on as a pupil. He was
going to dump her, and she didn't know how she'd be able to
bear it. This difficult old man, with his gnarled useless fingers
and his ugly face covered with dark brown liver spots, had been
her musical father for two years, two years in which this cluttered, scruffy room in a mansion block in St John's Wood,
which smelt of dust and cats and forbidden hoards of tobacco,
with its piles of music and its grand piano and its windows
which were never cleaned, had become her real London home.
She had worked long and hard for his praise, but she'd been
wasting her time and his. Now that the moment of truth was

approaching, her music had deserted her. Worse even than her own failure was the thought of how she'd let him down.

Silence.

This was worse than anger.

She waited for his dismissal. 'I was mistaken,' he would tell her. 'I thought you had talent but I was wrong. Our lessons are finished. Goodbye.'

And who would blame him? Why should one of the best teachers in Europe fritter away his time on a pupil who had no more talent than a metronome? Just a mechanical ability to hit the correct notes in the correct order, but no true gift.

Still he was silent.

Sam sighed. This was the end. She glanced across at Nadira, who was touching the piano keys with the tips of her fingers, as she often did when stressed, then leaned forward to place her bow in its case.

And then she heard him. 'Sam? What are you do?'

'I thought—' She didn't know what she thought, except that this time, he hadn't even bothered to be angry with her. She was no longer worth his rage.

'Sam.'

Just her name, spoken softly. Her eyes flew up to look at his face. There was no anger there. For the first time since she'd known him, he looked baffled.

He said, 'Sam, since your mother dies—'

'It's not that,' she interrupted him swiftly. She wasn't going to resort to the sympathy card because she knew that was false; in the first three weeks after Kirsten's death she'd played better than ever in her life before. Music had taken her in its arms and together they'd flown. Or so she had thought at the time. Now it seemed as if that must have happened to someone else.

'What, then?'

She was silent. How to describe the raw fist of pain that had ground itself into her heart? How to explain her rage at the lies that had poisoned her mother's death? Her reality was now so alien to everyone else's that all harmony had vanished. How could she make music when all she wanted was to scream down the lies and evasions, the platitudes and pretences, and shout, *you're wrong, wrong wrong*? And at the back of everything, buried so deep that she only touched it in her dreams, lay the terror that maybe they were right, after all: Kirsten had killed herself. She thought she'd known her mother, but she hadn't, not really. She'd been wrong about everything. If she could have found her journal . . . But it was gone. Maybe, even, destroyed. How to live with that kind of uncertainty, that kind of not knowing?

She didn't have the words to explain how she felt about it. In the past, she would have put it into her playing – but that didn't work any more. She shrugged and said, 'I don't know.'

'Sam, trust me. The music will return.'

She didn't believe him. How could she? Nothing like this had ever happened to her before. Always, no matter what was going on in the rest of her life – fights with her stepmother, trouble at school, boyfriends and boozy nights and getting into trouble – always the music had stayed true. It had been the single constant, the one thing she could rely on no matter what, but now, when she needed it more than at any time in her life, it had deserted her. Maybe this was what happened when you grew up. Maybe this was how she was going to be from now on and Grigory was just being kind because – and this was hardest of all – he felt sorry for her.

She didn't want pity, not even his. 'I'm wasting your time,' she said.

'I will judge that,' he told her sharply, the familiar asperity returning to his voice. 'But you, Sam, I think you must take a break for a couple of weeks. Exercises and scales, okay, but forget the pieces. Grieve for your mother. Clear the space for your head.' He hesitated, then a smile touched his lips as he declared, 'Cut yourself a slack.'

'What? But the Frobisher is less than two months away!'

'You don't have to do that competition, Sam. There will be others.'

'But—' Sam glanced across at Nadira, saw that she was just as shocked. The Frobisher had been their goal for over a year. If she did well in that – and Grigory had hinted once or twice that she had a chance of winning – she'd be launched in her career. It was what she'd dreamed of for so long that she couldn't turn her back on it now. She said, 'I have to do the Frobisher.'

'Sometimes,' said Grigory quietly, 'when you dip your bucket in the well and it comes up empty, sometimes, Sam, it is best to wait for the rain to fall again.'

'Is that a wise old Hungarian folk saying?'

'No. I think it up just now, for you.'

She looked out of the window. The sky over London was pale, cloudless and faded with the heat of late summer. Rain didn't look likely for a long time. She said, 'If I don't do the Frobisher then – all this will have been wasted.'

'Nothing is ever wasted.'

Sam thought this over for a moment, but really, there was no contest. Focus, she told herself. You just have to try a bit harder. Otherwise, what point is there to anything? 'I *have* to do the Frobisher,' she said. 'I won't be able to live with myself if I don't.'

'And if you're not ready to give your best shot? How will you live with yourself then?'

'Well, as you said, there'll be other competitions.'

Grigory shook his head and didn't bother to answer. They all knew that a bad performance in a competition with the stature of the Frobisher was worse than no performance at all. But, 'It's a risk I have to take,' she said firmly.

'Hm. You are stubborn fool. I do not approve.' He stood up, reaching for his stick. 'Now, where have I squirrel my comforts?'

Sam caught Nadira's eye, and saw the flicker of a smile. Grigory had been forbidden tobacco by his doctor, and his wife worked hard to keep temptation out of reach. The teacher hid little stashes of tobacco round his room, the pleasure of outwitting what he called 'the comfort police' as important as the tobacco itself. Sam had once found a pack inside her cello.

He shuffled around for a few moments, peered without success into a pottery jug on the mantelpiece, then lifted a flap of carpet with his stick. Then, 'Ah yes,' he said, triumphant, 'the Casablanca manoeuvre!' Delighted with himself, he went to the piano, lifted the lid and reached behind the prop. A small packet of untipped cigarettes slid out and fell on the strings. 'Ha! She never find it there.'

Sam stared at him. 'Casablanca?' she asked.

He was shaking a cigarette from the packet before replacing it behind the prop. 'The movie. Humphrey Bogart hides the documents under the piano lid – surely you remember that?'

Sam didn't answer. *Casablanca* – of course. Hadn't that always been Raph's favourite film? She was kicking herself for not having thought of this before. She was busy unscrewing the end pin of her cello and placing it in its case. 'Same time next week?' she asked.

'Yes. Same time next week.' He lit his cigarette, inhaled deeply and almost immediately started to choke. Still coughing, he said, 'I recommend that you stay with scales and exercises for a few days. But if you must play, go back to the Bach. The G major Suite. If anything can help you through this time, then Bach will.'

'Sure,' said Sam. But she was only half listening. Usually she and Nadira lingered while Grigory spluttered his way through the end-of-lesson cigarette; he often talked to them about his years as a young musician in Budapest, the greats he had worked with. But today Sam was clearly impatient to be gone. He wondered what had caused her sudden sense of urgency.

Still coughing, Grigory watched from his first-floor window as Sam and Nadira emerged on to the sun-baked street below. He expected them to turn right, heading towards the tube, but today, for once, they stood together. They seemed to be discussing something. He hoped that Nadira was reinforcing his advice, but he wasn't sure if it was possible to reach Sam right now. Which saddened him.

He had grown fond of Sam, not just because she was a talented and hard-working musician, but because she had that extra quality, a largeness of spirit, a willingness to take risks, that distinguishes the real artist from someone who is merely competent. He knew, without being told, how deep her suffering was right now. He would have known just by listening to her play that her mother's unresolved death had turned her life into a nightmare of jangling discord. He hoped she would find a way through her suffering, but he knew, knew from his own experience, that some types of hardship are too much for the fledgling musician to survive. It was quite possible that what she was going through now would break her, musically, and she would never reach her true potential. But in this life, to reach your potential is a rare gift.

He would do what he could to help Sam. So would Nadira. But ultimately, she had to find her own musical salvation. No one else could do it for her.

The two girls separated, Nadira heading towards the tube, while Sam flagged down a cab, leaned forward to give the driver instructions, then pushed her cello inside. Grigory had never known her take a cab before; he was curious to know where she was going.

Sam had not expected Raph to be at home. On a Tuesday morning the cleaner could let her in. She was excited, almost certain she now knew where her mother's journal – and maybe the poem as well – was hidden, but when she had paid off the taxi, leaned her cello against the balustrade at the top of the steps and rung the bell, Raph himself opened the door.

He did not look remotely pleased to see her.

'Sam, what are you doing here?'

'Just paying a visit,' she told him. Behind the stocky figure of her stepfather – her former stepfather – she made out Lola coming down the stairs. Tall and slim, Lola had a tumble of streaky, blonde hair and bee-stung lips. The words 'trophy wife' came into Sam's mind; she reminded herself that Raph and Lola were not even engaged, let alone married.

'Who is it, Raph?' Lola called.

'Sam.' Raph half turned to acknowledge the question, but he did not step aside to let Sam in, nor did he invite her into the house. Lola stopped at the bottom of the stairs, and waited. She was wearing platform sandals and a tiny tunic dress with a massive belt slung over her hips.

Sam said, 'Is it okay if I come in?'

'If you want.' It was ungracious, but Raph couldn't exactly refuse. He moved aside just enough to allow her to carry her cello over the threshold and into the hall. 'Johnny drove you back okay, then?'

'Yes. We stayed the night at Wardley.'

Raph made no further comment. Lola leaned a single bare elbow on the bottom of the banister and stared. If they had rehearsed this scene for a week, they couldn't have made her feel more of an interloper.

Raph said, 'Right. Look, Sam, this is rather an awkward moment. I'm just off to chambers and I'm dropping Lola off in Bond Street. Can I give you a lift somewhere?'

'I thought I might stay here for a bit. Have a glass of water. It's very hot.'

'Yes. When's this weather going to end?' said Raph. 'Sorry, Sam, some other time. We really are in a rush.'

'I can let myself out.'

'Not possible You know, alarms, and all the rest of it.'

'Isn't Mrs Crouch in?' From the basement kitchen came the noise of at least two domestic machines.

'It's her day off.' The hoover was silenced. Switching itself off, presumably. Raph looked at his watch. 'Did you come round for anything in particular, Sam? I hope it can wait.' He glanced down at the cello case. 'It can't be much fun carting that around in this heat.'

'I'm used to it.'

Raph picked it up, tested its weight. 'I think we can fit this and you in the back of the Audi, if we all squeeze in. Are you ready, Lola? I'm got to drop by chambers to pick up some papers and then I'm due in Camberwell, so we'd better get a move on.'

It wasn't like Raph to be in a rush, sounding disorganized. The one thing that was abundantly clear was his determination not to leave her alone – not even with the phantom cleaner as chaperone – in his house. Which might be because of Lola, of course, and her sudden possessiveness for his space – but then again, might be for a different reason entirely.

Lola still had not spoken a single word to Sam; she picked up her bag and sauntered past her into the sunshine. A small smile was hovering on her lips. A smile of triumph, perhaps.

Raph followed Sam and Lola out of the house, pulled the front door shut behind him and went down the steps to his car. Sam noted that he had not set the burglar alarm: presumably the cleaner, whose presence Raph had denied, would do that when she left. Lola draped her long body by the passenger door, waiting for Raph to let her in. Even her slightest gesture was made as though several people were watching her – and usually, Sam had to admit, this was the case.

They drove in silence until they reached Bond Street. Lola leaned over and gave Raph a lingering kiss on the lips, letting her eyelids flutter to a close as she did so, then let herself out of the car and walked away without a backward glance.

Sam was getting out of the car, too.

Raph said, 'I can drop you off at your flat if you want.'

She'd thought he was in a hurry, but, 'Sure,' said Sam. 'I'll sit up front.'

As they edged through the traffic approaching Piccadilly Circus, Raph said, 'It's probably not a good idea turning up unexpectedly like that. It's not for me – you know I'm always delighted to see you. But the thing is, all this unpleasantness with Kirsten has been a lot for Lola to deal with, you know.'

It was like being kicked in the stomach. *All this unpleasantness with Kirsten . . .* Since when did the appalling tragedy of her mother's death get pared down to 'all this unpleasantness'?

Before she could respond, Raph went on smoothly, 'In fact, it's probably best if you don't come to the house at all. Lola means a lot to me. Not the way your mother did, obviously, but all the same, I know we're very different, but I want this to work. That doesn't mean I don't want to see you any more. I know, why don't you and I have lunch together sometime? Are you free next week?'

'No,' said Sam at once.

'Ah. That's a shame.' But Raph couldn't keep the relief out of his voice.

Sam was sitting curled up, leaning against the passenger door, putting as much distance as possible between herself and Raph. He glanced across at her and said, 'Look, I know how difficult all this has been for you, but—'

'No, you don't,' said Sam in a small, hard voice. 'You've no idea what it's like. To you it's just an *unpleasantness*. My God, I can't believe you said that!'

'You know I didn't mean it like that. Kirsten was . . . she was . . .' As if by magic, his voice was suddenly hoarse with emotion. 'Jesus, Sam, I loved your mother. No one else will ever come close. But . . . well, now she's dead and my life is moving on and right now my life includes Lola.'

'You're just using her as an excuse.'

'Really? And precisely why would I want to do that?'

It was the patronizing way he asked the question that goaded Sam into saying, 'Because of Kirsten's journal.'

It hadn't been any part of her plan to mention her mother's journal. Raph winced, as though she'd struck him a physical blow, then instantly recovered his poise and said, 'Which journal would that be?'

'The one she was writing when she died.'

'We don't know for sure she was writing a journal.'

'Of course she was writing a journal. And it's missing, Raph. Just like the poem.'

He turned to bestow on her a look of studied incredulity. 'And you think I've got them both? Really, Sam, whatever gave you that idea?'

Sam turned away to hide her smile and looked out of the window. They were crossing the Thames; an excursion boat filled with tourists and people with ordinary lives having a good time was passing under the bridge. She said, 'I guess a little bird must have told me.'

'What little bird?'

'A little murder bird, perhaps?'

'What the hell are you talking about?'

'It's a figure of speech, Raph.'

'Well, you're wrong. I don't have any of your mother's papers. You took them all when we went to Gull Cottage that day.'

'Yes. Of course. Silly me.'

'Don't start making something out of nothing, Sam. I feel bad that I can't be more help to you right now, but . . . well, don't fly off the handle, but I've been talking this over with one or two people and I really think it might help if you had some kind of counselling. If money was a problem, I'd be happy to pay. It's the least I can do.'

'No thanks, Raph. You've been very helpful already.'

And he had, too, in a way. There'd been that brief moment when she asked him about the journal; in the split second before his immaculate barrister's mask came back into position, any doubts she'd had earlier had vanished: Raph knew exactly what she was talking about.

'About that lunch . . .' Raph said when he dropped her off outside her flat.

'Thanks,' she said. 'I'll call you.' She was pulling the cello off the back seat as she added. 'Don't worry, I'll only call you up at work. There's no point upsetting Lola, is there?'

'I'm sorry it's turned out like this,' said Raph.

I'll bet you are, thought Sam.

*

Nadira was hovering, anxious for Sam's return. She never really liked being alone in their flat, though she wasn't about to admit her fears to anyone. Her Sikh family in Leicester was convinced that she was in mortal danger from muggers and rapists every moment of her time in London. She ridiculed their fears. What were they talking about? She was perfectly safe and could look after herself; she was a modern, independent girl. But deep down, she shared their fear: London was a big dangerous city where people did get mugged and raped. And round here, flats were frequently burgled.

Every time footsteps sounded on the concrete walkway outside their front door – another dark-haired young man with a satchel full of flyers for pizza delivery or cut-price curries – her heart pounded and she slipped the chain in place. Her nervousness was getting worse; in the old days she fessed up to Sam, and her friendly teasing had helped get the risks back into proportion. These days, it wasn't so easy talking to Sam about anything.

They'd met on their first day at college. Nadira had noticed Sam right away, not just because of her natural gifts, but because, like her, she seemed to feel out of her depth in the hot-house atmosphere of the college. During those first days it was easy to imagine that all the other students were friends from way back. A good few had studied at the Menuhin School, others were from leading London academies or the National Youth Orchestra. She and Sam had registered each other as outsiders on day one.

Later, when the pressure from Nadira's parents to abandon her music and adopt a more conventional career reached a climax, it was Sam who gave her the courage to carry on. And it was through working with Sam that she discovered where her real talents lay, as an accompanist. She was getting regular work now, and money wasn't as much of a problem as it had been, but a gulf had opened up between her and Sam. Actually, it felt more like Sam had drifted away from her.

In the first few weeks after Kirsten's body was found at Gull Cottage, they'd grown closer than ever. Sam said she didn't know how she'd have got through without her. Nadira had cancelled her holiday and stuck to Sam like glue, making sure that she ate regular meals and slept at night, and that she kept on with the music. For Nadira, whose fiancé had broken off their engagement when she went to London to study, music was the solution to everything: no heart so broken that it couldn't be mended by a few hours' concentrated playing every day.

But in early August, about six weeks after Kirsten's death, a change took place. Nadira realized that Sam was turning a tragedy – her mother's suicide – into a complex drama that showed no prospect of ending. It wasn't that Nadira was crass enough to think that Sam should be 'over it' by now, but one or two remarks Sam let drop indicated she didn't accept the suicide scenario. Nadira thought she'd have to in the end; there was no possibility of closure otherwise. Neither of them came right out and said what they were thinking, but they became wary of each other, learned to censor what was said. It made them both unhappy, but it was hard to know how to resolve it. For the past couple of weeks, in the build-up to the inquest, they'd restricted their conversation to practical matters: what to have for supper on the rare evenings when they were both in, whose turn it was to clean the cooker, who'd go first in the shower. Maybe now that the inquest was over, their former easy friendship would be restored.

'Nad, it's me! Take the chain off, I can't get in!'

Embarrassed, Nadira hurried to open the door. 'Sorry,' she said. 'I must have slipped the chain on by mistake. How did it go?'

Sam leaned her cello case against the wall and took some bottled water out of the fridge. 'He wouldn't let me in.' She gave Nadira a brief account of her visit to Raph.

'Well, at least he gave you a lift.'

'It wasn't altruism, Nad. He wanted me as far away from his house as possible.'

'You don't know that for sure,' said Nadira, and regretted her honesty right away. The fragile trust that had been growing while Sam told her about Raph was wavering.

'You weren't there,' said Sam, turning away.

Trying to make up for her mistake, Nadira said swiftly, 'But why was he so unfriendly?'

'He's frightened of what I might find. Honestly, if you'd seen his face when I asked him about the journal, you'd think so too.'

Not having seen his face, Nadira was far from convinced, but she wasn't going to fall into the error of saying so. She tried a different tack. 'Has it ever occurred to you that Raph might have a good reason to keep the journal secret? If he's really got it, that is.'

'What kind of reason?'

'Maybe there's something it would hurt you to see. Something about you, perhaps.'

Sam stared at her for a few moments. Then she set down her glass of water very gently on the counter and walked through to their tiny sitting room. She sat down on the sofa and folded her arms.

'Sam,' Nadira had followed her through. 'I didn't mean to upset you.'

'No. You're right. It's a possibility. I've wondered that, too.'

'Then you can understand why he'd want to keep it secret.'

'Trouble is, I don't think that's the reason. And even if it was, it doesn't make any difference. I still have to see it.'

'But supposing you can't? If Raph has got it, and he won't let you into the house and Lola's there all the time and the cleaner won't help, then there's nothing you can do.'

'There's always something you can do.'

Nadira was silent. It was always a mistake to underestimate Sam's courage and determination, both of them qualities that she shared, but in a different way. Nadira could work hard and stick to her guns, but she was fundamentally conservative. She'd never do anything to draw attention to herself or challenge authority, if she could possibly help it. That's why opposing her family had been such torture and why she'd devote the rest of her life trying to prove she'd made the right decision.

Sam's freedom from those kinds of restraints had attracted her from the beginning. Sam, when she broke the rules, usually did so because she hadn't realized there were any in the first place. Her single-mindedness might have made her seem ruthless if it hadn't been combined with great kindness and generosity.

And now, she had that look on her face.

'What are you thinking?'

'Mm. Something just occurred to me.'

Nadira knew that expression. It meant Sam had just figured out a more direct route from A to B and planned to take
it, never mind the consequences. She'd had it last weekend
when she left the flat at eleven o'clock without saying where
she was going – and carrying a torch and a hammer. Hardly
items for a hot date. Nadira hadn't pressed her about her
plans then, not wanting to risk a rejection. But today they
were talking again.

'Sam, you're planning something.'

Sam turned and grinned, that old infectious grin that Nadira
hadn't seen in an age. She said, 'Maybe.'

'What is it?'

'I don't think you want to know.'

'You're not going to break in, are you?'

'No.'

'Thank goodness for that, anyway.'

'I already did.'

'What?'

'This time, I'm going to get someone else to break in for me.'

CHAPTER 8

The members of the jury were having a hard time making up their minds, which wasn't altogether surprising. A particularly vicious little robbery had occurred late one night at a pizza delivery place in Chingford. The amount of money stolen was small – less than two hundred pounds – but the proprietor, Mr Patel, had been beaten and kicked and his son, who had arrived back on a moped halfway through and rushed to intervene, was still unable to work as a result of his injuries. The prosecution implied that the three defendants had deliberately set out to inflict maximum harm, as a warning to other small business-men in the area. Certainly they looked like caricatures of small-time villains: with their crew cuts and their swaggering manner and exaggerated deference to the court. Various members of the Patel family attended each day; their quiet dignity and determination to see justice done demanded respect.

Unfortunately, however, Soli Patel, whether as a result of trauma or intimidation or confusion, had failed to identify all three of his attackers correctly at an identity parade. This was more than enough for Raph, who used it to sow the seeds of doubt in the jurors' minds. Never once did he state outright that his clients were innocent of the charges, but he repeated time and again that the prosecution case had to be watertight if his clients were to be deprived of their liberty. '*Beyond reasonable doubt*, ladies and gentlemen. Beyond reasonable doubt means that if you have any queries remaining, any niggling questions unanswered, then it is your duty to let these men walk free.'

By the second day, when the jury still had not reached a decision, it was clear that these niggling doubts were causing major problems. The judge called them back to let them know he'd accept a majority verdict. The jury retired again.

Mick was discovering that waiting for a jury to return a verdict was the least glamorous part of a barrister's life. After two and a half days spent in the robing room behind the court with only his laptop for company, he was on intimate terms with every crack in the plaster, every damp stain on the ceiling. In theory, as Raph had pointed out to him when he said he was going across the road to work in the pub and to text him the moment anything happened, this was an ideal opportunity to work on the Grace Hobden case. Having taken on the defence of the husband-stabbing housewife, Raph had deftly passed over the preliminary work to Mick.

Mick put his feet up on the low table in front of him, tipped his chair on to its back legs and examined the photograph of Grace Hobden carefully. Raph had been grudging with his advice and Mick, though he was obviously not going to admit it, was feeling out of his depth. He'd worked through the pile of papers several times already, but he still couldn't begin to figure

it out. Was she mad, bad or driven past all endurance by a bullying brute of a husband? Her own statement was a masterpiece
of non-information: 'I couldn't take it any more . . . It was like
it was happening in a dream . . .' and her photograph gave away
even less. She had a solid, almost wholesome face, and though
definitely not his type, she didn't look exactly the murdering
kind either.

Why had Raph insisted on handling this case himself?
Everyone knew he never touched domestic murders, while the
brief was exactly the kind Selina relished.

'*It was like it was happening in a dream . . .*'

Just what was that supposed to mean?

Mick tipped his chair back even further and stared up at the
ceiling. There was a Rorschach-type stain in the centre that had
recently acquired a weird ability to resemble whoever or whatever was plaguing him at that particular moment. Right now it
looked like a woman's face, though he was unable to decide
whether it was Grace Hobden's or Lola's it most reminded him
of. An amalgam of the two, perhaps – Christ, what a grim
thought.

If he hadn't known Raph better, Mick might have suspected
he'd guessed about his pupil's evening with Lola and had
inflicted Grace Hobden as a subtle form of revenge.

Not that Mick had anything much to feel guilty about. He'd
bumped into Lola quite by chance at Bill and Fi's party.
Recognizing his pupil-master's girlfriend he'd gone over to talk
to her; the fact that she was far and away the most attractive
woman in the room didn't hurt either. Later on, when he'd forgotten all about her, he'd noticed that she was so out of it she

was having trouble remaining upright. His motives in offering to see her home had been entirely altruistic: Raph was sure to be grateful if he heard about it.

Wasn't he?

The Rorschach blot had temporarily acquired a distinctly Raph-like appearance and its expression was not exactly grateful. Accusing, more like. Had it really been necessary for Mick to stay with Lola for four hours? Well, yes it had, because Lola had . . . well, Lola had wanted . . . well, she'd wanted him to stay. Why? Well . . . that was difficult . . . And then there was Sam.

Sam . . . in spite of his irritation with the general state of affairs, Mick grinned and tilted still further back in his chair. At this precarious angle he had to hook his feet under the desk to act as a counterbalance. The look on the girl's face when he stumbled on her in Raph's library was indelibly printed on his memory. That had to have been one of life's more unconventional introductions.

He was still grinning when his mobile rang. He removed his feet from under the desk and returned his chair to the vertical. 'Yes?'

A woman's voice on the other end of the line: 'Mick? This is Sam Boswin.'

Well, well, thought Mick. Coincidence, or what?

'Sam, hi. What can I do for you?'

'I have to talk to you.'

'Sure. How can I help?'

'Not now. We have to meet up.'

'Hm. Well, yes, I'll just check my diary—' Mick tipped his

chair back and looked up at the ceiling again. 'Umm . . . it's not looking good, I'm afraid.' He had an instinct that Sam Boswin meant trouble, and he needed to keep relations with Raph smooth. 'I'm kind of busy this week.'

'This evening,' she said flatly. 'When you get off work.'

Mick assumed that had been a question, though he had to admit it hadn't exactly sounded like one.

'Damn, I'd love to, but I can't. I've got a squash court booked and then—'

'So? Cancel it. This won't take long. After that, you can do what you want.'

'I intend to. What's this about?'

'I can't talk over the phone. I'll meet you at the pub opposite your work at six.'

'Oh, no!' The need to wrest back some control of the conversation made Mick tip back into an upright position; the last thing he wanted was a tête-à-tête with Sam taking place under the watchful eyes of his work colleagues. He was due in Notting Hill at about eight, so, 'There's a wine bar I know just off Westbourne Grove. I can meet you there at seven-thirty.'

'Okay, then.'

He gave the name and the street, before saying, 'See you at half seven, then.'

'You have to be there,' she said firmly, and hung up.

Mick wasn't used to being talked to like that. But still, if his pupil-master had a stepdaughter who lurked in his study in the dark when she thought the house was empty, it might be a good idea to find out what he could about her. Mick switched on his laptop and went online.

The jury foreman wore narrow, rimless glasses and had a fussy manner. But his verdict was unequivocal: 'Not guilty.'

Not guilty, or unable to reach a verdict, on all counts.

Mick had to fight down the urge to punch the air in triumph: their clients were free to leave and resume their lives. After the months of preparation, the endless obsession with detail and the delays it was like watching a pack of cards collapse. Against all the odds, it seemed, Raph and his team had won.

'Well done,' Mick turned to his pupil-master. Raph's expression was poker-faced professional, but his satisfaction was tangible. There was no one in the business who relished a good victory more than he did.

Then Mick glanced across the courtroom to where the seven members of the Patel family were sitting. Their faces were blank with disbelief. Mr Patel senior seemed to be explaining to an elderly woman, his mother perhaps, or an aunt, what had just happened. Soli Patel, who had lost the sight of one eye and would have headaches for many months still to come, was too shocked to speak.

Mick felt a stirring of unease. One of his clients, Shaun Boyd, who had been accused of stamping on Soli Patel's head when he was lying immobile on the ground, looked across the courtroom at him for the first time and met his eye. Nothing so crude as a grin or a thumbs up from the unexpectedly free Mr Boyd, but the message was there, all the same: We got away with it. Now you'd better watch your back. Mick saw Soli Patel clench his fists.

'A good day's work,' said Raph. 'This next bit will be easier than I expected.'

Mick busied himself putting documents away in his case, and did not look up again until the court was nearly empty.

It was a formality. 'Cheers, Mr Howes,' said Jason Franks when they met to debrief afterwards. The three defendants, who'd sweated out a three-week trial in jackets and ties, were now stripped down to short-sleeved shirts, tattoos glistening. 'You've been terrific. You and your team.' He grinned at Mick. 'Can't thank you enough. Any time you're passing through Chingford, look us up. We'd be delighted to give you a meal. You're welcome any time.'

'Yeah, that's right,' said Shaun. 'Any way we can thank you, let us know.'

'That's very kind of you,' said Raph.

'Or if we can help you at all. Someone you know who wants sorting, that kind of thing.'

'Shaun—' Jason said warningly.

'What?' Shaun's face was a picture of innocence. 'Only trying to be helpful, aren't I?'

Raph smiled indulgently, as though a small child had just offered him a particularly sticky and unpleasant-looking sweet. 'I didn't hear any of this,' he said firmly. 'Safe journey, gentlemen.'

'Has that happened to you before?' Mick couldn't help asking him as they were leaving the court. 'Villains offering to sort someone out for you?'

Raph chuckled. 'It's not usually so overt. But one does notch up credit in some very odd places. For instance, if you ever run into trouble in Ecuador, I know just the man to sort it out.'

'Thanks,' said Mick. 'I'll bear it in mind.'

*

The wine bar had been newly refurbished with lashings of stain-less steel and halogen lights and tortured-looking bamboos, but as it had no outdoor space it was less crowded than usual in this hot weather. Mick arrived ten minutes early, chose a table against the back wall with a good view of the door, and ordered himself a beer.

His time waiting for the jury to return its verdict after Sam's call had not been wasted.

Since Sam was connected with Raph through her mother, Mick had begun his researches with Kirsten Waller. The inter-net had thrown up its usual excess of irrelevant information, so he'd concentrated on the obituaries that had been written after her death, as well as coverage of the inquest. Obviously, since she had remained a US citizen, the major obituaries were from the States, but he was impressed by the attention she'd received on this side of the Atlantic too. He'd always been aware that Raph's estranged wife was a writer, but he hadn't realized she was such a big literary cheese – no doubt he turned to Lola for much-needed light relief after too many evenings with the wrong sort of heroic couplets. Lola probably thought Emily Dickinson was a cosmetics label.

The photographs showed Kirsten Waller to have been a good-looking woman in a Nordic, healthy-hippy kind of way with wispy long blonde hair and a broad smile, though the writer who kept on about her 'film-star good looks' was obvi-ously an old friend, and therefore prejudiced. As well as writing several volumes of poetry and getting through at least three hus-bands, she seemed to have involved herself in every radical cause from Greenham Common to animal rights. Mick could only assume that her marriage to Raph, who was conservative in his bones, was an attraction of opposites.

He concentrated on the details relating to Sam. In her early twenties, Kirsten had lived for a while in Cornwall where she met Davy Boswin, who was variously described as a farmer, a fisherman and a Cornishman. Their marriage lasted only a few years, during which time their daughter was born. When they parted, Kirsten had returned to the USA, presumably taking Sam with her, but was enticed back to England ten years later by husband number three – number two had been a union activist in Pittsburgh, but had lasted so little time none of the papers identified him by name. Husband number three was Raph; when this marriage also broke down she'd returned to America for few months, but she was back in Cornwall by the early summer. She'd been on holiday in a lonely cottage belonging to a friend, when, on midsummer's eve, just over two months ago, she ran herself a bath, took off all her clothes and got in. Unfortunately, she'd made sure that a small radio, plugged into the mains by an extension cord, was dropped into the bath along with the soap. Death would have been instantaneous. Any chance of it being seen as accidental was erased by the suicide note that was found on the kitchen table.

Those last details were merely alluded to in the obituaries, but everyone in chambers knew how Raph's wife had died. Apart from the origins of Sam's name, he'd been unable to find out much about her.

And now, here she was. Also early, she didn't see him right away but stood next to the giant ficus by the door and looked around. There was a ratty-looking green-and-red striped bag hanging from her shoulder and she was carrying an enormous cello case. She seemed to be wearing the same clothes she'd had on when they met the other night: khaki combat trousers, a black T-shirt and trainers. Medium height and slim, she had short dark hair brushed back from her forehead in a style that could have been urban chic gamine but was probably just convenience. She wasn't a Scandinavian-style stunner like her mother, but she was striking. Even the way she stood in the entrance to the wine bar was unusual: she was fierce and hard and wary, and looked as if she was casing the joint for an armed raid rather than searching for a familiar face. Mick sighed. He preferred to share his after-work drink with people who were light-hearted and fun – and neither of those adjectives looked applicable to Sam.

She saw him. Recognition, but not the flicker of a smile. She came over.

'Hi,' he said, half standing as she approached. 'You found it okay?' Automatically he slipped into a professional manner, friendly and efficient, but also detached. 'Is that your cello? I didn't know you played.'

'Yes,' she said, which seemed to answer all his remarks. She laid the cello case down on its side, then pulled out the chair opposite him. She was bristling with tension, the kind that makes you feel as if one touch and sparks might fly.

'What can I get you to drink?'

'Oh?' she said vaguely. 'Water's fine.'

'Sure you don't want something stronger? I'm having beer.'

'All right then, I'll have a whisky. Double whisky, ice but no water.'

No middle way with this one, then, thought Mick as he beckoned to the waiter and gave the order.

'So, Sam, how can I help?' he asked.

She didn't hesitate. 'That night at Raph's, I was looking for something that belonged to me.'

'Yes. So you said.'

'Well . . . I never found it. But I think I know where it is. I want you to get it for me.'

Mick smiled. She was so earnest, almost as if it was a matter of life and death. He said, 'It might help if I knew what this mysterious "it" is.'

'It's a notebook, pale blue leather, unlined. My mother had them made specially for her by a firm in South Carolina. She's been using the same ones for years. Kind of working notebook and journal combined. And there might be a poem with it.'

'You went to all that trouble to get hold of a poem?'

'It's . . . important.'

'I guess it must be.' He paused, giving her a chance to elaborate, but she didn't take it. He said, 'You're going to have to explain a bit, Sam. If Raph's got something that belongs to you, why don't you just ask him for it?'

She looked at him with contempt. 'He denies it.'

'So. Maybe he doesn't have it.'

'I know he does.'

'Then you should see a solicitor.'

'Oh really? Raph's only one of the sharpest minds in the legal profession. I don't really think I could fight him through the law and win.'

Mick had the feeling they were going round in circles. He

said, 'If you know where it is, how come you didn't get it the other night?'

'I didn't know then. But now I do. I think I do, anyway.'

'So, go back and get it.'

She shook her head. 'They'll have put a proper lock on that window by now.' Mick was staring at her blankly, so she explained, 'I broke in through one of the upstairs windows.'

'You don't have a key?'

'No. Lola doesn't like any reminders that her man once had a real partner. But I think Raph was just using her as an excuse. He doesn't want me in the house.'

Mick didn't say anything for a moment. It occurred to him that Raph might have good reason to be wary of his step-daughter. He glanced down at the strip of plaster on her palm. 'Is that how you cut your hand?'

'Yes.'

'Is rock climbing your thing?'

'I can't think of anything worse.'

'So?'

She shrugged. 'I had to do it,' she said simply.

Mick eyed her warily while the waiter brought over their drinks. *I had to do it.* Shades of the Grace Hobdens there. But Sam wasn't remotely like Grace Hobden, not really. Grace Hobden was a sub-urban crazy, the killer masquerading as Mrs Normal Housewife. Sam didn't look as though she'd ever be a normal housewife. And she did have the most remarkable eyes, grey-green and deep-set, with expressive dark eyebrows. If she hadn't been so relentlessly serious, he might have even found her attractive. She was more his type than that pink and blonde no-brainer Lola, that's for sure.

He said, 'Look, I wish there was something I could do to help you, but—'

'There is. Get the journal.'

'Sorry, Sam.'

'No, Mick. You haven't understood. I'm not asking this as a favour. You have to get it for me.'

'I have to?'

'That's right.' She raised her eyes to his, all weakness gone. 'You can't refuse.'

'Of course I ca—'

'Then I'll tell Raph about you and Lola.'

'Don't be pathetic. You know there's nothing between Lola and me. Never has been.'

'So? I can make it up. I'll bet neither of you have told him about that night you spent at his house, have you?' She waited for his denial, smiled when none was forthcoming. 'You and Lola would deny it, but then he'd expect that, wouldn't he? And even if he believed you, the doubt would always be there.'

'Are you threatening to tell Raph a bunch of lies about me and Lola?'

'Exactly.'

'You'd have to tell him you were there, too.'

'So? I've got nothing to lose. Besides, it's worth the risk.'

Mick stared at her. She returned his stare, unflinching, her eyes like hard green pebbles. Forget what he'd thought earlier about her being attractive. There must be piranha fish with more going for them. He said, 'That's blackmail. Not to mention lies.'

She shrugged. 'Whatever.'

'And it's not even true.'

'That's why they're lies.'

'Fuck. Are you serious about this?'

'I risked my life to get the journal, so a few lies and some blackmail, that's nothing. Yes, I'm serious, Mick. Deadly serious.'

'Fuck,' he said again. *Risked her life*, what nonsense. She was crazier than he'd thought. Furious, he shifted his chair as far from the table as the wall would allow. He was tempted to storm out, right there and then, having told her what she could do with her mother's sodding journal. But then he realized that, if she made good her threat, he might be looking for a speedy career change by the end of the month. 'Christ, Sam, you have to make life hard for yourself, don't you?' he said angrily. 'If you'd just explained how you felt about things, maybe even thrown in the odd please or thank you, I'd probably have helped you anyway.' It wasn't strictly true, but it made him feel better, helped with the sense of grievance. 'But no, you had to move straight to the thumbscrews.'

'Raph's your boss. Why would you help a stranger take something he wanted?'

'Because I felt sorry for you, maybe?'

It was the wrong thing to say. Her face, which hadn't been exactly open before, shut down like a trap. 'Stuff your pity. All I want is Kirsten's journal. You'll find it, if my hunch is right, under the lid of the grand piano in Raph's drawing room.'

'How do you know?'

'It's what they do in *Casablanca* – which just happens to be his favourite film. Raph likes those kind of parallels.'

It seemed like a long shot, and one he wasn't planning to take. 'I told you,' he said, 'going to his place that night was a one-off.'

'Well, you'll just have to make it a two-off, won't you?'

'Suppose it's not there?'

'For your sake, I hope it is. Just get the journal.'

She stood up and looked around for the waiter and asked for the bill. Mick said nothing: never had he felt less inclined to buy a round of drinks. When she'd rummaged around in her purse for the necessary coins, he stood up also and said coldly, 'Are you going to give me your phone number or is finding that out all part of the quest?'

'Here.' She pulled an address book out of her pocket and wrote down a couple of numbers on a blank page, then tore it out and handed it to him. Mick copied them into his palm pilot and chucked the paper into the ashtray. She hesitated, then, 'Thanks.' Her mouth drew back. The piranha fish was on the verge of smiling.

But as far as Mick was concerned, it was too late to start with the courtesies. 'Don't bother thanking me,' he said. Then he added, 'See you, Samphire.'

Her eyes widened. 'People call me Sam,' she told him. As he'd guessed, it was obvious she hated her full name, and he could see why. Turning up at a new school with a name like that – the other kids would have had a field day. Having a famous poet for a mother can't have been all plain sailing. *Samphire and Other Poems* had been Kirsten Waller's first volume, as he'd discovered in his researches. Dedicated to her only child. It was a pity the internet hadn't thrown up some kind of hazard warning; he could have used that.

'Shame about that, eh? Samphire's such a pretty name.'

She shrugged and turned without a word of goodbye and headed towards the exit, lugging the cello case beside her. Her shoulders had a dejected slump that made him feel almost sorry for her. Almost. Once out on the pavement, she straightened her back, as though forcing herself not to give in to weakness, and headed off into the late summer crowds.

Mick ordered himself another drink. He couldn't remember having ever been blackmailed before and beer seemed to help him get used to the novelty.

Not that he intended being bullied or threatened into doing anything against his will, but he'd have to work out a strategy. Right now it seemed to be a choice between caving in to blackmail or leaving for the South China Sea. Sam did look just crazy enough to carry out her threat, but Mick wasn't going to cave in. He was famous among his friends as a soft touch, would do almost anything if someone asked him nicely – as Lola had discovered – but he could be amazingly stubborn if pushed.

He'd meant what he said, in a way. Samphire was a pretty name. Some kind of edible wild plant, apparently. Not only attractive, but useful, too.

It didn't suit her in the least.

CHAPTER 9

Lola screamed.

She'd felt like screaming all morning, but that was because Raph's family were due to come over for supper that evening, and the imminent arrival of the Weirdo Brigade was enough to make anyone scream; this was different. There'd been no build-up to this scream; it was totally spontaneous.

She was standing in the doorway to the spare room. One of the prettiest rooms in the house, on the second floor, it had been Sam's room in the bad old days of Raph's marriage, and Lola had been planning to colonize it for some time. Unfortunately, Raph's mother also liked it, which was why Lola had gone up with a bunch of tulips in a vase. Now, what with the shock and all, the tulips and the vase lay on the ground.

The scream felt good, though, so she screamed again. Nothing like a good scream. Pity there was no one in the house to hear her.

She ran down the stairs to the master bedroom and dialled quickly.

'Raph, is that you?'

'Of course it's me.'

'Oh, thank God. Thank God you're there. I've never been so upset.'

'What is it this time? Broken another fingernail?'

'Someone's broken into the house. There's glass and stuff everywhere. It's terrible.'

'Someone's in the house? Have you called the police?'

'No–o.'

'Well. Call them.'

'Okay. Whatever.'

'Where's the intruder now?'

'I don't know. I think they've gone. I don't know when it happened. Oh Raphie, I'm so scared. Will you come home? Please?'

'You know I can't. I'm about to go into court. And don't call me Raphie.'

'Oh.' Lola started to make crying noises.

'Look, I'll see if I can get someone to come over. Just call the police, okay?'

'Okay.'

Lola dialled 999, gave a breathless account of the broken window in the spare room to a motherly voice on the other end, then went upstairs to get dressed. She didn't for a moment think the intruder was still in the house, if indeed they'd broken in at all. From the leaves that had drifted in through the broken pane, she'd say the damage had been done several days before, probably when Raph was away in Basle and had forgotten to set the burglar alarm and she was out partying. But it didn't hurt to stir things up a bit. The days could be quite long and boring when

Raph was busy with his work, which was most of the time, and a few burly policemen around the place might liven things up.

Another hot day. She changed into a bikini, just two wisps of fabric across breasts and crotch, wrapped a sarong loosely over it, touched up her make-up and went out into the garden to wait for the fun to begin.

'What the fuck are you doing here?'

Mick Brady was the last person Lola had expected to see when Raph said he'd send someone over. She'd forgotten he worked with Raph. Standing on the top step, he was wearing a white shirt, open at the neck, the regulation barrister's sober tie knotted low, suit jacket slung over one arm. He was carrying a briefcase and he didn't look exactly thrilled about this return visit to Raph's Holland Park house.

'Raph sent me,' he said coolly. 'He said you had burglars.'

'Oh. Right.'

Mick glanced sideways at the police car parked in front of the house. 'You called the police already.'

'Looks like it, yeah. Sorry to waste your time.'

'I might as well come in and check it out. So I can make a report to Raph.'

Lola stood aside to let him in. She'd forgotten how attractive he was, with his thick brown hair and tobacco-coloured eyes, which was a bonus, considering that neither of the police who'd shown up were her type. Anybody's type, really. The two police-men, one tall and skinny, one short and round, like a comedy duo, were just emerging from the drawing room as the front door closed behind Mick. The taller one, who'd been ogling

Lola's bare shoulders and long brown legs, said, 'We've got all the information we need for now. I'd get in touch with the alarm company right away if I were you. The system should have detected a missile being thrown through the window, even if no one actually broke in.'

'Okay officer. I'll do that today.'

The smile that accompanied this remark was mainly for Mick's benefit. She adjusted the sarong, which had slipped down over her breasts.

'If there's anything else you want,' the tall policeman offered hopefully, 'don't hesitate to call.'

'I'll remember that, officer.'

'We'll let you know how our investigations go,' said PC Short-and-round.

'Thanks.'

When she'd closed the front door behind them, she turned and said to Mick, 'Coffee?'

'A glass of water please.'

'Sure.' She led the way down to the kitchen. She was trying to remember, now that Mick had so unexpectedly turned up, exactly what had taken place between them that night at the weekend. So far as she could remember, they'd been attracted to each other – and seeing him again now, in daylight, it was easy to understand why – but nothing much had actually taken place. Though whether that was because she'd turned him down, or he'd turned her down, or they'd neither of them quite got it together to take the plunge, or whether they'd both just passed out and then he'd gone home, she wasn't altogether sure. Either way, she was glad he was here again, and glad that she'd changed into her bikini.

She was devoted to Raph, and hoped their relationship went on for ages, but he was kind of middle-aged and serious and sometimes it was fun to hang out with men a little closer to her own age.

She was aware of Mick's eyes on her back as he followed her down to the kitchen. She expected he liked what he saw; people usually did.

Mick said, 'Where was the break-in?'

'Upstairs. I'll show you if you're interested.' She reached into the fridge and pulled out a bottle of mineral water. 'Sparkling?'

He nodded.

She poured him a glass without speaking. The silence between them built up a pleasurable kind of tension.

As Mick took the glass he asked, 'Did you mention to Raph about me bringing you home from the party on Saturday night?'

'Bringing me home? Makes me sound like a package.'

'Did you?'

'Why d'you want to know? Has he been acting suspicious?'

'I just wondered.'

'No.' She regarded him coolly. 'Did you?'

'No. It . . . didn't seem important.'

Lola didn't like the sound of that. Like he didn't think she was worth mentioning. Piqued, she said, 'Raph might not see it that way. He can be quite jealous, y'know. Even when there's no reason for it.'

'He might be grateful. That I saw you home, I mean.'

'He might.' Lola held his gaze. His question, and the acknowledgement that neither had chosen to tell Raph, invested their encounter with a secrecy that was instantly sexual.

Even though nothing had happened between them – well, nothing much – it would be impossible to tell Raph about it now, after several days had passed.

Mick looked at her, then set his glass down on the granite worktop. 'You'd better show me where they got in,' he said.

'What's the rush?'

'I have to get back to chambers.'

'Chambers.' Lola spoke the single word with contempt. 'Chambers' was always getting in the way. Men like Mick and Raph just used it as an excuse, something to hide behind when they didn't want to fit in with her plans. In her mind, 'chambers' was a jumped-up version of her grandfather's garden shed, complete with electric kettle and paint-spattered transistor radio. 'Bo-oring.' Chambers was dismissed.

She led the way upstairs, past the first floor which was entirely taken up with the enormous bedroom she shared with Raph, with their two bathrooms and dressing rooms on either side, and up to the second floor, where the spare rooms were. 'In here,' she said, as she pushed open the door to the room which had once been Sam's.

Mick walked past her, stepping carefully to avoid the tulips which were still lying scattered on the floor where Lola had dropped them, then looked at the smashed windowpane, the glass on the carpet and the tendrils of creeper that had already wound their way through the gaps.

He peered through the jagged window to the patio below. 'Jesus,' he said, 'I never realized it was so high. How do you think they climbed up? Is there a ladder anywhere?'

'*We* haven't got one, that's for sure. And, call me old-fashioned, but it might look kind of suspicious, toting a ladder round in the middle of the night.'

He turned sharply. 'What makes you think it happened at night?'

'Must have done. That night we met at the party. D'you remember when we came back in and the alarm wasn't on? Raph forgot to set it when he left, but I wasn't about to tell the police that, was I?'

'Why not?'

'Insurance, of course.'

'Has anything been taken?'

'Not that I've noticed. In fact, I don't think anyone actually climbed in. Most likely it was kids mucking about, chucked a brick through or something.'

'Did you find a brick?'

'No . . . but . . . Maybe it wasn't a brick . . .' Her voice trailed away. They both knew it was stretching probability for even a small piece of brick to get lost in a room that size.

Mick was still peering out of the window, tugging at the creeper to see if it was secure. 'What a crazy risk,' he muttered again. 'Whoever climbed up here must have been insane.'

'*If* they climbed up,' corrected Lola.

'We'd better check the garden.'

'The garden?'

'To see how they got in.'

'Does that matter?'

Mick didn't answer. He was already heading back down the stairs to the kitchen, where double doors led into a conservatory, and from there into the garden. Lola was getting mildly pissed off by Mick's determination to waste time playing detective. He was standing in the middle of the patio, head tilted back as he examined the rear wall of the house. At this angle, his profile and the curve of his throat were shown to good advantage. It occurred to Lola that if she was ever tempted to be unfaithful to Raph – and, let's face it, it was bound to happen sooner or later – she could choose a lot worse than Mick Brady.

'More like the third floor,' he said. 'If you count the basement.' Did he want the burglars to get a medal for bravery, or what? 'Have you ever wanted anything badly enough to risk a climb like that?'

Lola laughed. 'Are you kidding? I'm not fucking mental, y'know.'

Mick was frowning as though trying to reach a decision. Lola guessed, with some irritation, that whatever the decision was, it had nothing to do with her. Then he grinned unexpectedly and asked, 'Is that coffee still on offer?'

'Sure. If you can spare the time.'

'I'm sure Raph would understand.'

Lola led the way back into the house. She took her time filling the kettle, grinding up fresh coffee beans, while wondering what exactly Mick thought Raph might understand.

While she was filling the cafetiere, Mick said suddenly, 'Can you imagine ever deciding to stick a knife in your partner? Actually kill someone?'

She turned slowly. 'Are we making small talk, here?'

'Raph's got me working on a brief which concerns a woman called Grace Hobden who stabbed her husband while he was sleeping. I can't get any sense out of her.'

'Maybe she doesn't know why she did it. Maybe it was –
impulse.'

'Either that, or very, very calculated. I can't figure it out.'

'What's she like?'

'Ordinary. On the surface at least. That's the whole problem.'

'Is she pretty?'

'Yes. But not my type.'

'Which is?'

Mick smiled. 'Oh, blondes with long legs who wear sarongs
round the house, that kind of thing.'

'Well, what do you know?'

She poured the coffee, handed him his cup, but he set it
down at once and asked, 'D'you mind if I use the bathroom
first?'

''Course not. There's one off the conservatory.'

Maybe he hadn't heard, because he went back upstairs, taking
his briefcase with him; after a few minutes she heard the
ground-floor toilet flush. When he returned, they took their
coffees out into the garden and chatted about the mutual
friends at whose house they'd met. Lola asked if he wanted to
stay for lunch – anything to help keep her mind off the arrival
of Raph's female relatives later in the day – but he said he had
to get back. Chambers, of course. No surprises there, then.

As she was seeing him out, she leaned against the doorpost,
her sarong slipping down over her breasts and dragging the
bikini top lower, too, and said, 'You won't tell Raph about
Saturday night without warning me first, will you? I mean, I
wouldn't want him to get the wrong idea.'

He glanced down at her breasts. 'Oh, I don't think you

need to worry about that.' He was grinning as he stooped to give her a peck on the cheek. 'I'm not about to tell him, nor will you, so who else is there? Bye, Lola. See you some-time.'

'Bye.'

His briefcase tucked securely under one arm, Mick set off briskly in the direction of Holland Park tube. As soon as he was out of earshot, he took out his mobile phone and keyed in Sam's number.

'Here, let me give you a hand with those.'

'Thanks.' Lola leaned forward to give Johnny a boxful of tea lights and a couple of the long flares she was carrying under her arm.

'Got enough there, have you?' he asked with a grin.

'You can't have too many. I want tea lights all along the path, so when it gets dark it'll look like a river of light.'

'Brilliant. Like this?'

'Or even closer. I've got hundreds.'

Working one on each side of the path, Johnny and Lola set the little lights all the way down to the table and chairs at the far end of the garden. They'd been banished from the kitchen, where Raph was cooking, aided – or at any rate, accompanied – by Miriam and their mother. Raph was a competitive and demanding chef, best kept away from unless you had a lifetime of training. A year ago, Johnny had spent summer twilights in the garden with Kirsten while their spouses hurled ingredients into pots and bashed and shredded and whisked. Now it was Lola. Given the way the Howes clan seemed to congeal into a single unit whenever all three were together, life was easier if their partners struck up a defensive alliance.

Lola contemplated her handiwork, while Johnny poured them each a glass of sparkling Saumur. 'Thanks. And cheers. I love candles, don't you? Raph won't have them in the house, not even the scented ones. He's got this thing about fire hazards.'

'It's hardly surprising.'

Lola tilted her head to one side and looked at him quizzically. 'Yeah? How come?'

'You must have heard the story.'

'What story?'

Johnny sighed. Raph hadn't told Kirsten either and Johnny had told her about it one October evening when they were all staying in the South of France and she'd been carelessly roasting chestnuts over a log fire. One had rolled out of the metal pan and burned a hole in the carpet. Raph and Miriam had both reacted in a way that a stranger might have considered unreasonable.

He said, 'Their father was killed in a house fire.'

Lola's eyes, not small to begin with, widened with disbelief. 'You're kidding me.'

'Raph was maybe five or six, so Miriam must have been about ten. Sunday afternoon, Dad goes up to the bedroom for an afternoon kip. Presumably he didn't put his cigarette out properly, or fell asleep with one in his hand. They think it was the smoke that did for him. Diana got the children out, but he didn't make it. The whole house was gutted, apparently.'

Lola looked towards the house. They could see Raph's silhouette as he zigzagged across the kitchen from table to cooker, back to table. 'Poor little tyke,' she said. 'I wonder if that's why he has all those nightmares.'

'He still gets them?'

'About once a week. He never told me about the fire, though.'

'He doesn't talk about it. I only heard from Miriam.' He hesitated. 'And that was when we'd been married a year.'

'I thought there was something, though,' mused Lola. 'Raph's different when his family's around. I mean, they're close, but it's not the usual kind of closeness, is it? Not what you'd call affectionate, not really.'

Johnny's opinion of Lola was going up, but he said loyally, 'They're a devoted family.'

'Well, obviously. But you don't get the feeling they *enjoy* being together, do you? More that they can't get out of it. Like a centrifugal force but the other way round. What's it called?'

'Centripetal.'

'That's the one. *Centripetal* – sounds like loads of feet, doesn't it? But with them it's like they couldn't get away from each other even if they wanted to.'

'That kind of tragedy often brings the survivors closer.'

'Does it? I guess you're right. And maybe that's why Diana always seems kind of, I don't know, kind of frozen. As though reality is too tough to deal with head on.'

'You're not just a pretty face, are you?' Johnny refilled their glasses. They sat in companionable silence for a few moments, the garden darkening around them. He said, 'I'm glad you and Raph got together, Lola. You're good for him. Kirsten always said the Howes partners had to stand shoulder to shoulder – because the three of them are so close, I suppose.'

Lola treated him to a dazzling smile. 'I'll stand shoulder to shoulder with you any time, Johnny.'

'Good. You don't mind me talking about Kirsten, do you?'

''Course not. I only feel threatened by women who are younger than me, and prettier. Why should I mind about some old dead saddo?'

'What?' Lola's casual bitchiness caught him unawares. He felt winded, the way he always did when people were gratuitously cruel.

She must have realized she'd gone too far – the Saumur speaking, probably – because she said defensively, 'Well, she *is* dead, and she must have been sad or she wouldn't have killed herself, would she?'

Johnny set down his glass. He was frowning. He said carefully, 'Kirsten was the most brilliant and amazing woman I have ever met. Her death was a terrible, terrible tragedy. Don't ever talk about her in that flippant, horrible way again. Okay?'

'Okay. Whatever.' Lola poured herself the rest of the bottle and looked towards the conservatory door. Miriam had emerged and was walking towards them. Lola said casually, 'Didn't you go to visit Kirsten last winter, when she went back to the States?'

'Yes. Why?'

'Just wondered. Hi, Miriam. How's it going in there?'

'Fine,' said Miriam, but she wasn't really concentrating on the question. She was looking round at Lola's handiwork with her usual anxious frown. She said, 'Is it really necessary to have so many candles?'

Johnny stood up and put a protective arm around his wife.

'Don't worry so much, darling,' he said. 'It's perfectly safe.' He was careful to keep his back to Lola, not wanting to see her knowing little smile. She thought she had them all figured out, but she didn't have a clue.

'Brandy, anyone?'

Raph laid his dessert fork on the side of his plate and sat back with a satisfied sigh. The meal was finished and it had been a triumph. He was a superlative cook, practically professional standard, proved once again, and he was satisfied.

Lola licked the last trace of chocolate off the back of her spoon and laid it down. 'That was bloody brilliant,' she said.

'Hm. Would have been better with unsalted butter,' he said. But he looked pleased with himself, she could tell.

'Tasted good to me,' she said.

He watched as her tongue circled her lips for the last traces of chocolate. For some reason, cooking always made him horny as hell. Otherwise she'd have insisted on a restaurant every time.

'I wouldn't mind a brandy,' said Johnny, pulling a fat cigar out of his pocket.

'I'll get it,' said Miriam, standing up to start clearing the plates.

'Leave those, darling,' said Johnny. 'You look exhausted.'

Lola knew this was her cue to leap up and start acting the busy hausfrau, but she hated to rush into the clearing up and besides, if Miriam wanted to get all stressy and play family drudge, who was she to interfere?

'No, I'll get it,' said Raph. 'You sit down, Miriam. Relax.'

Johnny said, 'Relax? That's not a word in Miri's vocabulary.'

Raph cast a glance in Lola's direction. An altogether approving glance. Lola was moulding soggy candle wax into little pellets. He said, 'She should take lessons from Lola, then.'

Lola flicked a pellet in his direction, but he'd already turned and was heading towards the house. It was Diana who looked disapproving, but she didn't say anything. Diana didn't believe in saying anything negative, which was fine by Lola. Especially when Raph was being super mellow.

Raph was gone some time. It was too much to hope that he'd started loading dishes in the machine, and tomorrow was not one of the cleaner's days, so Lola would probably have to stir herself at some stage, not that she was complaining. Johnny was talking about the work that needed doing at Wardley, how their plans to renovate the tower were being held up because of all the people they had to consult, because of its status as an ancient monument, a relic of—

'Miriam!' Raph's voice was like thunder. They'd been so absorbed in Johnny's stories they hadn't even noticed Raph coming down the path, but here he was, and Lola saw right away that he wasn't wearing his Mr Happy face, either. 'Miriam, have you been—?' He didn't finish his question, just glared at Miriam so furiously that for once Lola felt almost sorry for her.

Diana cleared her throat anxiously. 'So pleasant, these September evenings. And you can hardly hear the traffic.'

'Was it you?' Raph asked.

Miriam's eyes were bulging. Her broad, flat version of the Howes family face had always reminded Lola of some kind of amphibian; startled, she looked more frog-like than ever. But then suddenly, she smiled. 'Why, Raph, what's the matter? Is something missing?'

'Damn right it is.'

'What is?' asked Johnny.

'Miriam knows,' said Raph.

Johnny turned to his wife. 'Miri?'

She didn't answer, but miraculously her forehead was free of the anxious frown that had been there all evening. She looked almost excited.

Raph stood over them. 'What the hell have you done with it?' he demanded.

'I haven't got it,' she said.

'Got what?' asked Johnny.

Raph said, 'I don't believe you. When did you take it?'

'It wasn't yours anyway,' said Miriam.

'That's my business,' said Raph.

Diana had been fidgeting, the way she always did when there was a hint of trouble. Now she said, 'Is it ten o'clock yet? It must be time to watch the news.'

Miriam said, 'Johnny, we ought to make a move.'

'Not so fast,' said Raph. 'Not until I'm sure you haven't taken it.'

'Search our things if you want,' said Miriam.

'This is ridiculous,' said Johnny. 'What on earth is all this about?'

Raph slumped down into a chair and put his hand over his eyes. He said, 'Kirsten's journal. Her last journal. I took it from Gull Cottage when I went down with Sam just after Kirsten died. It's . . . I just thought it was best to keep it secret, that's all.'

Johnny was frowning. 'But doesn't all that kind of stuff belong to Sam now? I mean, since you and Kirsten were separated and—'

'We were never formally separated.'

'But all the same. Sam got all her other papers. What was so different about that last journal? Surely Sam should have that, too.'

Raph sighed. He said, 'In theory, yes. But in practice . . . look, this whole business has been hard enough for Sam, God knows. I was just trying to protect her.'

'Protect her? Why?'

Raph didn't answer. Then, 'Sam,' he said thoughtfully, and, turning to Lola, he asked, 'Who's been here today? Did Sam come earlier?'

'Of course not,' said Lola. 'I'd have told you if she had.'

'Who else, then?'

'Well, no one. Apart from those two policemen. I'm pretty sure they didn't take anything.'

'Not them.'

'What about that man who works for you?' Lola frowned, deliberately vague. 'Nick – Whatsisname.'

'Mick Brady.' said Raph. 'No, he's nothing to do with it. Sam must have got in somehow. But how did she know—?' He left the question hanging in the air.

Lola was utterly baffled. She'd seen Kirsten's journal, as it happened, when Raph came back from Gull Cottage right after she died. Raph had been pretty distraught and had left it lying in his dressing room and, since anything to do with his now-dead wife aroused her curiosity, she'd glanced through it, but had soon lost interest. If there'd been some juicy titbits about sex with Raph, or secret lovers, she might have persevered, but it was mostly fragments of poems about birds, and stuff of no interest to anyone at all, so far as she could see.

Diana smiled at no one in particular and said, 'Well, what a lovely evening this has been, Raph. Thank you so much. And Lola too. It's really been delightful.'

Raph poured himself a large cognac and swilled it round in the glass. 'That's right, Mother. We're just one big happy family, aren't we? Nothing ever really changes.'

'Yes, a lovely evening,' she said again. 'I wonder if we'll be able to sit out like this again this year.'

'The forecast is for thundery showers,' said Miriam.

Raph put his head in his hands.

Diana sat on the edge of her bed and listened to Raph and Lola moving around in the rooms below. She tried to keep her mind on practicalities – that excellent chocolate mousse Raph had made, the way the garden looked, all lit up with little candles, a small mark that had appeared near the hem of her skirt – but there was a fluttering of fear in the pit of her stomach that refused to go away. She made herself think about what she was going to do the next day. She had to go to Liberty's to look for fabric for one of her armchairs. She would collect up swatches and take them home and make her choice in a leisurely way. There was no point hurrying such an important decision. And there was wedding crystal to be bought for a neighbour's daughter. That would take up most of the afternoon.

The fear remained. She had a sense of things creeping through the darkness, danger, like a tide, lapping at the rim of her little family. There had never been a time when she didn't feel a little bit afraid – she couldn't imagine what a life without fear would be like – but recently it had got worse. Much worse.

She lay down in bed and pulled the covers over her. Then lay there, staring into the dark.

She had to keep everything on an even keel. But how?

That had always been the hardest question of all.

Raph put down the phone and unlaced his shoes. Lola, with remarkable tact, had retired to bed without asking him any questions and was sleeping, or pretending to sleep. It didn't really matter which.

He should have destroyed the journal right after he'd read it. Several times he'd been on the point of doing it – there was a shredder at work. Domestic rubbish is always the most efficient way to lose something – but he'd never been able to. When he'd read the journal through, first quickly, then slowly, the day after Kirsten's body had been found, he'd been astonished at the way it brought her voice back to life. Her wonderful, unique voice. Those slow, Midwestern vowels savouring each phrase, leisurely and purposeful, like a river making its slow progress to the sea. He missed her smile and he missed her laugh, and he missed the warm scent of her skin against his, but almost more than anything, he missed her voice. The voice he was never going to hear again. And each time he went to destroy the journal, he'd found he couldn't do it. It was the last thing of her that remained. He couldn't be a part of its destruction.

And now it was too late, anyway.

Was it weakness that had stopped him, when he still had the chance?

'I've got to make a phone call,' said Miriam, when she and Johnny were back in their tiny London flat. They'd had to sell their pleasant house in Ladbroke Grove after Anthony died, to pay for death duties, but luckily there'd been a little bit left over and they'd taken this tiny flat near Gloucester Road. Johnny used it quite a lot when he was in London during the week. On business, he said. Though she wasn't always absolutely sure about that. 'I won't be long,' she told him.

'Okay, darling.' He went into their bedroom, closing the door behind him. She looked at the blank door for a few moments, a familiar anxiety stirring in her heart. *Okay, darling.* They were automatic, his courtesies, these days. All the real tenderness and feeling had long since vanished. He was kind and loyal – she'd known that when she married him, it was one of the reasons she'd chosen him. Though not the most important one. The most important reason was that he was Raph's friend, perhaps the first real friend Raph had ever had, and she'd known instinctively that she ran the risk of losing Raph if his friendships excluded her. Raph had stood in for the missing father and given her away when she married Johnny, his best – in some ways his only – friend. Given her away. What a strange phrase that was. He'd never really give her away. Johnny had become part of the family, that was the only real change. The circle remained unbroken.

The circle must never break.

That's why she had to have the journal. Luckily, she knew someone she could turn to at a moment like this. She hunted through her address book, then came to the letter 'C'.

Well, it made sense. You called someone up when you wanted a pane of glass repaired, or a drain unblocked or the car serviced. So why not for this, too?

When she'd replaced the phone, Miriam sat for a while without moving. She felt drained. Not tired, exactly, but rinsed through, the way she always felt when she'd acted decisively, which wasn't often. No one could say she did it often.

It was a good feeling, though. A kind of floating relief.

When she was floating like this, the memories became almost bearable. She remembered the house they'd lived in when their father was still alive, a white-painted house with a door and five windows, just like the pictures little Raph used to draw with his new box of crayons.

Did it really look like that? Or was that just one of those memory tricks?

Another hot city night. It was getting hard to breathe.

Raph was coming across the lawn towards the house. The little dog was lying dead in his arms. Daddy's dog. Raph had known quite well that he wasn't allowed to play with him.

Had he forgotten what happened when he'd disobeyed before? There was no air in this room, that was the trouble. Miriam was choking. Suffocating.

'I'm going to teach you a lesson,' Daddy had said, that other time when Raph took the dog out without permission. 'A lesson you'll never forget. Bring me your guinea pig, Raph.'

Miriam never liked the guinea pig, not really. She pretended to, because Raph liked it, and because you were supposed to care about animals, but Tuppence had round black eyes that only had one expression and long claws that scratched you if you didn't hold him properly.

Raph fetched his pet, then stood beside Daddy while Daddy dug a hole in the garden, where the potatoes had been and the soil was still loose and easy to dig. It was a deep hole. Daddy put Tuppence in the box and put the lid on. You could hear Tuppence scratching around, trying to get out. Daddy held the lid firmly, then put the box in the hole and put the earth on top, smoothing it out when there wasn't any earth left. Miriam was crying, but Raph just watched. He didn't seem to understand what was happening.

He looked at Daddy when the last of the earth was smoothed. 'Can I play with him, now?'

'Tomorrow,' said Daddy.

That was when Raph started to protest. 'But he doesn't want to be in the box! Let him out! He can't breathe!'

Both the children were screaming as Daddy dragged them back to the house. He wouldn't let them out, even though Miriam was awake the whole night long, imagining. And in the morning, when they ran across the dewy garden to the old potato patch and dug the cardboard coffin out of the ground, Tuppence was stiff and cold.

Daddy found them and he was smiling. 'Let that be a lesson to you, Raph. Next time you disobey me, it'll be you in the box. You understand me?'

And now Raph had disobeyed again, and something had

happened to the dog. This time it would be Raph who was punished by being put under the earth . . .

'Are you all right, darling?' asked Johnny.

Miriam turned to him in the darkness. He couldn't see the
silent tears that streaked her face.

'Hold me,' she said. 'Just hold me.'

CHAPTER 10

I just couldn't take it any more.

'Why on earth didn't you tell us this right away?' Raph was bristling with frustration.

'I didn't think it was important.'

'Not important? That you had a lover? You do realize, don't you, that the prosecution will have a field day with this one?'

Grace Hobden stared at him blankly. At times like this, her broad pale face looked almost bovine. A prison diet, and no doubt liberal quantities of medication as well, had done nothing to improve her appearance. She'd put on weight and her hair hung drably on either side of her face. She picked anxiously at the skin round her fingernails. Mick watched her with a kind of embarrassed fascination and tried to imagine this ordinary-seeming woman picking up a kitchen knife and plunging it into her husband's somnolent stomach. The video footage he was trying to play in his head kept stalling. It just didn't work. He'd thought all along that a piece of information was missing; maybe the secret lover was the clue.

Alan Caulder, Grace Hobden's solicitor, said, 'Grace, you have to try to help us.' This was the second time they'd all met with her; it wasn't that she refused to co-operate, exactly, more that she seemed to have given up without a fight. 'We're trying to work out how to defend you, but unless you give us something to go on . . .' His sentence foundered on the reef of his certainty that Grace Hobden was looking at a life sentence. He'd said as much to Mick and Raph when they'd met up earlier.

'I'm sorry,' she said, her voice barely more than a whisper. 'I didn't think. Fergus was nothing to do with – with what I did.'

Raph leaned forward. 'You're telling me it was a coincidence?'

She nodded.

'I don't believe you,' said Raph.

Grace looked at the ground. For a few moments no one spoke. Somewhere far off, in another part of the prison, they could hear voices raised. Banging on doors and a woman's voice rising to a scream.

Suddenly Raph said, 'Grace, are you pregnant?'

She recoiled. 'How did you know?'

'A lucky hunch.' Raph smiled, as though his intuition had established a bond between them. 'Grace,' he said. 'Listen to me very carefully. I'm on your side. We all are. Maybe some people think you're a wicked woman and deserve to be in prison, but I believe there was a reason for what you did.'

'He beat me,' she said in a dull voice.

'Yes, so you said. But I think there was more than that.'

'I had to do it.'

'Why?'

Mick had never seen Raph like this before. He was talking to Grace as if they were alone together in a place more intimate and comfortable than this dreary windowless room with its peeling paint and its scratched table. Like a kindly father and a confessor and a doctor rolled into one, he was determined to peel back the layers with which Grace had learned to protect herself.

She raised her eyes to his face. Mick got the feeling she was sizing him up, wondering how much she could trust him. The dullness of her expression, which could make her look stupid at times, had been replaced with a calculating intelligence.

She turned away. Whatever test she'd set Raph, he'd failed. She said, 'You can't help me. I killed him and that's life.'

'Maybe not.'

Grace shrugged, but didn't answer. Silence.

Alan was looking embarrassed at Grace's refusal to co-operate with the best barrister he could find. He said, 'Grace, look, if you give us the information we need, we can get the charge reduced from murder to manslaughter. That carries a shorter sentence. You know that, don't you? If we can prove that you were provoked, or acted without premeditation, then you won't have to spend so long in prison. It may even be quite a short sentence. You'd like that, wouldn't you?'

A spark of animation, but, 'It's not going to happen,' she said contemptuously.

'Why not?' asked Raph.

Grace picked at her fingers, but didn't answer.

Raph said, 'Are you the kind of person bad things happen to?'

She nodded.

'How bad?'

She was turned so far away from them she'd almost twisted a hundred and eighty degrees on her chair. 'He was going . . .' She spoke into the corner of the room and the end of her sentence was inaudible.

'Going to—?' prompted Raph.

She whispered. Hand over mouth.

'Going to—?' asked Raph again. Now he was sitting so far forward on his chair he was almost touching her.

She whispered again.

'Kill you?' asked Raph.

She nodded.

'Why?'

She didn't answer. But she was panting, gripping the back of her chair.

'Why?' Raph asked again. 'Why was Paul Hobden going to kill you?'

Suddenly, without warning, she spun round to face her interrogators. Stood up, rage filling her like wind billowing a sail. 'Because of the baby! Because I was pregnant! Because it wasn't his!'

'Your husband knew you were expecting a baby?'

'Of course he bloody didn't! Don't you understand? He would've killed me if he'd known!'

'Because he wasn't the father.'

'No, he fucking wasn't.' Her face was transformed. Disgust and rage and despair. 'He hadn't been able to do it for months. Tried Viagra and everything but he couldn't do it. So he got violent instead, stupid tosser. He guessed there was something going on, but he never figured it was Fergus. All the same, he made sure I knew what'd happen if I ever left him.'

'And that was?' asked Raph.

Grace didn't answer right away. She sat down again slowly, deflating. Cowed again, as if events had left her numb. 'He told me if I ever tried anything, he'd track me down, me and the kids, and kill us. Then he'd kill himself.'

'And you believed him?'

'Oh, yes.'

'How would he have done it?'

'His brother's got a shotgun. He's got a farm outside Newcastle. He's supposed to keep it locked up, but he lent it to Paul last year when there were rats in the garage.'

'You think he'd have killed the children, too?'

'I know he would.'

'Ah,' said Raph.

Now she was angry with him. 'You think I'm making this up, just to get off, don't you? But it happens. You read about it all the time. Man goes and kills his wife, then the kiddies. Then does himself in. There was a case a couple of weeks before I did it. Asian fella. Lovely looking children, too.' Tears were streaming down her face, but she kept on, seemed like she wasn't going to stop. 'The littlest was only a baby. He killed their mother with a knife then smothered the children. Then did himself in, the stupid fucker. Well, I wasn't going to just sit and wait for Paul to come and get me. I might look stupid but I'm not a bloody idiot. What I did was wrong, but at least I'm still alive.

And the children, too. They're safe.' She was sobbing. 'That bastard can't hurt them now, no matter what happens to me. So
I'm not sorry I did it. I'd do the same again. And again and
again and again. I *had* to do it!'

Raph leaned back in his chair. 'Thank you, Grace.' He was
grinning, as though someone had just given him a gift. 'This
has been most useful. I think I'm going to be able to help you
after all.'

Alan asked eagerly, 'Provocation? Diminished responsibility?'

Grace rounded on him. It was getting easier to imagine her pig-
sticking her husband with a kitchen knife. She said, 'I fucking
knew what I was doing! No one's going to make out I was mental.'

'Grace—' Alan didn't want her to say anything she might
regret.

But Raph nodded approvingly. 'I'm sure you knew exactly
what you were doing, Grace. In fact, killing Paul was a calculated, rational act. You didn't have any alternative, did you?'

She had stopped crying and eyed him suspiciously, as if he
was trying to trap her into saying the wrong thing. 'I had to do
it,' she said, dully.

Alan Caulder said anxiously, 'Premeditation is the last thing
we want, Raph. That's murder. Mandatory life sentence.'

'You're forgetting self-defence,' said Raph cheerfully. 'Prove
self-defence and Grace walks free.'

'But—'

Raph stood up. 'Grace,' he said, stepping forward to shake
her by the hand. 'Keep the faith. I'm going to get you out of
here no matter what. Home with the children by Christmas,
how'd you like that, eh?'

Mick and Alan exchanged glances. A hopeful client was a co-operative client, but it was ethically indefensible to make promises when the outcome was so uncertain. They murmured their goodbyes and followed Raph out of the interview room.

As soon as they were out of earshot, following a wiry warder down the hall, Alan got in first. 'Raph, I know you felt sorry for the woman, but was it wise to raise her hopes like that? You know she's looking at a prison sentence, even if we can persuade the jury it was manslaughter.'

Raph was striding ahead. 'Lawful homicide,' he shouted back over his shoulder. 'Don't forget. If we can prove that she made a rational decision, based on her children's best interest, the court will have to agree self-defence. Grace has suffered enough, God knows. And those poor children of hers. Time for a bit of justice, don't you think? I want that woman home with her children by Christmas, and that's what I intend to achieve. Mick, work on it.'

'What?' Mick caught up with his pupil-master at yet another locked door where a warder waited with jangling keys. 'Looking at it realistically, I think our best line will be—'

'Bugger realistically. That woman has to get off. All or nothing. Drop the manslaughter defence, Mick. Why should she have to admit to that? What she did was lawful homicide. All we have to do is convince the jury that logically she had no other option.'

For a moment or two, he sounded so sure of himself that Mick was almost persuaded it was possible. Then the moment fled.

*

They parted outside the prison. Mick and Alan exchanged a few worried words about Raph's eccentric line of defence, and Mick promised Grace's solicitor that he'd keep pursuing the more traditional angles. Though neither man said anything, they shared an anxiety that Raph had overstepped the invisible barrier that separates the professional from his client. Mick wondered why. Surely Raph didn't fancy her, did he? It was hard to imagine that a man who was living with a babe like Lola would be distracted for a moment by the drab and hopeless, not to mention homicidal, Grace Hobden. But it was possible, he supposed. Like those men with gorgeous wives who pay to have sex with boot-faced whores. Obviously there was a whole lot about Raph he didn't know.

When he'd said goodbye to Alan, Mick caught a bus to Euston, then walked down Gower Street, stopping off to pick up a bottle of water from a café. There was still half an hour before he was due to meet Sam, so he went to sit on a bench in the shade in Bedford Square. He still wasn't sure about giving the journal back to Sam. When he'd phoned her earlier in the day, he'd said only that he wanted to talk. 'Have you got the journal?' she'd asked at once. 'We need to talk,' was all he'd said. Which was mean, keeping the girl in suspense like that, but then, since their last meeting, just thinking about Sam made him feel mean. After all, he'd tried the friendly approach and look where it got him. He might experiment with a little arm-twisting of his own. And there was no way he was giving it to her until he'd read it through himself.

Normally, Mick might feel some qualms about reading through private journals, but this time it didn't even occur to him. For one thing, his trawl of the internet had thrown up the information that the bulk of Kirsten Waller's papers, including all her early journals, were already part of some US university's archive, the property of scholars and biographers, as no doubt this one would be, too, before very long. So she must have written it in the knowledge it would become public property soon enough. If she didn't want that, she would have destroyed the journal before she killed herself. For another thing, Sam's own behaviour had been so unscrupulous that Mick felt justified in being the same. And for another thing – and this was enough on its own, really – he was curious.

And he was still curious. He'd read the journal through the day he'd liberated it from its hiding place in Raph's piano, and had paid particular attention to the final pages. He was left with more questions than he'd started with. The biggest question remained the simplest: what was all the fuss about?

Why had Raph gone to such lengths to keep the journal away from Sam and why was she so hell-bent on getting it back?

Kirsten Waller had large, old-fashioned handwriting that wove and danced across the pages, sometimes growing so large there was only room for a handful of words which might be obscure – probably notes jotted for a poem, like 'nemesis blue sky and water' – or else wonderfully mundane like 'Memo Sam's birthday'. On other pages her writing was tiny so that the paper was covered in words, fragments of poems and phrases, observations. Mostly these were formed in the normal way, but occasionally she played around with them: a long, detailed description of a farmer driving his cows back to the farm in slanting evening sunlight was written round the edge of the page, moving inwards as the spiral grew tighter and ending with a single word in the centre: 'Home'. A few pages later another version of the same prose poem was written in the shape of a cow's head. Next to it was what looked like a shopping list: marmalade, tea, batteries.

The bulk of the journal had been written during the previous winter, when Kirsten Waller was still in the States. She didn't always date her entries, but there were enough to give a general idea. The earlier entries hinted at the pain of leaving England, the need to submerge herself in work. People, when they were mentioned, were usually referred to with an initial. 'R' and 'S' presented no problems, but who were 'A' and 'M'? Who was the 'J' she met with and spoke to at length about 'D'? He supposed it was the kind of puzzle that kept research students busy; presumably it would make more sense to Sam than it did to him.

Kirsten Waller was intrigued by birds, no doubt about that. Mick had gone through a bird watching phase himself, when he was about eleven or so, just before his focus switched to Amy Taggart, siren of the lower sixth, and he forgot all about greater crested grebes and bar-tailed godwits. Kirsten was hardly a conventional twitcher; in fact, she didn't refer to birds by their traditional names at all. 'The summer sky bird' – what was that? A lark, perhaps? A buzzard? And 'the ice cream thief' might not even be a bird, though the other notes indicated that it was. There was mention, too, of a liar bird, a farewell bird, and a murder bird – well, that could be a magpie or an eagle, though another reference on the same page to broken shells made Mick think of thrushes. He wondered what had happened to the completed poems. Presumably Sam had them.

One puzzling aspect of the journal was the energy and enthusiasm that invigorated every page. She must have stopped writing it some time before she took her life, because there was no hint of depression or suicidal thoughts, but it was impossible to date the final entries. Mick was no expert on suicidal states of mind, but he had been expecting some hint, some clue, some poetic equivalent to that final painting by Van Gogh before he shot himself, those dark crows of death crowding over the path into the cornfield, the path that leads nowhere.

Mick put the journal back in his briefcase. He was in no hurry to hand it over to Sam, and not just because it went against the grain to give in to blackmail. He'd grown rather fond of Kirsten Waller as he'd got to know her through the journal. She came across as lively, interested, compassionate, humorous and quirky. Altogether likeable. It was a shame her daughter didn't appear to have inherited any of her excellent qualities.

He heard Sam before he saw her. She'd told him to meet her outside one of the shops in the Covent Garden Piazza; what she hadn't said was that she'd be busking. The clean, mathematical notes of a Bach sonata for solo cello rose above the warm hum of traffic and the laughter and talk of pedestrians.

Mick stood a little distance away and watched. Sam had changed from her khaki combat trousers and black T-shirt – at last! – and was wearing a flowery cotton dress with thin straps which left her shoulders and arms bare. The feminine effect of the dress was offset by her shoes – black canvas lace-ups – and her cropped dark hair, but actually she looked almost pretty in an urban waif kind of way. Her eyebrows were drawn together in a frown as she gave absolute concentration to the music, not even noticing when people stooped to put money on the rumpled jeans jacket which she'd placed on the pavement in front of her. This happened quite frequently, Mick noticed, and no wonder. Sam was good. He didn't know much about classical music, but he sensed the authority with which she tackled the piece.

When she finished, a little ripple of clapping ran through the gathered bystanders before they moved on. Sam flexed her shoulders, and smiled her thanks. Mick was surprised by the way her face changed when she smiled, making her seem much younger. And definitely attractive.

He moved forward and dropped a pound into the pool of coins. She glanced up, but the smile of thanks died as soon as she recognized him. Stony-faced, she leaned forward, retrieved the coin and handed it back to him. Her eyes lingered on the briefcase which he was still holding in his left hand. He could tell she was desperate to know if he'd got the journal, but far too proud to ask. Well, no harm in letting her sweat it out for a bit.

Sam leaned over and began to unscrew the peg that supported the base of her cello. 'You wanted to talk?' she asked, not looking at him.

'Yeah. Maybe over a drink.'

'Okay. I could use a beer. This is thirsty work.'

'How long have you been playing?'

'Just an hour. That's my slot.'

'I didn't realize busking was so organized.'

'Oh, yes.'

Mick watched as she put the cello in its case, folded the stool she'd been sitting on and picked them both up.

'Can I carry something for you?' he asked.

'I'm used to it.'

All the tables outside the pub were taken, so they made their way to the back of the bar. Mick ordered a couple of beers while Sam set her cello down out of the way. As he was waiting for his change, he glanced across to where she was sitting. Her face expressionless, she was tracing a pattern on the round table top with the tip of her finger. However poker-faced she pretended to be, he could see the tension in the line of her shoulders and the set of her jaw. Suddenly he felt mean about playing games with someone who was clearly so desperate, even if she had threatened him at their last meeting.

He set the glasses down on the table, pulled back a stool and sat down. 'Cheers,' he said.

'Cheers.'

'I've got the journal.'

'I guessed,' she said.

'You did?' Mick felt slightly cheated; he'd been expecting more reaction.

She nodded. 'Raph's been leaving me messages. I assumed they were about the journal.'

'I wasn't planning to. I don't like being threatened, and I didn't think you'd actually carry out the blackmail threat.' He paused, giving her time to agree she'd been bluffing, but she didn't take advantage of the opportunity, so he went on, 'Raph helped, as it happens. He asked me to go over to his place when they discovered the break-in, so it was easy enough. But the clincher, for me, was seeing the window you'd climbed in through. Bloody hell, Sam, you must have been crazy to do that.'

'I wanted the journal,' she said. 'I didn't think about the danger.' But she shivered, as though she realized the risk she'd taken. She drank some beer.

'I figured that if you were prepared to go to those lengths, the least I could do was help out.'

'Yes. And thanks.'

'It must be important,' said Mick. Experience had taught him there are times when it helps to state the obvious, but Sam didn't take the hint. Trying to get information out of her required the psychological equivalent of an oyster knife and he didn't seem able to find it. He wondered why he was even bothering to try. Suddenly impatient, he opened his briefcase and pulled out the journal and laid it on the table between them. Sam drew in a deep breath, then scooped it up greedily.

'Thank God,' she breathed. 'Was there anything else hidden there?'

'Just what I've given you.'

There was no real reason for them to spin this meeting out any longer, apart from the two glasses of beer that remained between them. Mick said, more to make conversation than in any hopes of discovering anything new about Sam and her mother, 'She must have been quite a woman.'

Sam nodded. She was hugging the journal to her chest, as if it were a hot-water bottle, or a comforter of some kind. Which, in a way, he supposed it was. He felt a sudden anger with Raph at having put her through this. He said, 'Why do you think Raph didn't want you to have it?'

'I don't know. Maybe there's something about me, though I don't believe that. More likely, she said things about him that he didn't want other people to read. Or maybe he's trying to protect someone else.' She thought for a moment, but this time Mick let the silence ride. Now that she had the journal in her arms, her whole manner had changed. While no one would describe her as expansive, exactly, she was becoming less prickly by the minute. 'Or maybe there's stuff in here that's not very flattering about him.'

'In that case, why didn't he just destroy it?'

'I don't know. When I've read it, I'll know more.'

Mick decided to change tack. He asked her about her cello playing and was not at all surprised to discover that she was about to launch on a professional career. 'There's a major competition coming up in a few weeks,' she told him. 'The Frobisher. If I do well in that—'

'You'll become a star?' he asked, only half joking.

She actually smiled, caught his gaze for a fraction of a moment before looking away quickly. 'No,' she said. 'I haven't got the extra touch of magic that separates the good from the truly great. But if I do well, it would mean some solo work, rather than just finding an orchestra to join. And chamber pieces, that kind of thing.'

'Sounds important.'

'Yes,' she said. 'I've worked a long time for it.'

He sensed the uncertainty behind her words. 'But . . .?' he asked.

'But . . . well, technically, I'm ready. More than ready, but . . .

it's hard to explain. Ever since—' She broke off, but Mick silently supplied the missing words: *my mother died.* 'Well, for a few weeks, anyway, it's like there's been a silence in my head where the music should be. I can hit the right notes, that's never been a problem, but somehow, the core of it is missing.'

'Is that so surprising, given what's happened? I mean, losing your mother and . . .'

She shook her head. 'It wasn't that. It's—' She broke off, glanced at him quickly then frowned into her beer. Mick was getting used to these fleeting glances, as though she were trying to decide whether to trust him or not. For some reason that he didn't altogether understand, he rather hoped she would decide he was worthy of her trust. She said in a low voice, 'It was when I discovered everyone thought she'd killed herself.'

'Yeah. That must have made it even tougher.'

She gave him a searching glance. 'It did,' she said simply.

He said, 'A friend of mine at university, his father killed himself and—'

'It wasn't suicide,' she said.

'What?'

'Kirsten Waller, my mother, did not commit suicide.'

'You don't think it was an *accident,* do you?'

'No.'

'Then . . .' Mick held her gaze, said slowly, 'You think someone killed her?'

'I'm sure they did.'

'But who?'

'I . . .' she faltered, for the first time. 'I don't know. It could have been a stranger. Someone who came into the cottage when she was in the bath – she never locked the doors – and killed her. But—'

'You think it was someone she knew?'

She nodded. 'And in a weird kind of way, I think she was expecting it.'

Mick was about to say, don't be crazy, people don't know about things like that before they happen, but then he remembered the notes in the journal, the phrases for the poem 'The Murder Bird', and a shiver went down his spine, in spite of the heat. He said, 'Expecting it?'

'Yes. The volume of poetry she was working on last winter was titled *The Murder Bird and Other Poems.*'

'So does the title poem give any clues?'

'It might do, I don't know. It was missing, same as the journal, when Raph and I went down to Gull Cottage – that's the house in Cornwall she was staying in when she died. I thought Raph might have it too.'

He shook his head. 'So you think that whoever killed her took the poem?'

'Maybe.'

'Raph had her journal.'

'It can't have been him. He was at a dinner party when she died.'

'So how does it tie in with the journal?'

'I don't know. The poem might have been in the journal. Or Raph could have noticed it as soon as we went into the cottage and then hidden it somewhere he knew I wouldn't look. That wouldn't have been so hard, right then. I was kind of in a daze—'

'I can imagine.'

'So I wouldn't have noticed, necessarily.'

Mick was thoughtful. Murder was something he dealt with in a professional capacity: he'd studied it, knew it as a legal entity, was preparing to help defend it in the Grace Hobden case. He knew the devastation it wreaked in people's lives. But that was during office hours, when he was being the trainee barrister. Murder wasn't supposed to spill over into your private life, that wasn't part of the deal. Not that Sam and her mother were his private life, exactly, but all the same . . .

The most likely explanation was that Kirsten had killed herself and that Sam was finding it impossible to come to terms with it. Still, if Sam was hoping to find evidence that her mother was not suicidal in the weeks before her death, she might well find what she wanted.

He said, 'Well, you could be right.'

Sam hadn't been expecting that. 'You think so?' she asked, her expression relaxing into a broad smile. It was extraordinary the way her face changed when she smiled. 'You really think so?'

'Sure,' said Mick. 'After all, if you want to kill someone, I would imagine it's always a good idea to make it look like suicide.'

'You didn't know my mother, but she just wasn't the suicidal type. She got low sometimes, same as everybody does, but she was a fighter. She never gave in to stuff like that. And I was going to visit just after midsummer. She was looking forward to seeing me, I know she was. There's no way she would have killed herself – just no way.'

Sam was transformed. All the prickliness had vanished. Mick

reached over and took her hand. He said, 'I wish I'd known her.'

She looked at her hand lying in his, but did not remove it. Smiling, she said, 'You would have liked her. I know the two of you would've got on.'

Mick grinned. 'I feel as if I know her a little bit anyway, from the journal.'

Sam was puzzled. 'From the journal?'

'And you're right. There's nothing in it that sounds like she was suicidal.'

As soon as the words were out, Mick could have kicked himself. With the thawing of the atmosphere between them, he wasn't the only one to have let down his guard, and he'd stumbled into a cardinal error.

Eyes like frostbite, Sam took her hand from his and snapped, 'You *read* it?'

'Well . . . sure . . . I glanced at it. You never said anything about not reading it, remember, and anyway, all her journals end up as public property, so—'

'You had *no* right to read it! It's private.'

'Hey, what happened to the gratitude?' said Mick. 'You've only got the bloody thing thanks to me.'

'Reading someone's private journal, that's about as low as it gets.'

'Oh really? That's rich, coming from a blackmailer.'

Sam stood up. 'Yeah. Well. Thanks.'

'Your sincerity is overwhelming.'

'I'm not very good at faking.'

'No? I'd say you were an expert. Aren't you going to finish your drink?'

But no, she was stuffing the journal into her red-and-green fabric bag and gathering up the cello and the stool. Obviously travelling light was never going to be an option for Sam. Under any other circumstances, Mick would have offered to help her get to a taxi, or public transport, but he had a feeling that any helpful suggestions would be instantly rebuffed and he was getting a bit tired of the Sam Boswin cold shoulder. Her shoulders, he decided, could be positively arctic.

'Thank you for getting the journal.'

'Don't mention it.'

She didn't.

Without another word, she walked quickly away.

Mick drank down the rest of his beer and pulled her glass towards him. He was still annoyed at having dropped that clanger about the journal. He might have guessed she'd be touchy as hell about anyone seeing it before she did.

But then again, he had a hunch that she'd have manufactured an argument sooner or later. She was probably the kind of spiky character who instantly regrets any uncharacteristic lowering of defences, and probably blamed him for having got her to open up in the first place.

Well, good riddance, he thought pettishly as he watched her through the open door of the pub. She was trudging across the piazza towards the buses, determined self-sufficiency in every step. It was remarkable the way Sam could make him react with a petty meanness he hadn't felt in years. Just as well there was no chance of them ever meeting up again. He liked friends who were easy-going and fun to be with and Sam scored lower on both counts than almost anyone he'd ever met.

CHAPTER 11

Sam emerged from the post office into the afternoon sunshine and took her mobile phone out of her bag. She had spent
the morning at a print shop, getting two photocopies made of
Kirsten's journal. She'd posted one to herself, c/o Davy Boswin
at Menverren; the other was in her shoulder bag, together with
the original. Now, for the first time since Mick had handed
over the journal the previous day, she was ready to deal with
stepfather.

She turned off into a side street and walked until the thunder
of lorries and buses on the main road had dimmed to a faint
hum before switching on her phone. It showed six missed
calls and answerphone messages. Without bothering to check
them, she punched in Raph's number. He answered at once.

'Sam, is that you?' She'd been expecting the bully, but to her
surprise he sounded worried. Take care. There's no one so
skilled at wrong-footing his opponent. Staying with the concerned parent act, he asked, 'Are you all right?'

'Any reason why I shouldn't be?' she asked, and, before he

had a chance to answer, she said swiftly, 'And by the way, I've got the journal.'

Silence, then, 'It had to be you,' he said.

'Why did you take it?' she asked.

'Reasons. Good reasons. I don't expect you to understand.'

'I might do if you bothered to explain.'

He changed tack.

'How did you get in? Lola says she never saw you.'

'That's not important, but—' Sam had no particular affection for Lola, but she didn't see why Raph's girlfriend should get the blame unfairly, so she added, 'Lola had nothing to do with it.'

'So how?'

'Did you take the poem too?'

'What poem? There was no poem. Sam, listen, you have to give the journal back.

'Are you kidding? Do you have any idea how much trouble it was getting it? Why would I hand it straight back?'

He didn't have an answer to that one. After a few moments, he asked quietly, 'You've read it?'

'Sure I have.'

He sighed. 'And now, if I'm correct, you're wondering what all the fuss is about. Right?'

'Maybe,' Sam said. She'd read the journal through from start to finish as soon as she'd got back after her meeting with Mick the night before, and, though she'd never admit so to Raph, she'd been bitterly disappointed. She couldn't find anything to explain why Raph had gone to such lengths to stop her from reading it. She said, 'I don't see why you lied about it. All this time, I've been imagining all sorts of reasons. And now I find there's nothing about me except how much she missed me and . . . and . . .' Sam felt tears rising suddenly. She swallowed, carried on, 'And that she wanted to talk to me about something.'

Silence again. Raph always the master of artful silences. When he spoke again, his voice was mellow, deliberately calm. 'Sam, believe me, I'm sorry it's been so hard for you but . . . look, now you've read it, please. Trust me. You have to give it back.'

'Why?'

'It's . . . I'm afraid you're just going to have to take my word for it, Sam. It's best for everyone that the journal remains in my possession.'

'No way. That's the reason I phoned. I've no idea why you're so obsessed with Kirsten's journal, but it's mine and you know it. All her papers were left to me, so you don't have a leg to stand on.'

'I am aware of that, Sam. And though this is probably hard for you to understand, I do happen to be on your side over this. Which is why I have to insist that you return Kirsten's journal to me at once.'

'Insist? Forget it, Raph. You can't insist about anything. Look, this is stupid. I only called you so you'd stop clogging up my phone with messages. As far as I'm concerned, we've got nothing more to say to each other.'

'Sam, stop! Don't be an idiot! And don't you dare hang up on me! Can't you understand that I'm only trying to protect you?'

Now she really did laugh. 'Protect me? Oh really? Are you threatening me, Raph? How dare you!'

'Sam, don't get upset. You don't understand any of this. Now listen.' Raph dropped his voice and spoke slowly and clearly.

'You have to trust me – I know it's hard and I can't give you the reasons. But believe me, please. You're not safe while the journal remains in your keeping.'

'Not safe?'

'No.'

'Why not?'

'You're not the only person who wants that journal.'

'Who else?'

'That's more than you need to know.'

Now it was Sam's turn to hold the silence. After a little while she said, 'I don't believe it, Raph: you really are threatening me.'

'I'm not threatening you, Sam. You're... you've always been like a daughter to me and now . . . well, I'm just letting you know how the land lies.'

'And what the hell is that supposed to mean?'

'Exactly what I'm telling you: while you have the journal—'

'Yes. Sure. I'm not safe. I heard you the first time, Raph. And guess what? I didn't believe you then and I don't believe you now. Don't bother trying to get in touch with me again because I've heard enough threats and lies from you to last me a lifetime.'

'Sam! Wait! Don't ha—'

She disconnected the call.

Then turned her phone off altogether.

If only it was as easy to erase Raph's voice from her life altogether.

Sam walked briskly down the street of tall white houses just to the north of Regent's Park. She had only visited Trevor Clay, who had been Kirsten's agent for many years, once before, but the memory of that day was still clear in her mind. It had been shortly after Sam had moved up to London from Cornwall and she'd been, at that time, curious about every aspect of her mother's life. It was during that meeting with Trevor that she'd gained some understanding of her mother's status as a poet. He'd been affectionate, interested and entertaining, but behind it all was a real respect for what Kirsten had achieved, and excitement for what lay ahead.

Number 44 was one of the smarter houses on the street. Others were subdivided into flats, but Trevor's wife Polly had inherited a substantial amount from an aunt and increased her wealth steadily by shrewd investments; they had the whole house, plus another in Suffolk and a villa in the South of France. Kirsten had told Sam that Trevor and his wife had an enduring and harmonious relationship, much to everyone's surprise, as the bookish Trevor had almost nothing in common with his socialite wife. Kirsten's theory was that she provided the financial security which he needed to champion literary works which, though widely praised, were never going to hit the jackpot, while Polly liked having artistic guests at her lavish parties. Their marriage straddled two worlds in a way that gave kudos to both. 'Besides, they keep out of each other's way, most of the time,' said Kirsten, 'so everyone is happy.'

Today, Trevor must have been watching for her, because he opened the door even before Sam had a chance to ring the bell.

'There you are, there you are!' he exclaimed in delight. 'Have you got it?'

'I've brought a photocopy. For safe keeping.'

'Wonderful, wonderful. Let's have a look. Come in, come in!'

Sam grinned. Trevor had never wasted time on pleasantries. When she'd visited before with Kirsten, he'd opened the door with a book of poems in his hand and said at once, 'Just listen to this! It's brilliant!' and had begun reading to them while they were still coming in and taking off their coats.

He was small and round and would have been fairly nonde-script if it hadn't been for his energy and enthusiasm. Kirsten once remarked that time spent with Trevor could feel like being stuck in a glass jar with a particularly insistent bluebottle buzzing round your head. She'd have wanted to keep swatting at him if he wasn't such a sweetheart.

Sam remembered this as she followed him through the immac-ulate hall and down the stairs to his part of the house. The basement gave the impression of an old-fashioned second-hand bookshop run by someone with no time and zero organizational skills – a totally false impression, as it happened. He moved a stack of books off a chair for her to sit down, then stood over her while she removed the envelope containing the journal from her bag.

She said, 'I've brought a copy for you to keep here.'

'Excellent. Of course, I would have given it back but—'

'I had to steal it from Raph.'

Trevor's eyes widened with surprise.

Sam explained, 'He's been acting very strangely about it. First of all he removed it from Gull Cottage and told me there was no journal. And now that he knows I've got it he's making out I have to give it back. For my own safety. I've just spoken to him on the phone and he was – well, let's say he put his case forcefully.'

'Strange. Very strange. I presume you've read it.'

'I read the whole thing last night.'

'And?'

She sighed. 'Honestly, Trevor, I can't understand what all the fuss is about. I didn't know what to expect, but I did have some ideas. First of all, I thought maybe my mother had written things about him that he didn't want to be made public. Then I thought she might have put in stuff about me which he thought I'd find upsetting. And then I wondered if there was anyone else that he might be trying to protect – like Lola, or . . . maybe even someone I don't know. But it's just the same as all her other journals: fragments of poems, notes, ideas, the occasional reference to conversations she had with people. But nothing that anyone could object to. I keep feeling as though I must be missing something – you know, as if there's some kind of coded reference that I haven't figured out. I thought maybe you might be able to spot something.'

'Well, I'll try. I'll certainly try.' Trevor had kept his eyes fixed on Sam while she was talking, but now he could resist the temptation no longer. Literally humming with anticipation, he pulled the sheets of A4 paper out of the envelope and began looking through them quickly.

'And another thing,' said Sam. 'There are notes in there for that poem we couldn't find, you know, "The Murder Bird". So far as I can make out, it's based on an incident we both saw, when a thrush and a lizard were fighting at Wardley and the lizard got killed.'

'That's right. I remember seeing an early draft when I visited her in March. She was very excited about it, said it would cause a sensation.'

'She showed it to you?'

'Oh yes. But she wouldn't let me take a copy. She said it wasn't finished.'

'What was your impression?'

Trevor hesitated. 'Well, of course, it wasn't finished. Just an early draft. But to tell the truth, I couldn't understand what she was so excited about. Usually her poems had a larger theme, but this one seemed to be just about the incident you both saw. In my opinion it wasn't really up to her usual standard at all. Presumably she came to the same conclusion, and that's why she destroyed it.'

'*If* she destroyed it.'

'What do you mean, "if"?'

Sam didn't answer his question. She said, 'The odd thing is that when she mentions "The Murder Bird" in the journal she says she has to ask me about it first.'

'She says that? Ah yes, here it is. "Check with S." I assume that must be you?' Sam nodded, and Trevor continued, '"'Murder Bird" will really put the cat among the pigeons." And there's an exclamation mark in brackets.' He stared at the page for a moment without speaking. 'God, I miss your mother's terrible jokes, Sam. I really do.'

'What do you think she meant?'

'I've no idea.'

'Didn't she talk to you about it?'

'No. She was actually quite secretive. Which wasn't like her at all.'

'You must have some idea what it was about? You'd worked with her for such a long time, and she trusted you.'

'Yes. Well.' Trevor hesitated. 'There was one possibility that did occur to me – and that would tie in with Raph's rather unusual reaction to the whole business.'

'Which is?'

'I think perhaps . . . When I visited her in the States—'

'You went out there, too?'

'I was in New York, yes. Who else?'

'Johnny. Raph's brother-in-law.' It seemed her mother had had a whole string of visitors to her winter hideaway.

Trevor went on, 'Well, it was obvious that she was missing Raph a lot – and you, too, of course. But she wasn't acting or talking like a woman who was happy with her decision to leave her husband. In fact, she told me that she was still as much in love with him as she'd always been. She told me there was a particular reason why they'd split up and until that was resolved, she couldn't see how they'd get back together.'

'Did she tell you what that was?'

'No. Absolutely not. But I got the impression it was to do with her poetry, something he disapproved of in her work. Or something that she was going to do which would make him angry. And since then I've wondered – and of course, there's no way now of ever knowing for sure, because we can't ask her – if perhaps "The Murder Bird" referred to Raph himself.'

'Raph?'

'Not literally, of course.' Trevor laughed at the very notion – a wheezing, buzzing kind of laugh. 'She wasn't about to suggest that her husband was in the habit of going around killing

people or anything like that. No, no. On the contrary. But . . .
well, look at the way she suddenly produced all those poems
once she had left Raph.'

'I assumed that was because she was unhappy last winter, and
alone.'

'Exactly. Unhappy and alone. Those were the circumstances
she needed in order to create her work. Like the amazing
"Samphire" poems after she left you and Davy. She was worried
by the fact that while she was living in London she'd produced
almost nothing. Life with Raph was just too comfortable, cosy
even. She had become too contented for her own good. She had
to leave him – just as she left you, Sam, all those years ago – in
order to protect her art. Raph stifled her creativity. He had
become "The Murder Bird". Murdering her poetry.'

'Which, to Kirsten, was more important than anything else.'
Sam pondered this for a moment. 'But I still don't see why she'd
need to talk to me about that. Or why Raph was so desperate to
keep it secret.'

'I might see something in the journal that you missed.'

'Maybe. And I'll read through it again. If only we knew what
had happened to that poem.'

'Most probably she destroyed it,' said Trevor.

'But then why didn't she change the title page of her book?'

'I can't answer that one. So, what are we going to call it now?
We can hardly call it *The Murder Bird and Other Poems* when
there's only "other poems". I've got the contents list here.
There's one poem – "The Farewell Bird" – which seems, under
the circumstances, to be appropriate. It's another of the ones she
was working on when I visited her in the States. I thought at the

time that it was a much stronger piece than "The Murder Bird".'

'Then I trust your judgement.'

'Good. I'll get the final copy off. Publication middle of next year.'

There was no reason to extend their meeting. Sam could tell that Trevor was itching to settle down with Kirsten's journal, just as she was impatient to read it through again. Somewhere, surely, she'd find an explanation for Raph's strange behaviour.

As she walked away down the street, the lowering sun warm against her face, Sam hugged her shoulder bag to her chest. Inside it was her mother's journal. Even with copies safely deposited with Trevor and at Menverren, she didn't like to let it out of her sight. She had to go home, now, and pick up her cello for an evening performance: the agency that sometimes got her work had phoned that morning to ask if she could stand in for a player who'd fallen sick. She'd have to try to forget the puzzle of her mother's journal and the missing poem for a couple of hours, and hope that the other players didn't notice that she'd be playing like an automaton.

It was rush hour and there was a crowd of people at the bus stop. Standing there, holding the bag close, she had the oddest feeling, as if she was being watched. She even looked around, trying to make out if any of the strangers nearby were looking at her. She told herself not to be so silly; she was imagining it, obviously.

She must be getting paranoid. Which wasn't altogether surprising after the conversation she'd had with Raph earlier.

The first bus that came along was almost full. Three people

in front of Sam got on, but she and several others were left waiting. She hugged the bag tightly. The bare flesh on her arms and
shoulders felt strange, as though smoke was drifting over the
surface, touching the fine hairs on her skin.

As though unseen eyes were fixed on her.

CHAPTER 12

'Resistance is useless. We won't take no for an answer, so you might as well do exactly what you're told for a change.'

'And if I don't?'

'Punishments. Dire punishments.'

Sam smiled for what felt like the first time in ages. This was a different kind of bullying, and welcome. Johnny had the sort of rich, sonorous voice that does forceful persuasion very well, and the prospect of being cosseted at Wardley for the rest of the weekend was distinctly tempting. She'd only called up because she wanted to talk to him about her mother – one or two references in the journal that only he could answer – but he would probably be more ready to talk at Wardley anyway.

'We-ell . . .'

'I'll be round in half an hour to pick you up. If you want to bring your cello that would be brilliant. You can serenade us by moonlight or leave it alone. You don't have to sing for your supper this time.'

'Hang on, I haven't said I'm coming yet.'

'No, I did. Look, Sam, we intend to look after you this weekend. Don't argue; it's a waste of breath. Be ready in half an hour or I shall simply have to bear you away by force.'

Johnny was grinning as he put down the phone. He didn't ask himself why he was so keen to have Sam at Wardley that weekend. In fact, he was careful not to reflect at all on his increasing reluctance to be alone with Miriam, even at his beloved Wardley. He was just glad Sam was coming to stay. Simple as that.

In the short time she and Johnny had lived at Wardley, Miriam had morphed seemingly without effort into a conventional country hostess. She was sitting under a huge cream sunshade on the terrace, a round table laid for traditional afternoon tea: freshly baked scones, curls of butter in little pots, home-made plum and raspberry jam in ceramic bowls, a Victoria sponge on a willow-pattern plate. Demure under a broad-brimmed hat and a flimsy flowery top, she poured tea from a generous pot. Only her shadowed eyes behind dark glasses, and the lines of strain round her mouth, spoiled the serenity of her image. She had apparently spent most of the day lying down indoors, pros-trated by one of her terrible blinders, and the headache was only just beginning to wear off.

'Glad you came?' asked Johnny, beaming at Sam across the table and helping himself to another scone.

'That's a tough one.' Sam pretended to consider his question. 'A tiny flat in Camberwell on a hot September afternoon or gra-cious living Wardley-style? I'll have to think about it.'

'Well, *I'm* glad you came.'

Sam could feel the tension slithering off her shoulders, like old skin curling off a snake's back. The journal was safe in her bag, leaning against her leg, and there were copies with Trevor Clay and in the post to Menverren. Her last conversation with Raph no longer seemed as threatening as it had done when she'd switched off her phone. Maybe she'd exaggerated his warning; maybe he was just eager to keep something that belonged to Kirsten. Even though their marriage had broken down, Sam knew he and her mother had never stopped caring for each other.

'More cake, Sam?'

'No thanks. That was a delicious tea.'

'Do you want to walk down to the lake before it gets dark?' asked Johnny.

Sam stretched her arms above her head. 'Mm, that would be brilliant. But you know what I'd really like? A long relaxing bath.'

'Excellent plan,' said Johnny.

'Dinner is at eight,' said Miriam, with a tight smile. 'It's just us. I hope you won't be bored.'

'Of course not. Can I help?'

'Not allowed,' said Johnny at once. 'I'm cooking tonight. Bangers and mash.'

Miriam was sweeping crumbs into a neat pile with the edge of her hand. A small cloud blotted out the sun. She said, 'Mother's coming for lunch tomorrow. I told her you'd be here.'

'Oh,' said Sam. And then, aware that her disappointment might have been too obvious, she said, 'That's nice.'

She doubted whether either Johnny or Miriam were convinced by her phoney enthusiasm. But even they must realize how difficult Diana was. She stood up and began clearing the plates.

'Leave that,' said Johnny, as sternly as he knew how. 'You're in the tower room again, same as last time. I'll take your bag. Remember, you're under strict orders to relax and enjoy yourself,' he added, frowning that sudden frown of his as he often did when aware that he'd been exuberant in the wrong place.

Some orders are really quite easy to obey, thought Sam, as Johnny picked up her bag and they walked briskly into the house.

Sam spent the next two hours with her mother.

That's what it felt like, anyway. When she'd got home after seeing Mick, she'd skimmed through the journal at speed, checking for references to herself or Raph, any mention of 'The Murder Bird'. She slowed up when she reached the final pages, and read carefully for clues about Kirsten's state of mind during those last days at Gull Cottage. Now, safe at Wardley, she could indulge in the luxury of slow reading.

She bolted the door on the bathroom, ran herself a bath and then sat on the bath mat, knees drawn up while she read. It was a habit she'd picked up when she was still at Menverren with her father and Linda and the boys, when privacy was hard to find.

She read slowly, carefully, determined to extract every last ounce of meaning from the seemingly random entries. Most of it, bits of poems, phrases, jottings and memos, was written while Kirsten was still in the States. A few longer passages described neighbours and friends in the Connecticut town where she was living; the long cold winter; her homesickness for England, missing Sam; someone called 'T' came to visit – Trevor, presumably – and others, a 'B' and 'N' and 'J'. Kirsten's habit of never writing a full name when an initial would do was frustrating. Sam knew Johnny had visited her during that time, so she assumed he was the 'J' referred to. She must ask him about it as soon as she got the chance – preferably when Miriam wasn't around. There were several references to 'M' trying to patch things up between her and 'R'. And then, at the end, mention of 'S' coming to visit – 'Check with S about MB.' And then, nothing.

When she was finished she got into the bath, which was stone cold by now, and quickly washed away her tears together with the sweat and the London grime. She wrapped herself in a towel and walked back to her room, pausing on the way to pull back the curtain of tarpaulin and peer into the empty tower: a dark column of empty space, smelling of damp and decay. A blackbird, or a pigeon, making enough noise for a whole flock of birds, rose up from one of the joists and flew out through a gap just under the roof. Sam stepped back quickly, vertigo kicking in. Kirsten would probably have created a poem from the startled bird and the empty tower.

Sam pulled a cotton skirt and a T-shirt from her bag and put them on, before settling down to examine the first part of the journal again. There was something she'd been avoiding, but she knew it had to be faced: Trevor had told her he'd seen the poem 'The Farewell Bird' – a draft of it at any rate – when he had visited Kirsten in the winter. Notes towards the poem, the phrases and images that Kirsten played around with when a poem was forming in her mind, occurred off and on through the early section of the journal, while she was still in the USA. The difficulty for Sam lay in the fact that the very same phrases, or ones very similar, appeared in the document that had come to be called her 'suicide note' by the coroner – the document which everyone except Sam saw as proof that she had taken her own life.

Sam could guess the official line: Kirsten was depressed already – and who would blame her? Alone in a rented apartment in a small town in Connecticut in the depths of winter, her marriage almost certainly at an end, no wonder Kirsten was contemplating her final 'farewell'. But Sam didn't buy it. There had to be another explanation, though right now she couldn't figure it.

The problem niggled at her through a supper which was marred only by the fact that Miriam's headache was getting worse again and any kind of conversation was obviously a strain for her. As soon as they were finished, Johnny insisted that his wife go to bed, even though it was only nine o'clock. Sam helped him with the clearing up, then they went out on to the terrace and looked up at the stars.

It was easy, companionable, sitting there in the darkness, the orange tip of Johnny's cigar glowing and fading beside her while they talked. Casually, joking about nothing in particular. Sam stretched and began to relax.

They watched for shooting stars.

Sam looked at the journal again before she fell asleep. She must have drifted off with the light still on because suddenly, when she was sliding into that space between waking and sleeping, the solution to one of the problems that had been nagging at her all day sprang clear and complete into her mind.

'The Farewell Bird' – of course! Sam sat up with a gasp, wide awake at once, and hurriedly checked back through the early section of the journal. She punched the air with triumph. There, if you looked closely enough, you could see the rough edge of paper near the spine where the sheet had been torn out. And the paper was an exact match. They were wrong, wrong, wrong! Those elegiac phrases that had been read out with such damning finality at the inquest were not Kirsten's way of taking her leave of the world as everyone so conveniently assumed; they were notes towards the poem she'd been writing as she prepared to quit her temporary winter home in the States and return to England. 'Flying to greyness' – wasn't 'greyness' a phrase she often used of Cornwall, with its ubiquitous granite and louring skies and sea like metal?

Kirsten had never written a suicide note, for the simple reason that she hadn't committed suicide. If she hadn't taken her own life, there were only two possibilities: accident, or murder.

Outside Sam's bedroom, the floorboards creaked. Footsteps tiptoeing down to the bathroom on her corridor. She wondered why, since their bedroom had an en suite bathroom, either Johnny or Miriam would use the guest bathroom; it must be Johnny, taking every care not to disturb his wife's sleep. After a few moments she heard the lavatory flush, the footsteps pad back over the creaking boards.

It was possible, but not likely, that Kirsten's death had been

an accident. It was also possible that Kirsten had been murdered and someone had made it look like suicide.

Someone?

Raph had removed the journal.

Presumably he'd torn the page out as well. Now that she
thought back, it was Raph who had 'noticed' the note, so
conveniently propped up on the table when they'd driven to
Gull Cottage together

Was Raph protecting someone? Or had the killer been acting
for him?

The more she considered the options – Lola? Miriam?
Johnny? who? – the more baffling the problem became. Sam's
moment of triumph when she connected the phoney suicide
note to the journal had given way to bewilderment.

She switched off her light and lay down, the journal slid
safely under her pillow, but it was impossible to sleep. It was
that time of night when silence becomes an absence of all
sound. Not a whisper of a breeze, not even the creaking of an
old house settling in the darkness. Not even . . .

The boards outside her room creaked again. Her nerves tin-
gled. There was a soft grunt of complaint as the handle on the
door to her room revolved slowly, and the door swung open
with a gentle easing of hinges.

Wide awake in an instant, Sam touched the spine of Kirsten's
journal, shunting it just a little further under her pillow as she
waited.

The dense shadow of a form moved through the darkness
to the chair where she'd left her backpack and her shoulder
bag. She waited only until she heard the chink of coins as

her purse was dislodged, then reached over and snapped on the light.

'Johnny! What the hell are you doing?'

'Sam!' He spun round, almost losing his balance and looking even more surprised than she was. He was wearing loose cotton pyjamas in a red-and-white stripe, his blond hair rumpled. Suddenly, ridiculously, Sam was reminded of a lumbering bear who had invaded their campsite one summer when she and Kirsten were travelling through the Algonquin National Park. That same look of almost comical guilt.

'What are you doing?' she demanded again.

'Sorry, Sam. I was trying not to disturb you, but Miriam can't shake her headache and we're all out of paracetamol. I thought you might have some. I didn't mean to wake you up.'

'You should have done,' said Sam. 'I wouldn't have minded, though I wouldn't have been able to help. I never carry painkillers. And anyway, I thought Miriam had more powerful pills than paracetamol.'

'She tries not to take them. Not unless she has to. I'm sorry.'

'That's okay.'

'See you in the morning, then. Good night.' Johnny was shuffling out of the room, his slippers scuffing the floor.

'Good night, Johnny. I hope her headache gets better.'

'Sleep well.'

But she didn't, of course. Not for a long time.

She was tingling with excitement. Johnny? She didn't for a moment buy the paracetamol excuse, but how was he mixed up in all this?

Had Raph put him up to it? Their friendship went back a

long way and it was easy to imagine Johnny trying to do a good turn for a friend, even if he didn't really understand the reason for it.

Johnny had been so welcoming, so warmly insistent that she come to stay, and she'd begun to relax, but it was the journal he'd been after all along.

Sam lay awake for a long time, planning how best to tackle him in the morning.

CHAPTER 13

'Watch out!' Miriam's tension levels were rising dangerously. 'You mustn't go in! The floor's rotted right through.'

'Don't worry about me,' said Simon Rednal, as Miriam held back the tarpaulin that hung over the opening in the wall opposite Sam's bedroom. 'All the original timbers – my God, what a treasure!'

'Oh, please be careful.'

'I shall be fine.' Unable to contain his excitement any longer, he stepped into the tower.

An authority on the preservation of ancient buildings, Simon Rednal had driven over from Bath that morning, arriving soon after breakfast. He'd been invited to advise them on the best way of conserving the fifteenth-century tower. In his mid-forties, small and wiry, he was brimming with enthusiasm. His lurid bow tie was just visible under the overalls he'd put on when he arrived. Sam had heard them approaching down the corridor that led to her room and had gone out to join them. Johnny, as Miriam never ceased lamenting, was nowhere to be seen.

'I can't think what's happened to him,' Miriam sighed, putting a hand to her forehead. Sam had never seen her looking so frail; her skin was luminous with the strain of her headache, her mouth a thin line, gritted against the pain. 'My husband knew you were coming and he's usually so reliable.'

Simon Rednal was too intrigued by the treasures of Wardley to be bothered by Johnny's absence or Miriam's worries. Standing just inside the tower, he twisted round to peer up at the ceiling. 'Just look at that,' he said happily, 'All the original vaulting is still in place. And just look at that fretwork!'

Carried away by the beauties being revealed, he took another step.

Miriam squeaked. 'Watch out! There's a twenty-foot drop!'

'Don't worry about me,' he called back happily. 'I'm indestructible!'

Sam joined Miriam at the entrance to the tower. 'Oh dear,' twittered Miriam wretchedly, 'it's not safe.' She was twisting her pale hands over each other in anguish.

'I'm sure he knows what he's doing,' Sam tried to reassure her.

Simon Rednal was treading carefully, testing each board with the toe of his well-polished loafer before trusting it with his weight. 'Ah yes,' he said, his voice turning sonorous with doom, like a doctor diagnosing some dread disease, 'it's not just woodworm, I'm afraid.' He peered up towards the ceiling again. 'Leaks,' he said emphatically. 'Leaks and—' Here he crouched down to gouge out a tiny edge of board with his penknife while Miriam held her breath. 'And here, if I'm not mistaken, is our old enemy, the death watch beetle. A serious infestation, I believe.'

'Will the boards have to be replaced?' asked Sam, since

Miriam seemed to have temporarily lost the power of speech.

'Good Lord, no!' Mr Rednal was so horrified at the very idea of such architectural sacrilege that he sprang to his feet at once, a sudden move that almost cost him his life. 'They'll have to be treated, of course, but—' He stopped mid-sentence, his enthusiasm turning to horror as, with a low tearing sound, the board he was standing on gave way like soggy cardboard.

Miriam screamed. Simon Rednal's left foot was disappearing from view as the wood crumbled. He tilted, losing his balance, but at the last moment he lunged towards the doorway, grabbing at the doorposts, gasping as he tumbled past the tarpaulin and into the corridor.

'What's happening? Are you all right?' Johnny's voice could be heard as he ran up the stairs. 'Miri, what's the matter?' He came into view and raced down the corridor.

Simon Rednal leaned against the wall while he recovered, but already he was smiling. 'Hardly a test that's recommended by the experts, but I suppose that tells us everything we need to know about that floor of yours,' he said. 'The floorboards will have to be removed for treatment. The joists we'll do *in situ.*'

'You could have been killed!' wailed Miriam, who was trembling helplessly.

'No, no. It was nothing,' said Simon, wiping the perspiration and a couple of cobwebs from his forehead. 'The joists would have held me, I'm sure. It was just that bit of floorboard.'

Miriam was not convinced. 'I should never have let you go in,' she said. 'I knew that floor was lethal. If you'd fallen—! And it's twenty feet on to stone flags. Oh, if anything had happened, I'd never have forgiven myself.'

'Johnny Johns,' said Johnny, towering over the historic build-ings expert and seizing his hand in a warm grip.

'Simon Rednal,' said the adviser, as his hand was pumped up and down. In spite of his protests, he was still looking shaken.

'Sorry I was late,' said Johnny. He was wearing shabby clothes and his face was grimy with dust and sweat. 'Got started clearing out one of the stables and lost track of time. A job I've been mean-ing to do for months. Has Miriam shown you what you needed?'

'I'd be interested to see the ground floor.'

'Of course. It's been used for storage for years, but we cleared it out last year. Beautiful old stone flags. Come and have a look.'

Johnny led the way along the corridor and back towards the stairs. He hadn't looked at Sam once; hadn't even acknowledged she was there. Which wasn't like him at all.

As soon as Simon Rednal had driven off, Sam followed Johnny into the kitchen and set the bottle of paracetamol down on the table.

Johnny drew back, shocked. Then he said, 'So, you did have some.'

'No. *You* did.'

'What?'

'These were in your bathroom cupboard.' While Johnny and Miriam were discussing dry rot, deathwatch beetle and heritage grants with Mr Rednal, Sam had taken the opportunity to do a little snooping of her own. It hadn't taken long. She picked the bottle of pills up and shook it gently.

'Really? I must have missed them.'

Johnny turned away and tipped some new potatoes into the sink. A roast of lamb was sizzling comfortably in the oven. A bunch of fresh mint lay on the large scrubbed pine table in the middle of the room. Usually this kitchen was the relaxed heart of the house, especially when Johnny was cooking. His style was the opposite of Raph's: simple food, cooked without fuss and with liberal quantities of alcohol for the chef.

'Sherry, Sam?' he asked.

'No, thanks,' she said. 'You can't have missed them. There were half a dozen other kinds of headache pills in there as well. Quite a little pharmacy, in fact.'

'Ah.' Johnny was staring intently at the new potatoes, as though they might be able to explain a way out of this situation. 'You've got a headache? Poor Miri's pretty knocked back, too. Must be this heat.'

Sam said, 'What were you really looking for last night?'

'Last night? Well, I told you. I just didn't want to wake you, Sam, and Miri asked me to see if you had any headache pills and—'

'Please, Johnny. It was a rotten lie to begin with, but now it's shot to hell.' In any kind of contest, Johnny Johns would probably emerge as just about the worst liar in the world. He was looking so miserable and embarrassed that Sam felt almost bad about questioning him – almost. She asked again, 'What were you looking for?'

'Yes. Ah. Sorry I woke you. Never meant to . . .'

'Was it my mother's journal?'

'What?'

Sam tapped the flat edge of her bag, held between elbow and hip. 'Kirsten's journal. Was that what you were after?'

Johnny cast a longing look towards the door leading out into the garden. He'd turned the colour of ripe fruit and was perspiring freely. 'Kirsten's journal? What are you talking about, Sam?'

'Did Raph tell you to steal the journal for him?'

'Raph?' This time his surprise was genuine. 'No, of course not.' Then he stopped, colouring even more deeply as he realized that his denial had been an admission of sorts.

'Who, then? I can't believe you wanted it yourself.'

'I wouldn't dream of taking your mother's journal.'

'Then who?' Sam had been so convinced that Raph was the culprit that she wasn't sure who else to suggest. When he didn't answer, just stared at her, she said, 'It wasn't Miriam, was it?' then saw by the way he drew back with shock that she'd hit the target first time. 'Miriam?' she said, suddenly remembering that fragment of conversation between Raph and his sister she'd overheard after Kirsten's memorial service.

'Look, Sam, I never said anything about Miri.'

'Stop bluffing, Johnny. You're really bad at it. Why did Miriam get you to try to steal Kirsten's journal?'

'Not steal,' he said, utterly wretched now. 'She'd never dream of stealing it.'

'So what would you call it?'

'Well, look here . . . the thing is . . . I mean, I'm sorry I woke you and I've apologized. What else can I do?'

'Tell me the truth?'

'But—'

'Please, Johnny. I have to know why you wanted it.'

He wiped his hands on a towel and sat down at the kitchen table. 'God, Sam, I'm so sorry about this. All right, then. But you must promise this won't go any further. Promise?'

'Why?' Sam pulled out a chair and placed herself opposite him. At last, they seemed to be doing business.

'The thing is, Miri did ask me to get the journal – not to steal it, you understand, but just to borrow it for a couple of hours, so she could have a look at it. I was going to put it back before you woke up.'

At last, it looked like he was telling the truth. 'Why did she want to see it?'

'I don't know.' He was looking shifty again.

'She must have given you some idea. I don't believe you'd do something like that without a reason.'

'Well, yes, I suppose . . . she said it was something to do with her family. I mean, Kirsten's journals are going to be published, aren't they? – or at the very least put in an academic archive where every Tom, Dick and Harry can go snooping through them – so it's understandable that Miriam would want to see what was in it, just in case. You'd feel the same, I'm sure. It's a question of privacy, really. That's all.'

'Then why didn't she ask me? I could have told her there was nothing to worry about. Kirsten hardly mentions Raph's family.'

'Well, that's a relief then, obviously. I'll pass that on, if you don't mind.'

'Why? What was Miriam afraid she might say?'

'I've no idea. The usual business, I suppose. Family squabbles, that sort of thing.'

'Secrets?'

'Maybe.'

'What kind of secrets?'

'Oh, just the usual kind of things that every family – ah—!'

Johnny broke off, his face breaking into a smile of relief as he heard the car coming down the drive. 'That must be Diana.' He glanced at his watch. 'Spot on time as always. I'd better get cracking with the vegetables. I think we've just about said all there is to say on the topic of – you know. Your mother's book.'

'No way,' said Sam. 'Not until you've told me what Miriam was afraid of.'

'Sorry, Sam. I'd love to talk more, but I really have to go out and say hello to Diana. You know what she's like. Good manners, and all that.'

Suddenly purposeful, he strode from the kitchen. Sam followed him as far as the hall and observed through the open front door as Diana's driver helped her from her car. She hadn't driven since the accident in which Anthony was killed and various young relatives had taken the post of chauffeur. Craig was the most successful so far. Slim and dark-haired, he'd had some trouble with the police in his teens but was now thinking of training to be a computer analyst. Bobbo erupted from the back seat and started living up to his name, bobbing around their feet and yapping with excitement. Johnny went over to greet her. Sam heard him ask Craig if he wanted to join them, but he said he'd go to the pub nearby. They conferred about when Diana was to be collected. Johnny took her arm and together they walked into the house. Johnny was explaining that Miriam had a headache and hoped to join them for lunch. He was the perfect host, not leaving Diana alone for a moment. She graciously talked on neutral subjects and sipped her fino sherry. Of course, that meant Sam had no opportunities for further questions. Presumably, that suited Johnny just fine.

*

Smoke was drifting across the lawn. As soon as lunch was cleared away, Johnny had returned to the stables and the bonfire he'd been building earlier from old boxes and junk. Miriam had retired to the drawing room, curtains drawn against the sun's glare. She was lying on the sofa, her dark glasses folded on her stomach. She opened her eyes when Sam entered.

'Sorry,' said Sam automatically. 'Were you sleeping?'

'Just resting,' Miriam murmured. A fan stirred the warm air.

'Is your headache still bad?'

'It's not good,' said Miriam. 'I've known worse, though.'

'There's something I wanted to ask you,' Sam began. Then she stopped. There was a movement in the shadows at the side of the room.

Diana was sitting in a blue-and-cream striped chair. A Sunday colour supplement had slid off her knees and she leaned forward to retrieve it from the floor. Bobbo, sleeping by her feet, opened one black eye and made a half-hearted attempt to nibble her hand. 'Nothing but rubbish nowadays,' she said bitterly, as Bobbo went back to sleep. 'Silly young girls no one has heard of. I remember when they used to have real articles. Things you could learn from.'

Miriam raised herself on one elbow. 'You wanted to ask me something?' she said.

Sam hesitated. Miriam wore an expression she'd never noticed before: hard and cold, like shards of ice.

If she was worried Sam was going to ask her why she'd wanted to see Kirsten's journal, she needn't have bothered. Sam didn't intend discussing it in front of Diana. Something about Diana always made her uneasy.

'It's okay,' said Sam. 'I'll leave it till you're feeling better.'

'Ask me now.' It was a command.

Sam hesitated. 'All right, then.'

Diana cleared her throat. 'What's that smell?' she asked. 'Is it smoke? Is something on fire? What's going on?'

Miriam sniffed, then swung her feet to the floor and struggled upright. 'Smoke,' she gasped. 'There must be a fire. Oh God, a fire.'

Their agitation would have been comical, Sam thought, only nothing about the two women that afternoon made her feel much like laughing. 'Johnny's lit a bonfire,' she told them. 'He was clearing out one of the stables this morning and he's burning some old boxes and bits of wood.'

Miriam was choking, as though the room had suddenly become thick with smoke, even though you could hardly smell the bonfire at all. 'Ugh, close the windows! How could he be so thoughtless! Quick, before we suffocate.' She was gripped by a fit of coughing that exhausted her so much she collapsed back on the sofa.

Sam walked over to pull the windows shut. Diana had stood up and was agitatedly gathering up her things, preparing for flight. Bobbo watched. 'Are you sure it's outside?' Diana demanded. 'Maybe it's in the kitchen. Fires spread so quickly. Get up, Miriam, get up. It might be dangerous.'

'It's outside. I promise you there's no danger,' said Sam, pulling the last window closed and fastening the catch. 'And it's quite a long way away. There's really nothing to worry about.'

Diana snapped, 'There's always worry when there's a fire. You don't know what you're talking about.' She was fanning herself with the magazine.

Miriam had subsided amongst her cushions again. 'A fire,' she muttered. 'How could he light a fire? He knows how much I hate fires. Oh, that smoke will kill me, I know it will.'

Sam drew the curtain back to cut out the light again. 'There,' she said. 'The smoke won't come in any more.' She turned to look back into the room. Miriam was moaning quietly, holding her forehead with a pale hand and rocking. Diana had sat down again and seemed to be keeping a lookout for the first signs of smoke.

Suddenly Sam was annoyed with Johnny for being so thoughtless. Fire had killed Diana's husband, the great tragedy of their lives, so no wonder they were distressed. She said, 'I'll go and see if he can make it burn faster. Then there won't be so much smoke.'

Miriam said in a low voice, 'Make it stop. Make him stop the smoke.'

'What smoke?' asked Diana, still looking all around. 'It's gone now, Miriam. There is no smoke.'

'I can smell it.' Miriam turned on her side and buried her face in the soft chintz of the sofa.

'Nonsense,' said Diana briskly. 'It's all gone. There never was any smoke.'

'There was. I know there was.'

'Think of nice things, Miriam. No point dwelling on unpleasantness.'

Miriam rolled over to face her mother. She opened her eyes just enough to throw her a look of such hatred that Sam felt a sudden shiver of fear. 'Is that the truth, Mother? Well, you should know, shouldn't you? You're the expert, after all.'

'I don't know what you mean,' said Diana.

'Don't you? See no evil, hear no evil, speak no evil. That's always been your motto, hasn't it?'

Diana reached down to pick Bobbo up and held the little dog close. He licked her face. 'I don't know what you're talking about, Miriam. All this talk of evil. It's just silliness.'

'Yes, Mother.' To Sam's horror, Miriam had begun laughing, a mirthless kind of laughter. 'And now, smell no evil. There is no smoke. There never was any smoke. I must have imagined it. Silly Miriam, to imagine the nasty smoke. Whatever will she think of next? Listen to Mother, Miriam. She knows how to deal with things.' And she laughed again, then stopped suddenly and pressed her fingertips against her forehead.

'You're being very foolish. That's enough, Bobbo.' Miriam was still laughing as Diana set the dog back on the floor. 'I intend to ignore you until you are sensible again. See, Miriam, now I'm reading.' And she picked up her magazine and stared intently at the first page she came to, her expression blank as only Diana knew how.

CHAPTER 14

Mick was in luck. He could hear the pure notes of a solo cello rising over the wave-like ebb and flow of traffic noise. He didn't recognize the piece, but as soon as he turned the corner, he recognized the player.

He walked forward slowly, then hung back, reluctant to be seen, at the edge of the semicircle of spectators, but caution wasn't necessary. Seated on her folding stool outside a coffee house, forearms circling the cello between her knees, Sam was lost in the music. She wore a black cotton dress which left her arms and shoulders bare. He could just make out her familiar green-and-red striped bag, held behind the cello, as though she was afraid of losing contact with it, even for a moment. Kirsten's journal was just visible, poking out of the top. Mick was struck by the way Sam's whole body was engaged in the music-making, from the graceful arch of her head and neck, tilted away from the bow arm, through her shoulders and down to her strong hands.

As people emerged from the coffee shop, they dropped coins

into the rumpled jeans jacket she'd placed on the ground, and smiled their thanks at the unexpected serenade. Sam ignored them. Gracious as ever, thought Mick; maybe he'd been wrong to come. But then she finished with a flourish and her informal audience burst into a spontaneous round of applause. Sam blinked, appearing surprised that she wasn't alone, then looked round slowly. Her face broke into a generous smile, a smile that reminded Mick suddenly of a photograph he'd seen of her mother. When she eased up and stopped being watchful as a cat, Sam was a real stunner.

Just as he was moving forward, an American couple who had placed a five-pound note among the coins, asked if Sam would have her photograph taken with them. She agreed at once, standing between them and grinning for the camera, the shoulder bag clamped to her side. The Americans moved away, the crowd dispersed and Sam leaned forward to unscrew the peg at the base of the instrument.

Mick hesitated. A lad in a green baseball cap had approached. He was holding an *A-Z* and pointing to the page, but Sam was frowning. It looked as though she had reverted to her habitual frostiness. Suddenly, what Mick had come to tell her didn't seem that important. Their acquaintance hadn't exactly been a barrel of laughs so far. Let someone else tell her. Come to think of it, she probably knew already.

He had only taken a couple of steps when a discordant movement snagged on his peripheral vision, causing him to turn swiftly. He wasn't sure what had caught his eye, unless it was some invisible force field connecting the baseball-cap-wearer with a cyclist, anonymous in his black helmet with visor pulled down over his face, who had appeared out of nowhere and seemed to be speeding straight at Sam. Something metal glinted in his free hand. Suddenly, Mick was running.

'Sam! Watch out!'

The cyclist swooped on to the pavement, leaning over the handlebars and to one side, his legs extended for balance. He slowed, reached over. Mick saw the flash of a blade as it plunged down, aiming at Sam.

'Jesus, no!'

Sam twisted round, raising her hands to protect her face. The striped bag swung free and the knife blade fell, slicing through its strap. She grabbed at it, but it slid through her fingers as the cyclist put a foot down on the ground to steady himself, secured his grip on the bag and pedalled furiously off into the traffic. The whole episode had taken just seconds and already the young man in the baseball cap, the casual decoy, was nowhere to be seen.

'Stop him!' Sam shouted at the top of her voice. She yelled into the cafe for someone to rescue her cello, then set off in pursuit.

But Mick was ahead of her by a few metres. He was a fast runner, though out of practice, but the cyclist was lean and fit and knew exactly what he was doing. He weaved through the traffic, missing cars and taxis by a hair's-breadth, judging distance with brilliant accuracy. Inevitably, the distance between them was increasing.

'Stop that bike!' Mick roared, but people stood back, watching.

Then Mick stopped shouting; he needed all his breath for the chase.

A red light ahead and the traffic had stopped. The cyclist skimmed along the narrow gap between cars and pavement towards the front of the queue. A woman, talking into her mobile phone, glanced across at the green pedestrian signal, then stepped off the kerb straight into the path of the cyclist who almost lost balance as she fell back, shrieking.

'Stop – him!' gasped Mick. The cyclist recovered his balance and shot through the red light, then veered round to the left where the road was clear ahead.

'Fuck you!' the woman vented her shock on Mick as he pounded past.

It was no good. Hunched over the handlebars the cyclist was drawing away; soon he would be out of sight, lost among the traffic way ahead. Mick slowed his pace. He didn't stand a chance against a cyclist on an open stretch of road, but then, just as he was about to stop and look round for a taxi, he saw something which gave him a glimmer of hope.

The near collision with the woman at the pedestrian crossing had caused the cyclist to loosen his grip on the bag. He grabbed at it, clutching it to his side with his right hand, but as he did so, the strap fell clear, and hung down by his foot. At the far end of the street, just as he was overtaking a dark blue florist's van, he tilted to the right, ready for the turn. He hadn't reduced his speed at all. Suddenly, the floating ribbon of strap vanished. A moment later the rear wheel of the bike rose up in the air, and the cyclist, graceful as a Minoan bull dancer in slow motion, soared in a smooth arc over the handlebars, then landed heavily on the tarmac.

A bus, coming from the opposite direction, ground to a halt

just inches away. The cyclist lay quite still as his bike toppled over on top of him. Sam's bag lay beside his outflung arm, its strap still tangled in the rear wheel.

People crowded round. Inevitably, someone asked the cyclist – secret and unmoving behind his opaque black visor – if he was all right. No response.

Mick pushed his way past a stout woman in a white embroidered blouse. He crouched down to retrieve the bag. A flood of nausea swept through him. The figure splayed on the tarmac could be dead, for all he knew. And for what?

Above his head, voices competed with instructions. 'Call an ambulance.'

'Loosen his helmet.'

'Don't move him.'

'Give him space.'

The bus driver climbed down from her cab. She was angry with shock. Sweat cascading down her face, she cursed randomly.

Mick lifted the rear wheel off the cyclist's chest, then started to unthread the strap from the spokes.

The woman, breasts heaving with indignation under her embroidered blouse, leaned down and put a hand on his shoulder. She smelt of mints. 'And just what do you think you're doing?' she asked, in a voice accustomed to obedience. 'I saw everything. If you hadn't been chasing him, this would never have happened.'

'The bag is stolen,' said Mick.

'What?'

'This bag – he stole it.'

'How do we know you're telling the truth?' she demanded. 'You can't just take it.'

'Watch me,' said Mick. He was still too short of breath for lengthy explanations.

'Oh no you don't,' said a small man with spiky hair who had clearly decided to take the woman's part.

'Oh, for fuck's sake,' said Mick, exasperated. 'The guy's a thief.'

'We've only got your word for that,' said the woman. 'We'll wait for the police to arrive and let them decide.'

A groan emerged from behind the visor and Mick broke into a sweat of relief.

'He's alive,' said the woman.

'Yeah. Let's ask him what he thinks.' The small man put his foot on the strap of the bag, which Mick had just succeeded in working free of the wheel.

'Can't you do something useful?' asked Mick. 'Like phone for an ambulance or something.' And then, as Sam joined them he said, 'Thank God you're here. These morons think I'm trying to steal your bag.'

Calling them morons was a tactical mistake, he realized as soon as he'd said it, wiping out any advantage gained by Sam's appearance on the scene.

'How dare you!' exclaimed the stout woman, as Sam fell to her knees and tried to reclaim her bag. The man refused to move his foot.

'Get off!' said Sam. 'Of course it's bloody mine.'

'Tell us what's inside then.'

'One blue notebook, for a start,' said Mick.

'We can all see that,' said the man with a satisfied smirk, and it was true: one corner of the journal was poking out at the top.

Sam was furious. She barrelled her shoulder against the man's knees, knocking him off balance long enough for her to pull the bag free of his foot. She hugged it to her chest.

'Just a moment, young lady,' said the officious woman. 'Tell us what's in that bag and we might believe you.'

'None of your business,' said Sam, turning away.

But an unhealthy alliance had sprung up between the two strangers, and the small man caught hold of the bag by one corner.

'Wait till the police arrive!' ordered the woman, seizing another corner.

'No way,' said Sam. 'Let go!'

But then, 'Oh, look,' said the man.

While they'd been absorbed in arguing, the cyclist, helmet still covering his face, had struggled to his feet and limped quietly away, leaving his bike in the road. They were just in time to see him climbing into a black cab.

'Would you say that was the action of an innocent man?' asked Mick.

He picked up the bike and moved it over to the pavement. The bus driver climbed back into her cab and restarted the engine. The spectators were drifting away.

The woman in the white blouse was still aggrieved. 'We were only trying to help,' she said.

'Yeah,' said the man. 'And look at all the thanks we get.'

A small hiccuping noise erupted from Sam. She had gathered all her belongings together and replaced them in what remained of her bag, hugging it close to her chest. Her eyes, peering at Mick over the top, were gleaming with amusement.

He realized that she was laughing.

'Lucky you were passing, or what?' she said as they returned to the café where she'd left her cello. 'Some coincidence.'

'Not really,' said Mick. 'I was looking for you.'

'You were? Why?'

'There's something I wanted to tell you. Not here, though. Let's find somewhere a bit more private. D'you fancy a drink?'

Sam looked around. 'Not right now,' she said. 'I feel like walking. Hang on a minute while I park the cello.' She went into the café, where the man behind the counter, whose biceps had not been built up making cappuccinos, promised to look after the cello and she told him briefly what had happened. Mick watched through the glass. She looked elated, almost radiant. Being mugged seemed to agree with her – weird woman. But he felt energized, too.

'Dan will keep an eye on the cello,' she said as she emerged into the sunshine. 'He says my music is good for his business, and gives me free coffees, so everyone is happy.'

'Sounds like a good arrangement,'said Mick.

'Mm.'

They didn't talk much as they walked towards Lincoln's Inn Fields: Mick made a couple of comments, just to be sociable, but she was lost in her own thoughts. By the time they'd reached the shady garden in the middle of the square, they were ready to find an empty bench and sit down.

'Thanks for chasing him, Mick,' she said. 'If I'd lost it—'

'I know. I lost all my credit cards once.'

'They're not important. Not like—'

'The journal?'

She nodded.

Mick said, 'Bad luck they hit on you.'

Sam looked at him oddly. 'Luck?' she asked. She held his gaze for a moment, then said, 'There was something you wanted to tell me?'

'Yeah. I've been trying to figure out a defence for a woman called Grace Hobden who stabbed her husband while he was sleeping and I thought the angle of the knife wounds might help.'

'I'm not exactly an expert on stabbing,' she said.

'No, but I've been talking to a friend who knows about forensics.'

'Did they help?'

'Not much, no. But then I asked her about electrocution in water.'

Now he had her attention. All of it. 'So?' Sam prompted him.

'Unlike ordinary forms of electrocution, which leave burn marks at the entry point, underwater electrocution leaves no marks. According to this expert at least, it's a near enough perfect way to get rid of someone. Once the victim is dead, you remove the electrical appliance from the water and dispose of it. Cause of death: heart failure. Foul play is hardly ever detected.'

'So you do believe me after all?' Sam asked eagerly. 'You agree that my mother was murdered.'

'No, just the opposite. Don't you see? This proves it must have been suicide.'

She frowned. 'How do you work that out?'

'Think about it, Sam. Just suppose for one moment someone did murder your mother by dropping a radio in her bath. All they had to do, once she'd died, was switch off the current at the mains, remove the electrical appliance and get rid of it, then switch the current back on and leave. Everyone would assume natural causes. End of story. Which means there was no reason at all for anyone to try to make it look like suicide. I know this is tough, but it really does look like your mother must have killed herself, after all.'

'Oh.'

You could almost see her retreating into her shell.

'I'm sorry, Sam. I know it's hard, but it's always better to know the truth.'

'Bollocks,' she said. 'I *do* know the truth – or at least, I know some of it. I'm only disappointed because I thought you agreed with me, that's all.'

'But why would someone try to make it look like suicide when it would have been so simple to make it look like an accident?'

'I can't answer that – yet. But I know it wasn't suicide. And it's not just a gut feeling. There's plenty of evidence for what I believe.'

'Such as?'

She hesitated.

Mick asked, 'Did you tell the police what you thought?'

'I tried, once. But they'd already made up their minds and they refused to believe anything that didn't fit with their version.'

Mick had some sympathy with the police view, but he said,

'Look, Sam. I am still prepared to believe you, if there is evidence for murder. But you have to tell me what it is.'

'Why do you think they tried to steal my bag just now?'

Mick stared at her. 'People get their bags stolen all the time. London's a mugger's paradise, or hadn't you noticed? Murder doesn't come into it.'

'Oh really? And if you were a halfway professional thief, would you really go to all that trouble for *this*?' She gestured towards the contents of her carrier bag. 'I mean, I'm really fond of my old bag because it was a present from my friend Gina when she came back from Guatemala but it doesn't exactly send out the message that there's valuable stuff inside. Did you notice that man with the green baseball cap who distracted my attention while the cyclist was coming up? That was a well-planned hit. Why would professionals go to so much trouble for this? Even my mobile phone is two years old. Handbag thieves generally go for wealthy American tourists, not scruffy-looking buskers.'

'Maybe they were amateurs. You know, sort of apprentice muggers.'

'Somehow, I don't think so.'

'You think he was after your journal?'

She nodded. '*They* were. There were two of them.'

'Hang on, Sam. Why would anyone go to all that trouble to steal your mother's journal? Apart from you, that is – and you've already stolen it. I know she was an ace writer and all, but this is ridiculous. Besides –' Mick grinned. '– those two goons hardly looked like literary types.'

'They wanted the journal.' There was no doubt in her voice.

'Okay, just suppose you're right about that. Does that mean you think they were the people who killed her?' Mick tried to keep his voice neutral, but the question still came out sceptical.

'No, but I think someone put them up to it.'

Who? And why all the fuss about her journal? It doesn't make sense.'

She was silent for a bit before asking, 'You know Kirsten was supposed to have left a suicide note?'

'Well, then. There you are.'

'Only she didn't. Look.' She pulled the journal out and opened it about ten pages in. Close to the spine, Mick saw the feathered edge of a torn page. 'The missing page is what was produced as a so-called suicide note. But in fact it was lines towards a poem she was writing just before she came over to England: 'The Farewell Bird'. Someone tore the page out and propped it on the table at Gull Cottage to make it look like she'd left a note.'

'Are you sure? Does the paper match up?'

'I've checked.'

'Okay, but that still doesn't prove anything. She could have torn the sheet out herself. To save time.'

The look Sam gave him was scorching. 'My mother was a *writer*,' she said with slow emphasis, as though that explained everything. 'There's no way she would have recycled some old notes if she was about to say goodbye to the world. Words were her passion and she would have wanted to get it right. And she would have written to me. I know she would.'

Mick saw the fire of utter certainty in her eyes. He wasn't sure if he believed her, but suddenly, against all his rational instincts, he realized that he wanted to. He said, 'So you think that whoever killed her just happened to find a page in her journal that looked a bit like a suicide note, tore it out and left it lying on the table to look like she'd killed herself? Why go to all that trouble when it would have been so easy to make it look like an accident?'

'I don't know. Maybe they didn't know about it looking like death from natural causes. I didn't until you told me. And you didn't either until that forensics person told you. But I reckon the person who faked the suicide note also took that poem I told you about, "The Murder Bird".'

'So what exactly are you saying, Sam? That your mother knew she was going to be murdered and wrote a poem about it in advance?'

'Maybe not. But there has to be a connection between them or why did someone remove the poem as well as the journal?'

Mick thought he could see where this was leading. He said, 'Raph had the journal. According to your theory, that means he must have taken it from the cottage. You think he's responsible for your mother's death? You think he *killed* her?' Mick spelled it out, hoping Sam would realize just how preposterous her theory was. 'You really think Raph travelled all the way to Cornwall, killed your mother, then went around trying to make it look like suicide?'

Sam didn't answer right away. A faint flush was spreading over her cheeks, but her jaw was set in a way that Mick was coming to recognize as dogged determination. She said, 'Raph was involved in the cover-up, sure, but I don't think he killed her. He couldn't have done, not unless they got the time of death wrong.'

Mick was relieved that she wasn't actually accusing his pupil-master of homicide. But it was a small concession to reality. 'So if it wasn't Raph, who was it? According to your theory, I mean.'

This time, Sam was quiet for so long that Mick began to hope she was beginning to see her hypothesis was fatally flawed. Eventually, she said, 'I went to stay at Wardley at the weekend, the place that belongs to Johnny Johns, Raph's brother-in-law. Johnny came into my room when he thought I was asleep and tried to take the journal. He said Raph's sister just wanted to have a look at it and then he'd have put it back.'

'Why didn't she just ask you if she could look at it?'

'That's what I wanted to know.'

'Did you ask her?'

'I was going to but I didn't get the chance.'

Mick was baffled. 'It doesn't make sense,' he said.

'My mother used to say things always make sense if you know all the facts. We just don't know all the facts yet.'

Mick thought of Grace Hobden. Would her behaviour make sense if he knew all the facts, he wondered. He wasn't sure if he really wanted to understand that kind of homicidal 'sense'. Then he thought of Sam, sitting so tense and determined on the bench beside him. In spite of his growing sympathy for her, nothing she had said changed the fact that the most likely explanation was the simplest: Kirsten Waller had taken her own life and her daughter, her only child, was concocting elaborate fantasies to obscure the truth.

It was best to be blunt – painful, but best in the long term. 'I'm sorry, Sam,' he said. 'But your theory just doesn't hold up.

Sooner or later, however hard it is, you're going to have to face up to the fact that you didn't know her as well as you thought. Otherwise it's going to eat away at you – and that's not good.'

'What makes you such an expert on my mother all of a sudden?'

'I guess it's because I'm not involved, so it's easier to see things in perspective.'

'But you are involved, through Raph.'

'That's got nothing to do with it.'

'So the fact that Raph is your pupil-master has nothing to do with your opinion?'

'Of course not.'

'I don't believe you. Jesus!' Suddenly she was bristling with rage. 'How could I have been so stupid! For a moment there, I almost trusted you, but I should have known you'd be on his side in this.'

'It's not a question of sides—'

'Isn't it? Why have you been asking me all these questions, making out you agreed with me, when all along you were just trying to find out what I knew.'

'I wanted to know if you had a case.'

'A case! Why, so you could report back to Raph and tell him all about it?'

'Now you're just being paranoid.'

She stood up. 'Oh, really? Did he set you up to this? Is this a bit of extra curricular help for the big white chief? Did he tell you to find out what I was planning to do next? Is that it?'

'Sam, I promise you—'

'Don't waste your time! I wouldn't believe anything you said anyway. And you can tell your precious boss that I don't know how he's involved, but I'm bloody well going to find out. And I can do it on my own. I don't need help from you or anyone else.'

'That's not fair!' Mick was on his feet as well. But it was too late. Sam was striding away across the park, a lonely, determined and utterly wrong-headed figure in her black cotton dress. He kicked the leg of the bench with frustration.

He was about to run after her, to persuade her that she'd read it all wrong. Then decided not to. The girl was so convinced the whole world was against her, he didn't stand a chance. No reason for him to feel bad about it.

Why should he waste time caring about Sam anyway? After all, a relationship that had begun with blackmail, then segued effortlessly into paranoia and accusations of murder, was never going to be his style.

It was way past time to put Sam Boswin and her sad obsession with her mother's death out of his mind.

Sam wasn't the only person to be struggling with paranoia that afternoon. Nadira had been fighting a losing battle with her big-city fears. They'd run out of coffee, but she didn't dare to leave the flat. She tried to focus on music-making, but for once, that distraction didn't work. Her home had become a place of siege. What had happened to Sam? She should have been home by now. They'd been planning to practise the Schumann. She'd texted her but there'd been no answer.

Did Sam know who the man was who'd called earlier? And what about those phone calls?

The letterbox crashed; another couple of cards for a minicab firm. Nadira was shaking as she stooped to pick them up and put them in the bin. Where was Sam?

At six-thirty she heard Sam's key in the lock, her familiar exasperation as the door was held by the chain.

'Nad! Let me in!'

'Okay. Sorry.' Nadira fumbled with the chain. 'I forgot I'd left it on.' It was the familiar excuse. Then she said, 'No, I didn't. Sam, someone's been trying to get hold of you and they wouldn't say who they were. A man keeps calling up.'

'Raph?'

'I don't think so. But – are you all right?' she asked as Sam carried her cello into the flat. 'You look terrible.'

'More compliments? It's okay, Nad. But someone tried to steal my bag and I had to leg it after him.'

Nadira glanced down at her bag. 'You got it back, then?'

'Yeah. I had help.'

'Sam, what's going on?' Nadira's eyes were huge. 'There's been all these phone calls, and this morning someone came round looking for you.'

'Who was it?'

'He didn't say. And I didn't let him in. He said it was urgent.'

'Did you recognize him?'

'No. What's happening, Sam?'

'I'm sorry you've been affected by this, Nad.' Sam was frowning.

'If I just knew what was going on—'

'I'm not sure I know exactly, myself.'

'Tell me what you do know.'

Sam hesitated, as if she was uncertain how much to say. Then

she went into their little sitting room and sat down. 'Let's have
a cup of tea and then have a go at the Schumann. That is, if it's
not too late for you.'

'Sure. But first I need to know what this is about.'

Sam sighed. 'I've just spent the whole afternoon with somone
who thinks I'm making it all up. I'm not sure if I can go through
the whole thing again. And maybe he's right. Maybe I'm just a
nutter who won't face up to the truth.'

'You don't really think that, do you?'

'No. I don't. But then, mad people always think they're in the
right.'

'You're not mad, Sam.'

'Thanks.' Sam smiled. 'Oh, Nad, you're the only person who
still believes in me, and look at all the thanks you get. You've
been scared out of your wits, haven't you? And it's my fault. I
can't keep putting you through this.'

'I wouldn't mind, if I just knew what it was about.'

Sam was thoughtful for a while, not speaking. At length she
said, 'I don't think I *can* tell you. It's not fair for you to be tied
up in this any more. Someone wants Kirsten's journal and they
won't give up until they get it. That's why my bag was stolen
and that's why someone came round earlier. I think I'm going to
have to get away for a few days – and I'll let them know I'm not
here any more. That way they'll let you alone.'

'Who will? And why do you have to go away?'

'I'll be back soon. Don't worry.'

'Where are you going?'

'I don't know.'

'Yes, you do.'

'Okay, but I'm not saying. I've got to do this on my own, Nad.'

'Can't I help you?'

'No. Well, maybe . . . yes.' Sam turned to her suddenly and the look she gave her made Nadira afraid all over again, but in a different way. Sam said, 'Nad, I want you to promise me something.'

'Sure, anything.'

'Promise me that if anything happens to me, even if it looks like an accident – or suicide – you won't accept that. You won't let them get away with that lie, not with me too.'

'Oh, Sam! You have to tell me what's going on!'

'I will, I promise. Just not right now. I've got to do this on my own for a bit.'

Nadira should have known, from the way Sam spoke, that her mind was made up. But it was impossible not to keep asking. Sam insisted they practise together, and said she'd be back for their lesson with Grigory the following week and that they'd still go in for the Frobisher in November, but Nadira could feel Sam drawing away from her. And there was nothing she could do to keep her there.

CHAPTER 15

Linda wanted to be kind. This summer had been difficult for everyone, what with Kirsten's death, the funeral and then the inquest, but it had been hardest of all for Sam, obviously. So when she'd phoned up and said she was coming down by train that afternoon, Linda had understood that Davy would drop everything to go and pick her up from the station, leaving her to sort out the bedrooms. Louis had to move in with Nathan and she tried to make Louis' room look like a proper spare room, even though there were pictures of fantasy lords and Britney Spears on the walls and box-loads of Lego under the bed. Not to mention that all-pervading smell of sweaty trainers that is the universal accompaniment to adolescent boys everywhere.

She squirted lilac-scented air freshener into the room from the doorway. Only a partial success: chemical-scented sweaty trainers, now. Well, she was sorry if it wasn't what Sam was used to but they could only do their best and she hadn't given them any warning, had she? Typical of her to expect everyone to run

round and put themselves out just because she was condescending to pay them a visit for the first time in over a year,
apart from the night before the inquest, of course, but that
didn't count because she'd had to stay with them then, hadn't
she?

Sam hadn't even arrived yet, and already Linda was feeling
cross and defensive, fragments of arguments playing in her
head. And why did Sam have to make such a mystery about it?
She'd said on the phone that she needed to get away from a
boyfriend – ex-boyfriend, presumably – who was getting to be
a nuisance. Not quite a stalker, but that was the gist. 'Don't tell
anyone I'm here,' she'd told her father on the phone. 'I just need
to get away from London for a bit.'

Linda had bitten back her scorn when Davy put down the
phone and repeated what Sam had said. With Sam, everything
always had to be a drama. Just like her mother, though Davy
wouldn't hear a word against either of them. Kirsten had given
Davy the run-around, going off and leaving him to bring up a
little girl all on his own. Even though his mother had been
around to help in the beginning. Linda had brought a welcome
breath of normality into their lives but she frequently wondered
if they realized what a lot she'd done for them.

When Linda first started going with Davy, she'd felt sorry for
the poor little dark-haired motherless waif and wanted to pro-
vide what she was sure Sam had been missing all along. The
only trouble was, Sam quickly made it clear she didn't feel she'd
missed out on anything. To hear her talk, you'd have thought
her life at Menverren had been a bed of roses until Linda turned
up. 'She'll come round,' Davy told her. 'Just give her time.' But

it wasn't true. And then when first Nathan was born, then Louis, Linda stopped bothering about Sam. She had her own family to look out for now.

When Sam went off to live with Raph and Kirsten in London, Linda had breathed a sigh of relief. She'd tried the best she could; now let someone else take the girl on. She and Davy and the boys were a proper little family at last.

And now, here she was again, getting out of Davy's car, and he was grinning like an idiot, so pleased she'd finally condescended to come home again. The boys were just as bad; they treated her like royalty – and what had Sam ever done for them?

Linda went down the stairs, pinned on a welcoming smile as Sam came in through the kitchen door, Nathan and Louis both competing for her attention. Davy followed, carrying her backpack and her cello. He looked pleased as anything.

'Hello, Sam,' said Linda.

'Hi, Linda. How's it going?'

'Oh, you know. Not too bad. I'm working at the—'

But Louis interrupted. 'I'm in the band, now, Sam. I play trumpet.'

'That's brilliant, Louis,' said Sam, smiling at her half-brother the way she'd never ever smiled at Linda. 'We'll have to work out some duets together.'

'I'll put the kettle on,' said Linda. In the commotion, she wasn't even sure that anyone heard her. She'd been going to tell Sam about her new job at the surgery, three mornings a week. She'd only been working there a couple of months but already she was on top of the computer system and getting used to filtering the urgent calls from the time wasters. But, of course, no one was interested in that. It was just an admin job, after all. Nothing so glamorous as playing a cello or writing poems that no one had ever heard of. Just a plain old useful job that brought in regular money and gave her faith in herself again, faith that she could be more than just a wife and a mother. All she wanted was a bit of appreciation.

'Thanks,' said Sam, hardly looking up when Linda set the tea on the table. 'And did Dad tell you that I don't want anyone knowing where I am for a few days?'

'Yes, he did. Said it was something to do with a difficult boyfriend.'

'That's right.'

Linda waited. It would have been nice to think they might talk about it later, woman to woman. Linda could have given her advice in a motherly sort of way and Sam would be grateful. Yes, and it wouldn't rain in Cornwall between June and September and she'd lose two stone in a week and never put it back on again.

'Sam will need the car tomorrow,' said Davy, smiling happily at his daughter. 'She's got a few people she wants to see.'

'Yes. Well. I do have to get to my job, you know.'

'I can drop you off,' said Davy easily. 'And Sam can pick you up. We'll sort it out somehow. All right, Linda?'

'All right,' she said.

And, *not all right at all*, she thought to herself. But she knew when to keep her mouth shut.

At any other time, this drive would have been a pleasure. Sam had travelled the narrow roads in this part of Cornwall a hundred times and in all seasons. She knew them in winter, when the hawthorns were bare and battered by gales, and in spring when the steep banks were speckled with the pale stars of primroses. In May, bluebells grew thickly among the pink campion, before the huge white umbels of cow parsley branched extravagantly and then flopped down into the road. But September was best of all, when the flowers and grasses had been cut back by the council trimmers and the banks were the pale colour of hay, with the new shoots of ferns emerging among the blue dots of wild scabious, when the trippers had returned home and the roads became drivable again and the sunlight faded and the first leaves of sycamore drifted on to the tarmac.

The Cornish roadshow, Kirsten always called it; there was a poem about it in the early 'Samphire' collection.

The last couple of days, Sam kept feeling as if she was jumping tracks, like some kind of schizoid tram. In the kitchen at Menverren at breakfast time, she'd slid effortlessly back into her old life: Nathan ate an enormous bowl of cereal and Louis ate nothing at all, while Linda fussed and Radio Cornwall chatted comfortingly of minor roadworks and British Legion fund raising. And now – jump the tracks – she was alone again in a world where murders went undetected by anyone but her.

Polwithick was a large village about a mile inland from Gull Cottage. It had a church and a post office and a bakery. Most of the old cottages in the centre of the village had been bought up by incomers, while the Cornish lived in the modern estates that had spread up the sides of the valley. Sam found a parking place near the war memorial and walked across the street to the narrow, terraced house which had been the home of her mother's friend, Judy Saunders, for the past twelve years.

She knocked at the door. The windows were all closed. After she'd knocked several times and peered in through the windows, an old lady, with the kindly, slightly condescending smile of a retired schoolteacher – which she was – emerged from the house next door.

'You can knock all you like,' the old lady told her with quiet satisfaction, 'Judy's gone away.'

'Where?'

'She didn't say.'

'Do you know when she'll be back?'

'Maybe today. But maybe not for a few days. A week, even. She said,' and here the old lady screwed up her face as though struggling to remember Judy's exact words, 'she said she was going to play it by ear.'

'Do you know her mobile number?'

'Her what, dear?'

'Never mind.'

The old lady watched without speaking while Sam wrote a brief note. She pushed it through the letter box and said, 'When she gets back, can you tell her Sam Boswin wants to talk to her, please? I'm staying at my dad's. She knows how to get in touch.'

'I'll tell her.' Just as Sam was turning to go, the old woman said quietly, 'And I'm sorry about your mother, Sam. She was a wonderful lady. Judy took her death very hard, and I'm not surprised. We're all going to miss her.'

Sam stood quite still. 'Thank you,' she said.

She went back to her car and sat for a few moments. It was

the unexpected remarks like that which could leave you feeling winded. An old man was walking his arthritic poodle along the narrow pavement in the morning sunshine. He looked so calm, at peace with the world.

Sam turned the key in the ignition. Time to get back on track again.

At the next place she visited there was no doubt that people were at home. Chickens ran squawking as she entered the farmyard and two large dogs came bounding out, barking loudly, followed closely by a short, stout woman wearing a faded flowered dress and well-worn wellington boots on bare legs. This was one of those farms where the buildings and animals are kept in immaculate order, at the apparent expense of the owners. Ann and Bob Wearne might look destitute, but they were rumoured locally to have paid for their new tractor with cash.

'Hello, Mrs Wearne,' said Sam, getting out of the car and stooping to pat the nearest dog, a large black and brown collie. 'Can you spare a moment?'

Ann Wearne took hold of the larger of the two dogs by the scruff of its neck, and grinned. A stout woman, she had sparse, curly hair which didn't look as though it had been brushed that day and when she opened her mouth to remonstrate with the dogs, her teeth were revealed: they jutted out at drunken angles, and two were missing entirely.

'Quiet, Dooley. That's enough, now,' she scolded the dog, who stopped pretending to be a guard dog and went off to flop down in the shade. Turning back to Sam, she said, 'I was sorry to hear about your mother, Sam.'

'Thanks.

'She was a fine woman. But you know that.'

'Yes.'

'D'you want to come in for coffee?'

Sam shook her head. 'I just wanted to ask you something. You and Mr Wearne. It won't take long.'

Ann looked at her for a moment, then nodded, as though she'd been expecting Sam's questions. 'Bob's down by the ponds. I've got to take him a message. We can walk down together, if you like.'

The track leading down to the valley was deeply rutted, packed with ridges of earth hardened by drought. Skylarks rose up singing on either side. From the bottom of the hill came the steady drone of a tractor.

'How are you getting on, Sam?' asked Ann as they were walking.

'All right,' said Sam.

'We could hardly believe it when your mother died like that. Such a terrible waste.' It was a simple statement of fact. She added, 'And she was always so proud of you, my lover.'

Sam smiled.

The Cornish terms of endearment, 'my lover', 'my bird' and 'my 'andsome', might be as randomly distributed as 'darling' among actors, and as meaningless, but they reminded her powerfully of her grandmother and all the Boswin uncles and aunts and cousins who'd surrounded her with affection, making sure she never missed out when Kirsten left

She said, 'And I was proud of her, too.'

'Quite right. She was a good woman, I reckon. You can be

proud of her, Sam. I know lots of people held it against her, the way she went off and left you when you were just a littl'un, but I reckon she must have had her reasons. She never talked about it much, but she did say once, when someone had been short with her, said something, I don't know what and I don't rightly want to know, but she looked at me and she said, "Ann, if folk knew what that cost me, they wouldn't be so quick to criticise." And I believed her.'

'Yes. I don't think she felt she had a choice about that.'

'She told me about some competition you were going in for. How was it?'

'The Frobisher? It's not happening till November. My teacher wants me to pull out because I haven't been up to form recently. He says it's too important to screw up. But I haven't made up my mind yet.'

'The Frobisher, that's right. She did tell me the name but I'd forgotten. She was looking forward to it.' Ann paused, then added thoughtfully, 'At least, it seemed like she was.'

They walked in silence for a while. Small butterflies danced beside them. Sam asked, 'Did you see much of my mother while she was at Gull Cottage?'

'Well, in a manner of speaking. She came by here maybe every other day when she was walking into the village or if she wanted some eggs or some milk. And once or twice I'd pop over with some scones or a pasty. Now, of course, I wish I had gone over more often. But she always said the solitude was what she liked about the place, so I didn't like to make a nuisance of myself. And she seemed content enough.'

'So she didn't seem depressed? Or worried about anything?'

'No, but I dare say she'd not have told me, even if she had been.'

'But you would have noticed.'

'Maybe.'

An invisible barrier had crept between them. It was possible that Ann felt in some way guilty because of Kirsten's death: she'd been her closest neighbour. Had she missed the signs? Was there something more she could have done?

They walked the last bit without speaking, then rounded a corner and pushed open the gate into the field Bob Wearne was harrowing. Ann waved, the tractor came round in a wide arc and stopped about ten yards away. Bob switched off the engine and climbed down from the cab.

In his fifties, Bob Wearne walked with a limp, the result of a misunderstanding with a newly-calved cow some years before. He wore a flat cap and a checked shirt and there was a mass of crows' feet round his eyes from years of working outdoors in all weathers.

He smiled. 'Hello, Sam. What brings you here?'

Sam was grateful for his directness. She said, 'I'm trying to find out who visited Gull Cottage shortly after my mother died.'

Bob Wearne shot a glance at his wife, then said, 'It was your father who found her body, wasn't it?'

'But before that. Earlier that morning. Someone else was seen.'

'Well, now.' He pushed his hat back and scratched his head. 'Gull Cottage is right by the coast path. You get all sorts walking past, especially in the summer. Can't keep track of them.'

'You might notice someone in a car, though.'

'Well. You might do. Yes.'

'Especially someone who looked like an outsider. A Londoner, maybe.'

'Yes. That's true.'

'And especially if they were driving a flash car. A TVR for instance.'

'Yes,' said Bob Wearne thoughtfully. 'I reckon you'd remember that all right.'

'So you did see someone at Gull Cottage earlier that morning, before my father went there?'

'I didn't say that, Sam.'

'But—'

'What's this leading to, anyway?'

Sam drew in a deep breath, restraining herself. 'I'm just trying to get to the truth about what happened.'

'Ah, the truth now. That's a slippery old thing, truth. They've had the inquest to find that out, my lover.'

'Yes, but the official version isn't always the right one. You know that.'

Bob Wearne looked at her intently. He said, 'You know what they say, Sam, about letting sleeping dogs lie. Sometimes—'

'My mother's not a bloody dog!' Sam blazed. 'And I'm not stopping till I know what's happened to her!'

Bob threw his wife a glance, as if to say, get this hysterical female off my back, and turned towards his tractor. As he walked away he said, 'Sorry, Sam. 'Fraid I can't help you. Best to get on now.'

'Thanks anyway.' said Sam, but he'd started the engine again and she wasn't sure if he'd heard her.

When they were walking back up the track, Sam said to Ann, 'You never gave him the message.'

'I'll tell him at lunchtime.'

'He did see someone, didn't he?'

'He might have done. But you know how it is. It's hard to be certain of dates and times. I'm sorry, Sam. Sorry for all of this. It must have been so hard for you.'

'It still is.'

Only when Sam was back in the car, the engine already running, did Ann feel safe enough to lean down and say, 'What your mother did, Sam, I reckon that was impulse. She hadn't intended it at all. That may be the best way to look at it.'

'Why do you say that?'

Ann looked away to the far end of the farm where her husband was still working. 'Well, see. The thing is, the day she died, she came over in the morning to buy eggs. Said she wanted some of my fresh eggs for when you came to visit. Looked like she was on top of the world. She was looking forward to it, see? So it must have been an impulse – what do they call it? – "While the balance of her mind was disturbed." That's what I think. She wasn't in her right mind at all. Tragic, that's what it is.'

'Yes,' said Sam.

Tragic: the one fact about her mother's death that had never been in doubt.

'Thank you. No, that's *absolutely* wonderful. You've been *most* helpful.' Raph's voice could drip like melted honey when he chose. He'd tried it with Kirsten once, but she'd laughed at him and thrown something – a slipper? a cushion? – at him and told him not to be such a pompous old hypocrite, and he'd laughed in his turn, and then . . . Forget about Kirsten. It's Sam who's important now. Smoothly he interrupted the anxious voice at the other end of the line. 'I'm *so* sorry to hear she's been having trouble with a boyfriend. No, she hadn't said anything to me about it. I would have tried to help, if I'd known. Yes, give her my love. I hope she has a good holiday with you and Davy. She needs it. Yes, yes, I was just checking to make sure she was all right. Thank you. Yes, same to you. Goodbye.'

Raph was thoughtful as he put down the phone. Memo: never trust Linda Boswin with any secrets – not that he was likely to – the woman's so indiscreet she ought to work for the Cabinet Office.

Still, at least he knew where Sam had disappeared to.

Not the best hiding place, if hiding had been her intention.

Anyone could find her, easily.

Even a murder bird.

CHAPTER 16

'Why didn't she just leave?' Mick asked.

Martha Irving weighed the question. She was sitting behind a desk piled high with files and leaflets. On the wall behind her posters were exhorting women to 'say no to violence' or informing their partners they wouldn't get away with it.

'Leaving a violent partner,' Martha said carefully, 'is statistically the most dangerous thing a vulnerable woman can do. Research studies show that more than three-quarters of battered women suffer violence *after* leaving their partner. Sometimes – too often – that violence is fatal.'

'I thought there were places they could go.'

'Refuges? There are – but sometimes their partners track them down and kill them all the same. And who wants to live in a refuge for the rest of their lives? Have you ever actually visited one?' Mick shook his head. 'No, I thought not.'

'What about the police? Restraining orders? The law is there to protect women, same as everyone else.'

'Hm. Tell that to the hundred plus women who are killed by their partners – or former partners – every year.'

'As many as that?' Mick was aware that his surprise must make him seem to her like just another ignorant barrister-in-the-making, but it couldn't be helped. 'Christ. D'you think Grace Hobden knew the figures?'

'I've no idea. But I do know that women in violent relation-ships often reach the point where they believe only one of them is going to get out of it alive. And if there are children involved, the stakes are that much higher.'

'You mean those men who kill their whole family? That's not very common, is it?'

'It's rare, yes. But it does happen. And the threat is there. My guess is that your Grace Hobden was in an impossible situ-ation: she couldn't stay and she couldn't leave. For women like her, killing their partner can seem like the only logical solu-tion.'

'You're saying that Grace Hobden made a rational decision?'

'Maybe not rational the way you or I would look at it, but from her point of view, yes. That's precisely what I'm saying.'

'And you'd be prepared to say this in court?'

'Sure I would. I'm not sure it'll do much good, as the law hasn't caught up yet with current thinking on the reality for bat-tered women. But each case we fight helps change the *status quo*. Bit by bit.'

'Brilliant. We'll be in touch, then, nearer the time.'

'Is that it?' Martha Irving seemed surprised that their meet-ing had been so brief.

'It's what I need to be getting on with.'

She shrugged. 'Okay. Anything I can do, just tell me.' The phone in her outer office was ringing shrilly. To Mick, it sounded almost like a woman screaming.

As soon as he was outside again, Mick breathed in big lungfuls of London air. He hoped his impatience hadn't been too obvious. In Martha's tiny office, listening to her talking calmly about the scores of women killed every year by their menfolk, he'd felt guilt by association, just for being a man. Which was obviously ridiculous, but uncomfortable all the same. Maybe campaigners for battered women always have that effect.

Guilty. An image of Sam appeared in his mind. Not for the first time, recently, either. It must be all this talk of violence and murder. Sam was turning out to be a hard person to stop thinking about. The most annoying aspect of this Sam-thinking was that each time he did, he felt bad, as though he'd let her down somehow.

Which was not logical. There was no reason at all for him to feel bad about Sam Boswin.

But all the same . . . Stop it, he told himself. He'd done what he could to be helpful: he'd taken the trouble to tell her about the effects of electrocution in water, he'd risked his neck in traffic retrieving that damn bag with her mother's journal inside, then he'd listened to her concerns about the possible explanation for her mother's death and given her his considered opinion. What more was he supposed to do?

Zero, actually. The logical course of action, if thinking about Sam just made him feel bad, was to think about something else.

Or some*one* else, to be more specific. As soon as he'd walked a little way down the street, he phoned Tara, an attractive, easy-going girl he'd met on holiday and gone out with a couple of times, and asked if she wanted to meet up for a drink after work. She was good fun so long as he remembered to keep her away from the twin perils of absinthe and karaoke. 'Only a drink?' she said. 'Sure, we can start with that, anyway.' 'Great,' he said. 'See you at eight.'

But as soon as he switched off the phone he was depressed by the prospect; he had no real interest in seeing her after all. She would laugh at his jokes and smile hopefully and gossip about mutual friends . . . his spirits sank at the prospect. He might as well phone and cancel right now. He remembered the withering glance Sam had given him when she said, 'My mother was a writer', as if that was everything he ever needed to know on the subject of Kirsten Waller, and then her fierce expression when she told him she knew her mother had been killed.

Hang on a minute, he told himself. Since when did Mick Brady find withering and fierce attractive in a woman? Was it possible he was turning into some kind of sad old masochist? This was against everything he believed in. He felt sorry for her, that was all. The poor girl had lost her mother, didn't seem to have much of a life apart from her music and was consequently obsessing about far-fetched murder plots. Anyone would feel sorry for her.

Well, *anyone* might, but knight errantry had never been Mick Brady's style. Damsels in distress had a tendency to send him galloping off in the opposite direction faster than a speeding arrow. If he knew what was good for him — and he always had done up till now – he'd make sure he had nothing whatsoever to do with Sam in future. A sad, deluded obsessive cluttering up his life was not a recipe for happiness.

On the other hand, Tara, even allowing for the absinthe and the karaoke, was exactly what the social doctor ordered.

He'd set out early and walk across the park. Chill out and get in the mood. But first he had to drop off his papers at work. Corinna on reception was wilting visibly; she complained that the fan which had been graciously installed on her desk by the senior partners only succeeded in bringing all the warm air down from the ceiling and wrapping it round her. Mick agreed that the high-ups were all inured to discomfort by hideous prep schools from an early age. The first thing he'd do when he became a senior member of chambers would be to install air conditioning. She said, 'Promise?' and he said, 'Promise', and walked down the corridor to Raph's office .

Outside the door, he stopped. Raph was on the phone. Nothing unusual in that. Usually, when Raph talked on the phone, he sat at his desk, facing the door. Or, if he needed to be particularly assertive, he stood. Very occasionally, when he was talking to Lola, or someone he was intimate with, he perched on the edge of his desk, his relaxed pose reflecting the informality of his conversation.

Never like this.

Raph was seated in his chair, yes, but crouched in a conspiratorial huddle. He was cradling the phone as if it was an infant, and talking in a low and urgent voice. Mick hung back, listening.

'No, listen,' he was saying. 'It's nothing. I only said that to scare you. It's really not that important. Yes, I know, but you have to believe me now. Because I'm telling you the truth, for God's sake, that's why. I lied before because I wanted you to stop, but . . . no, this is the truth, really it is. Just listen to me, will you! I'm telling you there's nothing in it. I've seen it, that's how I know. It does-n't matter that she's got it. It really doesn't matter, okay?'

Sweat was pouring down his face and he was pleading. That was the truly disturbing aspect of all this: Raph Howes, who could bully or cajole, command or seduce, depending on the need of the moment, right now Raph Howes was helplessly pleading.

'Look, I told you already, I lied,' Raph said again. 'Yes, I'm sorry, I know it was wrong, but I wanted to stop you . . . I know you were trying to help but . . . no, it was the wrong way. She never said that in the journal. No, I promise you, she didn't . . . yes, in the poem, but that's been destroyed. No need to worry about that. Listen, I mean it, there's no way Sam's getting hurt over this . . . no, and I wouldn't tell you if I did. Please, just back off, all right? It'll work out fine just so long as you don't do anything. Jesus, why the hell can't you just trust me, just once?'

Mick backed slowly away.

'Are you okay?' Corinna looked up as he came back into reception. He didn't answer, and heard her say as he left the building, 'It's the heat. No one's acting normal today. Mr Howes has been all over the place since lunchtime. I'll be glad when the weather breaks.'

Half a mile from chambers, Mick turned into a side street, away from the thundering traffic on Gray's Inn Road, pulled out his phone and punched in Sam's number. He was answered by the most annoying voice in the world for those with an urgent message: 'The Vodaphone you have called is switched off. Please try later.' Damn, damn, *damn*! Never had the bland female voice been so infuriating. He sent Sam a text: 'I was wrong. Please contact. Most urgent. Want to help. Mick.'

He stood for a moment, breathing deeply.

It wasn't enough. He had to do something right now. Find some way to contact her at once. *There's no way Sam's getting hurt over this*, Raph had said. What did that mean, exactly? And why the hell had she chosen to switch her phone off now, of all times? Maybe she was doing a concert, or busking. She'd switch the phone back on in an hour or so. He'd try again later, like Vodaphone woman advised.

He wasn't in the mood to wait.

He'd go to her home only he didn't have her address. Who would know? Raph, obviously. But Raph didn't know he and Sam had met, so why would he want her address?

Lola. He still had her mobile number. But just as he started to scroll down for her number, he paused. It was possible, just possible, that Lola was the person Raph had been talking to on the phone, the person he had instructed not to hurt Sam.

Get real, he told himself scornfully. You know Lola – not well, but enough. She might have her faults, but she's not exactly the kind of woman who goes around hurting people, let alone . . . let alone, killing them.

Mick stood very still. Catching up.

His pupil-master, the man he'd chosen to guide him through the labyrinthine paths of the legal profession, had just told an unknown someone that he didn't want Sam hurt. It didn't sound like he was talking about emotional pain either. And Sam believed her mother had been murdered and that Raph knew more about it than he let on. If she was right, there was a strong chance his pupil-master was accessory to murder.

'Oh shit,' he said out loud. Welcome to the world where nothing is how it seems.

The world that Sam had been living in, alone and unbelieved, for months. He couldn't begin to imagine how hard that had been, what it had been like sitting through an inquest where her mother's death was recorded as suicide. No wonder she'd been quick to flare into anger.

He began walking back towards chambers, then pulled into another side street while he tried Lola's number. This time the phone was answered after a couple of rings.

'Lola, hi, how are you? This is Mick. Mick Brady. I came back to your place after the Feilers' party, remember?'

'Yeah. Hi. I remember.' She sounded pleased to hear from him – good. But also cautious – not quite so good.

'Listen, something's come up and . . . I bumped into Raph's stepdaughter the other day . . . I know, quite a coincidence, isn't it? She plays the cello, doesn't she? Well, I've got a contact I think might be useful for her and I wanted to drop round her place and give it to her. Yes, I've already got her mobile number but I'm in south London and I thought I'd just call in.'

'It's somewhere in Clapham, I think,' said Lola. She was sounding bored now at the direction the conversation was taking. Or perhaps boredom was a façade to cover her unwillingness to help.

'Have you got her address?'

'No. Why should I? Ask Raph – he'll tell you.'

'He's tied up right now.'

She made an impatient noise, as though Raph was always tied up when people needed him. 'Well, you'll have to wait, then. It can't be that urgent. And I don't know it.'

'Okay. Sorry to trouble you. And thanks . . .' For nothing, thought Mick angrily as he terminated the call. Raph was the last person he wanted to ask.

When he got back to chambers, Corinna was spraying Evian water on her throat and face. 'I'm just off,' she said. 'You look like you could use some of this.' She helpfully squirted the cooling mist against his cheeks.

'Thanks,' he said. Then, 'You don't happen to know Sam's address, do you?'

'Sam?'

'Raph's stepdaughter.'

'Oh, Sam Boswin. Poor girl. She lives in Battersea. No, Peckham. Or maybe it's Camberwell. Sorry, I'm not being much help, am I? West London's my patch. All those bits south of the river get kind of blurred. You'd better ask Mr Howes.'

'You haven't got it written down, anywhere?'

Corinna shook her head. 'But Mr Howes is still around,' she said. 'He'll know.'

'I was hoping not to have to bother him,' said Mick.

Behind him a deep voice asked, 'What will I know? And since when did you have any scruples about bothering me?'

Raph was standing in the lobby. He looked tired, his face drawn and strained, but then most people did at this time of the evening after a long day in the relentless heat.

Mick hesitated, but Corinna spoke for him. 'Mr Brady's been asking for your stepdaughter's address. I told him to ask you.'

'Sam? I didn't know you knew each other.' If Raph was surprised at Mick's request, nothing in his manner betrayed the fact.

'We met a couple of weeks ago,' said Mick. 'At a party.'

'Really? You never told me. I wouldn't have thought your social circles crossed. She only usually hangs out with musicians.'

'Even the tone deaf have contacts.'

Raph eyed him curiously for a moment, then said, 'Thirty-three Chepstow Mansions. It's one of those council blocks near Clapham Common. Third floor. Dodgy lift.'

'Thanks,' said Mick, turning to go.

'But she's not there,' said Raph. 'I tried to get hold of her last night but her flatmate said she'd gone away.'

'Gone? Where?'

'That's what I wanted to know.'

Raph held his gaze, in the way people do when they're brazening out a lie. Mick got the feeling that Raph knew exactly where Sam was. Raph said, 'It's worrying, isn't it? After all she's been through in the past few months, to have her suddenly up and disappear without telling anyone where she's gone. I'm concerned about her.'

'Yeah. Sure.'

An hour ago, and Mick would have believed him. Not any more.

Chepstow Mansions was the kind of block, one of hundreds in south London, that you walk past without noticing, utterly lacking in character or architectural presence. Mick walked up the concrete stairway to the third floor. Two pale-looking little girls were dressing dolls on the top step. They broke off their game and stared at him in silence as he walked past.

Number 33 had a reinforced glass panel in the door. The wood was gouged and flaking round the keyhole; someone had been tampering with the lock Mick pressed the buzzer, but heard nothing, then knocked on the door. He saw a shadow move behind the glass. Good. Sam must be there after all. She'd probably told Raph she was going away to throw him off the scent.

The door remained firmly closed. Mick knocked again.

Still no reply. He began to wonder if he'd imagined the shadow moving within.

He crouched down and pushed open the letter box, peering through. 'Sam?' he asked. 'Are you in there? Sam, it's me, Mick. Listen, I've come to say I'm sorry. I was wrong about your mother. I overheard Raph talking to someone on the phone just now and I came over to tell you that I believe you now. Something's going on. Sam?'

From somewhere inside the flat, out of sight, a woman's voice, not Sam's, a voice shrill with fear, said, 'Sam's not here. I already told you. Go away and leave me alone.'

'Do you know where she is? I have to talk to her. I think she may be in some kind of danger.'

'No. Go away. Leave me alone!' The woman's voice cracked and he realized that whoever it was he was talking to was crying.

'Please. I'm a friend of Sam's. I want to help her.'

'Go away!'

'But—'

Mick had been so intent on trying to reach out to the woman inside the flat that he hadn't heard footsteps on the concrete walkway behind him. A man's voice shouted, 'Bastard! Get the fuck away from here!' Mick's arm was jerked viciously up behind his back and his head was rammed against the wall. He let out a yell of shock and pain, then struggled to free himself, but there were two of them, dark-skinned and angry. He lashed out with his feet, kicking blindly.

Inside the flat, the woman screamed.

The second time Mick's head struck the wall he blacked out.

Nadira pulled back the chain and opened the door just in time to see her younger brother using a stranger's head to punch the wall. She'd never seen him so angry.

'Stop that!' she yelled. 'D'you want to kill him?'

Dil, her older brother, said, 'That'll teach him not to come frightening you.'

He released his grip on the stranger, who slid down on to the ground with a low groan. Both the men looked down at him curiously.

'Are you okay?' asked Benj.

She nodded.

'Got your stuff? The car's downstairs, only we can't park long.'

She reached down to pick up a small holdall and a music case. She felt close to tears, as if she was running away from everything she'd fought so hard to achieve. But there were limits to what she was prepared to risk to follow her dream. When

Sam made her promise not to let 'them' get away with the accident lie, she'd thought she must be exaggerating. Murder? That kind of thing didn't really happen to people like her. She'd had second thoughts when she'd been woken at three o'clock in the morning by the sound of someone trying to chip away at the front door. Still fuddled with sleep, she told herself it must be Sam, who'd come back after all, but lost her keys.

'Sam?' she called out to the shadow beyond the frosted glass of the door. 'Sam, is that you?'

The shadow was quite still.

'Sam?' Now her voice was squeaky with fear.

The shadow melted into the darkness.

Not Sam. A burglar, maybe, who'd fled when they realised the flat wasn't empty. Or maybe someone who was looking for Sam and fled when they realised she wasn't there.

Either way, Nadira was thoroughly spooked. She'd had enough. As soon as it was light, she called home.

If someone was prepared to hurt Sam, it stood to reason that she wasn't safe, either.

The stranger, who was still slumped against the wall, opened his eyes and blinked. He put his hand to his head.

Looking up at her, he croaked, 'I have to warn Sam.'

'I don't know where she is.'

'I think she's in danger,' he said.

'Why?' asked Nadira. 'I don't understand.'

'Nor do I, not really.' He shifted his position. 'Something to do with her mother's journal.'

'Come on, Nad,' Dil said. 'Let's get going.'

'How do you know Sam?' she asked the stranger, who was
levering himself into a sitting position. He didn't look at all the
burglar type.

He said, 'I got her mother's journal for her. Twice, actually.'

No way was this the same person who'd been trying to break
in last night. Nadira was sure that she could trust him. She said,
'I'm sorry they hurt you.'

Benj took hold of her bag. 'We're wasting time.'

'We can't just leave him.'

'He'll be all right, won't you, mate?'

Mick held the side of his head and stood up shakily.
'Depends what you mean by all right,' he said. Obviously the
wall was playing an important role in keeping him vertical. 'I've
felt better, actually.'

Nadira said, 'This is a friend of Sam's. He's okay.'

'Mick Brady.'

Dil hesitated for a moment before shaking him by the hand.
'Sorry about your head,' he said.

Benj handed Nadira's bag to his brother. 'Go down and keep
an eye on the car, okay?' He lit two cigarettes and gave one to
Mick, while Dil went down to look out for traffic wardens.
'When we saw you shouting through the letter box, we thought
you must be the guy who's been hassling our sister. A case of
mistaken identity, obviously.'

'I've got some plasters in the flat,' said Nadira.

'I'll be okay.'

'Tell you what,' said Benj. 'We can drop you off somewhere
if you like. We'll be going through central London.'

Mick ignored him. He said to Nadira, 'Please, you have to

tell me where I can get in touch with Sam.'

'I'd like to help you, really I would, but Sam wouldn't tell me where she was going. She said it was better if I didn't know.'

'Damn. Look, if you talk to her, can you tell her to get in touch with me. Say Mick Brady overheard Raph talking to someone on the phone and he believes her now. I'm on her side.'

'Yes. I'll tell her. Are you sure you're okay?'

'I'll be fine.'

Nadira pulled the door shut behind her and double locked it, then edged past Mick and followed her brother along the walkway to the lift. She felt crushed and hopeless. When she phoned her brothers and asked them to come to get her, it had felt like the only sensible course of action. Now, it felt horribly like running away.

CHAPTER 17

'You *told* him I was here?'

Linda stared at her calmly. 'You never said that Raph Howes wasn't to know.'

'I said I didn't want *anyone* to know.'

'Did you? I thought it was just this boyfriend of yours. The one who's been making trouble.' Linda didn't bother to keep the scepticim out of her voice. 'I'd have thought Raph Howes would have wanted to help.'

'That's for me to decide.'

'Oh, well. No harm done, is there?'

Sam knew it was pointless trying to explain. Even if she told Linda and Davy her real reasons for wanting to lie low for a bit, they'd probably think she was making it all up. Besides, as she went upstairs to pack up her few things, she had to admit that Menverren hadn't been the most original place to choose. Some deep-grained homing instinct had drawn her back to this place.

That, and its proximity to Gull Cottage.

Twenty minutes later she reappeared in the kitchen. Linda was putting a quiche in the oven.

Sam said, 'Can you give me the number of a taxi, please, Linda? If I leave now, I can catch the last train back to London.'

'But you only just got here,' said Linda.

'Something's come up. I need to get back.'

Linda sighed. 'So what about that boyfriend you were trying to keep away from?'

'I think I panicked.'

'It's not Raph Howes, is it?'

'No.'

'Well, that's something, anyway. Your father will be disappointed.'

'Tell him I'm sorry. And I'll be down again soon.'

Now that Sam was about to leave, Linda seemed gentler. She said, 'No need to waste money on a taxi. I can drive you, Sam.'

'That's brilliant. If you're sure it's not a nuisance.'

'It's the least I can do,' said Linda. And later, when they were pulling into the station car park she said, 'I hope you come down again soon. You know we always like to see you.'

'Thanks.'

'And I'm sorry about telling Raph Howes.'

'Don't worry. He would have guessed, anyway. It doesn't matter.'

'That's all right, then.'

'I'll be back soon, I promise.' Sam got out of the car, removed her cello and bag and said, 'You know how much I've always hated saying goodbye and you must be anxious to get back. See you soon, Linda.'

'Goodbye, Sam. And good luck with your competition.'

Sam watched as Linda turned around and pulled into the traffic and disappeared up the hill. She stood for a few moments more, then, instead of going through to the platform, she went to the only taxi on the forecourt and gave the driver the address of Gull Cottage.

Breaking into people's houses was becoming a habit, Sam thought.

It was growing dark when the taxi driver dropped her off at Gull Cottage. He'd spent the journey trying to remember the details of the tragic death that had occurred there in the summer – 'Didn't you read about it?' he wanted to know. 'It was in all the papers.' In between parrying his questions, Sam had tried phoning Judy Saunders in Polwithick, to ask if she could stay for a couple of days, but as before, all she got was the answerphone. Since Judy had cancelled all the bookings at Gull Cottage after Kirsten's death, Sam was sure she would have no objection to her staying there for a night or two. Or maybe more.

She was all out of plans. From now on, she'd have to play it by ear – not a very good metaphor for a cellist who couldn't hear the music any more. She'd have to fly by the seat of her pants, then – whatever that meant.

On the drive over she'd got the taxi to stop at a supermarket and had bought some milk and bread and a few necessaries, but she didn't know how long she'd stay. Only that she had to find a place where no one would come looking for her, where no one she cared for would be hurt by their proximity.

Those text messages from Mick had tempted her, briefly, to break her self-imposed silence. *I'm on your side*, he'd said. *I believe you and I want to help.* If only she could have been sure that she believed him. His change of heart might be genuine, but then again, wasn't it too convenient? He worked for Raph after all and pupils were always anxious to get articles. Raph might have persuaded him to indulge in a few extracurricular activities. She was better off acting alone.

The sun had already gone down behind the cottage. Sam ate sardines out of the tin and made some tea, then sat in the doorway of the cottage and played the cello in the evening light. A couple of hikers, walking along the coastal path behind the cottage, stopped and listened, their faces shining. The unexpected combination of music and landscape and twilight: 'We'll never forget this,' they told her, before continuing on their way. Sam knew that it was far from real playing. She still could not hear the music inside, any more than she could hear Kirsten's voice.

At last, she could put it off no longer: she had to use the bathroom. Go into the room where her mother had died.

She climbed the stairs slowly, wishing all the while that she'd done it while the cottage was still filled with sunlight. She'd never been alone at Gull Cottage before. She'd visited often enough, when she was still living at Menverren and Kirsten used to come over most years and stay for a month or so, usually in May or June.

On the landing, she hesitated. It was very quiet. Kirsten had told her once that houses are like foreign cities: they never reveal themselves fully until you've spent time there alone. Now, with nothing but the sound of the waves softly breaking against the shingle and rocks below the house, Sam understood what her mother had meant.

There was a tightness round her ribs as she moved along the corridor which led between the two bedrooms to the bathroom at the back of the cottage. Its one small window was almost at floor level, under the pitch of the roof, and looked out over the Wearnes' far fields. Now, beyond the glass, all was darkness.

Had it been dark on midsummer's eve, when her mother ran herself a bath?

Sam stood at the entrance to the bathroom; it seemed impossible to go further. Her imagination was spiralling into visions she'd blocked for months.

Kirsten runs water into the bath. Kirsten takes the radio from the bedroom, where it's plugged in, and carries it through to the bathroom. She's got an extension flex, so the radio will reach.

She takes off her clothes and gets into the water.

She's lying there, relaxing. Does she think she's alone in the cottage? Or is it someone she trusts who comes up the stairs?

Someone who stands, where Sam is standing now.

Someone who picks up the radio, walks over the worn lino.

Kirsten starts to get out of the bath. She's reaching for her towel. But she isn't quick enough.

The radio sails through the air and Kirsten screams.

The murder bird is too fast for her.

But who? Who is it Kirsten sees as the electricity pours through her body, stopping her heart?

Forcing herself to cross the bathroom floor, Sam looked back towards the doorway, and almost imagined she could see a figure standing there. A shadowy figure. Impossible to make out who it was.

Sam made up a kind of bed on the sofa – no way was she sleeping upstairs, it was bad enough having to use the bathroom – then lay down with the sound of the sea coming through the open window, her mother's journal under her pillow. It was hard to sleep, and when she did she was disturbed by dreams of violence and death.

She was woken by sunlight and birds and the certainty that she had to act, do something, anything to break the deadlock she was trapped in. She got up, opened the door and walked as close to the edge of the cliff as she dared. She drew back. That old fear of heights – but the plan she'd decided on scared her even more than the vertigo did. Was it crazy? Almost certainly, but right now, it was the best she could come up with.

She had to discover who had killed her mother. If there was no other way, then she'd have to scare them into showing themselves.

She went back inside and sat down at the rickety table, where her mother would have worked every day while she stayed at Gull Cottage. First, she wrote a letter to Trevor Clay. Then she repeated the words and wrote copies to Mick Brady and her father, and then for good measure she wrote briefer versions to Grigory her teacher and to Nadira. If anything happened to her, some 'accident' or 'apparent suicide', then one of them must believe the contents of her letter. Not that she intended to let anything happen. The cottage had neither envelopes or stamps; she'd have to get those in the village.

She debated whether to see the letters safely posted before making her phone calls, but in the end impatience got the better of her. Its lack of a phone had always been one of the reasons Kirsten loved Gull Cottage; luckily Sam still had credit on her mobile.

She took her mobile from her bag, stared at it for a few moments, then punched in Lola's number. You've got to start somewhere, she told herself. As she listened to it ringing, drew breath to speak, she had the giddy feeling she used to get when, battling against vertigo, she'd forced herself onto the highest board during school swimming lessons. She was hoping for an answerphone message, but Lola answered after the second ring.

'Lola, this is Sam.' Going to the edge of the board.

'Yes?' Lola had her nail-buffing voice, the one that implied Sam was of less interest than a well-polished toenail.

'Lola, I just wanted you to know.' Leaning over the edge and looking down, far down at the waiting water. 'I've found the poem, "The Murder Bird".' Diving, now. 'I know who killed my mother.'

Water cold against her face. She'd done it.

There was a brief silence at the other end of the line. Then Lola said, 'What the fuck are you talking about?'

'I told you.' Sam was speaking very distinctly. She'd wondered before about Lola's powers of comprehension. 'I know who killed my mother. I've found the poem.'

She hung up before Lola had a chance to respond again.

Then she phoned Raph on his mobile. Just like with diving, it got easier with practice. This time she was in luck; he must be in court or in a meeting, because she got his voice mail and left a message. The same message: she'd found the missing 'Murder Bird' poem. She knew who killed her mother.

By the time Sam dialled the Wardley number, excitement was swelling inside her. The stalemate was over: now something was sure to happen. The phone rang eight times before Johnny picked it up. 'Sam! How lovely to hear from you!' He sounded almost normal and so friendly that Sam had to remind herself that this was the man who had come into her room at night, hunting for her mother's journal. And then lied about it.

She said, 'Johnny, I've found that poem of my mother's. "The Murder Bird". I know how she died.'

There was a pause, then, 'Where are you, Sam? Are you all right?' His concern sounded genuine. The man was expert at faking concern – he'd had years of practice with Miriam, after all.

'Yes, I'm fine, thanks. And I'm at Gull Cottage.'

'Are you on your own?'

She tensed. Why did he want to know that? Then she asked, 'I want to talk to Miriam now. It's important.'

'Yes, of course, . . . hang on. I'm just taking the phone through now. What are you doing at Gull Cottage? Do you want to come here?' And then his voice became quieter but still distinct as she heard him handing the phone over to his wife. 'It's Sam, Miri. She wants to talk to you. Something about Kirsten's death. See if you can persuade her to come here for a bit. I'm sure it's not good for her being alone.'

And then Miriam was on the other end, with her please-don't-say-anything-troublesome-because-you-know-I'm-not-very-well voice. 'Sam? What's happened?'

'Hi, Miriam.' Automatically, Sam was extra breezy, the way

one is when talking to an invalid. 'I just wanted to let you know. I've found that poem of my mother's, "The Murder Bird". I know how she died.'

Was she imagining it, or had Miriam's voice become a shade more breathless? 'Where did you find it?'

'I found it. That's all that matters. I know.'

She hung up.

She started to dial Diana's number, more to block the incoming calls than because she thought Raph's mother might have been involved in Kirsten's death. She might as well work through to the end of the list.

Diana answered almost at once. 'Good morning? Is that the new driver?' She sounded old and vulnerable and immensely formal.

Sam said, 'Hello, Diana. It's Sam Boswin here.'

There was a brief pause. 'Sam. Yes. Will you be able to drive me?'

'I'm at Gull Cottage.'

A longer pause, before Diana said cautiously, 'It's one of my bridge days. Twice a week, regular as clockwork. But now Craig's broken his arm. It's most inconvenient.'

"Oh. I'm sorry.' Sam steeled herself before saying, 'I've found my mother's poem. "The Murder Bird". I know how she died.'

'It's Emily's day to host the bridge. We all know how Kirsten died, Sam. Didn't you go to the inquest?'

'It wasn't suicide, Diana. And –' She almost believed it herself, now. '– I know who did it.'

'I would have gone to the inquest, but Raph said it was better not to.'

'Sorry to trouble you, Diana. But I had to let you know. Goodbye.'

She hung up. Most probably Diana would think she was insufferably rude and mentally unbalanced. But there was a slender chance that Raph's mother would know exactly why she had phoned.

Sam switched off her mobile. Energy whooshed through her. She should have taken this action ages ago. Already she felt better, and she jogged most of the way to Polwithick with her letters. As she emerged from the post office, just as she was about to shove them into the letter box, she saw a small Fiat pull up outside Judy Saunders' house. The next moment Judy herself, big-boned and tall, her grey hair wild about her face, climbed out.

Sam pushed the letters into the slot, then called out and began running towards the car.

'Sam!' Judy stopped dead in her tracks. She looked startled. 'What on earth are you doing here?'

'Looking for you,' said Sam with a grin.

'For me? Why?'

'Well, first off, I wanted to ask you if I could stay a few nights at Gull Cottage.' A closed expression came over Judy's face at the mention of her cottage, so before she could refuse, Sam went on hurriedly, 'I tried calling you, but as you weren't here I spent last night there anyway. Sort of camping, really.'

'How did you get in?'

'Through a window. Sorry, I just thought you wouldn't mind,' she ended, lamely.

Judy looked as though, on the contrary, she did mind quite a bit, but to Sam's relief she didn't say so right away. Her neighbour, the old woman Sam had spoken to the day before, was already emerging with bored inevitability from her cottage, ready to join in the conversation. Judy threw her a harassed glance before saying, 'Hello, Mrs Pearce. Yes, thank you, I had a lovely time. I'll be over shortly to see you, just as soon as I've had a chance to talk to my friend. It won't be long.' And then to Sam she said, 'You'd better come in.'

The front door led straight into the living room, which was cluttered with furniture, its walls a busy patchwork of Judy's Cornish paintings of cliffs, boats and jugs. Judy closed the door, then pulled back the curtains and opened the window to let in some fresh air.

She said, 'Gull Cottage isn't really habitable any more.' She managed to sound apologetic and defensive at the same time.

'It's fine by me,' said Sam. 'I'd like to spend a few days there on my own. It . . . it felt important.'

Judy threw her a look before saying, 'Coffee? I've just driven down from Bristol and I need a cup.'

'Thanks. Was that a holiday?'

'Not really.' Judy had gone through to the kitchen at the back, but the cottage was small enough so they could still carry on a conversation easily. 'Visiting my brother – mean sod. But better than nothing and I needed a break. Not much of a break, needless to say.' With Judy even the simplest statement sounded grudging.

Sam was looking round the room. There had been a time when Judy had been taken up by a London gallery. Back then, before Kirsten was published, Judy had been the successful one, encouraging Kirsten. Then their fortunes were reversed and their friendship suffered; Judy resented Kirsten's success. So far as Sam knew, she hadn't exhibited in years. She still referred to Kirsten as her 'best friend' but it had become an awkward, difficult friendship. Gull Cottage was Kirsten's main reason for returning to Cornwall.

Sam said, 'I guess all this has been difficult for you. Because of Gull Cottage.'

'Of course it has. But nothing like as bad as it's been for you. I'm glad you're here, anyway. I thought you'd been avoiding me.'

'Why would I do that?'

'You know, because of the cottage.'

'Is it okay me staying there?'

'I wish you'd given me some warning. I could have done a bit of cleaning.'

'Sorry. It was kind of an impulse thing.'

'I'm selling next year.'

'So I heard.'

'I love it, but . . . after what happened. Well, selling it seems like the best thing to do.'

Judy came back, carrying a tray, and set it down on the table. She looked troubled. She patted her grey hair, but it sprang up again at once. 'Sit down,' she said. 'Make yourself comfortable.' She waved irritably towards a chair.

'Thanks,' said Sam. And then, as soon as they were both sitting at the table, and before she lost her nerve, she said, 'I've found Kirsten's poem, "The Murder Bird".' The lie was harder, face to face.

Judy seemed unfazed. 'Powerful, isn't it?'

Sam was watching her expression carefully. 'I know how my mother died,' she said. And then, suddenly realizing what Judy had just said, she drew back. 'You've seen the poem, too?'

'Of course I have.' Judy sounded huffy. 'I *was* your mother's oldest friend, Sam, don't forget. We may have had our differences over the years, but she always valued my opinion.'

'And . . . what did you think of it?'

'To tell you the truth, I couldn't really see why she was making such a fuss about it. She said it would cause a stir, and she wanted it to be the centrepiece of her new collection, though I told her plainly "Sea Holly" was much stronger. Kirsten could be very stubborn about things like that. What did you think?'

'I . . . well, obviously "Sea Holly" is fine. But . . .'

'She said she had to ask you about it. I don't know why. I always thought music was more your thing.'

'She told you she was going to ask me?'

'Yes. She seemed to think people might be offended by it – can't think why, but she must have had her reasons. Poor Kirsten.' Suddenly her face softened. 'God, but I do miss her.'

Judy's heartfelt words would have moved Sam five minutes before. But now, suddenly, the stakes were impossibly high. Sam hesitated. Then casually, as if it were the most normal question in the world, she asked, 'You don't happen to have a copy of the poem, do you? It's just that Trevor and I think there may be another version and we're not sure—'

'Of course,' said Judy. 'She brought it over a couple of days before she died.'

Sam's heart was pounding. 'Can I see it?'

'It's here somewhere.'

Judy leaned back and reached across to a pile of papers on the heavy oak sideboard. She shunted a couple of old newspapers out of the way, and pulled out a yellow folder. Inside were typed pages. As soon as Judy drew them out Sam saw the title of the first one printed neatly across the top of the page. It was 'The Murder Bird'.

CHAPTER 18

Sam sat on the grassy hillside above the cliff. To her right and a little way below she could see the roof of Gull Cottage, the only building in sight. The sea lay ahead, its silvery blue streaked with dark channels where currents of cooler water flowed. A couple of fishing boats were moving near the rocks; buoys marked the spot where the lines of lobster pots had been dropped. Gulls swooped and called overhead. Half a dozen walkers trudged in single file towards the cottage, following the invisible contours of the coast path. The air was sticky-hot.

She'd copied the poem by hand while she was still at Judy's. She had the journal with her always; now, sitting in the warm sunshine, for the first time she had them both. She read the poem through again while she ate her pasty. Already she was getting to know sections of it by heart, especially those phrases she recognized from the journal as Kirsten's thoughts for the poem as it was forming in her mind. However many times Sam read them, those final lines still carried a lethal punch.

The first four stanzas described the encounter between the

thrush and the lizard which she and Kirsten had witnessed that summer afternoon in the abandoned vegetable garden at Wardley. The words brought back the shock of their life and death struggle; she remembered the thrush's beak stabbing and cutting, the lizard's increasingly desperate attempts to defend itself. Worse, the poem forced her to remember her own complicity in the slaughter. She had wanted to interfere, but Kirsten had stopped her. *It's nature's way. It's happening all the time; the only difference was that this time we saw it.* And she had accepted that, and stayed and watched.

With the fifth stanza came the real surprises:

> We watch and do nothing
> to stop the killing –
> beak stabbing belly,
> body hardly breathing
> on a garden path.
>
> A headlight glints in the sun
> as if it was on. Did he see it
> like the glitter of the thrush's eye
> before his lizard-thin limbs
> felt the second strike?
>
> Will there be a third?
> The words curl round the hand
> that lit the fire, round the foot
> on the accelerator. This murder bird
> does not make mistakes.
>
> Is that why I hesitate?

The fishing boats were moving away now, pots raised. Heading back to harbour. Tall cumulus clouds were massing in the west; parts of the sea were blackberry dark. Knees hunched in front of her, Sam surveyed the view, surprised somehow that it was the same one she'd seen that morning when she set out to Polwithick. She felt light-headed, as if she were floating. In this last hour, whole landscapes had changed.

The murder bird had a face now. An elderly, dignified face. Diana's face.

It had to be.

Hers had been the foot on the accelerator when Anthony with his lizard-thin limbs had been killed. And the fire that had killed Diana's husband – that had been no accident, either. Kirsten's poem made it clear that Diana had killed twice. Her own death meant she had killed a third time. This murder bird did not make mistakes.

And Raph had covered for her. What choice did he have? He could hardly turn in his own mother.

A familiar figure was striding across the field towards Gull Cottage: Judy Saunders. What did she want? Nothing Judy had said that morning indicated that she realized the significance of her mother's poem; it was possible, however, that Sam hadn't succeeded in hiding her excitement, and Judy had guessed something was brewing. Sam lay back amongst bracken and long grass: she didn't want to have to deal with Judy right now.

She had to act, and act quickly. As soon as she'd seen Judy leave the cottage and go back along the path towards the village, Sam switched on her mobile phone. It informed her she had

nine missed calls, and that her message box was full. She
punched in Trevor's number. He answered at once.

'Sam, where are you?'

She ignored his question and asked, 'Trevor, have you got a
pen? I've found the "Murder Bird ".'

Trevor whooped with delight, a sound she'd never heard from
him before. 'Brilliant! Brilliant! Where was it? Can you send it to
me? That's fantastic. No, e-mail it – that way I'll get it right away.
My God, this is the best possible news. Where did you find it?'

'Judy Saunders had a copy.'

Trevor swore. Sam could imagine him striking his forehead
with vexation. 'Of course! Why didn't I think of her? Never
mind. I sent the manuscript off two days ago but I'll phone the
publishers now and tell them the good news. This is terrific!'

'I haven't got e-mail down here, but I'll post you a copy, I
promise. But just in case . . . well, just in case anything happens,
I'm going to dictate it to you now.'

'Okay. Hold on . . . damn, why do pens never work when you
need them? That's better. Okay, I'm listening.'

It took longer than Sam had expected to dictate the poem and
while she was doing so, her phone signalled that she was almost
out of credit.

'Those final stanzas – I didn't see those in March.'

'Those were the ones she wanted to check with me before
publishing. She knew it would stir up a storm. I guess she
wanted to know I'd support her. Which I would have done, of
course.'

'A storm? I don't understand. What does it mean?'

'It means,' said Sam carefully, 'that Raph's mother killed

Anthony Johns.' Stunned silence on the other end of the line. Sam carried on, 'Probably Diana killed her husband as well. That fire wasn't an accident. At least, Kirsten didn't think so.' More stunned silence. 'That's why Kirsten said the poem would stir up trouble. And that's why she was murdered. By Diana. Before the poem saw the light of day and she went to the police.'

Trevor was making throat-clearing noises, but still seemed incapable of speech.

It was going to take him a while to get his head around this idea, and Sam couldn't afford precious time nursing him through the transition. So she said, 'You've got the poem now, that's the main thing. I'll call you again later.'

'Yes, but—'

'Sorry, Trevor. Can't talk now.' And she hung up.

Ignoring the missed calls, Sam went straight to the message box. There were three new messages from Mick asking, with increasing urgency, that she get in touch with him and repeating he believed her. Two hours ago that would have meant a lot, but now – well, now everything was changed. Soon, everyone would believe her. She sent him a message telling him to call her and, after less than a minute, he did.

'Mick, hi. Thanks for calling. I'm almost out of credit and—'

He interrupted, the words tumbling out. 'I owe you an apology, Sam. I overheard Raph talking on the phone and you're in danger. Someone is trying to hurt you.'

'Yes, and I know who.'

'You do?'

Sam told him. It was necessary to do a lot of explaining, and she read the poem out twice, but he was less incapacitated by the news than Trevor had been. Whatever he'd heard Raph saying on the phone had obviously prepared him for surprises.

'Wow,' he said, when she was finished. Which seemed a reasonable response. 'I knew there was something. But Raph's mother – that's kind of unexpected.'

Suddenly, Sam could picture him grinning.

'Hey, I've just thought of something. d'you think that was Diana on the bike? The geriatric mugger?'

'She's an old lady, Mick. Not bionic woman. It could have been her driver Craig, though, but she's got plenty of dodgy relations so it wouldn't have been hard for her to get someone else to do her dirty work.'

'What are you going to do now?'

'What Kirsten wanted, of course. I've already made sure the poem will get published. But that will take time. I think I'll post it on the net, so anyone who wants can read it.' She thought for a moment, then said, 'Now all that's left is to go to the police.' That would have been what Kirsten wanted, too.

'Where are you, Sam? I'll come to the police with you. Sometimes it helps to have a legal brain around, and a poem on its own might not be enough to persuade them. I can tell them what I heard Raph saying. Besides, now Diana knows you're on to her, you're even more of a target than before.'

'I know. But Gull Cottage is a three-hour drive from Exeter and it's six from London. And I'm sure none of Diana's relatives live this far down. If I go to the police now, I can make a statement before anyone can stop me. I'll call you when I'm through.'

'Isn't there anyone nearby who can go with you? Just in case.'

'Yes,' said Sam, wondering why she hadn't thought of this before. 'I'll ask my dad.'

Sam had been so absorbed in the poem and talking on the phone, that she hadn't noticed the change that was taking place around her. While she'd been talking to Trevor and Mick, the clouds that had built up over the western headland had turned an ominous pewter, and the temperature had dropped. She stood up and walked down the hill towards Gull Cottage. By the time she got there, a dark tower of cumulus had blotted out the sun.

She phoned Menverren and, as she'd feared, there was no reply. 'I'm at Gull Cottage and I need to go to the police,' she told the impassive answerphone. 'I can explain properly when I see you, but please come and pick me up as soon as you can. It's urgent. Really urgent. Thanks.' She only hoped it would be Davy who checked the messages.

Her phone was out of credit, so she couldn't even call the local taxi service.

Now there was nothing to do but wait.

Large drops of rain were beginning to fall. She made sure the journal and the poem were safely stored in her bag, then pulled on a sweater. What now? There was only one thing left to do. She found a stool, then took her cello from its case and set it in the middle of the floor, and played a few exercises. For the first time in ages, the music wasn't fighting her. Her whole body was responding to the ebb and flow of the notes, as though it was as much an instrument as the cello and bow she held in her arms. She moved effortlessly to the piece she'd

first heard with Kirsten, all those years ago: the Bach G major
Suite that she'd been working on for the Frobisher. And as she
played and the dry ground beyond the threshold darkened with
rain, she remembered Grigory's words during their last lesson:
*sometimes, Sam, when the well is dry, you have to wait for the
rain to fall again,* and she wondered what strange Hungarian
wizardry had made him pick that image. And then, while the
music flowed around and through her, she imagined her
mother listening, and she realized that when she'd been reading 'The Murder Bird' just now on the hillside overlooking the
sea, it had been Kirsten's voice she'd heard saying the words.
The strong, resonant voice that she'd been unable to hear for
weeks. And with the sound of Kirsten's voice in her ears she
was able to engage with the music, in a way that she'd feared
was lost for ever.

Losing herself, she was caught up by the music, and flew.

When she finished playing, she leaned back. So much tension
and emotion, and now it had dropped away, leaving her drained
and complete all at once. Then she looked up and realized that
Davy was standing in the doorway. She had no idea how long
he'd been listening. She set down her bow.

His face warmed into a smile. 'You're good, Sam,' he said.
'Really good.'

'Thanks, Dad.'

He came in. Behind him, the rain was falling steadily, straight
down, running off the gutters, soaking the parched earth.

'I thought you'd gone to London,' he said.

'I didn't want anyone to know where I was.'

'Hiding, are you?'

'Sort of.'

'Well then, what's all this about you being in trouble with the police?'

She stood up and walked towards him.

'It's not me, Dad. It's about Mum.'

'Kirsten?'

She nodded. 'She didn't kill herself, Dad. She was murdered.'

'Oh Sam.' He looked sad for her. 'I know you've thought that, but the inquest—'

'It's different now. I've got proof. I'm taking it to the police.'

'Are you sure?'

'Mum knew, Dad. It's all here, in this poem. She was going to expose someone, and that's why they killed her.'

Something in the certainty with which she spoke must have convinced him. He let out a long sigh, as though he'd been carrying an unresolved burden for months. 'I never thought she'd take her life. That wasn't her way. Kirsten had her faults, God knows, but she was always a fighter.' He put his arms around her shoulders and hugged her. 'Like you, Sam. Everyone doubted but you never gave up on her, did you?'

Sam fought down the tears. She said, 'We've got to make sure her killer doesn't get away with it. All right, Dad?'

'All right, Sam. Who was it, then?'

'I'll tell everything on the way to the police station. They'll have to believe me now.'

CHAPTER 19

Johnny poured himself half a tumbler of neat whisky, then set it down, untouched, on the sideboard. When the ground is opening up under your feet, it's advisable to keep a clear head.

At first he'd thought – hoped – that phone call from Sam had been a joke, or a sign that the poor girl had finally flipped. But one look at Miriam had been enough to tell him that this was horribly, deadly serious.

'What's going on?' he asked. In the background they could hear the workmen stacking the floorboards from the tower, ready for treatment.

'I have to talk to Raph,' Miriam said. She was shaking.

'Can't you talk to me? I am your husband.'

'I have to talk to Raph,' she said again, like a zombie, repeating things by rote.

Just then the phone rang. It was Raph, so she got what she wanted. It sounded to Johnny as if he was doing most of the talking, but when Miriam finally put the phone down, she said, quite calmly, 'Johnny, there's something I have to tell you.'

'Go on, then.'

'It's . . .' She couldn't meet his eye. 'It's about my father's death. I want you to know before . . . before anything happens to my mother.'

He took her hand and sat down beside her on the sofa; as he listened to her story of the two bewildered and frightened children he was filled with an overwhelming desire to help her, imagining what she must have endured on the day her father was killed. 'My poor baby,' he said, embracing her and wondering why she had never told him all this before.

'I didn't want to burden you with it,' she said in a trembling voice. 'Raph and I have lived with it for so long.' He almost believed her.

Sympathy ebbed, turned to disbelief and then revulsion when she progressed to the subject of Anthony's death. His brother had been murdered? He stood up, leaving her sitting alone and upright on the sofa. Her shaking was uncontrollable, now, but he could no more have embraced her than put his hand in a tarantula's cage. Somewhere, far off in another, more normal world, one of the workmen was whistling 'Che Sera Sera'.

'Diana – killed – my – brother?' He choked on the words. 'And you *protected* her?'

Miriam was gazing up at him with those large, flat eyes of hers, trying to win his sympathy, but by now he was only taking in a fraction of what she said. She wanted understanding and forgiveness; worst of all, she wanted assurance of his love. He couldn't even pretend any more. Her need was suffocating him. Blinding him. Her dependence had fogged his vision for far too long, but now, as the fog cleared, he remembered and was sickened. Kirsten had known.

His thoughts flew back to their last meeting, when he'd gone to visit her in March in that rented flat in snowy Connecticut. They'd talked, the way they always did, with easy friendship. And that afternoon in her temporary flat with the late winter snowfall lying thick on the ground outside, she'd confided the story of her failed marriage.

She hadn't intended to. 'This is between me and Raph,' she told him.

'But you still love him?

'I'll always love Raph.'

'So what's the problem?'

'Haven't you guessed, Johnny? Haven't you ever wondered about Diana?'

'Diana?'

'You must've been suspicious. Didn't you ever wonder about Anthony's "accident"?'

'What are you talking about?'

She told him her theory about Diana. It didn't take many words to turn a world upside down. 'You have to admit,' she said, with a wry smile, 'it's a change from the usual problems-with-mother-in-law complaints. Not many people realize their partner's mother goes around killing people.' Johnny was shocked, shocked by what she'd told him and shocked by her light-hearted tone. But her gallows humour was probably the only thing that had got her through the past months.

Diana was the reason their marriage hit the rocks. Kirsten told Johnny she had guessed early on, from one or two remarks that

Raph had let slip, from a phrase that had escaped him during a nightmare, from omissions and silences and a sense of something festering in their family history, that his father's death had not been the accident of the official version; Raph and Miriam had both covered up for their mother with their silence. They'd been so young at the time, Raph six and Miriam only ten or eleven, Kirsten had nothing but compassion for the two bereaved children. They had lost their home and their father in a single day; they were hardly going to risk losing their mother, too.

'Poor kids,' she said, sitting cross-legged on the rug. 'No wonder they grew up with a skewed kind of morality. You know how you always think whatever your parents do is normal? Besides, what could they do about it? They weren't about to turn her in. And, you know, I even felt some sympathy for Diana. It must have been terrible to live with a violent partner back then when no one wanted to know about it. Maybe it was even self-defence.'

'Can you be sure she did it?' Johnny asked. 'It could have been an accident.'

Kirsten stared at him, that calm, clear-eyed stare that was so much a part of her. 'Be honest, Johnny,' she said quietly. 'You've had the same hunch, huh?'

'Well,' he fidgeted. 'I sometimes wondered . . . but murder . . . I never imagined murder.'

'Didn't you?'

He said, mumbling somewhat, 'Accidents do happen.' But even as he spoke, he'd remembered a hundred little oddities that he'd noticed between Miriam and her mother and brother, a hundred little telltale signs he'd chosen to ignore.

Kirsten must have guessed what was going through his mind.

She said gently, 'I kept telling myself their dad's death could have been an accident. But after your brother died, I couldn't kid myself any more. When we got home that night, I was bursting with it. I came right out and asked him straight, "What happened today, Raph? Did Diana run him down deliberately?" Even then, I hoped I was imagining it. People don't just go around mowing people down. Not in my world.'

'Raph admitted it?'

She shook her head. 'Of course not. He denied it, made out that the whole idea was a nonsense, that I was being nuts etc. – but right at the beginning, before he had a chance to get going with the denials, I saw that look in his eye and it told me everything I needed to know. It was all there: guilt, panic, horror. He knew all about it.'

Johnny felt a sudden relief. 'A look in his eye? Is that all? It's hardly going to stand up in court.'

'Doesn't stop it being true, though, does it? Ask Miriam, Johnny, see what she thinks.'

'You think she knows about this?' Johnny was suddenly very cold.

'Sure she does. After all, she was right next to her mother while she was driving. When her father died she was too young to be responsible, but sure as hell she could have spoken up about Anthony.'

'There's no proof,' said Johnny. 'I'd never have taken Wardley if I thought . . .' His voice drifted into silence. They both knew that he would have turned a blind eye to almost anything to get his hands on Wardley.

'It's tough, isn't it?' said Kirsten, her voice suddenly gentle.

'You've no idea how many times I was tempted to let sleeping dogs lie in order to save my marriage. But it was too late for that. We'd opened Pandora's Box and you can't ever close that up again. Pandora's Box turned out to be a can of worms, eh?' They both smiled. 'Raph knew what I thought and it became like this huge mountain between us. Even when I wasn't trying to persuade him to do something about his mother, Raph knew I was thinking about it. Wondering why he couldn't come clean.'

'Did he ever admit to it?'

'No. But he started to have nightmares about fires and cars. And dogs. He said that on the day his father died their dog Chippy had been run over. His father had been out drinking and he passed out on the bed. Which was why he didn't escape from the house when the fire got going. For all I know Diana might have spiked his drink as well. Raph was right next to Anthony when he was knocked down, so he must have seen everything.'

Johnny was pacing up and down while Kirsten continued to sit cross-legged on the rug. He looked out at the snowy landscape, grey clouds heavy with snow, and wondered if Kirsten could be right. At the very least, his brother's death ought to have been investigated. By the proper authorities. Just in case. And so too with the death of Diana's husband. A definite possibility.

But when he was in the plane flying back to England, Kirsten's theory started to seem far-fetched. And by the time he got back to Wardley, his doubts were spiralling. He'd confronted Miriam almost at once, of course he had, but she had laughed at the very idea of her mother causing anyone's death deliberately.

'Oh Johnny!' she had exclaimed, not even taking his suggestion seriously. 'Surely you don't believe what Kirsten tells you! For heaven's sake, the woman's a *poet*. She makes things up for a living. I mean, you know I'm really fond of her, and if there's any chance of her getting back together with Raph then I'll do what I can to help, but really, she's been on her own too much if this is the kind of thing her imagination cooks up. How could you even *think* that my mother would hurt anyone, let alone go around killing them off? Well, really! I don't know whether to laugh or cry. The whole idea is utterly ludicrous. I'm surprised you even bothered mentioning it to me.'

There'd been more, along the same lines. Of course, Johnny could have persisted, but Miriam's version of events had been so much easier to live with. Just think of all the complications that would follow if Kirsten was right: the circumstances of Anthony's death would have to be dredged up again. Besides, once you're back in the familiar routine of your life it's hard to blow everything apart just because someone who is now three thousand miles away has told you nothing is as it seems. Without Miriam's support, what was he supposed to do about it? Go to the police? He didn't have any evidence. Talk to Raph? He'd risk losing his closest friend. Confront Diana? Somehow he couldn't quite picture the scene. He'd drive down to visit her – and then what? Stand in her chintzy drawing room with a glass of sherry in his hand and Bobbo snapping at his shoelaces and say, 'By the way, Diana, you didn't by any chance murder your husband, did you? Oh, and bump off my brother Anthony as well? No? Oh, okay. Just checking.'

She'd come to stay with them at Wardley the weekend after

he got back from the States, and it was impossible to imagine that slim, dignified old lady as someone who had killed, not once but twice. Besides, if Kirsten's interpretation of events was right, then surely someone would have worked it out by now. It didn't have to be up to him. And always, at the back of his mind, was the fear that he'd lose Wardley the moment a question mark was raised over Anthony's death.

Right now, the tumbler of whisky still in his hand, workmen banging in the tower and his wife informing him his brother had been murdered, the only person he blamed, apart from Diana of course, was the contemptible woman, some kind of stranger he happened to have been married to for fifteen years, who was staring up at him with such misery in her eyes it seemed to suck all the air out of the room.

He said coldly, 'I suppose Raph was in on this, too.'

'Raph was just a baby,' she said.

'He wasn't a baby when Anthony died, was he?'

She didn't answer.

'Kirsten . . .' Just when you think you've heard the worst, there's a new shock.

'What about Kirsten?'

Johnny was silent. Oh no, not Kirsten. All the familiar ground was falling away. He didn't want to go there but . . . the steps were plain: Kirsten had known about Diana; Kirsten had been prepared to expose Diana. And now Kirsten was dead.

He drank the whisky. Gripped his empty glass.

'Diana killed Kirsten,' he said.

Miriam stared at him.

'You knew, didn't you?'

She went on staring.

'And Raph was in on it, too.'

She started speaking then, something about wanting to protect Diana, had to do it, knew she'd never hurt anyone again, but he'd stopped listening. The whisky glass left his hand and flew across the room, smashing into a thousand pieces against the wall.

A man in overalls was standing in the doorway. He was just in time to watch the glass shatter. 'Sorry, bad time,' he said. 'I'll come back later, guv.' He smiled awkwardly, then disappeared.

'Damn you, Miriam! Damn you to hell! You knew about Diana, you knew what she was capable of, but when I told you what Kirsten had said you lied and lied and lied! It's your fault she's dead! My God, I'll never forgive you. Never!'

'Johnny, please listen to me.'

'No, Miriam. I'll never listen to you again. I'll never trust you again.'

She crumpled like a child, sobbing, begging him to forgive her, saying that she'd never wanted Kirsten to be hurt, that if she'd thought for a moment . . .

She was contemptible. No, she was beneath contempt. Johnny's righteous anger swept away his guilt at having let Kirsten down when she trusted him with the truth about Diana. His wife was to blame for everything.

He said, 'You and Raph could've stopped Diana. Did you tell him what Kirsten thought? Did you laugh about it together?' And then, as a still more terrible thought occurred to him, 'Did you tell Diana about Kirsten? Did you warn her?'

'No! Of course not! I promise you.'

'Then how in God's name did she find out?'

'I don't know!'

'You're lying again,' said Johnny. But this time it was a statement of fact, stripped of all emotion. He no longer cared that his wife was lying to him, no longer cared that she'd lied to him when he confronted her in the spring and that her lies had led to the death of a woman he'd loved and admired. He no longer even cared that their whole marriage had been, to some extent, a fraud, because Miriam had chosen never to confide in him the single defining fact of her childhood: the real circumstances of her father's death.

And the reason why this certainty was not the tragedy that it ought to have been was because it freed him. Invisible shackles were falling from his spirit. It was years since he'd felt any real affection for Miriam, longer since he'd actually loved her. He couldn't remember what that love had felt like. Apart from a few infidelities – which didn't count because they'd never been a real threat – he'd stayed loyal because that was the kind of person he was. He'd always been aware of her dependence, a dependence which had been more than just her physical frailty, the inability to have children and the crippling headaches. He had known that when she told him he was her whole life, she really meant it. But also he had relied on her, on her ability to manage the practical aspects of his life. Like making sure he got the family home that at one time had meant everything to him. Though if he'd been happier in his marriage, if he'd had a real family to care for instead of the impossible Howeses, he wondered whether Wardley would have been so important. Important enough to make him shut his eyes to murder.

All of which was academic now. His marriage was over in all

but name and if that meant losing Wardley also, well, he found suddenly that he was ready for a new start.

He said, 'Stop crying, Miriam. I'm calling the police.'

'Why?' she asked, looking up at him through tear-filled eyes.

'You know I have to. Before someone else gets hurt.'

'Wait. Don't do anything rash. Think of the publicity, the scandal. Is that what you want?'

'I'm not covering up for your mother.'

'What are you going to tell them?'

'The truth, for Christ's sake.'

'You don't have to tell them everything. Listen, tell them about Kirsten, that'll be enough to stop Diana. But don't tell them about Anthony. We can still keep Wardley.'

'We?'

'Please, I'm begging you. Don't throw everything away. Wait until you've calmed down and you can see things clearly again. There's too much at stake.'

Johnny hesitated. But waiting and considering was exactly what he couldn't afford to do, not this time. Once before he'd thrown away the chance to stop Diana's murderous impulse and he dared not risk it a second time. He had the feeling that if he acted courageously now, he might be able to wipe out some of the guilt of his earlier silence. Miriam knew how much Wardley meant to him; given time, she might still be able to reach him. He said, making it real, 'It's too late for that. Your mother has to be stopped before she hurts someone else. Before she finds out about Sam.'

'Just wait, please.'

'No.'

Miriam let out a long sigh, gave up the fight and leaned back against the sofa cushions. She looked utterly exhausted. 'Very well, Johnny. You're right, of course. We have to protect Sam.'

Miriam he had called her. Not Miri. To him she would never be Miri again. The worst had happened, just as she had always known it would, one day. There was no point trying to achieve the impossible. She must collect herself and face up to this strange new future alone.

He thought she was a frail, weak creature – everyone did – but he'd be surprised how tough she could be when necessary. First things first. She went upstairs to the bathroom where she washed her face and repaired her make-up, then changed into more formal clothes – a plain grey skirt and a navy blue blouse. In her experience, if the outward appearance was correct, it was easier to play whatever role circumstances imposed.

By the time the police car pulled up on the driveway, she was calm again. Cool, calm and very collected.

This was not turning out how Sam had expected. She had imagined more reaction when she and Davy walked into the police station with her revelation – 'I'm here to report a murder.' She'd expected wheels to turn, that there'd be energy and purpose. Instead of which she'd had to wait endlessly while the duty officer took down details of who she was and where she lived, all of which was totally irrelevant in her opinion. Even when she finally got to talk to someone who seemed fairly senior, he just treated it like an informal discussion, friendly and encouraging, yes, but hardly urgent. DS Jenkyns had perfected the art of appearing simultaneously sympathetic and deeply sceptical. Under his detailed questioning Sam felt her story begin to fray at the edges, then come perilously close to disintegrating altogether. Not that she doubted the truth of what she was saying, not for a moment, but she realized they were hardly about to send a police car, sirens flashing, to Exeter, to arrest Diana, drag her screaming off to prison, on the strength of what Sam was telling them. Had Kirsten known this would be the most likely response? Was this the reason she'd opted to make her theory public in a poem?

'So the main evidence you have,' said DS Jenkyns, professionally polite as he'd been since the beginning, 'is a *poem*? Is that correct?' He said the word 'poem' as if it were an item requiring verbal tongs and was definitely not an expected exhibit in a murder enquiry.

'I already told you,' said Sam. 'My mother was planning to use the poem to expose Diana Howes—'

'Who was her mother-in-law,' said DS Jenkyns.

'To expose her mother-in-law, yes. I expect she would have gone to the police as well. That's why Diana murdered her.'

'Because of the poem. I see. And then her son, the barrister Raph Howes, drove down from London and made it look like suicide.'

'Him, or someone else,' said Sam. 'He removed the poem and tore the page out of her journal to look like a suicide note.' She felt sick, the nausea that comes with not being believed. Raph's reputation was another stumbling block. A high-profile barrister from well-respected chambers was hardly the kind of citizen DS Jenkyns expected to pervert the course of justice. Beyond the window of the interview room, the rain which had

begun while Sam was playing the cello at Gull Cottage continued steadily.

'Very well then,' said DS Jenkyns finally. 'If you don't mind
waiting here for a little while, Miss Boswin, I'm going to send
DC Church to take down your statement. She won't be long.'
He stood up.

'Then what happens?' Sam wanted to know. 'Will you talk to
Diana Howes?'

'I expect we'll want to get statements from Mr Howes and
from his sister first,' said DS Jenkyns calmly. 'We may even do
that tomorrow.'

Tomorrow. Or next week. Or maybe never. 'They'll deny it,'
said Sam.

'We'll have to take it one step at a time,' he said. 'Don't
worry, Miss Boswin. The proper procedures will be followed,
you can be sure of that.'

Her heart sank. That meant they'd do it all according to the
book, just to make sure they were covered, and then they'd put
the file away, until – until when? Until Diana struck again? And
guess who her next victim was most likely to be. Damn her
stupid optimism; it had all seemed so straightforward when she
was sitting on the hillside overlooking the sea, when she had the
poem in her hand and Mick on the phone saying he believed
her.

DC Church turned out to be a thickset, earnest young
woman with a heavy fringe and freckles. She was obviously very
junior and definitely unimpressed by the task she'd been given.
It was clear she didn't believe for a moment that the statement
she'd been told to take down was going to result in the opening

of a murder inquiry. She was not about to risk her credibility among her male colleagues by getting a reputation for being gullible. And being interviewed by someone so junior proved Sam's story was not being taken seriously.

It was a bad beginning for both of them. After twenty minutes, Sam was more convinced than ever that this whole exercise was a waste of time. Her thoughts began to spiral. Why had she been so ready to trust Mick? He might have encouraged her to go to the police with her story because he knew all along they'd never believe her. If he was working with Raph, then he was all part of Raph's continuing scheme to protect Diana from the law. And Judy? Why had Judy come to visit her at Gull Cottage so soon after she'd given her the poem? Judy and Raph knew each other, so it was possible that she was somehow involved in all of this, too.

Outside, the rain was falling more heavily, a grey curtain, and bleak. Sam shivered, then realized that DC Church had repeated her last question at least twice.

'Sorry,' said Sam. 'I was thinking of something else. What was it you said?'

DC Church's sigh implied that if Sam couldn't be bothered to pay attention, then she didn't see why she was wasting her time. She said, 'I was asking why you thought your mother wanted to clear matters with you before she published this poem? Isn't that rather unusual?'

Sam, looking into DC Church's impassive eyes, reached the end of her patience. She said briskly, 'Okay. Let's end this now. You don't believe me and nothing is going to happen as a result of this.'

'It won't take much longer.'

'It's not going to take *any* longer,' said Sam firmly. 'I'm off.'

'But we haven't finished.'

'I have.'

'Will you at least sign what you've already said? There might be an issue of wasting police time if you sail off, just like that.'

'All right. Have you got a pen?'

'You've got to read it through before you sign.'

Sam fretted. Already the statement had run to four pages all covered in DC Church's round handwriting. She was just skimming through the third page when the door of the interview room opened and DS Jenkyns reappeared.

The change in him was tangible. Where before all had been torpor and scepticism, now there was energy and purpose.

'Right,' he said. 'How are you getting on, Kate?'

'Miss Boswin is just checking through her statement. But we didn't finish.'

'There didn't seem to be much point,' said Sam. 'Since you don't believe me and aren't going to do anything about it.'

'Is that the impression you got?' asked DS Jenkyns. 'In that case, I owe you an apology. In the last ten minutes I've been contacted by Berkshire police, who have informed me that a Mr Jonathan Johns has been in touch with them. His statement confirms everything you've been telling us, Miss Boswin. And his wife, Mrs Howes's daughter, says the same. It's beginning to look as if we might have a murder inquiry on our hands after all.'

CHAPTER 20

Mick was trying to concentrate on the Grace Hobden papers before the meeting he and Raph had scheduled with her solicitor that afternoon. He wasn't having much luck. The air was hot and sticky and late summer thunder was rolling across the sky. He kept wondering how Sam was getting on with the Cornish police, how Raph would react when he knew what was going on. He was still wondering when Raph returned from court and picked up the messages on his answerphone.

The first three he dealt with in his usual peremptory style. 'Yes, yes', stubby fingers drumming on the desk. 'Stop wittering on and get to the point, for God's sake.'

And then Sam's voice, clear and deliberate, and definitely keeping to the point. 'Raph, are you there? I've found Kirsten's "Murder Bird". I know who killed her. I know who the murder bird is.' Click.

Raph looked intently at the phone for a moment, then nodded, almost as though he'd been expecting it. He looked up and caught Mick's eye, watching him. He frowned. 'You're going to have to cover for me at this afternoon's meeting, Mick. We've been through the main points so you and Alan will be fine.'

'Woah, just a minute. We need you there, Raph,' said Mick. 'You know what we think about pinning everything on self-defence. Alan agrees with me that we need to keep manslaughter with provocation or diminished responsibility as an option – at least we have to keep it in reserve. It's not fair on Grace to drop that option. Self-defence is a long shot; lose, and the poor woman is looking at life.'

'Since when were you paid to have opinions of your own?'

Mick looked at him.

'Okay.' Raph turned away, emptying papers on to the desk. 'I don't have time to argue with you now. You'll have to cancel. Tell Alan we're rescheduling for next week.'

'He's not going to like it.'

'Tough. Something's come up. Family business.'

Mick thought for a moment. He was leaning back in his chair while the hugeness of what was happening to his pupil-master finally hit home. Then, 'If you're planning on damage limitation, then you're too late,' said Mick. 'Sam's talking to the police right now.'

'How the hell do you know?'

'She told me.'

Raph absorbed this. 'How well do you two know each other?'

'To be honest, I don't really know.'

'You know she's deluded, don't you?'

Mick didn't answer.

Raph picked up the phone and dialled quickly. He was frowning. 'Can't you stop him?' he asked the unknown person on the other end of the line. 'No, it's too late for that. Yes, I'm driving down there now. No, there's no need for us both to go. I can handle it. I know. I'm sorry, too. But we can't protect her any longer. Yes, I'll call you. Chin up.' He put down the phone. 'I have to go,' said Raph.

'Are you going to tell me what's going on first?'

Raph registered his change in tone. 'I'll decide about that. You concentrate on this afternoon's meeting.'

Mick stood up. 'You told me to cancel the meeting. I'll tell Alan and get a message to Grace. I'm taking this afternoon off.'

'What the hell—?' Raph stared for a moment, then shrugged. 'I'll deal with you later. Right now, I've got more important things to do.'

'Like warn your mother? Don't you think you ought to be worrying about Sam right now? Isn't she the one who deserves protection? What about some priorities, here? What about—?' His last question was shouted in an empty room.

Mick slammed his fist down on the desk. He'd been expecting Raph to stay to fight, to give an explanation that made sense. Now the full implications of Raph's vanishing act sank in: his pupil-master's mother was about to be accused of murder; Raph was most probably an accessory after the fact, if not actually involved; Mick's pupillage was up the spout; three weeks to go and the chambers he'd gambled his future on was about to be engulfed with scandal.

'Oh, fuck,' he said to the emptiness.

Mick had only been to Cornwall once before, a bucket and spade holiday with his family when he was about ten. He remembered white sand and rocks and a cold wind whipping off the sea. He'd forgotten how long it took to get there.

Before leaving London he left a message on Sam's mobile saying he was coming down. At Exeter, where he stopped for petrol, he phoned again to get instructions to Menverren. This time she answered. She sounded neutral, not surprised or pleased that he was coming, but not actively hostile either. In fact, she sounded numb. It must have been quite a day for her, too; he said he'd be with her in an hour. She told him he'd be lucky.

Two hours later, courtesy of roadworks and an overturned lorry, he was still crawling along the A30 in the pouring rain. It was hard to tell if dusk came earlier in these parts or if it was just the weight of clouds blotting out the light. By the time he reached the turnoff for Menverren his wipers were losing the battle against the rain and he was wishing he'd never come. Why travel all this way to see cactus-bloody-woman? Curiosity? She'd never shown much sign of being the confessing type. Because he wanted to help? Well, he'd tried that before and got his hand bitten off for his pains. Because he fancied her? That was a joke.

It was the need to act, do something – anything – that made him leave chambers just after Raph. Now that he'd made the gesture, and refused to cover for Raph while he charged off, presumably to his mother's rescue, Mick was ready to turn round and drive back to London again.

Menverren was a huddle of small, grey buildings on the edge of rain-grey heathland. It looked like the kind of place where Thomas Hardy would have felt right at home. Mick

wondered if the bleak landscape had given Sam her uncompro-
mising social graces.

And then, as ever, she confounded his expectations. It was a
welcoming Sam who ran through the rain as his car came to a
halt, a Sam who looked as though the burdens of the world had
been lifted from her shoulders. Even, amazing to relate, a grateful Sam.

'This is Mick,' she said, slipping her arm through his and
leading him into a warm kitchen that was crowded with members of a family he'd never even guessed she had. 'He's helped a
lot.'

He grinned at them, feeling about fifteen years old again.
The pressure of Sam's hand on his arm told him why he'd
driven so far.

He slept that night on the couch in the living room, listening
to the rain as it spilled out of the gutters and spattered against
the windows. An autumnal wind was getting up.

'Can I borrow your car?' Sam asked her stepmother the
next morning. 'I'd like to show Mick Gull Cottage.' She turned
to him. 'That is, if you don't have to go straight back to
London.'

'I'm in no hurry,' he said. 'But we can use my car.'

'You don't know the roads.'

'You'll have to navigate, then.'

'Okay.' She grinned.

They drove through winding lanes, steep banks on either
side, which all looked the same to Mick. It was obvious Sam
knew every curve and turning.

'You're different here,' he said. They'd slowed to a crawl behind a massive tractor which was pulling a trailer so wide sections of the hedge were being gouged out.

'It's not *here*,' Sam told him. 'It's *now*. I didn't realize until I found the poem, and people started to believe me, but thinking one thing when everyone else thinks another thing and they all think you're mad for thinking what you think, well, it becomes a kind of madness. Hm. I haven't expressed it very well.'

'Really badly, in fact. But I think I know what you mean.'

'I know you do,' said Sam, looking straight ahead. 'That's why you're here.' She reached over his left arm and jammed her hand on the horn. 'Just look at that maniac! Why does he have to pull that sodding great trailer through these lanes? He's just trying to destroy them.'

Sam glared at the trailer as it turned off into a field.

Then she said, almost casually, 'By the way, Diana's been arrested for murder.'

'How do you know?'

'I phoned the police station this morning when you were talking to my dad. They said she'd been taken in for questioning. But off the record, they said they'd be charging her sometime today. Apparently Raph and Miriam have both backed up what I told them yesterday.'

'They've decided to stop protecting her, then. About bloody time.'

'I guess so. Turn left at the end.'

'Where are we going?'

'Gull Cottage.'

'D'you have a key?'

'I don't need one.'

'Oh, I'd forgotten: Sam Boswin, famous Cornish cat burglar.'

'Yeah. But even you could break into Gull Cottage. It's a cinch.'

'You mean I don't get to watch you shinning up a vertical cliff face?'

'Only after dark.'

'I thought you had sticky pads on your hands and feet.'

She held her palms up for inspection. 'First rule of cello playing,' she told him. 'Always remove sticky pads first.'

But at Gull Cottage her mood changed again. She hardly spoke when she let him in – she was right: he could have climbed in through the ground-floor window she opened, but she went to the front door anyway – and showed him the living room and the kitchen where her mother had spent her last days.

They went upstairs in silence. Looked at the bedrooms. Went into the bathroom. The rain had stopped and sunshine was leaking feebly through the low window on to the wooden floor.

'This is the place?' he asked, feeling clumsy and stupid, but wanting to break through her silence somehow.

She nodded. She was hugging herself. Mick took a step towards her. His instinct was to put his arms round her, offer comfort. But that no longer seemed such a simple gesture of support. He stayed where he was and after a few moments they went downstairs without talking.

Back in the living room he said, 'Let's find a pub. I'll get you some lunch.'

She didn't seem to have heard him. She said, 'My mother loved this place.'

'It must be great in good weather.'

'I was going to come to stay. Two days after she died. She was looking forward to it.'

He waited. Maybe she needed to cry. It was only to be expected.

'I wish you'd known her. You would have liked each other.' She turned to him and her eyes were brimming with tears.

Mick felt as if he was made of stone. 'She must have been a great woman.' It was true, obviously, but it didn't really help anyone much, him saying it now. In fact, it was just a way to keep her at arm's length, and she knew it.

Sam stood quite still for a moment, then walked briskly out through the front door. Maybe the pub idea – and a place where they could joke together again and get away from all this heaviness – appealed to her after all. But she didn't go back to the car. The grass that led to the edge of the cliff was slippery with rain. He followed – for one crazy moment he thought she might be planning to hurl herself over – but she stopped some distance away. Curious, he overtook her and went and stood at the edge. The ground fell away, but it wasn't as dramatic or dangerous as it looked at first; if he stepped over – or fell – gorse and brambles and steep slopes would soon break his fall.

He began windmilling with his arms, as though he was losing his balance, then turned back, grinning.

'Don't!' she shouted. Her face was pale. 'Come away from the edge!'

'Come and get me!' he said, tilting precariously. 'Ooh, er, I'm going to fall.'

'Stop it!' she was almost sobbing. 'Stop it, Mick. I can't help you. I get vertigo.'

He stopped, hearing the raw fear in her voice. 'You do *what?*'

'I get vertigo, you bloody idiot.'

'That's what I thought you said.' He'd come to stand in front of her. 'You climbed up the back of Raph's house and you get *vertigo?*'

'I know. Crazy, eh?'

'Or brave.'

'Not brave enough to stand at the edge here.' She looked sideways, away from him. 'Not that I care what happens to you,' she said.

'Like hell you don't.' He touched the side of her face, and then swiftly, before he had a chance to think what he was doing, he reached down and kissed her. Lightly. Waiting for a well-aimed cactus quill to tell him he'd made a fool of himself.

She said, still not looking at him, 'Why did you do that?'

'I guess I must have felt like it.'

'Hm. So why did you stop?'

'Just pausing.'

The corners of her mouth whiskered upwards in a smile that mirrored his when he kissed her again. Her lips were surprisingly soft.

'Let's skip the pauses, shall we?' she asked, next time he drew back.

'If you insist.'

'Oh, I do.'

After a while, they went back into Gull Cottage. They didn't notice when the rain began again, in earnest.

CHAPTER 21

The tension in Court Number Two was palpable. No one was dropping pins that afternoon, but you could hear every squeak and shuffle of the jurors' shoes as they filed in and resumed their places. Most of them looked fairly stunned at the hugeness of the decision they'd spent two days collectively reaching.

Mick studied their faces, hunting for an indication of what their verdict was going to be. The woman with the straggly hair, whom he'd marked down as most hostile to Grace Hobden throughout, had an unusually soft expression around the mouth and eyes. Did that mean she'd got her way, and they'd agreed on conviction, or that she'd been won over by the arguments of the others and now saw the accused in a more forgiving light? Impossible to tell. The tension had finally got to him; he was almost forgetting to breathe.

Beside him, Raph sat impassive as a buddha. Given the storms he'd survived over the past six weeks, the man's self-control, on this and other occasions, was remarkable.

Diana Howes had been charged on two counts of murder.

Bail was refused, so for over six weeks she'd had to suffer the horror of a remand wing. From one or two remarks that Raph had dropped, it sounded as if she was disintegrating under the shock. She denied everything, said she couldn't understand what she was doing there and was frequently sedated. Sometimes she thought she was still at home. Occasionally Mick wondered if Raph was encouraging this picture of the pathetically senile old lady: the Pinochet defence had worked in the past and might well prove to be his mother's best chance of ending her days in freedom.

When news of her arrest became public, Raph had instantly offered to resign from chambers; his personal tragedy must not turn into a scandal for his colleagues. They suggested that he take six months off. Wait and see, lie low, play it by ear. Raph refused: he fully intended to resign, but if they wanted him to remain – and he was the highest earner in chambers, as everyone knew – then he would insist on continuing to work and expected their total support. Either he was a liability, or he was an asset, was the way he saw it. He'd quit or he'd carry on, but he wasn't going to sit idly kicking his heels waiting for others to decide his fate. Dermot had quiet words with several of the senior barristers. Raph's work continued without interruption.

He had more energy and relish for a fight than ever. Mick had been impressed by the way Raph had gambled with his own future, but to gamble with Grace Hobden's was different. Against all accepted practice, Raph insisted on staking everything on the murder charge, pleading lawful homicide. To allow even the possibility of manslaughter because of provocation or diminished responsibility would play into the hands of the prosecution. Mick, who now had a tenancy in chambers, had argued long and hard, but Raph wouldn't budge. So now, as the jury returned, Grace could expect either a life sentence or freedom. There was to be no middle ground. Mick guessed that this was how Raph like to play things.

Mick's criticism of Raph had been allayed to some extent by the brilliance of his summing up. He had decided against portraying Grace as a victim, brutalised by her husband, who'd snapped after years of abuse. Nor had she, according to Raph, acted when the balance of her mind was disturbed. No, when Grace had plunged the knife into the heart of her sleeping husband, it had been an entirely rational act, compelled by the harsh logic of her situation – hers and that of her children. Consider the circumstances she found herself in: she was expecting another man's child; she was preparing to leave a violent man for a kindly one. But Paul Hobden had let her know on several occasions that if she ever left him, it would be the last thing she did. He'd cut out stories from the newspaper about men who'd killed their wives and children – and then themselves – and stuck them to the fridge. Using – and this detail had produced a visible frisson in some members of the jury – a set of Teletubbies fridge magnets to display those blurred and heart-rending photographs of families that had been wiped out.

By Easter, as her pregnancy was starting to show, Grace was facing an impossible dilemma. She could stay with Paul Hobden, or she could leave him, taking the children with her. Either way, she was risking not only her own death but those of her three innocent children as well. (Raph had slipped up at this point, talking about Grace's *two* innocent children – Mick scribbled him a note and he corrected his error instantly.) Even if there had been only a 20 per cent chance of Paul Hobden carrying out his terrible threat – and Grace was clear in her own mind that the odds were much higher – what mother will allow that kind of death sentence to hang over the lives of her children?

Grace took the only step available that was guaranteed to safeguard their future. She knew that by doing so she was almost certainly sacrificing her freedom, but in her opinion it was what she had to do to give her children the chance of life. Raph asked them, 'If an armed raider had broken into her home and threatened not just her own life, but the lives of the three people who meant more to her than all the world, and she saw the chance to save them and took it, would she stand in front of you accused of murder today? No! A hundred times no! We'd be applauding her for her courage and swift thinking. Paul Hobden was that armed raider, ladies and gentlemen of the jury. If Grace had not acted as she did, then it is likely that by now we'd be lamenting the deaths of not just Grace but of Angus, Matthew and Susan – who, by the way, had her fourth birthday last week – as well. Given that choice, that impossible choice, what else could she do? Ladies and gentlemen of the jury, Grace Hobden does not deserve our pity or our scorn. Still less does she deserve the crazed punishment of an unjust law. Grace Hobden, ladies and gentlemen, deserves our respect and praise. She deserves admiration and honour. She deserves, above all, the freedom to return to those children for whom she was prepared to sacrifice everything that makes life worth living.'

Raph's summing up had made the front page of several papers. It would have hit the headlines anyway, even if his mother hadn't been on remand for murder. Luckily, none of the papers had so far drawn any parallels between Paul Hobden's death and that of Raph's father, since Diana was only being accused of the murders of Kirsten and Anthony. Maybe after *The Murder Bird and Other Poems* was published in the spring the situation might change. Mick didn't know if Raph's impassioned defence of Grace Hobden linked back to the circumstances of his father's death, and he wasn't about to ask. Maybe when he'd been in Raph's chambers for about fifty years that would be a possibility. But not now.

A door to the rear of the courtroom was opened and Grace walked in, a sturdy warder on each side. She looked remarkably composed for someone who was both pregnant and most probably going to receive a life sentence in about three minutes' time; maybe she had already accepted her fate. Her broad, stolid face looked almost bovine. Just as well; she was likely to need every ounce of stoicism in the years ahead.

The judge peered over her gold-rimmed glasses at the jurors.

'Members of the jury, have you reached your verdict?'

The foreman, a thin man with a tendency to smile at all the wrong moments, stood up. 'We have, your honour.'

'On count one alleging murder, how do you find the defendant, guilty or not guilty?'

The foreman hesitated. He grinned, then recollected himself and looked down at the sheet of paper in his hand. It was fluttering, like a bird, trying to break free.

'Not guilty.'

Silence.

The judge looked startled. Then she turned to Grace, who was still staring straight ahead, as though waiting to hear what else the foreman might have to say. The judge said, 'In that case, Grace Hobden, you are free to go. The court is—'

The end of her statement was drowned out by an explosion of noise from the public gallery. 'No! Murderer! She killed my brother!' And then, louder and more frantic as the ushers grabbed the speaker by the arms to hustle him out, 'The fucking cow! Hanging's too good for her! What about my brother? She killed my brother! She can't get away with this!'

A small group of women who had attended each day of the trial broke into a cheer. Still shouting, Don Hobden was manhandled from the court. They could hear his voice getting fainter as he was escorted down the corridor towards the stairs and the exit. The women's cheering died down. The court seemed quieter than ever.

'What do we do now?' whispered Mick.

'Congratulate our client, of course,' said Raph.

Grace Hobden had turned away at the first sign of unrest, expecting to be led back to the cells as had happened on the only previous occasion when the court had been cleared. But the warders had melted away and she was left standing uncertainly on her own. Raph strode over.

'Well done, Grace,' said Raph, extending his hand. 'We did it.'

'We have?'

'You're free. Acquitted. Not guilty,' said Raph.

Mick added, 'You can go home now.'

'Oh,' she said, in a voice hardly more than a whisper. And then, as though he'd just handed her a small gift, 'Thank you so much, Mr Howes.'

The sense of anticlimax was making Mick feel irritated. Perhaps to compensate, he grinned and extended his hand. 'Congratulations, Grace. I'm sure it was your testimony that won them over.'

'Do you think so?' she asked.

'Oh, absolutely,' said Mick heartily, wondering why the hell she couldn't at least crack a smile. Her hand, briefly folded in his, was limp.

'What happens now?' she asked Raph.

'We go back to my chambers,' he told her. 'You're in for a bit of a shock when you step outside. Some of the public will feel strongly about the verdict.'

'Oh?'

'This case has had more than its fair share of publicity,' he told her. 'And not all of it's because of you. I'll explain later. There's a car waiting, but we'll have to get through the press vultures first. Don't worry. I'll make a brief statement, and Mick will get you to the car.'

'All right,' she nodded. Trusting as a child. Mick had the feeling Raph could have told her that all they had to do now was hold hands and jump out of the third-floor windows, and she would have complied without question. He wondered how Raph was proposing to tell her that it wasn't the notoriety of Paul Hobden's murder that had attracted the publicity, so much as the fact that during the trial her defence counsel's mother had been charged with not one, but two murders. They had debated whether to tell her, but Raph figured Grace was in no state to take in that kind of information

'I'll go out first,' Raph told Mick as they reached the entrance, 'and deal with the journos. Grace can stand with me for a minute – you won't have to speak at all, Grace – and then as soon as we're done, get her to the car.'

The moment Raph pushed open the door, a barrage of flash-lights blinded them. As Raph had surely known, the journalists and TV crews were more interested in him than his client. He paused, smiling, and held up his hand. 'My client wishes to thank you all for your concern,' he began, ignoring the questions which were flying at him from all sides about his mother's case. 'As you can imagine, the events of the past months have been extremely difficult for Mrs Hobden and for her family. The consequences of that terrible day will be with her for the rest of her life, but for now, she is grateful that her long ordeal is nearly over and her only concern is to be reunited with her children again as soon as possible. She requests only that they be granted privacy so they can start to rebuild their lives. Thank you.'

'Let's go,' said Mick, taking Grace by the arm; together they walked briskly down the steps.

More cameras flashing; more shouted questions. Hello, fifteen seconds of fame, and goodbye, thought Mick as the photographers and journalists jostled to talk to them. But most were concentrating on Raph, the big fish, and Mick had little difficulty getting Grace safely into the waiting car.

Raph joined them a couple of minutes later, slamming the door behind him, and their car sped off through the rain-swept streets.

Back at chambers, Raph offered Grace brandy, which she turned down, and tea, which she accepted. While they were waiting in one of the interview rooms for Corinna to make the tea, Raph asked Grace if she wanted to phone her children now and tell them the good news.

She raised her eyes to look at him, as though this idea had never even occurred to her. 'May I?' she asked.

'Of course,' he said, handing her the phone.

Her hands were shaking as she pressed the first two numbers. She misdialled, then tried again. After the third failed attempt, she passed the handset back to Raph and said, 'Would you mind dialling the number for me, please? I don't seem able to manage.'

Her eyes were brimming with tears.

Raph checked the number, then dialled swiftly. As soon as it was ringing, he handed it to Grace. 'We'll leave you,' he said. 'I expect you want some privacy.'

'Thank you,' she whispered.

Mick stood up to follow Raph. As they reached the door, Mick heard her say, 'Angus, this is Mummy. Yes, darling, it's over, and . . . well, everything's going to be all right. I don't have to stay in prison, darling. I'm free and . . . I'm coming home.' She broke down and sobbed.

Raph and Mick walked down the corridor to their room.

'Brandy, I think,' said Raph, reaching into the cupboard behind his desk. 'A job well done.'

Mick said simply, 'Well, she got away with it. That's good.'

Raph showed no surprise at his choice of language. He looked at his watch and said, 'Once our Mrs H is on her way back to her children, d'you want to come out for a drink?'

An invitation from Raph, especially at a time like this, was not to be turned down lightly, but Mick said, 'Any other time, I'd love to, but if I leave now, I can catch the end of today's Frobisher.'

Raph smiled. Since September, he'd adopted a benign interest in the romance between his former stepdaughter and his former pupil. 'I'd almost forgotten the Frobisher. Wish Sam luck from me, will you? Though from what you say, she doesn't need luck.'

'Luck's always useful.'

'It's the final section tomorrow, isn't it? Saturday – I should be able to come along to that.'

'Her father's coming up from Cornwall.'

'Is he now? The entire Sam Boswin support team. Well, she deserves it. Off you go, then, Mick. I'll wind things up here.'

Mick loosened his tie. Anxious though he was to get over to the Frobisher, it felt wrong, after so much work, just to leave without any celebration of their success. 'Congratulations, Raph,' he said. 'I was totally against gambling everything on self-defence, but you did it. You must be very pleased.'

Raph cradled his brandy. 'You'd think so, wouldn't you? But one is always left with a strange sense of anticlimax, I find. More so with winning than with losing, which is odd. I don't understand it myself. But I've got used to it.'

'Well. Well done all the same.'

'Thank you, Mick. Now, bugger off and look after Sam. She needs you more than I do right now.'

Mick ran.

*

An hour later, Raph walked up the steps to his house. There were a couple of photographers to capture this unremarkable activity on camera, but their presence had become almost routine since Diana's arrest the previous month. He wouldn't have said he was used to it, exactly, but it didn't bother him the way it did when the news first broke: Mother of leading barrister is murder suspect. It was a good story, obviously, full of human interest and drama. 'The Proof's in the Poem' was one of the more inventive headlines. 'Famous writer murdered. Suicide was faked.' For a few days, the story got wide coverage. Now it was being kept alive because of the Grace Hobden case and Sam's entry in the Frobisher. It would flare up again when Kirsten's book was published. As a story it would never die away entirely. Every time Raph or Sam or any member of their circle did anything remotely newsworthy the 'facts' would be replayed with varying degrees of accuracy, while poor Diana languished – and for once the cliché was entirely appropriate – in some bleak women's prison.

The fact of her incarceration was like a stone lodged in his heart: there was nothing he could do to shift it. That she deserved to be punished was neither here nor there. She was his mother and he hated to see her suffer.

As soon as he had received Sam's call about 'The Murder Bird', he had known the chances of keeping Diana out of prison were evaporating. He hardened his heart, and forced himself to remain detached. He hired the best defence team; he kept on the case; he guided her every move, so far as he was able. It wasn't enough. It would never be enough.

There were beneficiaries, though, to this tragedy, even though he wasn't one of them. Kirsten's publishers were rushing through production of *The Murder Bird and Other Poems* with a speed unheard of in poetry publishing. A poem that had exposed one murder and precipitated another would have been widely read even if it had been doggerel. 'The Murder Bird' was anything but doggerel and it looked as though Kirsten's work was finally going to reach the audience it deserved. When Trevor Clay phoned to offer Raph sympathy for what was happening to Diana, he couldn't keep the excitement out of his voice: it wasn't often that a book of poems was a bestseller, but the publishers were talking about an initial print run of 20,000. And that was just in the UK.

Sam's career was similarly affected. Even if she didn't win the Frobisher outright, agents and producers were jostling to sign her up. Because of Kirsten's tragedy and Diana's notoriety, Sam's name would be recognizable to an audience who didn't usually listen to cello music. The fact that she was young and talented and photogenic didn't hurt either.

Raph paused on the top step, his key ready to press into the lock. The rain had stopped but the ground was damp, a scent of wet tarmac and earth. He'd take Lola out for a meal this evening. Life with him must have been difficult these past weeks. He'd make it up to her now.

As soon as he stepped over the threshold into the hall, he registered the change. It wasn't just the two large suitcases parked at the foot of the stairs or the unaccustomed silence.

'Lola?' he asked the quiet air, and then, more loudly, 'Lola!'

A moment later, she walked slowly down the stairs. She was wearing jeans and a black sweater, her suede jacket was slung over one arm and she gripped a small suitcase in her hand.

He watched as she continued down the stairs, her speed decreasing with every step.

'What's this?' he asked.

Her gaze was unflinching. 'What it looks like, Raph. Sorry. There's no easy way to say this but . . . I'm leaving.'

'Ah,' he said. And then, because that didn't seem enough of a response, he added, 'Why?'

She fiddled with her hair. 'I . . . I've met someone else. He's called Martin and you haven't met him. He's coming to pick me up in—' She glanced at her watch. 'Well, he's late. I was going to leave you a letter.'

'A letter?'

'Just a note, really. I've got it here. D'you want to read it?'

'Not particularly.' Raph was still adjusting to this latest turn of the wheel. 'I'd rather hear it from you.'

'Yeah, I reckon I owe you that much.'

'Is it because of . . . what's happened?'

'Well, yes. Obviously. But also, no. I mean, if it was just your mother being in prison, I'd stick by you. And it's not Martin either. He's just an excuse, but don't tell him I said that.'

'What, then?'

She hesitated, debating whether to fob him off with an easy excuse, then sighed and said, 'I've realized, this last week or two, what I guess I kind of thought from the beginning, only it didn't seem to matter so much then. But it does now. I wasn't ever really a part of your life, Raph. You shut me out. You never talked about anything that mattered, not really.'

'We already discussed that. I explained to you about my mother. How we'd always covered up for her. I told you, when my father died I was too young to understand what was going on. I trusted my mother and I trusted Miriam. I knew something bad had happened, but it wasn't until I was grown up that I really understood. And I never knew that she'd killed anyone else. I thought Anthony's death was an accident. Kirsten's seemed like suicide. It was Miriam who went down and found the note. I would have told you about my father, in time. How he died. These things aren't exactly easy to discuss, you know.'

'Yeah, I know.' Lola fiddled with her hair a bit longer, then said, 'Trouble is, Raphie, I don't believe you.'

'What?'

She shrugged. 'It's okay. I won't tell anyone. There's nothing to tell, really. It's just a hunch. But all that time you were telling me about your mother after Miriam went to the police, and you were making out like it was this huge confession and all, well, it just didn't ring true, somehow. I felt further away from you than I'd ever felt before. I think there's still loads of stuff you're not telling me. But it doesn't matter now, because I'm moving on.'

'I see.'

'It's kind of hard to say this, but I think we've just been using each other. Which is fair enough, I suppose. And now it's stopped.'

'I see,' said Raph again. He wondered if she wanted him to deny it, whether he was supposed to put up more of a fight. He knew that it would be unkind to show her how unemotional he felt, and he had no wish to be unkind. Lola had been a good diversion, when he'd needed one, and her timing now was just about impeccable.

They were both relieved to hear the sound of a car pulling to a halt in front of the house.

'That'll be Martin,' said Lola, superfluously.

'Do you mind if I don't meet him?' asked Raph. 'You'll let me know where you are, won't you? In case you've left anything. And because of post, that kind of thing.'

'I'll call you,' she said.

Raph put his hands on her shoulders and touched her cheek briefly with his own. It was like touching a stranger.

She said, 'Take care of yourself, Raph.' She was choking up. She must have been really quite fond of him, after all. Raph wished he could put on a similar display.

He said, forcing the words out, 'I'll miss you, Lola.'

She didn't answer. Maybe she knew that was a lie, too. He'd probably underestimated her all along. He'd needed her to be simple and uncomplicated, and had refused to see anything that didn't fit the fantasy.

He turned and went through the drawing room to his study. From there, the sound of the front door closing was hardly audible, and the noise of Martin's car pulling away was indistinguishable from the noise of all the other traffic on the road.

But the silence in the house, now that he was alone, really alone, was profound in a new kind of way.

He went to his desk, pulled open the third drawer and pulled out the gun he always kept there. His Walther, a present from a grateful villain, years before. Kirsten had found it once and asked him if he was really that bothered about burglars. He'd tried to make light of it and cracked some joke about being paranoid, and maybe she'd believed him. Or maybe she'd known, even then, that the only person he'd ever consider using it on was himself. It was his insurance policy, like the cyanide capsules operatives were given before being parachuted behind enemy lines. He put it back. No need of it yet, even though, already, a faint smell of burning hung in the air.

At the back of the same drawer, from under a folder of bank statements, he pulled out the framed photographs of Kirsten he'd put away when Lola moved in. He moved a few items on his desk and placed the photographs where he could look at them. There was Kirsten on her own, smiling that big smile that had first made him fall in love with her. There was the photograph of him and Kirsten in that restaurant in Barcelona when they'd gone away for a weekend soon after they first got together. And there was the photograph which Miriam had taken after their wedding, the picture in which both of them looked quite ridiculously pleased with themselves. Like cats that had found the cream. Or two people who'd fallen in love and intended to be together for ever.

Regrets crowded in, thick as flies. He had only himself to blame for the collapse of their marriage. Kirsten had realized right away that Anthony's death wasn't the accident he and Miriam and Diana all said it was. Being a clear-sighted woman who hadn't grown up in a jungle of lies and silences, she'd thought the only option was to expose Diana and let justice take its course. She couldn't understand why he, a barrister, was determined to subvert the law. It didn't take her all that long, either, to figure out that this wasn't the first time it had happened, to ask questions about his father's death. Putting two and two together, she had made four – or a close enough approximation, anyway.

Close enough to be dangerous.

He had, of course, done everything in his power to throw her off the scent. He should have known that was impossible; his silence and obstruction created the gulf which opened up between them. He'd never thought he had any choice about protecting his mother: it was just something he had to do. But now she was exposed anyway, an old lady banged up with common criminals; the press were camped on his doorstep; the whole family was subjected to the scrutiny not just of the law, but of public opinion as well. Everything he'd most feared was happening, but none of it turned out to be as difficult to bear as the loss of Kirsten. He should have sacrificed Diana when it would have meant he could still salvage his marriage. Now, it was difficult to remember what he'd been so afraid of. Exposure wasn't so very hard, after all – not nearly as hard as facing the rest of his life without Kirsten.

Worse still was the knowledge that by refusing to allow Diana's exposure after Anthony's death, as Kirsten had wanted, he had, in effect, signed his wife's death warrant.

Maybe, when that knowledge became intolerable, he'd come and find the gun.

Autumnal rain was falling in the garden and it was growing dark when Miriam found him.

He was still sitting at his desk.

'How did you get in?' he asked.

'Lola called earlier.'

'She told you?'

Miriam nodded. She said, 'Johnny's leaving me, Raph. He's going away next week and he won't tell me where. He wants to sell Wardley.'

She put her hand on his shoulder and he leaned over so his cheek brushed her fingers. 'Poor Miri,' he said. 'That's tough.'

'Yes,' she said.

'So what do we do now?'

'Carry on, I suppose. The best we can. Just like we've always done.'

'Do you think we can?'

'I'm sure we can. It'll be all right again, Raph. Just wait and see.'

Raph wanted to believe her. But he was beginning to wonder if now, after all that had happened, it was already too late.

CHAPTER 22

Sam walked out on to the stage. Her long black dress was tight around her bust and waist, then floated down to just above her thin heels. She'd let her hair grow since the summer; dark wispy curls were feathering her neck. Her shoulders were bare, but she wasn't cold. She was so keyed up she could have walked out into a blizzard and not noticed.

The applause took a long time to die down. If she'd been aware of these things, Sam would have known that she was a popular candidate, and favourite to win. As she set her cello down, Herman Schreiber, who was to conduct the Dvorak, caught hold of her left hand and gave it a squeeze of encouragement. Behind him the leader of the second violins caught her eye and grinned.

Sam had been preparing herself for this moment for days – in some sense, for years – ever since she'd learned that she was through to the final six, but even so, the experience of settling down between orchestra and audience was overwhelming. This was going to be a musical journey utterly different from the

times she'd played this with Nadira valiantly attempting to
reproduce the entire orchestra on the piano. Take your time, she
heard Grigory's words in her head. This is your big moment.
Enjoy it.

He was there, of course. As Herman Schreiber raised his
baton, a single glance was enough to take in the familiar faces
looking up from the front rows. Grigory was frowning; he
was almost as nervous about this performance as she was. Her
time with him was almost at an end; she was ready to move
on to another teacher, perhaps in Europe. Sam wasn't the
only person whose reputation was on trial over the next half
hour. She had to demonstrate that Grigory had taught her
well.

Nadira was sitting beside him. Her presence there meant
more to Sam than anyone else's; she would have pulled out of
the Frobisher altogether if it hadn't been for her. The public
attention after Diana's arrest had taken her completely by surprise; she would have gone into hiding and stayed there. But the
Frobisher was in three parts: unaccompanied cello, cello and
piano, and, for the final six, a concerto.

'You know I can't do it without you to accompany me,' Sam
had told her, shamelessly blackmailing, and then, just in case
she hadn't exerted enough pressure already, she went on, 'We've
got this far together. You can't abandon me now.' The thought
that her own dramas had meant the end of her friend's dream
was intolerable.

'Oh, can't I?' Nadira had demanded, half laughing and half
aggrieved. 'While you're at it, why don't you just put a gun to
my head and threaten to shoot me?' But she had arrived in

London two weeks before the first stages of the Frobisher were due to start. Sam could guess how much family pressure she'd had to confront in order to return to the wicked city, but looking at her now, her face radiant with enthusiasm, she was sure it had been worth it.

Davy drove up from Cornwall the day before and he wasn't alone. Linda and the boys had come up, too. The previous evening they'd all gone on the London Eye together, Nadira and Mick joining them. They'd had ice creams and watched a storm travel from the south-west to the Hampstead hills. A proper family outing.

One person Sam had not expected to see at the Frobisher was Judy Saunders, but there she was, looking just as grudging and uncomfortable as ever, but still, rooting for her in her own way. Judy was getting a lot of mileage out of her role as custodian of the missing poem. There'd been interviews, and Sam had overheard her when they'd all met up in the bar after the solo section asking Trevor if he could find her an agent as she was writing a book about her friendship with Kirsten.

Trevor wasn't there. He'd attended the first two sections and Sam had got him a ticket for this performance, but at the last moment he cried off, saying the tension was too much. He told her he'd listen to a recording of it later, when the result of the competition was known. As always, the immediacy of experience was something he preferred to avoid.

Mick was sitting away from the others and a little to one side. He looked as though his mind was not entirely on the concert that was about to begin. Sam was careful not to catch his eye. She knew what was distracting him and, right now, she didn't want to think about it. There'd been a coolness between them ever since she'd told him, the previous evening, that Raph had asked her if she minded him coming to the final day of the competition.

'You said *yes?*'

'I told him I didn't mind either way.'

'But you *must* mind!' Mick was incredulous. 'How can you not mind? After what he did? After what he didn't do?'

'So? You still work with him, don't you?'

'That's different. It's my career. It's not personal.'

Sam had tried before to explain to Mick her ambivalence towards Raph. Yes, he had covered up for his mother – but how did she know she wouldn't have done the same in his shoes? And in some ways she thought that he had been a victim of Diana almost as much as Kirsten had been. She didn't feel sorry for him, exactly; what she felt was not clear cut at all.

'Why does he have to come anyway?' Mick wanted to know.

'Ask him. He's always supported me. I'd probably never even have got to the Frobisher if it hadn't been for him.'

'Bollocks. You've done well because you're brilliant. Nothing to do with him. And this is all part of him trying to brazen out the scandal round his mother. It's for his own public image, not because he cares about helping you.'

'Maybe. But it's too late now, anyway. I told him he could come.'

She would have preferred it if he'd stayed away. For one thing, if the Howeses were absent, Johnny would certainly have come and she missed his cheerful, encouraging presence. But Miriam, who followed her younger brother like a shadow these days, was sitting beside him, and where Miriam went, Johnny was careful to stay away.

Raph and Miriam were sitting slightly to one side. Notoriety had affected them both, making it seem as though they were permanently apart from everyone else. Raph trying too hard; Miriam not trying at all.

One person was missing: one face among all the others that Sam would have wanted to see as she lifted her bow to start playing. But then, Kirsten would always be an absence, whenever and wherever Sam was performing.

Herman Schreiber raised his baton and the orchestra played the first few bars. Sam closed her eyes briefly to shut out the everyday world and the horrors of the past weeks. She shook back her hair, flexed her shoulders and lifted the bow, poised to strike the first note.

At once audience and judges vanished from her mind. As did the endless worries about Diana and Kirsten, Mick and Raph and everyone else. All that existed was the present. There was no past and no future, no people or conflicts or grief, only this soaring music. Starting to play was like stepping into an alien landscape, where everything was newly minted and yet utterly familiar, a world without words but filled with colour and scent and texture.

Mick was having trouble concentrating. Sam had avoided him all day; he knew why, but still, it hurt. She needed to focus all her energies on the music and didn't want to be distracted by his worries and doubts. And her focus was paying off. He didn't know much about music, but it was obvious she had the audience eating out of her musical hand.

Not surprising, either. It wasn't just that she played like a dream, or that she looked young and beautiful on the stage in that amazing black dress – though obviously those things were important – but it was now impossible to dissociate Sam from her story. Even before she played a note she was known to the audience as the daughter of Kirsten Waller, the famous poet who had been brutally murdered in a lonely Cornish cottage. The young woman now conjuring magic from bow and cello had stubbornly refused to accept the official verdict; her persistence had paid off: the killer had been caught.

If only, Mick thought, it was that simple.

He'd tried talking to her about it ten days ago.

'I'm probably way out of line, here,' he'd said, bringing coffee and getting back into bed with her in her crowded Clapham bedroom. He'd kept his own place, but more often than not he spent the weekends with her. It was more convenient, since her music was there. 'Something's been bothering me ever since Diana got arrested.'

'Can't it wait?' asked Sam, yawning and leaning over on to one elbow.

'I'm not sure that it can.'

'Tell me, then,' she said, but he could tell she was only half attending. Since Nadira had returned and she'd committed to the competition, she'd plunged back in the world she knew and loved, the world of music-making. It was as though the time she'd spent away from it, while she struggled with the problem of her mother's death, had only made her appreciation of it stronger, now that she had returned.

He said, 'Kirsten knew her killer, right?'

'Of course she knew her. Diana was her mother-in-law.'

'And she trusted her as well. After all, when her killer was in the house she ran a bath in a room that had no lock.'

Sam nodded. 'There were never any locks at Gull Cottage. Not until Judy closed it up. You knew that.'

'So why would Kirsten have exposed herself to Diana? She thought Diana was a killer, the murder bird. She was going to publish the fact. Don't you think she might have been – well, at the very least, a bit wary of her? I mean, you don't take off all your clothes and get into the bath when someone you know to be a killer, and whom you intend to expose, is in the house with you. Do you?'

'But that's what happened. We know it did. Or maybe Diana pretended to leave, then came back.'

'Or maybe Diana didn't do it.'

Silence, then, 'That's ridiculous.' Sam laughed. 'We know she did. She killed her husband; she killed Anthony Johns, and then she killed my mother. The woman is a cold-blooded murderer, Mick.'

'But six weeks ago everyone "knew" that your mother committed suicide. And that was wrong.'

'Yes, because Diana killed her.'

'But just suppose it wasn't her.'

Sam thought for a few moments before saying, 'Who else could have done it?'

'That's what I'm wondering.'

'Oh, this is ridiculous. Of course it was Diana. No one chooses to go to prison for something they haven't done.'

'Maybe Raph told her she wouldn't have to stay in prison. That she'd get a suspended sentence.'

'Why would he do that?' Sam frowned. 'Besides, Diana's in the poem.'

'But what if your mother got it wrong?'

'Then why was she killed? It doesn't add up, Mick. Sorry.'

It didn't add up. They were agreed on that much. He'd left it there, but still his doubt remained, a small, niggling worry at the back of his mind.

He tried to dismiss it, concentrate on the music.

So far as he could tell, from his position in the second row along from Raph and Miriam, Sam was doing well. She'd pointed out the judges and their expressions told him they were enjoying every moment. Gauging music judges, he decided, wasn't that different from analysing juries.

He smiled, and was just beginning to relax, when he happened to glance along the row to where Raph was sitting. Mick's first thought was that he'd had a stroke. His face was no longer turned towards the stage but was grey and inward-looking. Suddenly Mick was reminded of the time he'd overheard Raph talking on the phone, that strangely vulnerable man, so different from the public figure.

In the silence that preceded the final movement, Miriam also noticed the change in her brother.

She leaned towards him and asked in a low voice, 'Raph, are you all right?'

He shook his head slowly. 'It's no good,' he said. 'I can't—'

The rest of his reply was drowned by the opening chords of the final movement. But Miriam's expression was grim.

Precisely forty-one minutes after Sam had begun, the final note faded to silence and the applause began. For Sam, returning from the invisible space where the music was formed, it was an experience like no other. She blinked, let her bow arm fall to her side, then stood up and surveyed the audience. Grigory first. He was clapping slowly, and at first Sam was afraid that he'd been less than impressed by her performance, even though she felt it was the best she had ever given. But then she saw him struggle to his feet, still clapping. 'Bravo!' he shouted, and she saw that tears were streaming down his cheeks.

After that everyone was standing up and shouting. Davy and Linda and the boys, Mick and Nadira. Raph had been among the first to rise to his feet, and Miriam was there beside him, clapping as though her life depended on it. Even Judy Saunders had joined in, swept away by the power of the music. It was so unexpected that Sam didn't know what to do. She smiled, bowed, bowed again, and then she was rescued by the conductor, who took her by the hand, kissed her cheek and led her off.

Out of sight of the audience, Herman Schreiber hugged her and said, 'Well done, my dear. You were magnificent.'

'I was?'

Still dazed by the whole business, Sam had to be herded back on stage for another bow. As she came into view, the audience roared their support. The orchestra members were all clapping, too, and grinning with the euphoria of the moment.

Sam bowed again, and again Herman Schreiber kissed her and
she shook hands with the first violinist and grinned and
clapped the orchestra, and when she looked back at the audience, Mick was easing his way along the seats. Where was he
going in such a hurry? In spite of everything she was annoyed
that he wasn't staying until every last note of the applause had
died down.

The next time Herman Schreiber led her back on to the stage
for a final bow, it was Raph who was edging his way past the
people in his row and Mick was nowhere to be seen.

And when Sam left the stage for the final time and the audience subsided into silence, she realized that she finally
understood the cliché about 'applause ringing in her ears'. She
was floating, more a cloud than a person, and she wanted this
feeling to go on for ever.

The other contestants crowded round, offering their congratulations. A Scottish violinist, who was her main competitor
and who was going to play after her, said quietly, 'I guess it
helps if you're already a media heroine, eh?'

Sam was too euphoric to be offended. She hugged him and
said, 'Good luck anyway. I'll be rooting for you.'

'Thanks,' he said, and grinned. 'You played bloody well,
actually.'

Sam hugged him again.

Mick was coming towards her, his face grim. He pushed his
way through the crowd that had gathered round her and said,
'Sam, I've got to talk to you. Privately.'

'Was it okay?'

'Wonderful. But we have to talk.'

'Later,' she said. Right now all she wanted to hear was the praise she was soaking up like a sponge as the orchestra members filed past, each one smiling and adding their own few words to the torrent of approval.

'This is urgent, Sam. I think—'

But Sam didn't want to know what he thought, not yet at any rate. God knows, she'd waited too long for this moment – a whole lifetime, it felt like – to have it cut short by Mick or anyone else. She wanted to enjoy her success with Davy and Linda. She was glad she'd arranged to go out and have a pizza with them and the boys while the final contestant played; she'd meet up again with Mick for the final announcement, and for the party and razzmatazz that would follow.

She said, 'Leave it till later, Mick. I'm meeting Dad and Linda now.'

'Can I come?'

'No,' she told him. 'We need a family moment. Just the five of us.' Truth was, she didn't want his dark mood spoiling her party.

'But—'

'I mean it, Mick.' She turned away, only to see Raph coming towards her from the front of the hall. He looked as morose as Mick. Why couldn't they just be glad for her? Mick still looked as though he wanted to administer a particularly unpleasant dose of medicine. Damn them both. She had no intention of being trapped between two people who were determined to ruin her moment of glory.

She said, 'I've got to find Davy and Linda. I'll see you later.'

Mick shouted, 'Sam, wait!' Just in time, she slipped between the tuba player and a couple of violinists and headed into a corridor she didn't recognize, but which she guessed must lead to a side exit. She was still carrying her cello and holding up the skirts of her dress with the hand which held the bow. Footsteps echoed behind her, coming closer.

There was an outside door she hadn't notice before, and she headed that way. If this came out at the back of the theatre, from there it was just a five-minute trek in her black dress and high heels to where Davy and Linda would be waiting with the boys at Pizza Palace. As she emerged into the damp grey evening air, she was surprised to see Miriam coming towards her.

Miriam looked startled, then pleased. 'Congratulations, Sam,' she said. 'You were tremendous.'

'Thanks.'

'Can I give you a lift somewhere?'

'That's very kind. But I'm going for a pizza with Dad and Linda.'

'I know. Davy asked me to give you a lift. It's further than he thought. And the cello, of course.' Miriam smiled.

'Oh. Well, in that case, thanks.'

'The car's right here.' They crossed the road and the ignition lights on Miriam's small Audi flashed.

'Are you sure there's room for the cello?' asked Sam.

'No, you must leave that here.'

'What?'

'Get in this side,' said Miriam. 'You're driving.'

'What's going on?' asked Sam, staring at the gun Miriam held in her hand. 'Is this some kind of joke?'

Miriam shook her head. 'Surely you've guessed,' she said.

Sam's eyes were on the gun.

'*Tweet tweet*,' said Miriam.

Sam gasped. Gripping the gun in her right hand, Miriam was transformed. All trace of tension had vanished; she was radiant with power.

'I fooled you, didn't I? Just like I fooled your mother. The last thing Kirsten heard was my pretty song. And now it's your turn. *Tweet tweet*.' She giggled, a chilling sound, and then was sober again. 'Now, Sam, do exactly what I say or . . .' She gestured with the gun. 'Remember what it says in the poem? *This murder bird does not make mistakes*.'

CHAPTER 23

The Pizza Palace was only half full when Mick walked in; he saw Davy and his family right away. They were sitting at a table near a large palm, plates of half-eaten pizza in front of them. They were silent and uncomfortable; that was the first surprise.

'Hi,' said Mick, walking up to them. 'Where's Sam?'

'We assumed she was with you,' said Davy.

'Yes,' said Linda, setting down her knife and fork. 'We booked a table, just in case lots of people had the same idea, but now it seems she's too grand even to have a meal with her own family.'

'Linda—' Davy placed a warning hand over hers.

'Well, it's true,' complained Linda. 'We went to a lot of trouble to come up and support her. I know she's busy and there's a big party afterwards, but this was agreed on days ago. We'll have a pizza together, we said, and have a chance to catch up. Spend time with the boys. And now she can't even be bothered to show up.'

'Linda, please—' Davy's protest was half-hearted.

'Where is she?' asked Mick.

'We thought you knew.'

'All we got,' said Linda, 'was a text message. Couldn't even tell us face to face.'

'A text message? What did it say? Have you still got it?'

'I was that angry,' said Linda, 'I erased it right away. She just said she'd been called away and would be in touch later. Something like that. Enjoy the pizza. Didn't even say sorry.'

Davy, less caught up in his own sense of grievance than his wife, noticed Mick's expression and said, 'What's up, Mick? Where's she gone?'

'That's what I'd like to know.'

Linda smiled. 'You're getting the brush off too, eh? Maybe there's someone else.'

'Somehow, I don't think so,' said Mick, scrolling down to Sam's number. Her phone was switched off. 'Damn,' he said.

'What is it?' asked Davy. 'Is Sam all right?'

'I don't know,' said Mick. 'I hope so.'

Without another word, he strode from the restaurant. Once out in the street, he broke into a run.

Sam had never driven an automatic before. Her left hand kept reaching instinctively for a non-existent gear leaver. Each time this happened, Miriam, who was seated beside her and holding the gun almost casually, waved it for emphasis and said brusquely, 'Hands on the wheel, Sam. Keep them there. Or else.'

The third time this happened, as they were approaching the

first sign for services on the M4, Sam asked, 'Or else what, Miriam?'

'Or I shoot you, of course,' said Miriam.

Sam considered this. 'What, going at this speed?' Sam glanced down at the speedometer. As soon as the traffic permitted, her passenger had insisted she put her foot down, and Sam didn't object. Being pulled over by the police seemed like her best option right now. She said, 'I don't think so. Not unless you want us both to end up dead.'

'I don't mind,' said Miriam calmly. 'It's a solution, isn't it? With any luck, there'd be a massive pile-up. Lots of people would die with us.'

Sam gripped the steering wheel more tightly.

'Sometimes,' Miriam continued thoughtfully, 'when I can't sleep, I imagine dying in an almighty crash. Going faster and faster and then suddenly – boom. All those mangled bodies, all that destruction. A good way to finish, I think.'

Sam threw her a look, to see if she was joking. She wasn't.

Miriam caught her eye and, seeing her expression of horror, she asked, 'D'you know who I envy most, Sam?'

'I can't imagine.'

'Suicide bombers.'

'Because they think they're going to heaven?'

'I don't believe in heaven. This is all there is. But what an exit! What a way to make people sit up and take notice for once. A human firework. And all the carnage. Brilliant.'

'You really think so?' Sam had an idea – she must have read it somewhere – that in a hostage situation, which is what this surely was, the secret was to keep your captor talking. Establish a relationship. She didn't know if the same thing applied in a situation like this, where she already had a relationship with the hostage taker. Or thought she had.

Miriam looked out of the window at the driver of a removals lorry they were overtaking. He glanced down at her and smiled, obviously thinking she was just an ordinary passenger in an ordinary car on an ordinary journey. Sam felt he might as well exist on another planet. Miriam turned away with a small shrug. 'Certainly,' she said, her tone offhand, as though wanting to die in a motorway pile-up was the most natural ambition in the world. 'I often think about it.'

'Why would you want to die like that?' asked Sam.

'It's just an option, that's all. I never said it was my first choice.'

She leaned forward and began fiddling with the dials on the stereo.

Sam said, 'You killed my mother, didn't you?'

'Uh huh,' Miriam acknowledged. 'I told you already.' And then she muttered, 'Damn. The reception is always so bad on this section.'

Sam hesitated. It was still hard to believe she was having this conversation, but in the circumstances she didn't feel much in the mood for small talk. After a moment she said, 'Why? After all, she was wrong about the murder bird. She was planning to expose your mother. You would have still been free.'

'Mm. I know. Poor old Kirsten. She thought she was so clever, but she got it completely wrong. Just like they all do.'

'So why?'

'Do you mind if we don't talk about it?'

Sam almost laughed. Miriam's polite little question was so

out of context. 'Do my wishes count for anything right now?'

'Not really.' Miriam had found Classic FM and the stately chords from Handel's *Water Music* filled the car. It was so inappropriate that Sam felt real panic for the first time: the world had gone mad and here she was, driving through the dusk with the woman who had killed her mother, listening to Handel. Miriam sat back in her seat and said, 'Kirsten got one thing right, though.'

'What?'

'Sometimes – times like this, for example – you do feel . . . *birdlike*. Soaring high above everything, like an eagle. "My lady's a high-flying bird." She hummed an old tune quietly, and her features seemed to be lit from within, as though the petty concerns of ordinary people would never trouble her again.

'Is that why you do it?'

'Do what?'

'Kill people.'

'Oh, that.' Miriam gazed at her thoughtfully for a moment, then looked away and gestured with the gun. 'I don't want to talk any more. Not to you, anyway. You're not important. Just drive.'

'And if I refuse?'

'Then I kill you, of course. Easy peasy Japanesy.' Suddenly, she sounded about ten years old, as if they were playing at cops and robbers in a school playground. 'I've already killed,' she counted off her fingers, 'four people.' She flexed her thumb. 'Someone has to be number five. It might as well be you.'

It was only when they had turned off the motorway and were on the narrow roads leading to Wardley that Sam realized the significance of what Miriam had said. 'Four people?' she asked, breaking the silence. 'Your father, Anthony and my mother – so who was the fourth?'

But Miriam wasn't to be drawn. 'Drive,' she said.

Raph had just reached his car when Mick caught up with him. He caught Raph by the shoulder and spun him round.

'Where's Sam?' Mick demanded at once.

'I thought she was with you.'

'How come?'

'She sent me a text message.'

'Fuck!'

'What's the matter?' asked Raph.

'Something's going on. I tried to phone but her phone's switched off. I can't get any answer. Have you seen Miriam?'

'Miriam?' Raph's face was suddenly ashen.

'You bastard!' shouted Mick. 'What the hell's going on?'

'I – don't know.'

'It's Miriam, isn't it?'

Raph nodded. 'Yes,' he said.

Johnny was in the kitchen when Sam and Miriam arrived at Wardley. Queen's 'Bohemian Rhapsody' was playing and he was just starting on a plate of oven-ready Thai food, a bottle of claret, half finished, on the table beside his glass. His address book was by his left hand, open at the letter 'M'.

His good-looking, florid face displayed first surprise, then delight at seeing Sam in her black evening dress. This changed quickly to dismay when Miriam followed close on her heels, and then, when he saw the gun in Miriam's hand, the gun that was pointing directly at Sam's back, there was slow, horrified comprehension.

He said, 'Sam—' and then he was speechless, his mouth remaining open in an O of stunned disbelief.

Miriam said quietly, 'Good evening, Johnny.' Then she frowned and said, 'How can you bear to eat that muck? There's proper food in the freezer, you know.' She reached across to the dresser and switched off the stereo. Silence echoed.

'I forgot,' said Johnny, and then, to Sam, 'How was the competition?'

'What?' It seemed incredible to Sam, after her journey at gunpoint, that she had ever played in the Frobisher, let alone that very day. And worse than incredible that Miriam and Johnny were talking about freezer food and music at a moment like this. She said, 'Does it matter?' and gestured with her hands towards the gun that Miriam was still pointing at her.

'Ah,' said Johnny. 'Yes, I see.'

He pushed his chair backwards, to stand up, but Miriam said swiftly, her voice like the snap of a whip, 'Don't move! Stay right where you are!'

Johnny froze. He was staring at her, his eyes huge. 'Is this some kind of joke?' he asked, but you could tell, from the catch in his voice, that he knew it wasn't.

Miriam pulled out a kitchen chair and told Sam to sit down, then stood behind her, so that she and Johnny were facing each other across the kitchen table. Sam could see Miriam's face in a mirror on the dresser in front of her. She couldn't see the gun but she sensed it with every nerve in her body. And she didn't doubt for a moment that Miriam would use it, if thwarted.

'Listen, Johnny. Pay very careful attention,' said Miriam quietly. 'I'm not going to say this more than once. Don't leave me. I can't live without you. I *won't* live without you.'

'Right,' said Johnny at once. Miriam's demands were hardly negotiable. 'That's settled then. I won't leave you. Now, put the gun down and let Sam go.'

'Don't be an idiot,' snapped Miriam. 'This whole mess is Sam's fault. I'm not letting her go now.'

'*My* fault?' asked Sam, trying to turn round so she could look at Miriam and receiving a warning tap on the side of her head from the gun. She gasped, then asked, 'Just how do you work that out?'

'You know perfectly well what I mean,' said Miriam tersely. 'I do not intend to discuss it with you.'

'So what are you going to do?' asked Sam.

The phone rang before she got her answer.

Miriam asked her husband, 'Are you expecting anyone?' She leaned past Sam to look at the open page of Johnny's address book. 'Pamela Moore, perhaps? Fixing up a little soiree?'

Johnny shook his head, never for a moment taking his eyes off his wife, her strange, flat face and her hand holding the gun.

Miriam walked around the end of the table and, keeping the gun pointed at Sam, she picked up the phone in her left hand. It was a voice Miriam recognized. She handed the phone to

Johnny. 'Answer it!' she mouthed. She gestured towards Sam. 'Not a word or—'

He said, 'Raph? Hello. Johnny here.' And then, after a pause he said, 'Sam?' Miriam was still shaking her head, and Johnny said, 'Er, no, actually, I've no idea where she is. Or Miriam, no. Yes of course, if I see them, I'll let you know. Sorry not to be able to help. 'Bye then.' He put the phone down.

'Well done,' said Miriam. 'We don't want any visitors tonight, do we?'

'What are you going to do?' asked Johnny.

'That depends on you,' said Miriam.

'Me?'

'Yes. You. You have to prove you'll never leave me. Never never never.'

'Fine. That's fine by me. Just tell me what you want and I'll do it. Anything, Miri, anything at all.'

Miriam smiled. 'At last,' she breathed.

'Just tell me what I have to do.'

'It's perfectly simple, really. All you have to do is kill Sam, Johnny. She's got to die, but this time I want you to do it for me.'

Raph clicked off his mobile phone and replaced it in his breast pocket. 'They're at Wardley,' he said.

'How d'you know?' asked Mick.

'Johnny's voice. I've known him twenty years and I can tell. He has to be the worst liar in the world.'

'How long will it take to get there?'

'An hour. Forty minutes if we drive fast.'

Mick looked at Raph. Right now his mentor didn't look capable of driving across a car park without crashing into something. He said, 'Give me the keys. I'll drive. And you can tell me about Miriam.'

Raph looked at him with disbelief. 'No,' he said.

'Yes, now. Get in. We're losing time.'

'It's too late,' said Raph.

'Get in the goddamn car,' said Mick, grabbing his arm and steering him round to the passenger door. 'I need you for directions.'

'It's hopeless,' said Raph. 'We'll be too late.'

Mick pushed him in, slammed the door behind him, then went round to the driver's side. He got in the car and started the engine. Raph was slumped hopelessly on the passenger seat. 'Where to?' asked Mick.

'The M4,' said Raph. 'Newbury turn-off.'

'Put your seat belt on,' said Mick. 'We might have to speed a little.'

'You'll never do it.'

'I can try.'

For the next fifteen minutes all Mick's attention was given to getting through the traffic as quickly and safely as possible. But once they were on the motorway, and Raph's car was cruising at a steady 110, Mick turned to his passenger and said, 'You've known all along your sister's a murderer and yet still you keep protecting her. Why?'

'She saved my life,' said Raph. 'What choice did I have?'

Mick glanced at him with disbelief. 'Kirsten Waller was threatening your life?'

'Of course not.' Raph waved the suggestion aside impatiently. 'That was different. But when we were children – she saved my life then. I owe everything to her.'

'Tell me about it,' said Mick. 'I need to understand.'

But Raph couldn't tell him, would never be able to talk about it. The necessity of silence had been a part of him for so long he couldn't change now. The memories were there; the memories would always be there, but about this, the central fact of his childhood, the central fact of his whole life, Raph Howes the smooth-tongued barrister would be for ever unable to speak a single word.

His sister, too. She'd tried, once, long ago. About six weeks after the fire that had destroyed their home and killed their father, when they were living with their mother in a rented flat, he'd heard Miriam tell Diana one evening when she was laying a fire in the grate, 'I did it, Mummy.'

'Did what, darling?' Diana looked up, a smudge on the side of her face. She'd still been beautiful, then.

Raph, his head bowed over his colouring book, had listened, hardly daring to breathe. Now the world really was about to come to an end.

'I dropped the match on the bedclothes.' Miriam's voice was hardly more than a whisper. 'I started the fire. It was my fault Daddy died. So he wouldn't put Raphie in the box, but I didn't mean him to die for ever.'

Diana had laid down her kindling. She brushed a strand of hair from her face and a second smudge appeared on her cheek. She looked up at her shy, timid daughter who was so frightened of new situations, so afraid of any place where she might be expected to

act. Diana's face was expressionless as she took in what Miriam was
trying to tell her, took it in, and then rejected it.

'Don't be silly, Miriam,' she said firmly. 'The fire was an accident. No one was to blame. We all loved Daddy very much and
we never wanted to harm him.'

'But he said he was going to kill Raphie. I had to stop him.'

'That's enough now, Miriam. It is very, very, *very* naughty to
make up these stories. I never want to hear you talk about it
again, do you understand? Never.'

'But Mummy—'

'The subject is closed. If you bother me any more with this
silliness, you'll have to go to your room and stay there till you
know how to behave.'

Even now, Raph ached at the memory; it felt as though his
whole life since then had been a silent scream of anguish for the
opportunities missed, the lies piled on lies, the deceit and
destruction from which there had been no escape.

Mick heard his groan and said, 'What about your mother?
How could you let her take the blame for what Miriam's done.'

'Diana?' Raph's voice was bitter. 'She deserved to take the
blame. It was all her fault, really.'

'Just how do you work that out?'

But Raph couldn't tell him. He said simply, 'Because that's
how it was.' And lapsed back into silence.

Mick said, 'Miriam killed your wife.'

'D'you think I wanted that? Kirsten was everything to me. I
never even wanted her to leave.'

'Jesus,' said Mick. 'How do I know you're not helping her
now? Maybe they're not at Wardley at all and you're just feeding

me all this to keep me out of the way so Miriam can take care of Sam as well.'

Raph shook his head. 'I don't want Sam to get hurt,' he said. 'I tried to protect her—'

'You did? That's the first I've heard.'

'But I did. I told Miriam Kirsten's journal contained evidence that would link her to Kirsten's death. I thought that way I'd be able to control her, stop her from hurting anyone else.'

'What kind of evidence?'

'There wasn't any. It was just a way to frighten Miriam, to make sure she stopped acting like a crazy person. I told her if anyone else got hurt, then I'd take the journal to the police and she'd be exposed.'

'So that's why she was so determined to get it from Sam.'

'Yes. By the time I told her there was nothing in it, she didn't believe me.'

'But Kirsten thought Diana was the murderer.'

'Yes.'

'How come she got it wrong?'

'Because we told everyone Diana was driving when Anthony got run over.'

'And it was Miriam?'

'Of course.'

'Why didn't Diana tell people the truth?'

'You don't understand, do you?' Raph sighed, then went on, 'Tell the truth? Talk about family? Why would Diana change the habits of a lifetime? She wouldn't know how to begin. When she was arrested, I told her she just had to keep quiet for a bit and everything would work out. It wasn't hard; after all, she'd been keeping quiet all her life. And it worked. She thinks the police are going to realise they've made a terrible mistake and let her go.'

'You think she knows about Miriam?'

'She must do, deep down. But she'll never admit it. Our family has to stay perfect.'

'Jesus,' said Mick. 'What a fuck-up.'

'Yes,' said Raph.

'I still can't believe you let Sam be in danger.'

'Yes, I can see how it might be hard for you to understand. But Miriam is . . .' Raph was silent for a moment, searching for words to describe the bonds that bound him to his sister, but it was impossible. He said, 'While Sam was playing just now, there was so much of Kirsten in her, that intensity and beauty of purpose. That was when I knew I had to make sure that she was safe.'

'Even if it meant sacrificing Miriam?'

'Yes. Even so.'

'Do you think Miriam guessed?' Mick thought back to what he'd seen during the concert.

'She must have done.'

'What's she planning to do?'

'I don't know.'

'You're lying,' said Mick.

'Maybe. You'll find out soon enough,' said Raph with a shrug. 'Slow down now. We're coming up to our turn-off.'

CHAPTER 24

She was the murder bird and she was flying high and free in the clear air, far above those feeble, stumbling creatures of dirt and earth. She was invincible; no one could stop her now, not Johnny, not Sam, not anyone. They looked at her with respect and they were afraid, because her great truth was in the open at last.

It wasn't just the gun nestled snug against her palm that gave her this power. Courage and clear-sightedness, those were her secrets. She could save and she could destroy. She'd done it before. Sometimes you had to destroy so that you could save.

She'd learned that lesson early.

Learned it the first time she'd felt herself change. Learned it the first time terror and confusion had been swept away by her brave action.

Some memories of the day her father died were muddled. Most shone like crystal. Had she wanted him to die? Yes, surely, but she hadn't known what dead meant, not really.

She remembered Raph stumbling across the field, the little dog lifeless in his arms, sobbing as he ran. Sobbing with grief for Chippy, but even more with fear for himself. How many times had his father threatened him for crimes far less serious than the death of a favourite dog? This time he would surely carry out his threat.

Their father was in the hall when Raph got in. He was waiting.

'Daddy, I didn't mean . . . Please—'

'Shut it.' Their father's face altered when he saw the little dog. He snatched it out of Raph's arms and held it aloft by the scruff of the neck, staring at the bloodied bundle of fur. He didn't seem able to believe what he saw.

Then he looked down at Raph.

'What did I tell you about taking the dogs out?'

Raph hiccuped, stifling his sobs.

'What did I say?'

'Please Daddy,' said Miriam.

'Keep out of this.' Very calm. It would have been better if he'd shouted. 'Remember what happens to naughty boys? Remember what happened when we buried the guinea pig? This time it's your turn. When I come downstairs, I'm going to put you in a box and bury you under the earth. So you'll learn to do what you're told.' He was breathing like a bellows, but he still hadn't raised his voice.

Silence. Raph was too frightened even to cry.

'Wait in there.' The big man dropped the little canine corpse and bundled Raph into the cupboard under the stairs, then shot home the bolt. 'Wait for your punishment.'

He set off up the stairs, the big black Labrador called Major lolloping up beside him.

And Miriam had watched it all. How long would Raph have to wait before Daddy carried out his threat? The rest of the day? All night? But Raph was frightened of the dark, had nightmares even when he was tucked up in his own bed with a nightlight burning in a saucer. Alone in the cupboard, alone with the monsters of the dark and the knowledge of the worse terrors ahead, her baby brother would lose his mind with fear.

Surely their mother knew that too.

'Mummy,' she pleaded, hearing the stifled sobs leaking out from under the stairs, 'do something. Don't let Daddy bury him. Please, Mummy. You have to *do* something.'

Diana watched from the doorway into the kitchen as her husband disappeared from view. She was wiping her hands on her apron.

She smiled brightly at Miriam – that bright, empty smile they dreaded so much because it meant she'd switched off and wasn't their mother any more, just a wax doll masquerading as a mother – and she said, 'I think I'll make us some scones for tea. That would be nice, dear, wouldn't it?'

Couldn't she hear Raph crying? Couldn't she feel the ground shifting beneath their feet, the deafening roar of a disaster about to happen?

'But, Mummy—'

'Go upstairs, darling, there's a good girl and make sure Daddy's put his cigarette out. We don't want any accidents, do we?'

'Accidents?'

'We don't want the house burning down.'

Obediently, Miriam nodded. Placed her foot on the first stair.

And then suddenly, she was moving in a bubble of light. It was all around and inside her, and it was telling her what to do. A commandment, a clear instruction. She, Miriam, had to save them.

She had ceased to be a little girl, weak and powerless and afraid. She had become an avenging angel, a giantess; she was all-powerful.

The white light lifted her up the stairs. She couldn't hear Raphie crying any more, or her mother singing as she pulled bowls and pans out of the kitchen cupboards. She could hear her father's snores, like some big old farm animal that's fallen down in a field, and she knew that it was up to her to make sure he never got up again.

There was no need to tiptoe. When Daddy was sleeping like this nothing woke him up, not even Major barking. Major was on the bed next to him. The black dog looked up and growled at Miriam. Sometimes she was frightened of Major. Once, when she'd taken the burning cigarette out of Daddy's fingers while he slept, Major had nipped her hand.

This time there was no fear. The white light was her shield. She wasn't even afraid of Daddy, who lay on his back, sleeping. He was going to sleep until he couldn't hurt Raph ever again. Daddy had stubbed his cigarette out in the saucer on the bed-side table. No fear of accidents this time, then . . .

Feet hardly touching the ground, she floated to the side of the bed and looked at him. The skin on his face was all different colours; she'd never noticed that before. It was yellowish and pinkish, but also a bit blue round the eyes, and his cheeks were threaded with tiny red veins, and round his mouth it was a bit mauvy. She didn't like mauve. And the stubble was disgusting.

She shook a cigarette from the packet lying next to the saucer, then lit a match and put it to the end of the cigarette. She held it there until the flame was about to burn her fingers, but it didn't catch light, not properly, because she wasn't sucking it. She blew the match out before it burned her fingers.

She struck a second match and held it between finger and thumb, watching the flame, watching the way her father's face went all watery-looking where the air was hot above the flame. At the last minute, just as the flame was about to touch her skin, she let it fall without blowing it out.

A small brown hole appeared in the quilt. The hole grew, though it didn't look as if it was burning. Major growled. She lit another match, let that one fall. And then another. More little brown holes.

And then suddenly there was a whoosh of flame. She threw down the matches and ran out of the room, slamming the door behind her. White light bore her down the stairs. She was running, she was flying, she was pulling back the bolt on the door to the cupboard under the stairs and shouting at Raph to come out, he was safe now, he was free. He didn't understand, just cowered further into the darkness and she had to take hold of his arm and pull him out. 'Fire!' she yelled, and together they stumbled out into the garden.

The middle of the lawn was safe. They could watch from there.

Major was barking, barking like she'd never heard him bark

before. No! The big black dog was shut in the bedroom with Daddy. 'Jump, Major, jump!' They saw the outline of a man appear briefly in the smoke, a hand flapping, then it vanished and there was nothing but smoke. Thick smoke was pouring out of the upstairs window. Their mother came running from the kitchen, a wooden spoon still in her hand.

She was shrieking, but Miriam felt calmer than she'd ever been. She had changed the destiny of the family and saved them. She was all-powerful.

Of course, the feeling didn't last. Afterwards, quite soon afterwards, when she realized that Daddy wasn't coming back, not ever, she was bewildered, then terrified by what she had done. It scared her that a little girl could make such a big change in a family, could make men come running with hoses and engines and ambulances, could make all those grown-ups cry round a fresh grave, could make someone go away and never come back. She was terrified of her power, terrified that she might one day do the same thing again.

She tried to tell her mother once, but her mother said it had never happened. Sometimes Miriam wondered if she'd dreamed it. Mostly she felt trapped and tangled and afraid, and sometimes she even tried to tell herself that she had imagined the whole thing.

The scariest part of all was when the feeling came back, maybe when Raph was being teased at school, or when she was scared of someone, that white light feeling, as though she was floating and all-powerful.

She learned to be careful. It was best not to speak much, or do anything which was unusual or different. When people teased her at school she learned how to make herself go deaf. When her teachers told her off she kept her head down and never complained. She made sure that Raph didn't bring friends home, because it made her angry if they were mean to him and she was scared of her anger. She didn't have any friends of her own, not really, but she didn't need them; she and Raph were happiest together.

Until their mother met Leo Tyler, and Leo thought Raph ought to be at boarding school. Miriam didn't say anything about that, but she knew boarding school for Raph would be the end of everything. She got a headache just thinking about it. There had to be some way to stop this new disaster.

Her father's death had been an accident – well, sort of an accident. And Leo's was, too. Though maybe she could have saved him. She was fifteen years old and Leo was teaching her how to sail. He was good like that. They were on his dinghy in the Solent and they'd been practising the man-overboard routine. She'd already been in the water three times and her teeth were chattering with the cold and her head was pounding. Leo said now it was his turn. She had to know how to handle the boat on her own in an emergency.

It was when she saw him in the water, waving his arms and ordering her how to manoeuvre the boat, that the feeling came back. White light and an inevitable sequence of events. She didn't even have to make any kind of decision; it all happened naturally. She just turned the boat towards the shore. Leo thought it was a joke at first, and laughed and said, 'Hurry up, Miriam. It's bloody cold in here.' Then he thought she was being pathetic and he started yelling and screaming at her to come back, but she just kept on going, and all the while his cries got fainter and fainter, and then she couldn't hear him any more.

Later, she was so shocked by what had happened, that she became hysterical and the doctor came and she was put to bed and given something to calm her down. And there she stayed; she couldn't move at all, couldn't get out of bed for a month. People were sympathetic at first and said she must have been very fond of Leo Tyler.

Anthony's death was different. Miriam prided herself on her ability to take advantage of any opportunity when it arose. She knew he'd have to die, because he was hurting Johnny and she had to take care of Johnny, just like she'd always taken care of Raph, but she hadn't worked out how to do it. And then she saw him walking along by the drive talking to Raph and she realized that his death was meant to be. The car seemed to steer itself towards him, knocked him over as if by magic, and then, when he was struggling to get up, moved for a second time. The car had known what she wanted.

Kirsten's death had been the hardest. Miriam never wanted her to die. She'd taken the trouble to drive all the way down to Cornwall to make her see why she couldn't expose Diana. But Kirsten refused to see sense. It was her fault, really, for being so stubborn. Once again, Miriam had had no choice. She had to protect her family, had to make them safe.

It must have been Kirsten's destiny, anyway, or the radio would not have been sitting there on the wooden floor of the bathroom, its long flex snaking through to the socket on the upstairs landing. The murder weapon was waiting for her. Simple as throwing someone the soap.

Simple, because she was powerful. She could change people's stars. She could make them cease to be.

Now it was Sam's turn.

And she knew it. You could tell by the look in her eye, the way her skin had gone all tight and puckered-looking with fear. Sam knew she had to die. Her busybody nosying around had wrecked Miriam's life. Johnny had turned against her; Diana was in prison, and now Raph was planning to go to the police and tell the 'the truth' just to keep Sam safe. She'd known what he was thinking, seen the way he changed when he watched her playing that music. He was going to try to break away from her, but she wouldn't let him, not ever. And she'd make sure he was too late to save Sam.

Johnny was still sitting at the kitchen table, just as he'd been when she and Sam first came in. He said, 'Miriam, look. Let's talk this through calmly.'

'I am perfectly calm.' It was true. She was always calm when she knew what she had to do. 'Say you love me.'

'I love you.'

'Say you'll never leave me.'

'I'll never leave you. Look—'

'Say it again. Say it as if you mean it.'

'Of course I mean it. Now, put down the gun.'

'Say it! Say it properly! Say you love me!'

'I love you, dammit.'

Miriam shook her head. This wasn't how it was supposed to be. She could feel her power slipping away, white light dissolving, fear nibbling at the edges. Ground was slipping. She waved the gun angrily. 'No, not like that. You have to mean it. You

have to say you'll love me for ever – and you have to mean it.'
She was gasping.

Johnny took a step towards her. 'Miriam, please, I'll say anything you want. Just put down the gun.'

Darkness was closing in all round her. She fought it. 'No. Go
upstairs. Sam, too. Single file. I'm following. The gun is right
behind you. Move!'

When they were halfway down the corridor, Miriam barked at
her to stop. Sam held up the skirt of her long black dress. She
was level with the tarpaulin that hung down over the open
doorway. An icy sickness lay in the pit of her stomach. As if she
had known for weeks, had known ever since she first saw the
huge and empty space on the other side of the flapping tarpaulin, that one day, she'd have to go in there.

Johnny had led the way and he stopped about a metre
beyond the doorway.

'Turn round,' Miriam told him.

He did as he was told. Seeing the expression on his face, the
paralysis of disbelieving fear, Sam knew she could expect no real
help from him.

Miriam said, 'Pull back the tarpaulin.'

He did so.

'Now, Sam,' she said, nudging the butt of the gun in the
small of Sam's back. 'You're going in.'

'Miriam, wait,' said Johnny, head jerking like someone who
is just waking up. 'She can't do that. The floorboards have all
gone. It's a thirty-foot drop. She could be killed.'

'Precisely,' said Miriam. 'Go on, Sam.'

Again Sam felt the gun jab against her spine.

'No, stop,' said Johnny again. 'I don't understand. Why are you doing this, Miriam? What's wrong with you? I said I won't leave you. What more do you want?'

Behind her, but quite close, Sam heard Miriam's quiet sigh. 'It's not enough, Johnny. You're saying it now, but you don't mean it. There's nothing left any more – and it's all because of Sam.'

'But why? I don't understand,' said Johnny again. Grasping at anything to gain a little time. 'What about Anthony? Was that you? I thought it was Diana, and now—'

'Of course it was me. I killed your brother for you. Wasn't that what you wanted, really wanted? In your heart? I did it for you, Johnny. I'd do anything for you.'

'Dear Christ, I don't believe it.'

'But it's true,' said Miriam. 'And Kirsten too. But that's all over and done with. Sam, walk forward.' Sam shuffled forwards slowly; she put out her hands, trying to keep the open doorway away. Impossible. She was there. 'Now, stop,' said Miriam.

A cool draught of air from the tower grazed Sam's cheek, blew across her bare shoulders and the tops of her breasts.

'Turn right,' Miriam told her. 'That's enough. Now, walk in.'

'I can't,' said Sam, staring into the darkness. 'I'm frightened of heights.'

'Walk,' said Miriam.

'Stop it,' said Johnny. 'This is crazy.'

And then they all fell silent, listening. Sam wondered if she was imagining it, if it was the rush of fear in her ears, but she could hear the sound of a car approaching down the driveway. She glanced at Johnny; he'd heard it, too.

And so had Miriam. 'Hurry!' she shouted. 'Walk in there!'

'No!' said Johnny, stepping forward. 'I won't let this—'

The end of his sentence exploded in the noise of a gunshot and his howl of pain as the bullet struck his leg and he fell backwards, sprawling on the floor and clutching his calf. Blood was everywhere. Sam spun round, but the second bullet whistled past her ear and Miriam screamed out, 'Walk, damn you, *walk*, *WALK*' and the next moment Sam was standing in the tower room and all around her was nothing but blackness and cold air.

The floorboards were gone. Sam stood in the emptiness, one bare foot behind the other, on a wooden joist that was too narrow. She held her skirts with one hand, put her other arm out for balance. Behind her came Johnny's howls of pain, but the roar of fear through her skull was louder than that.

Concentrate. Look straight ahead. Don't look down.

No mistakes.

Miriam was screaming, 'Go on, damn you! Go on!'

Sam didn't move. All her energy, every nerve in her body was focused on the single task of keeping her balance. The space around her was huge, a vast cavern of blackness and emptiness, and the dark was entering her heart and she couldn't move, was going to slide off the beam and fall, fall and never stop falling.

'Move!' shrieked Miriam, and she fired into the darkness and the sound of the shot seemed to lift Sam off her feet and she was running, flying along the beam and then she lost her foothold, her foot slid, her ankle grazed the edge of the joist, and then her calf, as she fell, and she screamed and hurled herself forwards and her chest struck something solid. She reached; she gripped. Ahead, in the bitter darkness, there were floorboards and her body was on them and she clung on, splinters slicing into her hands. Her feet were dangling into space, her long skirt dragging her down, but her body was on flat boards.

'Sam!' A man's voice was calling to her. 'Sam, are you all right?'

Mick's voice. Below her. Far, far below.

Another gunshot. Sam hauled herself on to the boards and lay there, not moving. Her arm was pale in the darkness. She tugged the fabric of her skirt to cover the white skin.

Looking back to the oblong of light in the doorway she saw Miriam in silhouette, peering into the tower, the gun still in her hand. How many bullets? She seemed confused by the darkness. Sam pressed herself against the boards.

Footsteps echoing through the house. Men's voices shouting, Mick and Raph, and Johnny calling to them. Mick's voice rose up from the empty blackness below her.

'Sam, where are you?' he asked again.

She didn't answer.

But Miriam's eyes were getting used to the dark. She raised her right hand and pointed the gun at Sam.

'No!' Raph's voice blasted through the doorway. The next moment he appeared at Miriam's side; he reached out to grab the gun from her hand. She sidestepped him neatly, and the next moment, she was in the tower room, too, body wavering on the narrow joist.

'Miriam, no!'

She half turned towards him, but as she did so, she lost her balance. Her body leaned at an impossible angle and she screamed. Raph's warning rang out, then he stepped forward to reach out and grab her, but she was already falling, catching hold of his arm, pulling him with her as her gun went off for the last time.

Silhouetted against the light for a moment, and then plunging through utter darkness, brother and sister fell together.

CHAPTER 25

It was never going to be a conventional book launch. *The Murder Bird and Other Poems* had generated more publicity than any volume of poetry since *Birthday Letters*; the media attention was balanced by a couple of carping reviews by critics who assumed that a well-known writer was necessarily second-rate, but Trevor had told Sam not to worry about them. He was certain that once the hullabaloo had died down, the poems would be valued for their unique voice, for Kirsten's humour and perception and lyrical gifts. She might have been wrong about the identity of the murder bird, but she was a shrewd observer of human nature and the natural world; her poems could be enjoyed on a first reading as well as repaying further attention.

Kirsten's publishers had hired a gallery in Bloomsbury for the launch, and guests stood around in front of black-and-white photographs of household objects taken from such odd angles, or in such unusual juxtapositions, that they looked like strange sculptures.

At four o'clock on the day of the launch Sam had phoned

Mick to tell him she wasn't going. 'I can't face it,' she said. 'It doesn't make sense. How can we celebrate the book when Kirsten's not there? The only reason everyone is making such a fuss about it is because she was murdered – it feels like we're capitalizing on her death. I just don't feel right about it.'

'I know,' said Mick. They'd had this same conversation several times during the previous weeks. Sam was developing a strong aversion to any kind of publicity. She'd withdrawn from the Frobisher and let it be known she wouldn't be available for public performances for at least a year. She had a horror of being listened to simply because her mother had been murdered, and she herself had almost suffered the same fate, rather than because of her abilities as a musician. She was going to use the money from *The Murder Bird* poems to study in Paris for a year. 'Going to this launch will be tough,' he agreed. 'But if you don't go—? Won't that be worse? Kirsten wanted her work to reach out to people, and that's just what's happening. This evening will be a celebration of your mother, of her life and her work. You have to go.'

'You'll be there, won't you? You won't be late?'

'Of course I'll be there.'

And so he was. Sam worried, sometimes, that she was leaning on Mick too much, but in the days after Miriam's death, while Raph hovered between life and death in intensive care, she had needed someone to lean on. It went against the grain, since she had tried, all along, to be as self-reliant as possible, but Mick was there when she needed him and she was beginning to realize that letting someone else take care of you is sometimes a different and harder kind of strength.

But she still found their closeness almost scary. It was one of the reasons for the year in Paris. If their relationship was solid, so her reasoning went, then they'd survive the time apart, and if not . . . well, better to know sooner, rather than later, was how she figured it.

He'd been talking to Trevor, but came over to stand beside her while Trevor made a short speech about Kirsten and the book. Then it was the turn of the publisher.

Mick slipped his arm around her waist. It felt permanent, and immensely reassuring. Sam was hardly listening to the speeches, since what they said was predictable: Kirsten's tragically early death – at the height of her creative powers – strange prefiguring in the title – work which will endure.

'And now,' she said, turning to Sam. 'Kirsten's daughter Sam would like to say a few words.'

Sam walked forward. Her cello was already leaning against its stand. She said, 'My mother was a poet, and so she understood, perhaps more than most people, the limitations of words. She told me once that the best response to a work of art is another. And so, instead of talking about my mother, I would like to play a piece that was important to us both, the Bach Suite number 1 in G major. And please, as this is a book launch and not a concert, carry on talking while I play.'

The silence in the room was absolute as she took up her bow and prepared to play the music which had meant so much to Kirsten, the music which had launched her own career and which, she would always believe, had saved her life when she stood terrified over the abyss.

And then, she began to play.

Not so very far away, and yet for ever out of reach, Raph lay in his hospital bed. Out of danger, between operations, not knowing yet if he'd walk again. Wreathed in every kind of pain.

A copy of the book lay on the thin coverlet: *The Murder Bird and Other Poems* by Kirsten Waller. Trevor had brought him a copy and told him about today's launch. At least the publishers had had more taste than to put a picture of a bird on the cover: simple lettering on a blue background. Kirsten would have liked that.

'Still reading that book?' Diana had asked when she came to visit. 'I've brought you some magazines. More cheerful, don't you think?'

She was sitting beside him now, flicking through the magazines and reading out any bits she thought might interest him. So far as he could tell, she'd emerged from her prison ordeal remarkably unscathed. She'd taken to wearing hats when she was visiting him, and, for all he knew, at other times as well. Today she was wearing a jaunty little number in hyacinth blue with the wisp of a veil on her forehead. There was a lot to be said for not facing up to reality. He should try it himself some time.

He might start by pretending Miriam was still alive, and Diana was still in prison. That was how it should have been. Their mother was to blame. Why had she not protected them when they needed it? But Raph had seen enough sadistic, bullying husbands during his career as a barrister – now over – to know it's never that simple. Probably Diana had been trying to survive the only way she knew how, trying to placate her husband, anticipate his outbursts, soothe them away with cakes and platitudes.

So Miriam had stepped in. Poor Miriam, his loyal sister, his dark angel. He'd grieve for her for ever, but all the same, there was guilty relief in knowing she'd never again act out his murderous fantasies.

He'd wanted his father dead, that terrible afternoon when he was crouched in that airless, smelly cupboard with old boots caked in mud and sharp-pronged tools and mouse droppings. He'd imagined killing him, seeing him burn. 'Don't play with matches,' Diana used to tell them gaily. 'We don't want the house to go up in smoke.'

Yes, he did. He wanted the house to burn down with every fibre of his six-year-old body. He wanted it so badly that Miriam had picked up his murderous energy like a poltergeist and made his fantasy real.

Was that how it had happened?

She'd done it again when the new man in Diana's life wanted to send him away to school. Raph had fantasized about watching him drown. Miriam had done it.

But what about later? Had he wanted Anthony dead, too? He hadn't been aware of wanting that, but maybe Miriam had picked up on his unconscious desires. And what about Kirsten? He was certain he hadn't wanted her killed – he'd still loved her, for God's sake – but that was the trouble with fantasy wishes. You couldn't control them. Sometimes you didn't even know what they were.

Miriam spun out of control. He'd thought he could threaten her with Kirsten's journal, but it hadn't worked. She'd got away with it so often she thought she was invincible, and Sam had been next on her list, he knew it in his bones. When he saw Sam playing in the concert, he'd realized that if he didn't stop Miriam, Sam would pay the price with her life.

Miriam. Diana. Raph. Which of them was really the murder bird?

Diana looked up from her magazine. 'There's an interesting article here about otters. Shall I read it to you?'

'No thanks, Mother. I may sleep a bit.'

'In that case I'll pop out and give Bobbo a run in the car park. Can I get you anything before I go?'

'Thank you. I've got everything I need.'

'That's nice, dear.' Diana said. And smiled.